Charles

J. E. Tyler

J. E. Tyler

Table of Contents

Dedicated to Kimberly; my best friend, lover and fellow horror
fan.

"Live as if you were to die tomorrow. Learn as if you were to live forever." ~Ghandi

Chapter 1: November 10th, 1981 - Age 14

Snow stretches across the yard in a flawless sheet, cold and silent beneath the early dawn sky. In its center, a single blemish. It is a rabbit, gray and trembling, a fragile spark of life against winter's frozen canvas. It hops once. Twice. Three times. Then freezes, every muscle locked, every nerve electrified. Its glassy eyes flick left, then right, scanning the stillness for the whisper of danger. The tiny pink nose quivers, tasting the air, pulling in the sharp scent of frost and distant wood smoke. Nothing moves. Nothing breathes. Yet the rabbit knows the truth: it is alone, exposed, a living target painted on winter's pure-white skin.

Behind it, a dotted trail of prints scars the snow; a breadcrumb path of vulnerability. Ahead, salvation. A garden crouches against a weather-beaten picket fence, its faded slats leaning tired and grey. The harvest is long dead, but scraps of green cling stubbornly to the earth, a promise of life in a season of death. Hunger gnaws at the rabbit's belly, urging it forward. Three more hops. Stop. Listen. The world holds its breath. Even the birds, moments ago singing dawn's golden hymn, fall mute beneath the rising sun. Its first rays lick the treetops, igniting them in fire, but the warmth never touches the snow, or the rabbit.

It coils its legs, ready to spring, ready to dash across the last stretch of white. One heartbeat. Two. Then—stillness shatters. A whisper of steel. A pellet screams through the frozen air and punches into the rabbit's eye. The world ends at once. The body collapses sideways, limp and graceless, staining purity with violence. Crimson bleeds into the snow, spreading like spilled wine, soaking deep until the white is gone.

Charles

From a distance, a rifle lowers, its barrel gliding down from the scope's narrow world of death. Through the glass, there is nothing now but snow. Endless, merciless white snow.

Chapter 2: November 10th 1997 – Age 30

The boyhood memory fades. A man now stands in front of a heavy, pure-white steel door. His nose is close enough to feel the cold coming off the metal. His face is hard and unshaven, but his head of formerly blonde hair has been recently shaven clean. The man is only thirty, but he looks to have lived a hard life. His face is creased and weathered. There are deep lines in his forehead. Dark circles are formed under his eyes like roadside puddles at night.

His eyes are an explosion of brilliant emerald.

A scar in the shape of an inverted cross adorns his neck, front and center.

He is thankful for the childhood memory that the cold, white steel door has just afforded him. He is puzzled that such unsuspecting things as a door have sparked so many vivid memories from his past lately.

On the cold steel door, chips and pits of various depths and widths from decades of service over decades of repainting have been recently covered once again in a fresh coat of clean, glossy, industrial white paint. The man's nostrils flare a little as he sniffs twice and then takes one deeper breath in through his nose. Though it is faint, the man can still smell the paint's freshness. He stands there for only a few seconds, but to him it feels like time has stopped. He is surprised at how much detail in the door he is able to study and take in. The bolt patterns... The hinges... They all seem so very interesting to him at this moment and he wishes he could stare at them forever.

Charles

He is amazed at his newly discovered ability to appreciate things and to come up with philosophical analogies inspired by seemingly meaningless items. This door for example certainly has history. There is no doubt it is scarred, but here it is in front of him, washed in a fresh coat of white, hiding the sins of the past as if nothing has ever happened here. Fitting, he supposes, considering his current circumstances.

There is a loud buzzing sound. Almost simultaneously, a large, hairy hand slams against the door right in front of the man's face, startling him back to reality. There is a grunt and a push and the heavy steel door swings open. It takes only a second or two, but everything is moving in such slow motion for the tired man. As the huge door slowly swings, he has time to soak in every little detail of the space that is unfolding and being revealed before him.

The room is all white and extremely well-lit from above with rows of fluorescent tubes that produce a sickly green-tinged, institutional light. He can hear a humming sound, maybe from the ballasts in those lights. The electrical hum makes him feel sick to his stomach and the contents within churn a little. He can taste the steak and lobster he had consumed only hours before. It feels as though it is trying to come back up. It tastes like low tide.

On the far end of the room there is a huge plate glass window. It is almost as large as the entire wall. On the other side of the glass are seated about twenty people. The room they are in is less brightly lit than his own, but the man can see almost every face. The people are all intently peering at him through the glass. He knows some of the people. They all know him. The man knows he is about to put on the performance of a lifetime for this audience.

The man is suddenly aware of the grip tightening around his left bicep and then his right. He is led forward into the room by two men who are flanking him.

The man is wearing a light grey jumpsuit and his escorts are wearing dark grey uniforms. Their faces are stern and as hard as stone. Their eyes seem dark, dead and emotionless and they make no eye contact with anyone as they robotically go about their tasks and move the man into position.

As he nears the large window the man has an opportunity to more closely see the faces of those in the audience. He doesn't find it strange that none of them look happy to be at such a joyous spectacle as the one they are about to witness. The man does his best to engage as many of them in eye contact as possible. One at a time he scans their faces, attempting to make contact. He wants to look into their eyes. He wants them to look into his. He wants them to see him. Some of them won't even look at him, but for those that do, the man conveys his message the best he can for as long as they will keep eye contact. This man's message to them is clear. He doesn't care. He smiles at them all. He winks and blows a kiss at an older lady in the front row. He sees a familiar man in a suit and nods his head upward. He smiles as he does so as if to convey smarmily "Hey! What's up, man? How have you been?" The observer just stares stone-faced back at him. The man engages his audience the entire time he is being helped across the room by his escorts. He is barely aware of the sound of his leg chains dragging on the floor or the mumbling going on around him in this room. All he can hear is that damn humming and all he can see are the faces of his adoring audience.

The handlers begin helping the man into a seated position in a wooden chair in the middle of the room. The chair is crafted of a heavy, red mahogany. Leathers straps hang like eels, pinned to the wood with rivets. As he is seated, the man no sooner makes contact with the chair when he is yanked backward and pinned to the back by two more sets of hands, one set on his left shoulder and the other on his right. Almost simultaneously he sees and feels the leather strap being tightened around his chest by yet another set of hands that seemingly comes out of nowhere. As the strap is yanked tight with a strained creak, the four hands that pin him to the chair release their grip. The man feels immediate relaxation.

And then the sound rings out.

It is a small sound that reverberates massively in the room, or maybe just in his head. The sound comes from everywhere and nowhere all at once and folds in on itself, like glass unbreaking in slow motion. It's a tiny implosion, a note that eats its own echo.

The man's eyes begin to dart around. He searches faces. None of them seem to have heard a thing unusual.

He starts to lose focus on his audience and begins thinking about where he is sitting and how he got here. As the men in the dark grey uniforms move busily around him, he begins slipping into the recesses of his own mind. As his situation becomes more and more real around him, like stripping layers of paint from the steel door, he slips further and further back into the dark memories of his past.

He hears voices, muffled at first, echoing like ghosts in the cavern of his mind. They sharpen, syllable by syllable, until the words strike clean:

—

"On both counts, we, the jury, find the defendant, Charles Belial Watkins, guilty of murder in the first degree. So say we all."

The verdict reverberates, heavy as iron bars slamming shut.

Blackness envelopes Charles as the walls of his own mind wrap around him. Another voice rises—calm, cold, absolute. The judge.

"The court, having reviewed the jury's verdict, hereby sentences you, Charles Belial Watkins, to death by electrocution for the murders of Sheriff Paul J. Dobson and Howard B. Rangle."

The words fall like a guillotine and so does the gavel: final, merciless.

—

And then the sound comes again, reverse reverberation followed by a hollow click collapsing instead of striking.

Chapter 3: August 1995 – Age 27

Charles is on his knees. His hands are in the air. His ski mask is pulled up. There is a dead officer on the floor about five feet from him to his right. Another officer stands in the doorway. Charles can only see a silhouette because there are bright headlights shining in from behind the still-standing officer.

Exhaust fumes from running police cars swirl around the headlights. Red and blue strobe lights flash and color the smoke. Blinding light is emitting from the officer's Maglite and causing Charles to squeeze his eyes almost shut. Thick smoke fills the room and the flashlight's beam appears to become a glowing extension of the officer's arm, reaching into the store and grabbing Charles by the face.

The officer screams to Charles, "Get on the ground, face down!"

Charles doesn't even bother looking around for a way out. A fire blazes 15 feet behind him and certain suicide by cop awaits him should he decide to make any other move. He knows he has nowhere to run. He doesn't want to die this way. He is not afraid to die. He welcomes death most of the time, but for some reason that he cannot explain even to himself, he just doesn't want it to be like this. He knows that this is not the way he's supposed to go down. It can't be. He is only twenty-seven years old. He has his whole life ahead of him still and he has grandeur plans for his future. He still has business to attend to. Charles wants to live another day.

Charles lowers himself slowly, face pressed to the scorched tile, arms and legs splayed wide like a crucifix. He is immediately relieved by his decision. The air down here is cooler, easier to breathe as thin ribbons of oxygen thread through the smoke. Relief flickers in his chest, absurd and fleeting, but real.

A violent hiss erupts. The extinguisher detonates in a blizzard of caustic snow, its hiss a dying serpent. Boots hammer the tile: black leather veined with ash. Then gravity becomes a weapon: a knee drills his neck, grinding his cheek into grit until pain blooms like molten blown glass.

Hands seize his arms, wrenching them backward with savage force. Steel bites his wrists. The cuffs ratchet tight.

A voice near his ear, low, almost kind: "Easy." Fingers lift the collar so metal won't cut skin.

The smallness of the mercy burns worse than the knee.

Sirens wail in the distance, growing louder, closer. Tires shriek against pavement, short, sharp chirps slicing through the roar of flames.

Then the world spins. His body jerks backward, chest scraping tile as he's yanked by his ankles. The officer drags him hard, fast, out of the smoke, out of the fire, out past the dead officer sprawled in crimson silence. Charles's chin bounces against the floor, sparks of pain flashing behind his eyes. He doesn't fight. He doesn't speak. He just slides like dead weight across the burning threshold.

Night air slams into him like a slap. It's cold, sharp, alive with sirens and chaos. The fire's orange glow flickers behind him, painting the dark with hellfire. His face skims the pavement now, close enough to taste the concrete. He sees nothing but blacktop, concrete, the slick rubber of parked cruisers, the scarred brickwork at the base of the building.

A truck exhales nearby—a deep, mechanical sigh as air brakes hiss and pop. More boots thunder past his head, storming into the inferno he left behind. The fire devours everything inside. Ahead, only cold pavement and the weight of judgment.

14

Charles

—

A hand yanks back on Charles's forehead and pins his head to the hard wooden back of the chair. A strap is yanked tight around his forehead and clasped. The anonymous hand releases its grip on Charles's forehead and Charles again immediately relaxes his muscles. He cannot move his head at all and his eyes must do all the work themselves as they scan the faces in the audience.

The sound reverberates in Charles's head again, too loud for its size. It begins where it should end, with an echo, like air being sucked through teeth, cut short by a tongue.

He begins to slip back into the safe confines of his mind and as far from his current reality as possible.

—

"Freeze!"

The word cracks through the smoke like a gunshot. Charles doesn't move. He stands in the back of Rangle's Pharmacy, his face glowing orange in the firelight. How long has he been here, staring into that blazing glare? How long has the heat been licking his skin, hypnotizing him? He doesn't know. He doesn't care. He just stares, his face brightening as the flames climb higher.

"Put your hands in the air—NOW!" The voice behind him is sharp, commanding, but Charles doesn't flinch. His hands stay buried in the pockets of his sweatshirt. His body is a statue carved in shadow and fire.

The voice barks again, louder, harder: "Three Tango Niner requesting backup—fire and ambulance at Rangle's Pharmacy. Possible two-seventeen and code fifty-two. Suspect at gunpoint."

"DON'T YOU MOVE!"

Boots shuffle behind him. The officer is closing in. Charles finally breaks his gaze from the inferno, moves nothing but his eyes to the left. Through the smoke, a figure slides into his peripheral vision—a uniformed officer, pistol raised, eyes darting like trapped birds. The muzzle points at Charles, but the cop's attention splits between the motionless suspect and the fire extinguisher hanging on the wall five feet away. He's closing fast, head jerking left and right, desperate to control a scene that's already lost.

"I said take your fucking hands out of your pockets and put them where I can see them—NOW!" His voice cracks as he lunges for the extinguisher, panic bleeding through the command.

The brief hesitancy in the officer's decision and focus is all Charles needs. The flash comes like lightning. A muzzle flare bellows from Charles's midsection. He's been aiming the .38 across his own belly the whole time, hidden in the folds of his sweatshirt. Without moving anything but his trigger finger, he fires through the pocket. One shot. Two. Three. The extinguisher erupts in a violent white plume, choking the room in chemical fog.

Charles keeps firing into the cloud until the revolver clicks dry. He moves fast, forward and left, ducking behind a shelf of canned goods. He crouches low, heart pounding, while the dust settles like ash after a storm.

Shapes emerge through the haze. Four black stars puncture the wall behind where the officer stood. Charles lowers his gaze. A single dark hole marks the center of the extinguisher's powder-coated top. White dust trickles from the breech, falling in a slow stream onto the officer's cheek, which is already slick with blood. The body lies crumpled beneath the extinguisher, face frozen in a grotesque mask of surprise.

Charles

Charles rises, steps closer, and stares. The falling powder reminds him of sand slipping through an hourglass, and for a moment, time feels suspended. A smile curls his lips. The first bullet did the job: clean, perfect, right between the eyes.

He crouches beside the corpse, lays the empty revolver on the officer's chest, and studies the wound like an artist admiring his work. His eyes drift to the pistol on the floor, three feet away. He reaches for it, fingers brushing the grip—

"FREEZE! PUT YOUR HANDS IN THE AIR!"

The command detonates from the front of the store, booming through smoke and fire.

—

A leather strap jerks tight across Charles's lap, biting into his flesh. He exhales slowly, the sound almost a hiss, and lifts his eyes to the glass. Beyond it, shadows of judgment, ghosts of his past hover in the dim gallery.

Second row. An old woman. His eyes find hers, soft with something that looks like pity. Maybe forgiveness. He glares back, a silent snarl curling his lips. He doesn't want her mercy. He wants her fear. He wants her shame. And he gets it—at first. Her gaze drops, folding inward like a wounded bird.

But then, slowly, defiantly, she rises. Chin lifts. Eyes climb back to meet his. One inch. Two. Her arms cross like armor. She holds his stare, unflinching now, and for the first time, Charles feels the weight shift. He can't break her. He can't bend her.

The sound echoes in his head.

The woman begins to blur. Her face dissolves into shadow as Charles's focus slides, drawn to the dark pane of glass itself.

It hits him like a slow, cold tide: this isn't simple distraction. It isn't a lapse in concentration. Something inside

17

him is pulling, hard, dragging him backward through memories in time. He feels it now, the way a man feels undertow clutching his legs. He can't stop it. He can't fight it. The present is slipping, bleeding out of his grasp.

His own reflection now stares back at him from the gallery, warped and ghostly in the glass. A sullen face framed in black. Behind it, the hum of fluorescent lights fades, replaced by the whisper of wind.

———

The reflection sharpens. The glass is no longer the chamber window. It's a small, framed residential window, slick with night. A single low-watt bulb burns above and to his left, bleeding orange into the dark. Outside that circle of light, the world is nothing but pitch. A breeze stirs, brushing his skin like a phantom hand. He inhales deep. The first breath tastes sweet, almost clean, then rot slams into his nostrils, rancid and sour. Garbage. Decay. He huffs it out hard, turns his head, breathes shallow until the stench drifts away.

When he looks back, the reflection is crueler now, hollow eyes glaring from the glass. Disgust twists his mouth.

Slowly, silently, he slides the vinyl seal of the air conditioner open. Fingers snake inside, searching for the cord. He finds it, yanks it free, feels the socket surrender.

The window groans as he lifts it, smooth and careful, keeping one hand locked on the unit. He tips the machine outward, lowers it to the ground like a corpse, then climbs onto the milk crate. Head first, he slips through the opening, a shadow bleeding into deeper shadow.

Inside, the air is stale, heavy with the scent of dust, old grease and years of food spills stained deep into the fibers of wood. Charles pulls a small flashlight from his pocket, cups it in his palm, and flicks it on. A dull red glow leaks through his fingers. He peels the edge of his hand back, letting a thin blade of light escape.

A pantry. Shelves tower around him, stacked with dry goods and cans that glint like tiny eyes in the gloom. He smothers the light again, presses his foot to the glass-paned door, and eases it open. Beyond, a kitchen sprawls: industrial steel and silence.

Dim glimmers pulse from refrigerator indicators. A digital clock bleeds green numbers above the door leading out of the kitchen: **5:15 A.M.** The world is asleep. Everything is so quiet that Charles swears he can hear the building breathe. Motors hum low. Vents whisper white noise. Somewhere, a valve clicks and water trickles into an ice maker.

The silence feels sentient. Watching. Waiting.

Charles crouches low, sweat slicking his skin, as he slips from the pantry into the kitchen's cavernous dark. He moves in a slow duck-walk, keeping beneath the gleaming steel counters and hulking appliances, his breath shallow, his pulse tapping at his ears.

The door leading from the kitchen to the main store looms ahead. It is a narrow, vinyl and aluminum rectangle with a glass eye. He rises inch by inch, vertebrae clicking like a lock being picked, and peers through the small portal. Nothing. Just blackness beyond. Then, he sees himself. His own face floats in the glass, ghost-pale under the jaundiced green glow bleeding from the clock above. Hollow eyes ringed in bruised shadows. A face that looks borrowed, stretched too thin. He touches his cheekbones, fingers trembling, and pulls at the flesh as if testing its hold. The lids drag down, revealing raw, glistening seams. For a moment, he wonders if the skin will tear away like paper.

A sound snaps the trance—a clink of glass, sharp as bone against tile. Charles drops fast and silent, heart skipping a beat, and scuttles behind a prep table. New light blooms faintly from the far side of the room, a cold parallelogram spilling across steel. Shuffling. Another clink. Then a dull thud, like meat hitting a block. The light dies. Silence breathes, then drawers whisper open and shut. Another flare of light.

Charles lifts his head, slow as a corpse rising. An obese old man stands before the open fridge, his back a pelt of coarse hair, briefs sagging like spoiled fruit. A bald spot gleams amid greasy black strands, dye clinging like rot to visible scalp. He moves with lazy certainty, plucking a carton of milk, setting it down, sipping as he works. A sandwich takes shape: ham, cheese, lettuce, tomato, each layer an ode to hunger. Charles's mouth floods. His stomach knots and growls, a beast clawing its cage.

The man reaches for a knife. Charles sinks, breath locked, ribs aching. Silence stretches, taut as wire. Then—scrape, slice. The blade divides bread and flesh-red tomato. Charles risks a glance. The sandwich waits, perfect, obscene. His gut roars again, louder, and he clamps his arms around it, squeezing until stars burst behind his eyes.

He peeks once more. The man is gone. Vanished like a warlock. Only the sandwich remains, glistening under the dim light.

"Who the hell are you?" booms a voice at his right.

Charles, still crouched, spins on the balls of his feet toward the voice. The old man stands only a few feet away, knife raised, steel flashing like a sliver of moonlight. His knees bend in a stance that draws from memory—combat drilled into bone. One hand grips the blade, the other floats forward, a crooked shield. For a flicker, Charles sees past the sagging briefs and greasy hair: this man is not a joke. He's a relic of violence.

Charles lifts his hands slowly, palms open, surrender bleeding into his posture. He rises inch by inch, vertebrae stretching like a rack, and takes a single step back. The clock above ticks, its green glow dripping across steel like poison.

"Don't move," the old man barks, stabbing the air with the knife. His voice cracks like a whip, slicing the silence into ribbons.

Charles raises his hands higher, his face melting into pitiful defeat. He feels the weight of time pressing down, every second another nail in his coffin.

"What are you doing here?" The words grind out, gruff as rusted gears.

Charles turns his head, slow as decay, toward the sandwich waiting on the counter. It is a monument to hunger, disgusting in its perfection. The old man follows his gaze, and something flickers in his eyes.

"You want that?" His mouth twists into a grin that doesn't belong. "Hungry, huh? Broke in for food?" A laugh erupts, feigned and hollow, echoing off steel. It dies as fast as it came. His face hardens, stone slammed over fire.

"Not a chance," he spits, jabbing the blade again. "You want a meal? How about three hots and a cot? State-sponsored hospitality! You're welcome!"

He sidesteps, reaching for the phone on the wall. That single motion cracks the tension wide open. Charles moves, arms drop, hand dives into his sweatshirt pocket, fabric pinched and yanked. Metal flashes like a Moray eel.

Three bounding steps. The muzzle hovers inches from the old man's forehead, black and menacing. The man freezes, breath hitching. Without looking, he fumbles the receiver back onto its hook, then lowers the knife to the counter with trembling care. His hands rise, slow as surrender in a war long lost. His eyes lock on Charles. There is no rage now, only the hollow weight of defeat, like a flag lowered at dusk.

Charles jams the muzzle into the old man's ribs and moves at once. His right hand keeps the weapon steady; his left sweeps down, snatches the soup can, and whips upward. The tin connects with the man's brow in a dull, ringing thud. He never sees it coming. His legs go out from under him, and he topples into a daze, breath knocked sideways. Red leaks over his right eye and trails down his cheek.

He clutches his face and screams, a ragged, animal sound that scrapes the room raw. He crab-walks backward on hand and heels, skidding across tile toward the swinging door that separate the kitchen from the main store. His tortured screaming is relentless. Charles needs silence. Needs the world to stop. He scans wildly—steel, tile, glass, shadow—and his sweat runs cold.

The old man vanishes through the door, still wailing. The panel flaps twice, stutters, and settles shut. Charles bursts through in pursuit. Fluorescent lights hum above; the aisles stand rigid and bright. The shop owner claws at a shelf of canned goods, trying to drag himself upright. Cans clatter to the floor by the dozens, rolling away like coins. Metal rings. The shelf shivers.

Charles closes the distance and stops short, watching, just a second, as the man fights to stand. The moment he turns, Charles brings the can down again, hard. The blow lands across the bridge of the nose. Something gives. The face warps, collapses crooked. The man folds over himself, hands flying to his ruined center.

Charles swings and smashes the can across those hands. Knuckles crunch. Fingers buckle. The old man jerks his hands back and stares at them in horror, one eye blown wide, the other swelling shut, red pooling beneath the brow. His hands tremble uncontrollably. His breath saws in and out. He tries to speak and only sobs come out.

He slides down the shelf and lies face up on the floor, still screaming, still staring, transfixed by what his hands have become. Charles can't stand the sound. It chews the air, chews his nerves, chews everything. He drops to his knees beside the man, lets the pistol fall, and clamps both hands around the soup can. He lifts it high, takes a breath that tastes like metal, and brings the tin down with all the strength he owns.

The impact crushes the mouth. There is a pop of enamel, a wet cough. The old man gags and claws at the air, choking. Red froth bubbles and spatters. Warm spray freckles Charles's face and hoodie. He hits again, angling for the temple with another hard crack, clean and merciless. The sound travels through the shelf into the floor.

He strikes again. The can finds the cheek, the orbit, the soft places humans are built to protect. There's only dull resistance now, then a give. He hits the mouth one more time, and the jaw slackens, hanging crooked. The screaming continues, higher, thinner, like a siren winding down but never stopping.

Shut up!—Charles screams in his mind, and then, louder: Shut up! He swings and swings, the can rising and falling, rising and falling, each arc carving a notch in the night. The noise keeps going, keeps splitting the world open.

For a moment, he isn't inside his body. He's outside, looking through the small window in the swinging door, watching a man kneel over another and hammer light into darkness. The glass gives him back a dim reflection of a figure spattered and shaking, eyes like holes punched in paper. The clock's green glow bleeds across the scene, time dripping down the shelves like poison sap.

He lifts the can again, arms shaking, lungs burning, sudden silence and a realization pierces the din: the scream is his. It has been his, spilling out of his own mind like steam from a broken valve.

He stops. Breath shudders. The tin hovers above his head. Below him, where a face should be, there is only a ruin—wet, unrecognizable, a smear of light and red and hair against the tile. The shelf above rattles with the aftershock. Cans roll in slow circles and come to rest like spent planets.

The lights buzz softly. The clock ticks somewhere behind the counter. The refrigeration unit kicks on and throbs like a distant engine. The air smells like copper and dust and something from the bowels of an outhouse. A fine grit floats in the glow from the ceiling fixture, drifting through this new gravity.

Charles stares at what he's made. He is suddenly, terribly aware of it and of himself. Hunger brought him here and is what kept his hand moving. He can feel it still, a slow pulse in the wrists, an echo of impact that refuses to fade.

Charles lets the can fall. It skitters across tile and fades beneath a gondola shelf. He scoops the pistol, buries it in his hoodie pocket, and springs to his feet. He scans the aisles in a frantic zigzag—labels, warnings, caps—his hands knocking boxes and bottles to the floor. He is hunting for erasure, for a way to wipe himself out of this place.

There. Two plastic bottles with hazard diamonds and a smell that cuts the sinuses. He twists both caps off fast, thoughtless, and upends them. Clear liquid splashes and slicks over skin and clothing, pooling beneath the body, streaking across tile in pearlescent sheets.

Charles moves, feverish. He bolts to the counter and snatches a cheap lighter from the display, then cuts and returns, grabbing a two-pack of paper towels off a shelf as he passes.

24

Plastic tears. Paper unspools. He crouches, presses one rolls into the churned mess beside the body, and the towels drink deep. He thumbs the spark. A tongue of blue appears at the end of one roll, then edges orange, nibbling the paper's rim and then ignition.

He tosses the burning weight. Fire crawls first, then takes, drawing thin lines along the wet paths like veins lighting up. The glow blooms. The body flowers into orange, then into a rolling glare that pushes the shadows back to the corners. Heat licks Charles's face, painting it with an unholy warmth. His breath tastes chemical. His eyes sting.

He watches the glow find the hands. Those ruined knuckles look like a failed prayer. The flames gather, wrap, swallow. He feels the air change. The hum of the coolers is thinning under a new rush, the oxygen turning greedy. The smell rises heavy and sweet, edged with copper and singe, not food, not anything the living name. It is simply the scent of endings.

The fire dances, and for a moment Charles sees in it a ritual: the clock's sick-green light ticking out along the ceiling, the aisles like pews, the counter a simple altar. He stands at the center of it, a shadow crowned by heat, and the flames write his silhouette in flicker and ash.

He takes a step back. The blaze roars a little louder, not explosive, just relentless, a mouth widening as it learns to breathe. Light swims across his hoodie, his hands, the steel edges of the counters. Bottles reflect like candles in a chapel. The floor shines like a polished stone, and in it: a warped version of Charles looking back, eyes dark and hollowed by glow.

He is almost mesmerized. The orange stutter paints his features into something he does not recognize. The fire moves with purpose, with choice, selecting shelves, licking labels, kissing cartons until they curl. Heat presses his skin. The ceiling flickers.

Somewhere behind him, a voice snaps the spell.
"FREEZE!"
—

The leather bites his wrist as the strap cinches tight. A buckle snaps. Charles watches the motion. A metal tongue slides into its slot, a hand pulling hard.

Charles lifts his gaze to the glass. Rows of faces blur until one set of eyes locks with his: a white-haired woman in the second row. Her beauty is a ghost now, buried under years of grief and sleepless nights. Her expression is stone. No tremor. No mercy.

Charles mirrors her emptiness. Two statues staring across a gulf of glass while men fuss with straps, threading leather through loops, tugging until it creaks.

Then the sound in his head again and the drift begins.

It starts like a whisper in the cathedral of his skull. A single word, echoing down the nave:

"Guilty."

The juror's voice rolls through him, hollow and booming, and the sound opens doors he cannot close.

Yes. Guilty of what they know. Guilty of what they proved. But what of the rest? The things no badge ever touched; no courtroom ever named? The atrocities that live in shadow, stitched into the seams of his memory like rot in old wood?

He feels the pull—hard, relentless, dragging him backward through corridors of thought. The chair dissolves. The straps vanish. His body is a husk left behind as his mind plunges into the black vault where the real ledger waits.

Images flicker. Not scenes, but flashes. Teeth. Fire. A scream that never belonged to him but somehow did. A hand clawing at air. A face folding inward like paper soaked in rain. Fragments whirl and collide, each one a shard of something unspeakable.

And then the darkness swallows everything.

—

Charles pushes the wheelchair through the great room, wheels whispering over polished stone. The space is a museum of someone's victories: a high ceiling hung with a vast alabaster chandelier, triangle skylights around its base forming eight even slices of pale day, shelves of antique books running forty feet along the back wall, their spines like a choir of muted colors. Marble busts watch from between the volumes, unfamiliar faces holding their breath.

A voice runs beside the breath of motion. It is an older voice, warm, gruff, practiced. Charles listens in fragments. He's more interested in the room and how it glows. He looks down at the man's crown: gray strands thinned evenly, a starched canopy over a scalp freckled by years of sun. No bald spot, just age made visible.

"Thank you again for working so late," the man says, with a small laugh. "Unusual night. I hope it was worth your while."

He adds, softer, sincere: "You've been there for me, Chuck. I mean that."

Charles wrinkles his nose as if something sour rises from the floor, and guides the chair toward the elevator alcove. A button gleams under his thumb.

The man keeps talking while they wait, voice rising with promise. "Thank you, Chuckie. You'll be rewarded. Your loyalty will not be forgotten. You saved this family bringing me that package. We won't forget it."

Charles says nothing. The man sweetens the pot, sounding almost joy-drunk on relief. "We can do this right now. A check. Name it, son."

The doors part—polite, lying. No car. Only depth: a throat of steel ribs and cables, machinery breathing cold.

Everything happens fast and strange. The chair jolts forward; it tips; casters hang; the old man locks onto the frame, knuckles chalk-white, tendons strung like wire.

"Help me, Chucky! Help me!" he gasps, voice shredded thin over the drop.

Charles stands behind the teetering chair and watches. The man draws strength from somewhere deep, working himself inch by inch toward upright. He might make it. He might pull back into the room's soft light, leave the shaft to its darkness.

"Chucky! Please!"

For a suspended breath, everything holds: skylights haloed, alabaster glowing, books and busts watching, the two of them posed in a picture of mercy and gravity. The room seems to tip with them, a cathedral leaning toward a decision.

Charles steps in.

One cruel, clean motion: a driving kick to the chair's back. The grip loosens; fingers peel from the frame like wax under heat. Momentum takes the rest. The chair tilts and goes, and the man with it.

The scream tears upward, raw and primal, unraveling down the shaft like a frayed ribbon. Hands claw at cables, but they slide away, cold, indifferent. The body separates from the chair, both shapes tumbling in a grotesque duet, glancing against unseen ribs and ledges that make dull, tolling sounds. The architecture answers with its own voice.

Charles

Charles leans in, no expression on his face, and watches gravity finish what intent began. The figure below folds, twists, becomes something unshaped. A final collision reverberates up the shaft—a sound that belongs to more than metal. Then the chair skitters into a corner, clanging like a slammed prison cell door, and everything settles.

Far below, stillness arranges itself. Metal sprawls across flesh. A dark sheen spreads beside the head and pulls light into itself, gleaming black from this height like crude oil waking from stone. The skylight reflections tremble in it—eight slices of daylight fractured in the pool.

Charles breathes in and tastes gear oil and pennies. The chandelier hisses above him, soft as distant applause. The busts remain neutral; the books keep their secrets. The room's grandeur refuses to break.

He draws a breath sharper than the last and spits into the shaft. The sound vanishes before reaching the bottom. His lip curls—not triumph, not regret; only a feral, wordless thing.

He turns away. It is raining now. In the skylights, eight measured panes continue their quiet ticking, unchanged by what has fallen.

———

The strap bites down on his left wrist, leather creaking as the buckle locks. Charles feels the jolt of reality in the metal, pressure, restraint, and looks at the shaved skin beneath it, hairless and exposed. The escorts release their grip. His arms are his own again, though only for a breath. He exhales slow, closes his eyes, draws in air through his nose and holds it until his chest aches, then lets it seep out like steam.

The chamber vibrates around him. He shifts in the chair, the weight of it pressing like judgment. For a moment, he slackens. His lids lower, muscles loosen, posture almost indulgent, as if waiting for a warm towel and a practiced touch.

But the hands working here are not gentle. They cinch, they bind.

The sound reverberates in his head again, louder this time, coming straight from the fiber of his skull— a single burst of steam from a pressure cooker's valve but it is being sucked, not blown.

Darkness blooms behind his eyes. From that darkness, another face rises—close, too close. A girl's face, young and soft, framed in shadow.

—

"Sir... are you okay?" Her voice carries a note of compassion, a thread of light in the black.

The thread snaps.

Charles rolls on the pavement without thought, a violent swing of muscle and iron. The tire iron connects with a sound that silences specters. She drops, folding into the damp pavement next to him, eyes wide and fixed on his. They do not blink. Blood, black in the pale of night, slides across her temple, threads down over lashes, pools in the hollow where moonlight should live.

He stands slowly, breath steady now, and looks down. The moon washes everything in silver, bleaching color into monochrome. Her face is a mask of black gloss, her eyes two white coins glowing against it.

Charles steps over the body and walks to the car waiting with its door ajar, engine murmuring like a conspirator. He slides in, drops the gear shifter, spins the wheel hard. Tires shriek. The tunnel ahead yawns open, swallowing him whole as he rockets into its throat.

—

Charles

Two men ride side by side, knees in the breeze, engines pulsing like twin hearts. Dusk drapes the mountain road in violet haze. The Harleys rumble steady, their riders half-lost in the trance of wind and throttle. Ahead, the first tunnel appears. Its mouth a black hole.

They glance at each other, grins flashing in the dim. One blips his throttle; the other answers. The echo inside the tunnel blooms like thunder trapped in stone. They love this. They don't know why, only that it feels primal, like calling to something buried deep.

The left rider drops a gear, pops the clutch, and the bike leaps forward with a savage BRAAAP that ricochets off concrete. His partner follows, twisting hard, exhaust trumpeting raw and unbaffled. The tunnel spits them out into starlight, and the mountain exhales cool air across their faces.

Another bend. Another tunnel ahead, this one longer, darker. They nod, a silent pact, and twist again. Eighty-five miles per hour as they dive into the hollow. The walls blur. The roar swells. They downshift in unison, throttles wide, engines screaming like war horns. Neck and neck, each nudging ahead, then falling back. No cops here. No rules. Just speed and pride.

The exit rushes toward them, a purple rectangle framed in black. Beyond it, the straightaway gleams under the night sky. And there—a shape descending the grade: a military truck, hulking, its headlights burning holes in the dark.

They see it. They don't brake. Not yet. The left rider holds his lane, jaw locked against the wind as tight as his resolve, refusing surrender. Chicken is the game now. He'll yield only after the tunnel spits them out and the race is settled.

The night explodes around them as they burst free. The right rider wins by a length. The loser jerks hard into the right lane, throttle easing, heart pounding. The truck looms, massive, close enough to taste its diesel breath, but the rider is clear in time.

Then—wrongness.

The truck veers left, sudden, intentional and brutal, crossing the center line like a lion lunging. Metal meets metal in a shriek that splits the night.

The first bike slams the bumper. Momentum dies in an instant. The rider rockets forward, body a ragdoll of flesh and leather, vanishing into the truck's grille with a sound that isn't a sound but a sentence. The Harley crumples, sucked under, sparks vomiting from steel on stone.

The second impact follows a heartbeat later. The front wheel bites the bumper, and physics snaps its jaws. The bike jackknifes, rear wheel whipping skyward, folding the frame like a rattrap sprung. The rider is crushed between machine and machine, pinned in a geometry of ruin. For a breath, the motorcycle hangs embedded in the truck's front end, seat-first.

The truck rolls on, engine dead, silence broken only by escaping steam and the creak of torn metal. Then the air brakes slam. Tires shriek then broken chirps. The jolt flings the mangled bike and its rider free. They hit the asphalt together, spinning in a slow, savage pirouette, sparks fanning out like dying stars. Twenty feet of grinding slide before stillness claims them.

The night exhales. Steam coils from the truck's shattered nose. Only one headlight still functions. It burns through the fog, not as a beam but as a wall of light, painting the air in ghostly white.

The driver's door groans open. A boot drops to the step. A figure descends, black against the glow, smoke wreathing his silhouette.

Charles steps out of the pungent haze, tire iron dangling from his fist. The headlight crowns him in harsh light as he walks toward the two dark shapes sprawled on the road ahead. An engine ticks down like a dying clock.

—

Leather cinches his calves; brass jaws bite until the frame vibrates under him. Charles watches the hands work. They toil efficiently, impersonal. He studies the pale patch of skin where hair was shaved away, a sterile island on his thigh. Another strap snakes around the other leg, its ends meeting like jaws before they clamp shut.

He lifts his gaze. Beyond the pane, the gallery blooms in sickly haze with rows of faces turning to silhouettes, then to shadows.

Only the nearer rows are clear. There, in the third row, corner, two figures hold shape: her face drowned in his chest, his eyes red-hot lasers fixed on Charles. Hate has a stare; it does not need a sentence.

Charles stares back, unblinking, and pushes, hard, from his mind through his eyes, as if thought could pierce glass and brand itself into the man's skull. Images he's carried for years, vivid and bright, surge forward like sparks hurled against stone. He wills them to stick, to scar.

The straps cinch tighter. Hands check buckles. The hum of fluorescent light thickens. And then the sound again—like an airy voice saying "heeet," only instead of exhaling, the word is thunderously whispered on the inhale.

The room begins to dissolve. Edges soften, colors drain until all light is consumed into the center. Blackness blooms, vast and soundless, and from its depth something stirs: a memory, spike-sharp, rising to meet him.

Chapter 4: October 31st, 1983 – Age 16

Charles scrambles down the cliff, sneakers skidding on loose shale, breath sharp in his throat. The river glints below, black glass fractured by moonlight. At the bottom, only a few steps carry him to the spot where a figure sprawls among stones. It is a boy, older than he by a few years, leaner but taller, jersey bright against the dark. Orange with white trim. A name stitched in white across the shoulders: **James**. Below it, the number **12**, stark as a street sign.

The broken boy claws for a half-buried boulder, fingers slick, trembling. He hooks it, hauls, and a scream rips out— gurgling, shredded. His body jerks an inch before collapsing under its own ruin. One arm dangles uselessly, a dead weight dragging through river stones and sand. His legs are just wrong. Angles where no angles belong. Shadows hide the worst, but the shapes speak for themselves.

Charles steps closer. The boy's muscles knot and strain, veins standing like cords as he fights to move. His whole frame quivers. Charles crouches, tilts his head, and peers into the boy's eyes. They're wide, glassy, burning with something that isn't just pain.

Charles smiles.

"Please…" The word scrapes out, brittle as dry leaves. Trembling, bloody fingers reach for him. "Please. Take my hand. Pull me up."

The smile deepens. His chest lifts, chin tucks, a posture fashioned from quiet triumph.

Instead of the pleading hand, he reaches down, grabs the shattered arm by the wrist and yanks. The boy screams a sound that blows out and dies in a strangled gasp as air evacuates his lungs at once. Stones clatter under their weight as Charles drags him ten feet up the bank, leaving a slick trail that threads toward the river. Blood beads and runs, weaving through pebbles like spider silk caught in a current.

Charles drops the twisted arm. It hits the ground with the thud of wet rope. The boy lies face-up, gasping, eyes wide and pleading, mouth working without sound. His body writhes in broken convulsions, trying to knit itself back together through sheer will. It doesn't.

Charles crouches again, gaze locked on eyes that beg, eyes that accuse. His own expression doesn't change. His hands find a boulder, heavy and cold, its weight boiling through his bones. Slowly, he rises. He lifts, trembling with effort, and holds it high above his head.

The rock falls like a heavy sentence.

Impact silences the night. A wet, blunt concussion. Fragments of dark fluid and pale shards spray, flung in twin arcs across stone. The boulder settles with a dull scrape, half-burying what remains.

Charles exhales, bends, and rolls the rock aside. The ruin underneath barely resembles a face. Eyes still in their sockets, skewed inward like broken compasses. Nose collapsed into shadow. Teeth scattered like dice across a tongue that droops grotesquely from an open jaw. The geometry of a life, undone.

He leans closer, breath fogging in the cold. The thick, sweet smell of iron and earth rises. He inhales, slow, deliberate, as if memorizing it. His lips part. A tongue flicks out, tasting the edge of what drips from the ear, the gesture quick, bestial, and gone.

Charles pulls back a foot, staring into those crossed eyes, their final focus locked in eternal contradiction. He has a look of disgust on his face brought on by the scene, history and the salty, metallic taste lingering on his tongue.

—

Charles finally blinks. As his lids flutter open again, his eyes lock on a man beyond the glass, a glare stretches tight between them. The man's stare doesn't waver. It is hard, white-hot, a furnace banked behind human eyes.

Hands tug at the leather restraints, testing buckles, cinching straps tighter against Charles's arms and chest. The chair emits a faint frequency under his weight, felt but not heard, a machine waiting for its purpose.

A woman lifts her head from the man's chest. Her face is drained and long from grief and rage. For a breath, she hesitates. Then, her gaze hooks into his. She wants to look away. She doesn't. Hate roots her there, holding her eyes open like toothpicks of torture. Hate makes her watch.

Charles meets her stare, unflinching. The silence between them thickens, a black rope pulling tighter.

The sound echoes in his head again, even louder this time.

He feels the room dim at its edges, the glow bleeding out, faces dissolving into shadow. Only these two remain, they're eyes burning through glass, through distance, through memory.

The chamber fades. The straps vanish. Darkness consumes all behind his lids, vast and soundless, and from its depth something stirs. A memory reaches upward like a claw from hell, dragging him back into the black corridors of his past.

Chapter 5: November 10th, 1980 – Age 13

The morning breathes fog across the river valley, an opaque veil clinging low to the earth. The sun is climbing, bleeding gold into the mist, but its warmth hasn't reached the ground. The air bites, sharp and clean, tasting of stone and leaf rot. Fall is in full swing. Trees are stripped bare, their crooked arms clawing at the sky.

Charles picks his way down the cliff, the toes of his sneakers seeking any small crack for anchor. His skinny frame strains against gravity, muscles tight as piano strings, every slip a whisper of death waiting below. His breath drags in his throat, white puffs breaking against the chill. The sun paints his face in golden light, but the cold still owns him.

The slope softens near the bottom. He hits level ground and doesn't stop. Momentum hurls him forward into a sprint along the riverbank. Stones crunch underfoot. Water murmurs beside him, black and glassy, carrying floating shards of sky. To his left, the cliff rises higher with every stride, a wall of broken bone climbing into the clouds. He runs harder, faster, lungs clawing for air, chest burning like a furnace stoked too hot. He runs and runs.

Finally, the fire wins. He stops dead, hands clasped on his crown, sucking breath in through his nose, blasting it out through his mouth in forced bursts. Circles carve themselves into the frost as he paces, pulling life back into his lungs.

When the ache dulls, he cuts sharp toward the cliff. His sneakers crunch over gravel until he finds the perfect spot—a flat stone waiting like an altar. He stacks smaller rocks on its back, one by one, a crude monument marking something only he understands. Then he steps away, back to the river's spine, and stands in the hush of water and wind.

A few more breaths. Then he moves again—slow at first, then faster—jogging upriver, chasing something unseen, something that waits beyond the bend.

Ten minutes of steady jogging and Charles halts, shoes grinding into frost-streaked gravel. His breath comes quick but controlled. He could run forever at this jogging pace. Practice has carved endurance into his bones. He comes here every chance he gets.

To his left, a familiar cairn rises from the riverbank—a stack of stones that nature didn't make. Charles bends, grips a boulder nearly as big as his frame will allow, arms stretched low and wide, back bowed under its weight. His fingers burn, tendons screaming, but he waddles forward, bow-legged, toward the pile. At the last moment, he veers right and drops the stone before a patch of shrubs clawing a sand mound near the cliff wall.

He returns for another. And another. Ten times he hauls rock, each trip heavier than the last, until his muscles quiver and his breath rasps like torn paper. On the tenth, he collapses to his knees, sweat chilling on his skin. He crawls now, dragging himself toward the shrubs, then flattens to his belly and slides into the green tangle, vanishing like a creature retreating to its burrow.

A hand shoots out, snatching a smaller boulder, pulling it into the foliage. Then two arms reach, rolling another stone into the hollow. One by one, the rocks disappear, swallowed by the shrubs as if the earth itself is eating them. Charles emerges halfway, grabs another, drags it down into the hidden depression. Again. Again. Until all ten are gone.

He rises inside the secret hollow—a pocket carved between cliff and shrub-covered mound. From the river, nothing betrays its existence. The mound curves in a semi-circle, its ends kissing the cliff face, sealing him in. Here, his work waits: a stone wall, rough and rising, its L-shape jutting from the cliff like a broken tooth. Three feet thick in places, three feet high in others—a fortress in progress.

Charles grips a boulder, hefts it up his arms, arching backward to gain height, and slams it onto the wall's crown. He fetches another. It's too heavy. It thuds to the ground between wall and cliff. He leaves it, grabs another, almost as big, and hauls it around the wall's rear. He steps onto the dropped stone, a makeshift pedestal, and pauses; chest swelling, chin tucking as pride flickers through him. Smart. Strong. Building something no one will ever see.

The boulder shifts beneath him in a slow, treacherous tilt. Sand grinds under his sneakers, and gravity yanks him sideways. He lunges to steady himself, but the stone he's carrying slips from his grip. It crashes down, pinning his right hand against the jagged crown of the wall.

A sound pops inside him, wet and sharp. He feels it before he hears it: the fingertip giving way, something inside bursting like a ripe fruit under pressure. Pain ignites in his nerves, a white-hot flare that blinds thought. He can't scream. He can't even breathe at first. The world narrows to a single pulse hammering in his skull, ticking like a warped clock. His vision narrows to a single pinpoint.

Charles clamps his jaw until his teeth ache, eyes squeezed so tight the darkness blooms red, then white. Seconds stretch into eternities. Each heartbeat is a strike of iron against bone. He fights the black edge of unconsciousness, dragging air into his lungs in broken gulps. Finally—finally—his mind claws back enough control to act. With his free hand, he heaves the boulder aside.

Shock freezes him. His finger is a ruin. The skin is peeled, nail shattered, pale tissue bulging through a split that shouldn't exist. It looks wrong, vulgar, like something that belongs inside, not out. Warm, relentless blood slicks his palm. Instinct takes over. He shoves the finger into his mouth. Copper floods his tongue, thick and salty, but there's something else: fibrous, alien. He tastes what he saw, and it makes his stomach lurch.

He stumbles, searching for anything, just anything to bind the wound. His thoughts scatter like startled bats. Wrap it. Stop the bleeding. That's it. He singlehandedly yanks his filthy white tank top over his head in one violent motion, twists it around his injured hand, and squeezes until the fabric darkens with spreading red. He balls his fist inside the cloth, pressure his only weapon against the pounding agony.

Charles scrambles up the mound, one hand clawing for purchase, the other clutched like a secret. He bursts from the shrubs, staggering toward the riverbank. Rage boils under the pain. It is rage at the stone, at himself, at the stupidity of it all. He kicks at pebbles, thrashes his arm, and expels a sound that shouldn't exist. A tormented burst of air shreds from a throat that never speaks. It scrapes past scar tissue like rust grinding on steel, a hollow, broken thing that claws at the air. No words, no voice; just a guttural exhalation warped into something primal. It's the sound of pain made physical, a breath turned weapon.

He spins, breath short, vision tunneling. Run home? No. Damn it! He clamps his ruined hand under his opposite armpit, bouncing on his toes like a child desperate for relief. Nothing helps. The pain is a furnace, and his blood feels like molten lava.

Then—water. The thought slices through the chaos. Coolness. Silence. He lunges forward, splashing three steps into the river, and plunges his hand beneath the surface. The shock of cold is salvation. It bites, then soothes, numbing the fire. His pulse slows. His breath steadies. Around him, the water lies unnaturally still, deep and quiet, as if holding its breath. Too quiet for morning. But maybe that's because his scream just shattered the world.

A soft squeak breaks the hush, then a gentle kerplunk from the opposite bank. Charles turns his head slowly. A frog glides across the misted surface, its tiny head slicing the water like a scalpel through gray flesh. Behind it, the river parts in a wound that closes almost as soon as it opens.

He crouches motionless, watching. Ripples fan out, brushing his ankles before kissing the bank. One, two, three hops and the frog claims a flat stone just waking to sunlight. Steam coils upward from the warming rock, curling around the amphibian like a spirit's breath.

Charles notices that the amphibian is missing its left, rear foot. The small, green stump long ago healed. He rises without sound, water dripping from his hands in slow, deliberate falls, each drop landing with a quiet certainty. The frog doesn't flinch. It sprawls belly-down, basking in its fragile kingdom. A shadow swallows the stone. The frog shifts, then settles again, trusting the stillness.

The stillness betrays it.

A boulder descends doom, striking with a crack that shudders through the bank. For an instant, the world holds its breath. Then color erupts—dark, green, and something that should never see daylight. Fragments scatter, some vanishing into the river with tiny plunks that feel strangely counted. Charles grins, small and crooked, at the sound.

His finger throbs faintly now, almost forgotten, thanks to this distraction. He nudges the stone aside with his foot and crouches low, knees hovering around his ribcage. The frog lies flattened, crude in its silence. For a heartbeat, Charles imagines it springing back, cartoon-perfect, top hat and cane in hand, ready to dance away. But the pooling red at its mouth kills the thought cold.

He scans the ground, finds a sharp, slender twig. He prods the limp body once, twice, then leans close, inhaling deeply as if the scent might tell him something. Closer still. His tongue flicks out, tasting the membrane clinging like a yolk. Disgust twists his face, but only for a breath. Then he moves with purpose.

Charles scoops the carcass into his bare hand and pinches its jaw until the mouth gapes wide. The stick slides in, piercing through with a single brutal thrust. Entrails dangle like broken threads, swinging wildly as he turns and bolts toward the shrubs—toward the place where secrets wait.

Charles drops to his knees at the shrubs, then flattens to his belly and slides down the sand like a shadow. Without pause, he springs up and darts behind the L-shaped wall. There, the cliff offers a secret. Low on the ground, protruding from the sand, a triangle-shaped crack, jagged yet perfect, like a doorway carved by something older than time. Four feet high at its peak, three feet wide at the base. His sanctuary awaits within.

He crawls through on elbows and knees, one arm clutching the frog impaled on its stick, the other bound and throbbing beneath a blood-soaked shirt. The passage squeezes him, stone scraping his ribs, until—light.

He emerges into a hollowed world: a vast sandy chamber encircled by sheer walls that curve upward into a ceiling pierced by a single round opening. Sunlight pours through like liquid gold, painting the western rim in amber as morning climbs. Above, the sky burns blue. Below, silence reigns.

This is his place. Hidden from every eye but the birds that might pass overhead, and even they would see only trees masking the rim. At the far end, a crescent wall rises, five feet high and thick as a fortress. It is fashioned by human hands, much like the smaller wall outside the cavern. Its curve hugs the cliff, leaving a narrow gap like a mouth waiting to swallow him. Charles slips through and enters the heart of his creation.

He plants the frog at the base of the wall, the stick stabbing sand like a flagpole. Fifty now. Fifty frog trophies in a grim amphibian parade. His fresh kill gleams beside relics that time has gnawed to bone. Some frogs slump in the first stages of ruin, their skins dulled and shrinking, their eyes clouded like old glass. Others are brittle husks, hollowed and weightless, clinging to sticks like paper lanterns. At the farthest edge, only skulls remain, pale and grinning, with stray bones scattered like punctuation in the sand. Charles steps back, arms lifting in a silent V, his chest swelling with pride. His art. His order. His truth.

He turns slowly and steps back to take in more of his handywork, scanning the voids between stones. Eyes stare back glassless, lifeless. A chipmunk slumps in a crevice, two more flanking it like guards. A snake coils stiff around a protruding stick, frozen mid-strike. Fish heads crowd the gaps, a school forever suspended in rock. From three jutting branches hang three cats, their ropes frayed, their bodies long surrendered to decay, their fur sloughed away, limbs rigid, faces collapsed into grimaces of bone. Beyond them, a beaver props grotesque, an otter beside it, both skewered, posed as companions.

Every creature faces the same way. As if drawn by gravity, their ruined gazes converge on a shadowed recess at the farthest wall. Charles follows their silent chorus to the cubby carved in stone. There, spread like an ancient relic, lies the cat— the first. Its flesh hardened to leather, its white fur mostly gone, leaving only a hint of a tail and the unmistakable curve of a skull. Time has stripped it bare, yet it commands the room like an idol.

Charles kneels. His breath slows. His eyes soften with something that almost looks like reverence. He nods once, a gesture heavy as a vow. This cat began it all. The axis on which his secret world turns.

Charles lingers at the threshold of his secret world, reluctant to leave. The air inside feels heavier than the forest beyond, as if the walls themselves hold their breath. He turns from his grim gallery of small trophies and steps out from behind the crescent wall, his movements slow, deliberate, like a boy savoring the last seconds of a ritual.

The open chamber stretches before him, its sand glowing pale under the shaft of sunlight pouring through the ceiling's round eye. At its center rises a monolith of stone, jagged and immovable, thrusting upward like the spine of the earth. This monolith appears to be the main chunk of granite that fell from above, its stalactites now facing upward, transforming them to stalagmites.

Charles approaches, his sneakers whispering across the sand. Perched atop that spiny stone is the carcass of a deer, or what remains of one. Its body sprawls in a posture that suggests surrender, limbs stiffened into unnatural angles, hide dulled to the color of old parchment. The smell is faint now, dry and brittle, but it lingers like a memory that refuses to die.

Charles pauses, studying the ruin. He cannot fully claim this kill. Nature delivered it here, broken and bleeding, one wrong step sending it tumbling from the cliff above. He remembers the way it landed and how the rock became its altar, how its breath rattled like a washboard in the dark. Paralyzed. Barely alive. A gift, though he never asked for it.

Charles

He stands motionless, eyes tracing the contours of bone beneath the shriveled flesh, the way time has gnawed the edges of what was once vibrant. Around the deer, under the light layer of sand, the top of the stone altar bears faint scars—marks of struggle, grooves etched by hooves that once clawed for escape. They lead nowhere. They end here, at this monument of stillness.

Charles exhales slowly, a soundless breath that feels heavier than words. Then he turns toward the triangle-shaped crack. He begins to crawl back through the narrow throat of stone. As he moves, his mind drifts, pulled backward to the day he first saw the deer lying there, its eyes wide and wild, its body shattered against the rock. That memory waits for him like a shadow at the edge of thought.

The sound bellows from within his mind again. The reverberation begins before the sound—a pinhole of vacuum leak being plugged with a fingertip.

heeet

Chapter 6: January 1980 – Age 12

The pull is stronger now. Charles doesn't feel the mahogany chair beneath him at all anymore. He is no longer being snapped back to the chamber. The truth of his present reality fades, and when his eyes open, they belong to a boy, twelve years of age, sneakers crunching frost-bitten leaves in the woods behind his home. He isn't searching for anything; not really. Just wandering, scouting like boys do, chasing the quiet thrill of discovery. He is miles from home, deep in the vast forest that adorns the clifftop.

Then he hears it.

A sound that doesn't belong to the forest's rhythm. A broken bleat, thin as rice paper. It rises, falls, then rises again, pulling him toward the trees like a voice calling from under the earth. Charles moves faster, weaving through trunks, breath clouding in the cold air. The sound grows sharper, desperate. He bursts into a small clearing and stops dead.

The ground gapes open before him—a hole in the world, rough and dark, its rim fringed with roots, slate and frost. Sunlight spears down through the opening, illuminating a hidden chamber far below. Sand sparkles in the cone of light, and at its center, sprawled across a massive stone, lies the source of the cries: a deer. Its body is twisted, legs splayed at wrong angles, eyes wide and wild. Stalagmites protrude from its right hip, left shoulder and through the flesh surrounding the ribs just below that shoulder. The deer kicks feebly, hooves scraping stone, but the effort is futile. The animal is broken. Trapped. Doomed.

Charles kneels at the edge of the abyss, peering into the secret place he never knew existed. The deer's bleat echoes upward, thin and hopeless, and something shifts inside him. He feels a weight pressing against his mind, a thought he can't name. He stays there for a long time, watching, listening, feeling the cold bite his cheeks while the sun crawls higher. The deer doesn't stop. It can't. And Charles knows, with a clarity that feels older than his years, that no one else will come. No one else will help.

It takes him hours to decide what to do. His mind turns the problem over and over, searching for an answer that feels right. When it comes, it feels like a light flicking on in a dark room. Simple. Brutal. Sure.

Mid-morning finds him back at the rim, arms aching from the weight of stones he's just finished dragging through the underbrush. He lines them up like checkers, five in all, each one heavy enough to matter.

Forty feet below, the deer lies on its altar of rock, still breathing, still waiting. Charles grips the first stone, hefts it to the edge, sends mental apologies to the deer and lets it fall.

It misses, thudding into sand with a loud, muffled whoomph. The second does the same. But the near misses teach him the angles, timing, the way gravity pulls. The third stone finds its mark. It crashes into the deer's ribs with a sound that cracks the silence, splintering bone and snapping spine. The animal's rear legs go limp at once. Its front hooves thrash wildly, trying to drag its broken body in a frantic, hopeless crawl. The cries tear upward, desperate and serrated, then falter into gasps.

Charles doesn't stop. The fourth stone drops, striking close to the last, jolting the deer sideways a little. He waits, breath steady, eyes locked on the target. There is still silent movement below. The fifth stone is the end. He lifts it high, feels its weight press into his palms, then lets it go. The boulder plummets, strikes the deer's skull with a sound that is both thud and sharp crack, The body jerks once, then stills. The stone rolls half a turn and settles in the sand below, leaving silence in its wake.

Charles stares down into the hollow, chest rising and falling. The altar gleams faintly in the morning light, the deer draped across it like an offering. Around the surface of the rock, the sand is scarred with marks of struggle; grooves that lead nowhere. He feels something then, something he can't decipher, as the echo of that last impact fades into the trees. It isn't triumph. It isn't grief. It's heavier than both.

And above the hidden chamber, the boy stands alone, staring into the place that will one day hold his secrets.

The sound again—*heeet* booming so loud inside his head that he instinctively smashes his palms to his ears. It is a futile attempt.

Chapter 7: November 10th, 1973 – Age 7

The pull drags him deeper. The chair, the buzzing of the chamber lights, the present—they're gone now. When Charles blinks, he's seven again, knees bent on the center of the splintered floor of the shed, his back to its rough wooden door. The air inside is stale, thick with the smell of oil, must and rust. The light slicing through the gaps in the boards paints stripes across his damp hair. He works in silence, hunched over something on the floor, his small hands moving with frantic precision.

From the distance comes the squeak of the house's back screen door. The sound is long, then short, culminating in a slam of aluminum on wood. A woman's voice floats across the yard, thin and searching.

"Charles?"

His head snaps toward the shed door behind him. Wide eyes fix on the slivers of daylight between the boards. He waits, breath held, listening for footsteps. Nothing. Only the birds beyond the walls, chirping like nothing is wrong. Slowly, he turns back to his task.

The voice calls again, closer now, edged with worry. "Charles! Where are you?"

He whips his head around once more, muscles twisted, every nerve straining for sound. The house door squeaks again, quick, then quicker, and slams shut hard. Silence settles like dust. Charles stares at the shed door, motionless, until the quiet feels safe. Then he bends low, returning to his work.

Sweat beads on his forehead, sliding into his eyes, burning them raw. His hair clings to his temples, damp and matted. He grunts softly as he tugs and pulls, trying to keep the noise down. The effort is fierce, but his lips stay sealed. No words. No sound. Just the scrape of metal against wood and the wet drag of something that resists him. He reaches for a green-handled box cutter that sits just within reach.

Then—a creak. Long, loud, splitting the hush like a hatchet. The shed door groans open, flooding the tiny room with blinding light. Charles jerks his head around, squinting against the glare. A silhouette of a man fills the doorway. His shadow is broad and towering, framed in sunlight like a second coming.

Charles throws up his left arm to shield his eyes. The hand he raises gleams slick and crimson, blood glistening in the full spectrum of daylight. The color is vivid, foul, dripping from his fingers like paint spilled on a canvas.

"What the fuck have you done? What the fuck is wrong with you?" The man's voice booms, bursting with fury.

Two strides and he's inside, boots pounding the floor. His hand clamps around Charles's blood-soaked wrist and yanks hard, lifting the boy clean off the ground. Charles's legs buckle, useless, dangling like windchimes. He flails for balance, his other hand clutching a green box cutter. The blade flashes once before the man seizes that wrist too, shaking it until the knife clatters down, biting into the wood beside a dark stain.

In a blur, the man hurls the boy toward the shed door. It explodes open, slamming against the outer siding as Charles's small body rockets through. He clears the ramp, hits the ground hard, and rolls, head cracking against earth, momentum carrying him two more feet before he slams into the birdbath. Water erupts, drenching his hair, cascading down his face. The concrete basin wobbles, teeters, then tips. Charles stares up, dazed, as the heavy disk tilts toward him in slow motion. He jerks his head aside just as it crashes down, gouging the dirt an inch from where his skull had been.

Charles

He scrambles upright, blood mingling with water, streaming down his cheeks in thin, diluted rivulets. As his eyes regain focus, he sees his foster brother dart into the house through the back door.

As the house door slams against the frame, the shed door bursts open again, slamming like a gunshot into the outer siding. The man storms out, rage radiating off him like heat. He grabs Charles by the back of his shirt, fist knotting the fabric, and hauls him toward the house, shoving him forward in jerks that make his feet barely skim the ground. The grip on his collar is iron, the only thing keeping him from collapsing entirely.

Behind them, the shed door swings shut, hiding the floor where blood still glistens in the thin slices of light.

The door to the main house slams shut, swallowing Charles and the man in a single violent sound. Brief, brittle silence settles over the yard—until the shed door groans again. Slowly, cautiously, a woman pulls it open. The rusty spring stretches with a long, aching creak as sunlight begins to invade the darkness.

The light crawls across the floor in slow increments, revealing the scene piece by piece; a cruel unveiling. First, the edge of a thick, wet blood stain, dark and glistening. Then a hammer, lying askew. Four nails scattered like dropped teeth. More blood. Thicker now. She feels her breath catch, her chest tighten. She wishes the light would stop moving, stop peeling back the shadows. But her own hand keeps pulling the door wider, as if it belongs to someone else. She feels outside herself, detached, powerless.

The light flashes off the metal of the green-handled box cutter, its blade buried in the wood beside a smear of red. Her stomach knots. Her eyes widen. And then the door swings fully open, flooding the shed with rays of truth.

The scene is complete.

She clamps a hand over her mouth, inhaling in short, sharp bursts that never seem to reach her lungs. Her other hand trembles against the doorframe as her gaze locks on the horror at the center of the floor.

A blood-star glistens on the boards. In its heart lies Snowflake; her cat—his cat, quartered with a maniac's malice: head, tail, four limbs set an inch off fate.

She moves in.

The fur is ruin, matted and wine-dark. Nails crucify each paw to the grain. Twine leashes the tail to a hammered-flat anchor. The eyes sit before the severed head like coins for passage; two zinc spikes spear the sockets, fixing the skull to wood. The heads of the spike are different than the rest of the nails.

The woman stumbles back, colliding with the door so hard it bursts wide and flings her onto the ramp. She tumbles down, landing on her rear, then crab-walks backward across the grass, her eyes locked on the shed as if expecting the crucified thing to rise and lunge. Her breath comes in choked gasps, but the terror clawing at her chest isn't just for the dead animal. It is for the boy. For what he is. For what he's become.

Her stomach heaves. She rolls to her knees and vomits into the grass, choking on bile. She sobs. Three more convulsions wrack her body before she staggers upright, never once looking back. Then she runs; screaming, crying, toward the house. Sunlight swallows her for an instant before she vanishes into the black mouth of the doorway. Hinges shriek. The spring exhales. The door slams shut behind her, sealing the darkness inside.

The yelling, crying and gnashing of teeth continues inside the house. Charles brings his palms to his ears and presses hard to block out the chaos. He squeezes his eyes shut tight.

Voices muffle, their sharp edges dulled. The voices begin to descend into complete, black silence.

And then the sound comes, loud as a thunder roll, inside his head. He squeezes his eyes shut tight, palms press harder to his ears, to no avail. The reverberation begins to roll to a deafening crescendo—*heeet*.

—

Charles opens his eyes. A bright yellow Tonka dump truck gleams before him, its pressed steel body radiating the morning light. It's no hand-sized toy. This is the big one, the kind you can ride. His birthday gift. Brand new. Charles runs his fingers along the cool metal, then reaches for Snoopy, his stuffed companion, and settles the dog in the truck bed like a passenger ready for adventure.

He grips the undercarriage and begins rolling the truck in wide half-moons across the rug. No engine noises. No shouted commands. Just silence and motion. Charles never needs sound to play. His imagination runs louder than any motor. Today, he's a racer. Snoopy completes the laps like a champion.

After a few circuits, Charles stops. He lifts the bed of the truck, dumping Snoopy onto the rug. A quiet, private smile flickers across his lips. He circles the truck once, then rolls it backward, then forward, stopping just short of the doll. Back and forth, teasing the edge of collision. Then Snoopy climbs aboard again, and the race resumes.

Charles straddles the truck now, short legs pumping, hands gripping tight as he propels himself faster and faster. The wheels lift, the frame tilts, and for a moment he feels airborne. Then—slip. The truck body hinges open, metal levering apart. His weight crashes down on the bed, and pain explodes in his fingers: sharp, searing, immediate.

Charles jerks upright, clutching his right hand in his left. Breath hisses through clenched teeth, harsh and fast. No scream. Just air, hot and furious. He stares at the finger. Blood beads at the nail. A black bruise stains beneath. He shoves it into his mouth, tasting iron. Anger flares. Snoopy flies across the room, smacking a tub of Lincoln Logs. The tub topples, spilling wood across the hardwood in a clattering rain.

The door bursts open.

Charles spins, hiding his injured hand behind his back as his eyes lock on the figure in the doorway.

Todd. Arms folded, grin sharp as broken glass.

"What's up, Chuck?" His voice drips mockery.

Charles says nothing.

"You are!" Todd unfolds his arms, pointing like a judge delivering sentence. "You're up-chuck, puke face! What's all the noise?"

Charles stands frozen, pitiful, both hands hidden behind him. One is gripping the other like stolen money.

Todd steps in, circling. "What are you hiding, up-chuck? Did you break something? Something of mine?" His tone hardens. "Let me see."

Charles pivots, trying to keep his back turned, but Todd moves like a quarterback, cutting angles, closing gaps. His words coil tighter, squeezing the air from the room. Charles knows what's coming. He's known for years. Todd has perfected the art of cruelty—pain without marks, lies without cracks. Every bruise, every broken thing, every dead creature on this property—Todd's shadow lurks behind them all. But no one sees it. No one hears it. Charles can't speak. Todd speaks for him. Always.

"C'mon, up-chuck. Show me." The grin widens.

Charles

Charles braces, face muscles flexed, breath shallow. He knows what is coming.

The slap comes fast and sharp, an open-handed crack that sears against his cheek, but when it lands, its sound is not of a hand slapping the meat of a cheek. It is the sound.

An echo ending in a *heeet*.

The sting of the slap is white-hot, blinding. And in that instant, the room fractures. The rug, the truck, the sunlight all vanish in shards pulled to nowhere. He's falling again, backward, spiraling into a memory older and darker.

—

A hairy hand, aged well beyond the years of his brother. Another slap. Age five.

Blackness again and another *heeet* explodes in his head.

The pull tightens, dragging him further back. The sting of the slap fades to a dull heat, cooled by the chill of autumn air on his cheek. Charles blinks and finds himself standing on the front porch, small and silent, his shoes dusted with dry leaves. Beside him looms a man in a black suit, polished shoes gleaming like obsidian. The man smells faintly of leather and ink. His hand rests on Charles's shoulder; not heavy, not gentle, just there.

The storm door creaks open. Charles's foster dad, David, fills the frame, one hand gripping the handle, the other braced against the jamb. His eyes drop to Charles first, scanning his face, then snap upward to the man in the suit. Anger flickers like a struck match.

"What happened?" His voice is low, tight, teeth barely parting.

The man's expression doesn't change. "Mr. James," he says evenly, "there was an incident during group play. Young master James became… unruly. We had to intervene."

David's jaw works. "Intervene?" He repeats the word like it tastes wrong. "I told you before—no marks. I don't want questions."

A pause stretches between them, long enough for the wind to rattle the brittle leaves in the gutter. The man reaches into his coat, smooth and deliberate, and withdraws a checkbook. The gesture is practiced, almost ritualistic.

"We appreciate your discretion," he says, flipping the cover open. "And we'd like to offer a little extra for the inconvenience. Two hundred should suffice."

David's eyes sink, shame pooling in their depths. His gaze drops to the porch boards, then snaps back up, sharp and sudden. "No more," he says, voice hard now. "You understand? No more."

"Yes, Mr. James." The man's tone is calm, almost soothing. "We'll do our best."

The check tears free with a crisp snap. Paper slides against paper; a sound too loud in the quiet huddle. David hesitates, then takes it, his fingers curling slow around the edge.

"Good day," the man says, already turning. His shoes click against the porch steps, measured and precise, as he walks toward the waiting car; a long black shape idling at the curb like a shadow.

Charles watches without blinking, the wind tugging at his hair. The door closes behind him with a hollow thud, and his vision begins to blur, pulling him deeper still.

The world tightens, then snaps. Todd's palm flashes white, and the sting detonates across Charles's cheek. The circular rug skews, spins and the Tonka truck blurs. When it steadies, he's here, seven again, breath broken, finger throbbing from the pinch under steel.

Todd looms. "What's up, Chuck?" he says, voice sweet as spoiled milk.

Charles keeps his hands behind his back. His right hand pulses heat. He can taste metal in the back of his throat. Swallowed tears? He says nothing. As always.

Todd steps closer, circling, a lazy predator tracing loops around prey that pretends not to tremble.

"You're up-chuck. Puke face." His grin shows teeth but no warmth.

Charles angles away, guarding the hand, guarding himself. Todd cuts in, quick; a practiced move, and seizes Charles at the shoulders. He gives him a rough shake that rattles air from his lungs.

"Let me see your little secret," he whispers, and there's a kind of glee under the whisper, a bright hunger that makes the room colder.

Charles clenches. He won't show the hand. He won't give it up. Todd laughs under his breath with a delighted, private sound and releases him just enough to make him stumble. "Birthday boy," Todd says. "Got you a present."

The words should feel kind. They feel like a hook.

Todd circles fully behind him, clamps an arm across Charles's chest and covers his eyes with a dry, warm palm.

"No peeking, stain." His breath grazes Charles's ear; his body presses Charles forward. The grip is confident, almost casual. The pressure isn't enough to choke; just to steer. Charles takes short steps, careful, heels brushing spilled Lincoln Logs, then hardwood, then the colder linoleum of the kitchen floor. The house is a corridor of sound: the drag of sock on floorboard, the soft slap of a screen door, the open air beyond. He hears leaves crackle. Hears Todd's shoes scuff. Smells damp wood and the faint sweetness of cut grass going brown.

He wants to move slower. He can't. Todd keeps him gliding, nudging, directing. The ground changes underfoot, first plank, then ramp. A hinge complains in a long, aching groan. The palm leaves his eyes in a burst of light and a shove, hard enough to send him stumbling forward into a dense musk of oil and old lumber.

—

The shed is darker than he expects, even with sunlight lancing through narrow seams between boards. Dust hangs in the air like a held breath. Workbenches rise around him, tall, heavy giants in the dim. Somewhere above, a tin hood dangles with a bulb hidden inside, a chain swaying gently from motion he didn't see.

Charles blinks. His eyes adjust. Behind him, metal scrapes. The latch on the outside of the door works with a click; the sound of a door deciding what stays in and what comes out. Todd's outline fills the gaps and then disappears as the shed door rattles.

Charles is alone.

He pushes himself to standing. The space stretches long in the dim, corners deep as pockets. He moves a step and lands on the edge of a hammer, the steel rolling under his weight. His ankle twists. He drops to one knee, breath hissing through teeth, and finds himself face-to-face with Snowflake.

The cat looks back.

Except—no. Not a look. Something arranged to feel like one.

Charles's breath stops. The universe narrows to the small circle where he kneels. Snowflake lies in the center of a shape painted across the floor—lines and angles in a red that's too dark to be paint, forming a geometry that makes the boards feel violated. The body is laid out in parts that do not belong apart:

58

head placed with precision, limbs near but not connected, tail set like a separate statement. The white fur is no longer white. Hardware pins pieces to wood flooring. Twine tethers what shouldn't need tethering. It is carefully done. Intentionally done.

The sight cracks something inside him. The scene sprawled before him breaks into shards that immediately, magnetically pull back together.

He falls the rest of the way to his knees. Hot, prickling tears surge. He reaches with both hands, forgetting pain, forgetting the throbbing finger. He wrenches at a nail holding a paw in place; it doesn't move. He slips. Blood slickens his grip. He reaches for the hammer, hooking its claw under the head the way he's seen in passing, not understanding leverage, only understanding that together belongs together. He pulls straight up but nothing gives. He tries again and still nothing. He pants, silent, a small machine running out of power.

"Charles?"

The name floats through the seams, thin as mist. Annie's distant, uncertain voice calling from the yard.

He freezes. Eyes dart to the door. He waits. No more sound. Only birds. Only the faint murmur of wind pressing the boards. He wipes his face with the back of his hand and leaves smeared red across his cheek. He goes back to the nail. Back to the claw. He adjusts. He tries.

He notices twine at the tail. Pulls. It won't give. A green utility knife sits nearby, blade buried in flooring, bright handle glinting like a warning sign. He takes it and brings it close to the tie, careful. He wants the twine off. He wants the cat whole. He wants the geometry to stop being geometry and go back to being Snowflake.

"Charles? Where are you?"

The call is closer now, its edges sharpened with worry. He turns again, eyes wide at the shed door, and holds still as if stillness can turn him invisible. The yard breathes. A screen door sings and snaps. Silence resets.

He looks back to the knife. To the twine. To the shape on the floor that is both his cat and not his cat anymore. He lifts his forearm and presses his cheek into the crook to wipe the sweat, breathing the clean ghost of laundry soap that clings to cotton. For a blink, he is seven and safe. Then the green handle glints again and the world remembers what it is.

Light erupts as the shed door blasts open. The sun is a sword. He flinches, lifting his left arm to shield his eyes. A broad-shouldered silhouette fills the frame, a stance held like a statue. It's David. He doesn't move. He almost vibrates with not moving.

His gaze lands. He sees the transgression. The arrangement. The boy kneeling in the middle, hands wet, knife in one, hammer hooked to a nail in the other. The conclusion forms faster than thought.

"What the fuck have you done? What the fuck is wrong with you?" The man's voice thunders, heavy and full of disbelief.

Two strides and he's inside, boots pounding the floor. His hand clamps around Charles's blood-soaked wrist and yanks hard, lifting the boy clean off the ground.

Outside, somewhere he can't see, Todd's footsteps drift away in a rhythm that feels practiced, measured, unhurried; as if he knows exactly how the scene ends.

Inside, Charles presses his palms to his ears, trying to drown out the booming sound—a reverse echo followed by *heeet*.

Chapter 8: November 10th, 1967

Pitch black. The sound of a small, rapid heartbeat. Fluid pumping through tiny arteries. The muffled sound is a woman's quiet moan from somewhere else.

She sits on the worn concrete floor, back pressed to the cold rail of the prison rack. Bare feet on cold, dusty stone, heels tucked against her hips. A thin blanket drapes over her knees making them two low humps of shadow.

Night holds the cell in its clutches. The only light is a slit of moonlight through a horizontal window too high to meet even if she stands on the rack. Everything is grey: walls, ceiling, uniform, dust in her hair, her skin in the pallid wash. The world is ash. She raises her head toward the window and the moonlight, and then she opens her eyes.

Emerald fire. Green, living, impossible under all this iron.

Beads of sweat and stray tears catch the moon's edge and glitter like frost. She knows the moon will scoot off its track in a few minutes, a luminous coin sliding from the slot. She inhales slowly, deliberately, a measured breath, and for a heartbeat she's content. Then her face tightens; jaw grinds; she folds forward, knuckles whitening on the blanket. She pushes the corner of it between her teeth to stifle sound.

She is in labor, and she intends to stay invisible. The infirmary would rearrange the story, would take the one thing she can still choose. She waits out the contraction, letting the breath become a metronome: in through the nose, out through the mouth, measured, disciplined. When the pain recedes, she leans back and lifts her gaze to the window's slice. Emerald meets silver. The moon inches toward the frame's edge—

tick. The sound resounds from everywhere and nowhere at once.

She allows a crooked half-smile, the right corner of her mouth rising. She challenges the moon to a race and stakes her useless life on winning.

Today someone will be born and someone will die.

She thinks of the forms she filled out months ago, the letters as neat as she could make them: **Charles Belial Watkins**. Born to a dead father and a Death Row mother. Born in grey.

Another wave grips her. She folds, breath controlled, sound swallowed. She reaches down and feels the bulging pressure; crowning. She rides it with intent: push when the urge crests, breathe when it slides away. Veins stand in her neck. Her eyelids stay shut until the burn fades. When she opens them again, the green returns, brighter as the moon slides—

tock. Resonation. Time isn't a clock in this cell; it's a body insisting.

She keeps the cadence: count the breaths, guard the silence, watch the moving coin of the sky. Emerald against iron. Mother against the moon.

The next contraction takes her like a fist. She bears down, controlled, chin to chest, hands bracing on the blanket. The crown becomes a head; slick, heavy, real. She supports it with one hand and blinks to focus. There—a dark loop at the throat.

A cord.

She keeps breathing. With her thumb and forefinger, she tries to ease the loop over the baby's head, calmly. It holds tight. She stops pushing for two steady breaths to reduce tension, then rotates the head slightly, looking for slack. The cord doesn't give. Another contraction surges; she can't halt it. She bears down and guides the head close to her body, using the baby's natural turn to bring the anterior shoulder through. The burn is bright and hot.

The shoulder slips; she finds just enough slack to lift the loop, half off, then the second shoulder turns and is born. The cord loosens. She frees it, quick and clean.

The infant spills into her hands with a wet, startling weight. She draws him forward onto her belly, face down and slightly sideways to keep the airway clear, primal instinct guiding her hands. She wipes his mouth and nose with the corner of the blanket, then rubs his back briskly from neck to hips. No cry. She rubs again, firmer. She gives a light flick to each sole.

Nothing.

"Come on, baby boy," she whispers, voice trembling but steady in intent. "Wake up."

She cradles him into the crook of her arm, keeping him warm with the blanket and her body heat. She checks for chest movement—slow, shallow, almost not there. She lifts him slightly to improve the angle of his airway and rubs again, rhythmic, insistent.

"Come on, little Charles. Please wake up for mommy."

The ritual frays. Her voice swells on panic; the emerald in her eyes flares. The cell block hears her.

"Now you listen to me, young man—wake up **now**!"

Her pleas become shouts, then raw sound. Doors pound in answer, voices echo. A mechanical clunk and the block floods white. The buzz of the lock; her door jerks open. Four guards and a doctor spill into the grey.

"Don't take my baby! Please don't take my baby! He's mine! HE'S MY BABY!"

Two guards pin her wrists, a third her ankles. The fourth scoops the infant, the doctor moving with practiced hands: clamp, cut and the cord separates. The baby vanishes through the doorway in the guard's arms. Her voice scrapes the fluorescent light.

"Bring him back! He's my baby!"

The doctor draws up a syringe, fast. He taps the side three times and then the needle slips into her forearm; the fight drains out of her with frightening speed. Words tumble into fragments, nonsense, prayers. The contraction is gone; the afterbirth remains. The doctor guides the placenta free, presses dressing, working with brisk, efficient care.

A gurney rattles in. Two guards lift her, the doctor places the placenta in a grey bin; just another piece of the cell's monotony, and sets it atop the blanket at her thighs as they roll her out. Keys jingle like a clock's second hand with every step.

Two prisoners in grey step in with mops and a bucket of hot, soapy water. A guard watches from the threshold. They set to the red slick, swabbing in broad circles, letting it all blend: water, soap, crimson and gray, into a duller shade. Not one of them notices the fine lines beneath; the intersecting strokes sketched on the floor. A symbol hidden in the swirl, erased by their rhythm, lost to the room's endless grey.

Outside the cell, somewhere unseen, a child takes his first breath. Inside, the moon slips out of the window's frame. Tick. Tock. A thrum. Prisoners continue to mop. Grey and red water swirls across the floor, spiraling like a wheel that's already in motion.

Chapter 9: August, 1968 – Age 9 months

A polished whitewall tire rolls almost soundless along a ribbon of fresh asphalt, its rotation hypnotic in the early light. Chrome flashes like shards of sun on the black 1968 Lincoln Continental as it glides over the country road—a dark shark fin slicing through a golden ocean of grain. The car moves with the hush of authority, a wraith in daylight.

Far ahead, a lone farmhouse clings to the horizon, small and stubborn, like a lifeboat adrift in a sea of wheat.

On the porch, Annie James smooths the hem of her blouse for the fifth time, then fusses with the waistband of her skirt. Everything is perfect—no wrinkles, no stains, but her hands won't believe it. She clasps them tight against her belly, willing them to be still. Her nails are clean; she spent forty minutes scrubbing last night. Still, she checks again.

Beside her, David James stands in his best jeans and a red-and-black flannel shirt. The August heat presses like a hand against his back, but the flannel stays; because it has a collar, and collars mean class. He wishes for a tie, something to finish the illusion. In his right arm, he balances a toddler with sun-warmed cheeks and a mop of blond hair. Todd wriggles, points a chubby finger toward the horizon.

"Car!" he chirps, voice bright as a bell.

Annie and David follow his gesture. At the far end of their half-mile dirt drive, a dust plume rises behind a black speck. The Lincoln eats distance like time itself, shrinking the gap with silent menace. Annie feels excitement surge, sharp and dizzying. She hopes she won't make a fool of herself.

David and Annie own this small house. They used to rent it, from Annie's parents. They worked the fields in exchange for the roof over their heads. When Annie's parent died, the house and land were willed to her. It's not much, but it is theirs. They have what they need. Nothing is new, but it suits them just fine. The house is small, but solid. It is a perfect little home in a perfect little town. It is a perfect place to raise children, open and safe.

But it's the out-of-the-way places in small, unassuming towns that can hold the darkest, most twisted secrets. Town's where people can get away with anything from fishing with dynamite to—well, to just about anything. The eyes of the rest of the world tend to skim right over little towns like this. A dot unnoticed on a map.

This sleepy little town offers the basics to its citizens, a grocery market, flower shop, shoe repair, garage. You can get what you need here, but it's not extravagant.

Most of the people here either work the farms and fields, or they work at the privately-owned prison. The rest either run a local shop, or work for one. It's a simple town, with simple people.

But this little town contains a heart of evil at its center, with black, slimy tentacles that branch out and can touch anywhere else in the world. Though most of the people of the town live quietly, according to their means, and don't have much, there is money here; old money. Much of the town is owned by one family, the Kerringtons. They own the prison. They own the preschool and they own a foster care and adoption agency, as well as many of the local business ventures in town.

It is for that foster care agency representative that Annie and David anxiously await.

The time it takes for the car to span the drive stretches cruelly, but finally, the car is there—sleek, black, perfect. It rolls to a stop before the porch. Its windows are onyx, swallowing the sun. The engine dies. Silence falls. Dust drifts past like smoke after a gunshot.

The driver's door opens. A tall man steps out on the driver's side, uniform crisp, chauffeur's cap angled low, shadowing his face. He moves with mechanical grace to the rear passenger-side door and swings it wide. A glimpse of silk stocking, then another. A white-gloved hand rises to meet his. With a subtle tug, a woman emerges. Her sun hat is a halo of yellow and white daisies, her silhouette a study in elegance.

Annie steps down from the porch, heart thudding. The woman advances, and time slows enough for Annie to drink in every detail: the sundress, yellow trimmed in white lace, hem flirting with the knee—classy, daring. Pearls at throat, ears, wrist. Hair sculpted into perfection beneath the hat, daisies woven like a crown. Makeup soft, flawless. Wealth radiates from her like heat. She carries a swaddled bundle in her hands.

David joins Annie at the foot of the steps. The woman smiles, voice smooth as cream.

"Hello, Annie. Hello, David—and hello to you, young master James." She wiggles a fingertip against Todd's chest, coaxing a giggle. "Are you ready to meet your new baby foster brother?"

Annie's hands rise instinctively. "Can I please—?"

"Of course." The woman transfers the bundle with practiced care. "Here you go. That's it—that's all I came to do. The paperwork's done, every 'i' dotted, every 't' crossed. You are officially parents again. Congratulations!"

Annie cradles the child, breath catching between the spaces of her excitement. After Todd's birth and the verdict from her doctors, she thought this joy was gone forever. She looks up at David; their eyes meet, and something tender passes between them—an extra weight of love. Together they gaze down at the sleeping infant.

"He's so precious," Annie whispers.

Her eyes find the pale scar at his throat, shaped like an inverted cross. She recalls the agency's words: a birth injury, an emergency tracheotomy, a life saved at a cost. No future care required, they said. But Charles will likely never speak.

Annie tucks the blanket higher, hiding the scar. David slides an arm around her waist, bends to kiss the baby's brow. He lingers, studying the tiny face. It is innocent, perfect. For a moment, the world feels whole. He is pleased at his decision to allow Annie to bring this child into their home. He is pleased at his decision to use this agency—an agency that walks on the edge of the law and oft times overlooks certain regulations in order to match baby with family.

A click and whir break the hush—the Polaroid's shutter, its motor spooling. The woman shakes the developing photo, smiling.

The infant stirs. His eyelids lift.

Dazzling emerald green amplified by the sun's rays.

David exhales softly, almost reverent. "Well… hello, little one."

The woman steps closer, extending the photo like an offering. "To remember this day by," she says, her pearls catching the sun.

Annie and David lean together, eyes fixed on the Polaroid in Annie's hand. At first, the image is a ghost—faces drowned in milky haze, shapes barely there, like spirits caught mid-breath. They watch in silence as the chemicals work their quiet alchemy. Colors fade in, shadows sharpen, the fog dissolves. The picture exhales clarity. Annie smiles, soft and certain. For a moment, everything feels still. Decision made, future unfolding.

The stillness shatters.

"No! Me!" Todd's scream rips the air like a siren.

Annie jolts; feet skittering, heart vaulting. David's arm clamps around her waist, steadying her, but her mind leaps ahead of her body. She imagines the infant flying, arching high above her head, suspended in cruel slow motion before plummeting toward the earth. Her hands fumble, clutch, recover. The baby presses tight against her chest, safe. Disaster averted by a breath. Charles doesn't stir. His face remains serene, as if the world's chaos is none of his concern.

Relief floods Annie, warm and dizzying; then drains, replaced by a cold wash of embarrassment. Heat prickles her cheeks. Her eyes snap to Todd, anger flaring.

"What is WRONG with you?" The words crack like a whip in a sort of whisper-shout, sharp with shame.

"Oh, that's alright," the woman interjects, voice smooth as balm. "Todd didn't mean to startle anyone and frankly, your reflexes are impressive." Her tone is light, almost playful, and it works. Annie's rigid brow softens; a sheepish grin tugs at her lips.

"Thank you, ma'am. Sorry," Annie murmurs, shoulders lifting in apology.

"No need." The woman's smile is gracious, her words almost ceremonial. "May your hands always be as quick, your eyes and ears keen, and your feet swift for these little ones."

With that well wish, she pivots, silk and daisies swaying, and slips into the Lincoln's shadowed interior. The chauffeur folds himself in with insect precision, door thudding shut. The engine ignites and idles with a low growl, smooth and certain.

The rear window hums down, revealing the woman's face framed in pearls.

"Now remember," she calls, voice carrying like a bell. "You're still in the fostering phase of the process. We'll visit twice monthly until he's three. Then quarterly until seven. After that; you're on your own, sweetie. You got this?"

"I got it, ma'am." Annie's voice is steady now, almost proud. "We'll look forward to your visits. Thank you—for everything."

Annie finds it odd that the fostering phase should last so long, but she is willing to sacrifice anything for this moment and lets the thought flutter from her mind as quickly as it came.

The woman nods, winks—a flash of warmth, and turns forward. Glass slides up, sealing her away. Tires bite dust, spin, and the Lincoln floats backward in a graceful sweep, cutting the grass like a scythe. A quick shift, a surge, and the car lunges down the drive, trailing a storm of earth. At the road, it turns, black slicing gold, and vanishes into the horizon. The dust lingers, swirling like a thought that refuses to settle.

Annie and David lower their arms, the farewell still tingling in their fingers. For a moment, they simply stand, staring at the empty road, the silence thick with newness. It feels strange; turning back toward a house that now holds more than it did minutes ago. A life added like a sudden note in a familiar song.

Charles breaks the spell with a quiet suggestion, delivered in the language of need.

"Pew! Stinky!" Annie laughs, nose wrinkling. "Somebody needs a change."

David grins, Todd giggles, and together they step inside, carrying the weight and wonder of the rest of their lives.

Annie lays Charles on the changing table and moves with practiced calm: wipe, fold, fasten, while David sets Todd down on the living room carpet to run his small kingdom.

The moment Todd is free, he barrels through the doorway and plants himself against Annie's leg, cheek pressed to her skirt like a flag finding its pole.

He hugs harder and looks up. "What you do to baby, Mommy?" His voice is curious and crowded with need.

Annie looks down and smiles. She wrinkles her nose and waves her hand in front of it. "Pew! Stinky poopy."

Todd imitates the face, delighted by the sound. 'Stinky poopy!' He tries it louder, testing how the word fills the room. 'Stinky poopy!'

'Mommy is changing baby's diaper like she used to for you,' Annie says, keeping her tone warm, steady. 'But now you wear big-boy undies and go poopy in the potty.'

'Poopy in the potty!' Todd chirps. 'Stinky poopy in the potty!' He beams at the rule, the way saying it makes him part of the grown world.

"That's right, Teej—stinky poopy in the potty. You're a big boy. That's what big boys do."

Annie finishes, lifts Charles from the table, and turns toward the hall. Todd is still fused to her leg, a barnacle of devotion.

"Todd, sweetie, come on. Let's go into the living room and play together," she suggests, shifting the infant and smoothing the blanket near his chin.

"No," Todd says, sliding down her calf to sit on her foot. His arms lasso her shin, fingers pressed white. He holds on as if the floor is a river and she is the only raft.

"You can show Charles your favorite toys," she tries, pointing toward the track laid out in the living room—the looping rails, the wooden engine, its little red wheels.

Todd's face tightens, "No! No Charles! My toys!" He tucks his head toward his chest and presses closer to her leg, making himself small, trying to vanish where her weight begins.

Annie steps forward with her free foot, then drags the foot Todd anchors. The movement is clumsy; half-step, half-drag. She takes another measured step and wobbles, catching herself with two quick hops. Frustration pricks. 'Let go,' she says, gentle but firm.

Todd holds tighter.

"Let go!" she scolds firmly. "David? A little help?"

David appears in the doorway, taking in the scene— Annie balancing the baby, Todd wrapped like a rope around her leg. He can't help a soft chuckle. "And it starts," he chuckles, smiling. "Toddie… Teej… The Toddler! Come on, son." He kneels and reaches with careful hands.

Todd refuses to yield. A long cry rises from him, a single note that climbs in pitch as if he's trying to reach the ceiling. "Nooooo," he sings, breath stretched thin.

Annie feels heat in her cheeks, a mix of fatigue and the sting of being pulled in two directions. David keeps his tone easy, but his hands steady. He lifts and loosens Todd's grip finger by finger, patient, murmuring reassurances while the cry trembles and wavers.

"My mommy. My mommy," Todd repeats, not angry so much as desperate, as if the words will anchor him.

David frees the small hands and gathers Todd against his chest. "I've got you," he assures, and carries him toward the living room. Todd kicks a few sharp, unhappy flicks of his feet, then sags in David's arms, the fight thinning. Charles remains quiet, eyelids heavy, mouth soft—the calm center of the storm.

———

High noon arrives like a golden coin. David is in the driveway, the hood of his pickup propped open as he checks belts and fluid, hands moving in easy rhythm. Inside, Annie sits in the recliner with her Bible open across her lap. The living room smells of sun-warmed wood and laundry soap. Todd, after hours, a snack and a nap that was mostly just quiet time, builds a small city from his wooden train set. He moves the engine along the looped track, then back again, then forward—circles and reversals, as if practicing the difference between keeping and sharing.

Charles sleeps in the bedroom, a steady rise and fall under the blanket. The house seems to breath just as softly, a gentle pause between one life and the next.

Annie glances at the wall clock. The second hand sweeps like a small blade. "Charles sure sleeps good, don't he, Teej?" she asks, breaking the hush with a smile.

Todd looks up, eyes unfocused for a moment; measuring whether this is praise for him or for the newcomer. He offers nothing back, expression flat, then returns to his track with a set mouth. He nudges the engine harder, making it rattle over the joints. He looks a little pouty, but more than that, possessive.

Annie rises, unable to resist checking on the baby again. In the bedroom, Charles lies awake in the bassinet, cooing softly, his attention bright. Their eyes meet. Charles smiles; a small, private curve of the mouth. Annie's heart loosens. She smiles back. They hold that gaze for a quiet moment, foster mother and new child getting to know each other. A tiny sound murmurs from his diaper; the smile breaks, then returns in a lighter way, and the cooing continues.

Annie carries Charles into the living room. With her toe, she hooks the spring frame of the bouncinette hidden behind the recliner and drags it into view. Two gentle taps of her foot and it slides closer to Todd's rail city. She lowers Charles into the seat and tucks the blanket around him, then settles on the carpet at her boys' level.

Todd reaches out as if to welcome the baby to his realm. He grips the top edge of the bouncer and begins to move it. The springs answer with a pleasant, rhythmic squeak. Within seconds he's bouncing higher than good sense allows, trying to feel the edge of the device—how far it will go, how much it will obey him. Annie's palm finds Charles's chest, steady and reassuring, and the motion settles.

"Easy, Teej," she says, softness held on a firm line. "Gentle."

Todd nods but watches her hand—the way it settles the motion and the way it belongs to the baby now. He lets go of the bouncer and picks up the engine again. He pushes it in tight circles, faster and faster, until the little red wheels blur. His face muscles set. The room is bright, but the feeling shifts.

Annie studies him, then leans into warmth. "You built a good town," she says. "Maybe you can show Charles the bridge. He'll like that."

Todd's eyes flick to the bridge, then to the baby, then to the hallway where shadow gathers at the bathroom door. He returns to his train. "My town," he says softly and whiny, almost to himself.

Annie hears the claim and hears the ache inside it. She reaches to smooth Todd's hair. "It's yours and we're just sharing it is all," she answers, careful, hopeful. "That's what big boys do."

Charles

She rocks the bouncer with two fingers, just enough to keep Charles content. The springs tick like a quiet metronome. In the corner, the clock's second hand keeps its sweep. Todd runs the engine across the bridge and back, then halts it as if deciding whether the track should bend or break.

Outside, David closes the hood with a firm, satisfied thump. Inside, the house breathes. Annie lets the warmth continue, but a small current moves under it—Todd's need to own, to define, to keep.

Todd looks toward the hall again, mapping distances in his head: from carpet to tile, from play to plan. Annie notices the glance and chooses not to name it; she draws both boys closer with her voice, with her presence, with the slow rhythm of a day becoming a life.

Charles's eyelids part. For an instant, emerald green catches the window's sun and flashes—a quiet reminder of something rare threading through this ordinary room. The color fades as his eyes close again. The moment passes, but the house remembers.

Todd presses the engine forward one last time, then lifts it off the track and holds it in his palm, turning the little wheels with a thumb. Circles within circles; round and round. He watches them spin, and his expression settles into a thought no one else can hear.

Todd plays with his toys for nearly an hour, the rhythm of wheels and tracks soothing the earlier storm. The house still with quiet. David is still outside under the hood of his truck again, Annie inside watching the clock's second hand sweep like a tadpole in a bowl. Todd glances at his mother, then at the baby. Charles smiles, a soft curve of lips, but Todd does not return it. His eyes hold something flat, something measuring.

A muffled sound escapes from Charles's diaper. Todd wrinkles his nose. "Stinky poopy!" he declares, voice sharp with displeasure.

Annie laughs, bright and easy. "Oh oh! Stinky poopy! Someone needs a change!" She rises, smoothing her skirt, and heads toward the bedroom for supplies. Halfway down the hall, Todd's voice follows—high, insistent.

"Poopy in the potty!"

Annie chuckles over her shoulder. "You tell him, Teej!" Her tone is warm, unaware of the current shifting beneath.

At the changing station, Annie gathers a fresh diaper, a soft cloth wipe, ointment, powder; the ritual tools of care. She turns back toward the hall, speaking as she walks. "I don't mind doing this for baby Charles, but I'm sure glad you're potty trained because—"

The sentence dies. Annie stops cold at the mouth of the hallway.

Todd is gone.

The bouncinette is empty.

Everything in her hands falls—diaper, powder, cloth, fluttering like pale birds to the floor. She runs. Behind the sofa— nothing. The kitchen—nothing. The front door; unsecured, its wooden frame a mouth. Annie lunges, shoving the storm door wide, and bursts onto the porch.

"Todd!" Her voice cracks the summer air.

David's head jerks up from the engine compartment. He sees her face is white, frantic, and drops his tools. "Honey?" he calls, already moving.

Then Annie hears it.

The flush.

Water rushing, a hollow roar from the bathroom.

"Charles!" The name tears from her throat as she spins and bolts down the hall. Her feet skid on carpet; her hand snags the doorframe, swinging her into the bathroom with a force that rattles the hinges.

Todd stands in the center of the tile, small and still, his eyes wide and doe-like, guilt swimming in their dark pools. His voice is calm, almost ceremonial.

"Poopy in the potty."

Annie's heart slams against her ribs. Blood drains from her face. She lunges for the toilet and wrenches the lid up.

The world elongates and snaps back smaller before returning to normal.

Charles is there—folded small, water lapping at his chin, eyes open and glassy. The bowl is a whirlpool, water rising, circling like time sped up. Annie plunges her hand into the cold and grips the sodden fabric of his sleeper. She hauls him free, cradling his head as his body clears the porcelain edge. Water streams from him in silver ribbons, splashing the tile like shattered glass. Annie clutches him to her chest, rocking, her breath bated, her tears hot.

David bursts in, filling the doorway with panic. "Annie!" He lunges toward her, toward the dripping infant.

"He's okay. He's okay." Her voice shakes, but she presses a trembling hand to David's chest, holding him back as if to steady the room. "Just a little wet is all."

David bends close, eyes scanning the child. Charles blinks, then coos a soft, airy sound, as if nothing in the world has changed. His face is serene, almost smiling. No sign of distress in those emerald green eyes.

Annie and David lock eyes, a silent exchange of terror and relief. Then, together, they turn to Todd.

He stands where he was, small hands loose at his sides, expression smooth as glass. His gaze meets theirs without flicker, without fear. He exudes only a quiet, unreadable calm.

The clock in the hall ticks once, loud as a piledriver.

tick.

Chapter 10: November 10th, 1973 – Age 7

Tock.

Todd stands in the shadow of his doorway, one shoulder pressed to the frame, watching sunlight spill across the rug in Charles's room. The rug coils outward in a spiral of color—threads braided tight from the center, red and orange and yellow wound like a fuse. Morning light makes it glow, a bright sunburst against the hardwood. Charles sits in the middle, where the spiral begins; a pin holding everything down.

The new Tonka dump truck gleams in front of him. It is big and heavy, with yellow steel and bulbous black tires thick enough to chew earth. A birthday gift, fresh from its box. Snoopy rides in the bed, floppy ears bouncing as Charles pushes the truck in slow circles. Always left, always tracing the spiral. No engine noises, no pretend commands. There is just silence and the scrape of wheels on braided fiber. Todd thinks it's strange, the way Charles plays without sound, like he's saving his breath for something else.

Today is the last visit from the agency. Seven years of check-ins, questions, and quiet notes end after this. After today, Charles belongs to the house for good. Todd feels the weight of that thought settle like dust on his skin. No more strangers asking how they get along. No more car rides for Charles alone. Just family. Just rules. Just Todd.

Charles dumps Snoopy out. The doll rolls across the rug like cargo gone rogue. He grins, small and private, but doesn't laugh. The truck reverses, then lunges forward, stopping short of the doll as if teasing it. Back and forth, then another load-up, another lap. Todd's fingers curl against the doorframe. Charles is good at alone. Too good.

Then Charles straddles the truck, gripping the undercarriage with one hand, Snoopy clutched in the other. His legs pump, pushing him faster around the spiral track. The metal frame rattles under the strain. Todd's eyes narrow. He sees the moment balance gives way—the truck tilting, the body dropping. A sharp clink of steel on steel. Charles jerks upright, breath hissing through clenched teeth. His left hand clamps over his right like a vise.

Todd's gaze flicks across the room as Snoopy sails through the air and smacks a tub of Lincoln Logs. The container topples, spilling its wooden cargo in a scatter of brown sticks. Charles stands frozen in the center of the rug, shoulders hunched, hands clenched. Todd can almost feel the pulse of pain radiating from that guarded fist.

He steps into the room, slow and deliberate, letting his shadow stretch ahead of him.

"What's up, Chuck?" His voice carries a lilt, casual on the surface, sharp underneath.

Charles doesn't answer. He never does.

Todd unfolds his arms and points, grin curling like a hook. "You are! You're up-chuck, puke face! What's all the noise?"

Charles shifts, turning his body to keep the injured hand away. The spiral rug seems to conspire with him, guiding his feet in a slow orbit as Todd circles closer. Todd's thoughts tick steady and certain, like the hall clock. He knows that look. He knows the pattern. Charles hiding something means opportunity.

"What are you hiding behind your back, up-chuck? Did you break something? Is it mine?" Todd's tone sweetens, coaxing now, but his eyes stay hard. "Let me see it."

Todd knows exactly what Charles is hiding behind his back.

Charles

Charles edges away, silent as ever, his breath shallow. Todd feels the old rhythm begin to settle between them. It's the same game they play every time. Charles guarding, Todd prying. Todd has learned how to make stories fit, how to keep his own slate clean while Charles takes the blame. He has learned how silence works in his favor, how bruises can speak when mouths can't.

He closes the gap, steps tracing the rug's spiral like a hunter following tracks. Charles's shoulders stiffen. Todd sees the flicker of panic in his eyes, the way his weight shifts toward escape. He almost smiles.

Outside, a car door slams—a sound carried from the drive, maybe real, maybe imagined. The agency woman will be here soon, pearls and papers and congratulations. She will ask if they are getting along. Todd already knows the answer he gives.

He stops just short of Charles, close enough to catch the scent of metal and birthday cake frosting. His voice drops, soft as thread pulled to the brink of snapping. "C'mon, up-chuck. Let me see what you've got."

The clock ticks in the hall. Sunlight slides another inch across the floor. The spiral waits for its next turn.

Todd stands closer now, circling. Charles stays in the center, shoulders tight, hands locked behind his back. Todd knows that posture. It means the game begins.

His voice is light, teasing, but his eyes measure every twitch. "C'mon, up-chuck. Let me see what you have."

Charles shifts and continues his slow rotations, his breath shallow. Todd allows the familiar tempo to settle in deeper—the one that has shaped years of mornings and nights. He has been perfecting this dance since Charles first came to the house, a quiet baby turned quiet boy.

Todd remembers the day he tried to flush him down the toilet, the way the water swirled like a clock winding fast. That was the start. Since then, Todd has learned things such as how to hurt without leaving marks, how to twist silence into blame, how to answer for Charles when questions come.

He thinks of the stories he has told, smooth and quick; the way adults nod when words sound certain. He thinks of the broken lamps, shattered glass, missing trinkets that were all laid at Charles's feet. He thinks of the small bodies found in the yard: birds, mice, frogs, turtles. Even the goldfish that hissed in a pan one summer morning darts through his memory. Mom never understood. She searched sheets for sharp edges, puzzled over cuts and bruises that bloomed like dark orchids on Charles's skin. Accident-prone, she said. Always falling. Always bleeding. Todd let her believe it. He helped her believe it.

Now he watches Charles guard that hand like it holds a secret worth keeping. Todd steps closer, tracing the rug's spiral, feeling the pull of its pattern. His thoughts tick with the hall clock; steady, certain. He knows how this ends. He knows how to make it end.

Charles keeps rotating, trying to keep his back turned, but Todd is quicker. He feints left, then right, closing the gap until there is no space left to hide. The air between them shivers with heat and quiet fury. Todd's grin sharpens. His voice drops, soft as thread pulled taut.

"Let—me—see."

Charles doesn't move.

Todd's patience snaps like a twig underfoot. His hand flashes out, open and hard, and the sound of the slap cracks through the room like a struck match.

Charles stiffens, his eyes wide, then distant—like he's looking past Todd, past the walls, into something far away. Todd sees it. He feels the air change, heavy and strange, as if the house itself is in a trance.

Todd doesn't know what Charles sees now, but as the blood rushes to Charles's cheek, he knows what he remembers: the porch, the man in the black suit, the bruise blooming like a purple stain on pale skin. He remembers standing in the hallway, pressed to the wall, watching his father's jaw, clenched, as words cut the quiet.

He is drawn further into Charles's glossy emerald eyes and into his trance.

—

Todd presses his forehead to the cool edge of the hallway wall, peering through the narrow slice of glass beside the door. The storm door stands open, sunlight spilling across the porch like molten brass. Outside, Charles is a small figure next to a man in a black suit. His face is turned just enough for Todd to see the mark blooming on his cheek. It is an ugly smear against pale skin.

Todd's pulse ticks with the hall clock. He knows that look. He knows what bruises mean. They mean trouble for someone, and Todd is already deciding who.

David stands in the doorway, one hand gripping the frame, his shoulders squared like a wall. His voice cuts the quiet. "What the hell happened to his face?" The words grind through his teeth, sharp enough to slice.

The man in the suit doesn't flinch. His tone is smooth, almost bored. "Well, Mr. James. Charles here got a little bit unruly during group play and we needed to discipline him. Is that a problem?"

Todd watches David's jaw tighten, the muscle jumping like a live wire. "Is that a problem?" David repeats, slower now, heavier. His eyes lock on the man's, disbelief simmering into heat. "Are you kidding me?" David's voice rises, still low but dangerous. "A problem? Yeah, it's a problem! I already told you—don't bring the kid home with marks. I don't like having to explain it to Annie."

Todd shifts his weight, bare feet silent on the hardwood. He imagines Annie's face when she sees the bruise. He imagines her questions. He imagines the answers—his answers; ready to slide into place if he needs them.

The man dips his head, words oiled and easy. "We are certainly sorry that it came to that." His hand moves inside his coat, slow and deliberate, like a magician about to reveal a trick. A checkbook appears, black leather flashing in the sun. "I'm sure you've been enjoying the extra compensation the agency has provided for your discretion, but I'd like to offer you a little more for this recent inconvenience. Shall we say another two hundred dollars?"

Todd sees David's eyes drop, shame pooling dark in their corners. His father's voice comes out flat, almost hollow. "Yeah… Two hundred will be fine." Then, sudden as a whip crack, David's head snaps up. His stare drills into the man's face. "But no more marks! You understand?"

"Yes sir, Mr. James. We'll do our best." The man's tone never wavers. He slides the check free, crisp paper whispering against the book, and hands it over. David takes it like it burns.

Todd watches the exchange, the way money moves like water, washing things clean. He files it away—how silence works, how deals are made, how bruises can vanish under the weight of bills. Outside, the man turns without waiting for a word, his shoes clicking against the porch boards. The limousine waits at the curb, black and gleaming like a beetle in the sun.

The door closes. The hall clock ticks. Todd steps back into shadow, thoughts curling tight like the spiral rug upstairs.

Some things are better seen than said. Some things are better learned than told.

—

Todd has had enough of Charles's trance. His palm cracks against the seven-year-old boy's face again, a sharp slap that echoes in the room and snaps Charles out of it. Before the sting fades, Todd lunges forward, wrapping Charles in a crushing bear hug. He hoists him off the ground and slams him hard onto the rug. The impact drives air from Charles's lungs in a hollow expulsion. Todd watches him writhe, small chest heaving, and feels a surge of control. He pries open the fingers of Charles's left hand and finds nothing. Empty. His jaw tightens. He reaches for the right, but Charles flails, desperate to keep it hidden. Todd's strength wins. The fingers unfold easily this time. Blood glistens at the nail bed, a black spot lurking beneath. Todd's lips curl into a grin.

"Aw. Did up chuck hurt his widdle finger? Oh! Let me kiss it and make it better!"

Charles struggles, but Todd clamps the injured finger between thumb and forefinger, lifting it close to his eyes. The wound pulses, crimson welling under pressure as Todd squeezes harder. A bead escapes, dark and slick. He stares at it, transfixed by the color, the promise. Slowly, his tongue grazes the tip. Salt and iron flood his senses, pennies on his tongue. Then he sucks the finger deep, pulling the blood clean. When he releases it, another dot blooms. He takes it again, savoring, then lets go.

"That's nothing, puke face. Hardly any blood. Didn't even make you cry." His smile is sharp, angry. He bites down hard, teeth grinding bone beneath flesh. Charles's face contorts, silent agony ripping through him. Breath sucks between clenched teeth, but no scream comes.

Todd releases him suddenly. Charles crumples, clutching his finger, tears streaking the rug fibers. Todd's sneaker lashes his thigh. "You want to see some real blood, you little devil worshiper you? Come out here a minute, up chuck."

Todd strides to the door, rage simmering under his skin. Behind him, Charles curls tight, eyes squeezed shut, tears spilling unchecked. Todd looms, kicks again. 'Let's go, Satan!'

Charles doesn't move. Another kick. Then another. "Get—up—Chuck!" Each word punctuated by a blow. Finally, Charles stirs, crawling upright under Todd's relentless strikes. "Get up, Chuck, up chuck, up chuck!"

They stumble down the hall, Todd driving him forward with kicks, through the kitchen, out the back door. One last boot sends Charles sprawling down the steps. Todd's grin widens. "You're going to love what I got you for your birthday, Devil spawn."

He clamps an arm around Charles's neck, palm sealing over his eyes. "No peeking, shit stain." The words drip like venom as they cross the yard.

Todd grips Charles tight, his palm sealing over the boy's eyes like a brand. The November wind slices across the yard, cold and sharp, but Todd feels only the heat of his own pulse pounding through his arm. He presses his chest against Charles's back, driving him forward with steady force. Each shove sends dry leaves crackling underfoot, brittle veins shuffling and snapping like tiny bones.

Charles stumbles, feet scraping the earth, but Todd doesn't ease up. He wants speed, wants control. The boy's hesitation grates on him; the way he's always resisting, always dragging his heels. Todd clamps harder, fingers digging into the soft skin around Charles's eyes. "Move," he growls under his breath, voice low and full of hatred.

Charles

The shed looms ahead, a black silhouette against the angled rays of sunlight washing over the yard. Todd feels the boards underfoot now, the hollow thud of wood echoing through his shoes. The air smells of damp earth and old rot, a scent that wraps around his senses like a dust devil. He shoves Charles harder, savoring the jolt that runs through the boy's frame.

A hinge groans, long and metallic, as Todd wrenches the door open with his free hand. Shadows spill out like a tipped can of black paint. In one swift motion, he rips his palm from Charles's eyes and drives him forward with a brutal shove. The boy pitches into darkness, and Todd's grin flickers in the gloom.

Charles pitches forward and stumbles, palms scraping rough wood as the door slams behind him. A metallic clink follows. It is the sound of the outside latch locking him in. His breath stutters. The air tastes of dust and rust, thick and stale. He blinks hard, eyes straining against the dimness until razor-thin streaks of sunlight carve through the gaps in the boards, slicing the gloom into jagged shards of gold.

He knows this place. It is the forbidden shed. He's never crossed its threshold until now. He should run, should pound on the door, but Todd is out there. Todd is worse than anything that waits inside.

Charles rises slowly, legs trembling. The space feels enormous, alien. Workbenches loom as altars, tools scattered like relics of a cruel ritual. A tin hood dangles from the ceiling, cradling a dead bulb. A thin chain hangs from it, swaying gently as if stirred by breath. He scans for something to stand on, spots a stool, and steps toward it.

He steps on something that rolls under foot, causing his ankle to twist. He drops to one knee as quickly as Newton's law allows to save the ankle from catastrophic damage. There, on the floor in front of him lies the culprit. It's a hammer that has been carelessly sprawled on the floorboards.

Pain flares. He rubs his ankle hoping to coax the discomfort out of it and that's when his gaze locks on something wretched—

Inches away, his cat; or what's left of it.

The eyes come first. Two glassy orbs on the floorboards, staring without lids, without mercy. They pin him in place, silent accusations gleaming in the slotted light. His own eyes flood, vision warping through tears as grief hits like a tsunami inside him. He jerks back, then forward, scrambling to touch, to undo, to make it right.

The cat's body is nailed down, limbs splayed like a grotesque diagram. Pieces: tail, paws, head; all pinned separately, each bound by twine as if cataloged for study. Charles's face contorts, tears stream unchecked. No sound escapes him, only frantic motion. He claws at nails with bare fingers, skin splitting, blood slicking his grip. He pulls until his muscles scream, but the nails do not yield.

His left hand drips crimson now, painting the wood in desperate strokes. He snatches the hammer; the same tool that betrayed him once already, and hooks it under a nail. He's seen this done before, but leverage is a mystery. He yanks straight up, knuckles whitening, breath tearing through clenched teeth. Nothing. The nail holds fast, indifferent to his agony.

He wipes sweat from his brow, smearing blood across his face like war paint. His gaze catches on the tail, tethered by twine. He tugs, but the cord bites back. Then he sees the green box cutter lying near the cat's midsection, blade glinting faintly in the fractured light. Salvation in steel. He grabs it, presses edge to fiber, sawing at the twine with trembling hands.

Charles

A voice slices the silence. Annie. Distant, calling his name. "Charles?" He freezes, eyes darting to the door, heart pounding against lungs. He waits, breath shallow, then turns back to the task. The twine frays but holds. He works harder, frantic.

'Charles, where are you?' The voice again, closer now. He stares at the door, wide-eyed, sweat and blood mingling on his skin. The back screen door slams. Silence swallows the yard. He bends again to the box cutter, to the tail, to the impossible hope of repair.

Then, light explodes. The door yanks open with a shriek, flooding the shed with brilliance. Charles twists, reels, throwing up his bloody hand to shield his eyes. A silhouette hardens in the glare. It's David. Motionless; a monster glowing with rage and disbelief. His voice trembles, rough with fury and fear: 'Charles, what the fuck have you done? What the fuck is wrong with you?'

He lunges forward, boots pounding, and reaches for the boy. The hammer clatters to the floorboards. David never notices Todd's signature slip knots in the twine; knots that Charles could never tie.

Chapter 11: November 10th, 1980 – Age 13

It is early morning. The sun bleeds slowly over the horizon, casting a fiery edge across the low-clinging fog. Charles stands at the cliff's rim, drinking in the view. This is a ritual he knows by heart. Yet today, something feels wrong. The colors of the leaves blaze too bright, almost feverish, as if autumn has sharpened its palette overnight. The air bites cool against his skin, but beneath it hums a strange warmth, like breath on the back of his neck.

He lingers, soaking in the beauty, though it prickles at him now. The river below glimmers with a sheen that seems thicker than water, a mirror that might swallow light whole. After a long moment, he turns right, pacing along the cliff's edge for twenty feet before pushing through the heavy brush. Branches claw at his sleeves as he slips into the tree line, twenty feet deep, until the roots of an old tree jut like knotted fists from the cliffside.

Charles crouches, fingers hooking under the hidden coil of rope wedged between roots. It feels heavier than usual, as if the earth resents giving it up. With a grunt, he tips it over the edge. The rope slithers downward. Tied firm to the largest root in the knot, it waits. Charles grips it and begins his descent. His breath holds, muscles straining, every fiber pulling. The sun flares orange against his face, but its warmth never reaches him. Light and chill are locked in silent war.

He hits the gentler slope below and breaks into a run along the riverbank. The cliff looms to his left, sheer and towering, its shadow stretching longer than it should. Charles sprints until his lungs burn, until it feels like something inside him might burst free. He stops abruptly, hands clasped on his head, circling, dragging air in hard through his nose and blasting it out through his mouth. The rhythm feels strange today. Each breath echoes louder than the last, as if the trees are listening.

His pulse begins to steady. He veers left toward the cliff and stacks some small rocks on top of a larger stone. It is a marker of progress. He ran at full speed much farther today than he did last week. That should feel good. It doesn't. The silence presses close, thick and expectant. He jogs on, further upriver, the ground whispering underfoot.

Ten minutes or more pass. Time feels slippery, like water through fingers. Charles halts again, not winded this time. He could run forever. He glances left at another pile of rocks, his own handiwork. This one matters. He bends, hefting a boulder almost too big for him. Muscles scream, grip falters, but he waddles bow-legged to the pile and drops it near a row of shrubs crouched at the cliff's base. One stone becomes two, then ten, each dragged and stacked with stubborn resolve.

Spent, Charles collapses to his knees, then crawls toward the shrubs. The earth smells different here. It is sweet and sour, like something rotting beneath the roots. He slides on his belly into the hollow between two bushes, vanishing into green shadow. A hand darts out, snatching a boulder, dragging it into the hidden depression. Then both arms reach, pulling another, then another, like a trapdoor spider feeding its lair. One by one, the stones disappear into darkness.

The river murmurs behind him, but its voice sounds wrong. It's too low, too deep, like words forming under the current. Charles freezes, listening. Nothing. Just water. Still, the unease lingers, pulling tight in his chest. He shakes it off and reaches for the next stone, unaware that the day has already begun to edge toward something strange, something waiting just beyond the shrubs.

Charles stands in the hollow between the cliff and the sandy mound, shrubbery curling like green arms around him. The mound forms a semi-circle, its ends kissing the cliff, hiding him from the river's gaze. His secret place. His work.

The wall rises before him. It is L-shaped, rough-hewn, a fortress in progress. Three feet thick in most spots, four feet high where his ambition outpaces his strength. He bends, grips a boulder, and rolls it up his forearms, chest straining as he hoists it high enough to drop onto the wall. Stone thuds against stone. He exhales hard, sweat streaking his temple.

Another boulder waits. It's too big, too heavy. He wrestles it, fails to lift it high, and leaves it sprawled between the wall and the cliff. He fetches another, nearly as massive, and carries it around the back side. His eyes flick to the earlier boulder and fancies it his improvised stepping stool. Smart, he thinks. He climbs onto it, balancing on its sandy surface, and braces to set the new stone.

A sound resounds in his head—too loud.

tick, tock, tick, tock, tick, tock

He wants to crash his palms over his ears to drown out the increscent sound, but the weight of the stone holds them prisoner.

tick, tock, tick, tock, tick, tock.

A *click* and a hollow, metallic *pop*, thunderous for what should be small sounds, reverberate to silence in Charles's skull, or possibly from everywhere but.

The ground betrays him. The rock stool shifts, sand sliding like ball bearings under his sneakers. His foot skids, his balance shatters. The boulder slips from his grip and crashes down onto his right hand, pinning it to the gnarly crown of his wall.

Pain detonates. A white-hot explosion that blanks thought, blanks sound. Charles feels and hears the tip of his middle finger burst open with a wet, sickening pop. He doesn't scream. He can't. His jaw locks, teeth grinding as his eyes clamp shut so hard the darkness blooms red, then white. His body curls around the agony, breath strangled in his throat.

Seconds stretch like hours. When his mind claws back, he grips the offending stone with his left hand and heaves it off. His gaze drops and shock slams him anew. The fingertip is mangled, split wide. Blood wells in thick rivulets, pooling fast. Beneath the torn nail, pale tissue bulges: fatty, stringy, glistening. The pulp of life exposed.

Instinct takes over. He jams the finger into his mouth. Copper floods his tongue, metallic and hot. His tongue experiences more than just the taste of blood. He feels the shredded anatomy against his palate, every slick thread, every torn edge. His stomach lurches, but he holds on, sucking hard as his eyes dart wildly. What? What now? Wrap it. Stop the bleeding.

He tears at his jacket, stripping it from his frame and whipping it to the ground. It lands crumpled, streaks of blood glistening on the material. He yanks his dirty white tank top over his head in one violent motion and winds it around his hand, tight, tighter, until the pain spikes like lightning. Blood soaks through instantly, blooming crimson across the cotton. He clenches a fist inside the shirt, squeezing, trying to stem the flow, trying to cage the agony. His breath comes in staggered bursts, each one tasting of copper and panic.

Charles scrambles up the sand mound, his body jerking with pain, one arm dragging dead weight. He bursts from the shrubbery and staggers toward the riverbank, breath tearing through clenched teeth. His injured hand throbs like a living thing, pulsing heat and agony. He kicks at pebbles, flails his arm in an attempt to fling the pain off, and unleashes a scream so raw and primordial that it splits the morning air like lightening.

He spins, wild-eyed, scanning for escape. Run home? No. No! Rage boils under the pain, scalding his thoughts. He clamps his good hand over the ruined one, squeezing hard. It doesn't help. He jams the ruined hand under his opposite armpit, locking it tight, bouncing on his toes like a child desperate for relief. The pounding won't stop. The finger feels huge, grotesque, every heartbeat another boulder's blow to the tip. Steam rolls of the slickened skin of his bare shoulders as he stands alone on the river's bank.

His gaze suddenly settles on the river's smooth-as-glass surface. Mist curls like the breath over his skin. Cool. Soothing. Salvation. He lunges forward, splashing three steps in, and plunges his hand beneath the surface. The shock of cold bites deep, numbing fire into ache. Blood ribbons out in thin, crimson threads, swirling like smoke before vanishing into the dark water.

Relief seeps in, slow and fragile. His pulse still roars in his ears, his face flushed with pressure, but the water's calm begins to seep into him. Too calm. The river lies unnaturally still, its silence heavy, as if holding its breath. Morning should be alive with chatter, wings, rustle, but nothing stirs. Maybe they heard his unearthly scream. Maybe.

A soft squeak breaks the hush, then a plunk. A frog leaps from the far bank, slicing the surface with surgical precision. Charles watches, mesmerized. The frog glides, only its head exposed. Ripples bleed outward, lapping his ankles then licking the sandy bank.

Charles

One, two, three hops and the frog claims a flat rock kissed by the first rays of sun. Steam coils upward, ghostly tendrils rising from damp stone as warmth seeps in and wet cool finds a place to hide for the day. The frog settles, still as carved jade. Charles stares, breath shallow, sensing something shift— something unseen, waiting just beyond the veil of ordinary morning. Everything seems just a little weird today, even this frog.

He notices that the frog is missing its left, rear foot, the stump now sealed, healed long ago. Charles rises slowly from his crouch, water dripping from his hands in rhythmic plinks, merging with the river's hush. The frog remains on its sunlit rock, indifferent, a jade trinket basking in warmth. Charles bends, fingers curling around another boulder, muscles strained as he hoists it high above his head.

The boulder falls. The shadow over the frog grows.

The world turns black, for the frog and for Charles.

———

A black telephone handset slams onto its cradle with a violent crack. Charles jerks from darkness. There is no river, no frog, no boulder. Instead, leather straps bite his wrists and ankles. The chair looms beneath him, cold steel, leather and oak, waiting to be put to good use. His audience waits, faces pale islands in a sea of shadow.

From behind, a hand reaches around, clutching a microphone, its cord snaking like a vein. The mic hovers before his lips. A voice, flat and merciless, drips from the darkness: "Do you have a last statement?"

Last statement? They know he doesn't speak. They know. Charles lifts his gaze, sweeping the room, locking eyes with those who dare meet his stare. He memorizes them—every flicker, every twitch. The silence is palpable.

He closes his eyes, inhales deep through his nose, and exhales slow, a smile ghosting his lips. He shifts as far as straps permit, settling as if for a long ride.

The straps creak. The vibration deepens.

On the wall, the industrial clock ticks, louder than it should, filling the chamber and Charles's cranium. The red second hand crawls toward twelve. In eight beats, all hands will align. High noon.

Three-click... Two-click... One... The air swells, pregnant with voltage, as time itself holds its breath.

He lights a small candle in memory: his foster-mother, Annie, at the sink, sunlight on her cheek, a laugh he never learned to say back. He holds that light in his chest until the hum grows teeth.

A hand grips the switch. Metal clinks. The lever slams down. Voltage screams through copper veins, flooding the chair. The hum rises—a swarm of angry bees trapped in steel. Charles convulses, every muscle locking in violent unison. Tendons rope his neck; veins bulge like cords ready to snap. His jaw clamps, lips frothing as bubbles spit and burst. Smoke coils from his skin, ghostly and ghastly. The stench of burning flesh fills the space. His world expands into infinite white heat.

—

A crack splits the silence as the boulder slams down. The frog is pulp, a grotesque smear against granite. Blood pools, dark and slick, threading into the sand.

Mist curls low over the riverbank. His smashed finger throbs, but rage pounds louder. Charles grins, breath short, scanning for a stick. He finds one, perfect length, and snatches it up.

—

Charles

In the chamber, the current surges. Charles's spine bows, ribs straining against leather straps. His eyes bulge, pupils blown wide, staring at nothing. Foam spills from his mouth, mingling with smoke. The clock ticks with sonic, echoing booms—red hand crawling toward twelve again:

Three-*tick*

Two-*tock*

One—

—

Charles jams the stick through the frog's slack jaw, ripping down hard. Entrails slither free, dangling like wet ribbons. He hoists his trophy, grinning like a wild animal, and spins toward the shrubs—

—and slams into something solid. A thud, a breathless gasp. Pain detonates in his tailbone as he crashes to the ground. He gulps air in shallow bursts, eyes clawing at the sky. Sunlight blinds him, a burning sword cleaving his vision. He throws up an arm, shielding his gaze.

A silhouette eclipses the sun. Tall. Still. Robed. It looms like a monolith, casting a shadow that swallows the sand. Charles freezes, frog skewered in his fist, blood dripping onto his wrist. The figure does not move. The air thickens, humming with something older than time.

Behind young Charles, the chair fades. The hum, the smoke, the straps all dissolve into silence. The clock never strikes twelve in the chamber. That path is ash now, burned away. Ahead, the robed figure waits, and destiny jumps tracks.

Charles thrusts the frog-skewered stick forward like a sword, his breath short and forced in and out of his teeth, his pulse a machine gun in his ears. He shuffles backward on his rear, scraping sand, desperate to carve space between himself and the looming silhouette.

The figure moves; two deliberate steps closer, robe whispering against the earth. It bends, skeletal hands unfurling, veins like blue rivers beneath parchment skin. Wrinkled fingers reach for his face. Charles braces to strike, muscles cocked, but terror roots him to the ground. He cannot move.

The hood peels back in slow motion as the figure bends forward, sunlight spilling across a face forged by time. An elderly woman emerges, her skin rice-paper thin, mapped with veins and age spots. Her lips, cracked and furrowed, writhe like a pale millipede across her mouth. Wisps of hair cling to her scalp, white as frost, revealing the scalp beneath.

Her eyes—one a blind, milky void, sagging deep into its socket; the other clouded but glimmering faintly with hazel, a ghost of color clinging to cataract fog. That flicker snags Charles's breath, though he cannot name why.

Her hand cups his cheek, papery warmth pressing into his skin. The other glides down his arm, over his trembling fingers, to the stick. She grips it gently, gaze locked to his. He yields without thought. In a blur too swift for her years, she flings the stick aside. It arcs through sunlight and splashes into the river.

Simultaneously, another sound cleaves the silence—a metallic tap-snap, sharp and hollow, echoing from everywhere and nowhere. It vibrates in the air, in the sand, in Charles's bones.

And then the familiar sound again. Loud, booming way too loud for such a tiny source.

tick tock tick tock.

The woman reaches, reclaiming his empty hand. Her grip is firm yet tender as she rises, drawing him up with her. They ascend together, eyes locked, breath mingling in the cool morning haze. She turns his palm upward, cradles it between both of hers. Something rests there now: small, solid, warm. He cannot look. He cannot break her gaze.

The cataract clouds swirl in her eyes, but that ember of hazel glows faintly, like memory flickering through fog. Charles stands frozen, the weight of the unknown pressing into his palm, as the river murmurs behind them and the world skews toward something irreversible.

The old woman's grip lingers, her papery fingers pressing warmth into Charles's skin. She leans close, breath whispering against his ear—words too soft, too strange to hold. Then her hands slip away. Empty air replaces her touch.

Charles stares into her eyes for one suspended heartbeat longer. Cataract clouds swirl, but that ember of hazel still glows faintly, a secret flicker in the stirred fog. At last, his gaze breaks. He looks down.

The object in his palm steals his breath. A pocket watch, but not like any watch born of this world. Gold, heavy, warm as if alive. Its cover gleams with a luster that seems to drink the sunlight and give it back in even brighter rays. Symbols are scrawled across its surface; arcane, elegant, etched so fine they look spun from threads of shadow and fire. Jewels stud the rim, tiny constellations of crimson and sapphire, each facet catching light and fracturing it into long needles of color that dance across his trembling fingers.

It is beautiful. No—beyond beautiful. It is impossible. The most exquisite thing Charles has ever seen, and somehow it feels like it has always belonged to him. His pulse slows, syncing to the silent rhythm of the watch.

tick tock tick tock

He lifts his eyes, seeking the woman, but her gaze has shifted, eerie and distant, fixed past him. One decrepit hand rises, pointing toward the river. Charles whirls, scanning water and opposite bank. Mist curls like smoke over the calm surface. Nothing moves. No figure. No sound.

He spins back—

—and the woman is gone. Vanished. Not walking, not retreating. Simply erased. The sand lies undisturbed where she stood. The air holds no trace. Cliff ahead, river behind, open banks stretching endless to the left and right, and she is nowhere. Charles turns in a full circle, heart pounding, mind clawing for reason. How could she even reach him here? How could she leave so fast?

Silence presses in. The world feels hollowed out, as if sound itself has fled. Charles stands frozen, dumbfounded, the weight of the watch anchoring him to this impossible moment.

Then, a soft plunk. From across the river, a frog leaps into the water, ripples whispering outward. The sound slices the stillness, delicate yet jarring.

Charles looks down again. The watch rests in his palm like a captured star. He feels an attachment blooming, fierce and unexplainable. It is his favorite thing now. It is his only thing. Peace washes over him, strange and deep, as if the world has folded into this single gift. He needs nothing else.

The sound continues, booming in his head.

tick tock tick tock.

Charles no longer desires to cover his ears. He soaks the sound in, letting it envelope him in its embrace like warm water.

tick tock tick tock.

It is calling him now.

He turns the watch in his fingertips, marveling at its secrets. His fingers trace the jeweled rim, searching, and find a latch disguised as a gem, cunning and perfect. He presses. A click echoes—heavy, resonant, like the opening of a vault, a sound that again comes from everywhere and nowhere, maybe from the cosmos, or maybe from his own head. The lid springs open.

Charles

A deafening silence encompasses all. No more ***tick***. No more ***tock***.

The face steals his breath anew. His focus pinpoints on this single object. There is nothing else for him now. There is no river bank. There is no sound. There is only this watch now. Ornate filigree coils across a field of gold, studded with jewels that glint like frozen tears. The hands—oh, the hands. They are carved from something pale, something that looks like bone. Each is sculpted into a skeletal finger, extended in eternal point. The minute hand has a small appendage at the end, creating a tiny claw. They do not move. Time here is a corpse. No ticking, no winding stem, no pulse but his own.

Charles runs his fingertips over the glass, feeling the chill of perfection, the weight of mystery. His eyes drink every detail, drowning in beauty.

A flicker at the edge of vision draws him back. A familiar frog emerges from the river, slick and green and hops onto a misted stone kissed by sunlight. It settles, still and serene, steam curling around its tiny body. Charles smiles, slow and strange, like a boy with a secret that is dying to get out. Without breaking his gaze from the amphibian amputee, he bends, fingers closing around a heavy stone.

Chapter 12: November 10th, 1983 – Age 17

Rain lashes against the kitchen windows, a gray November curtain swallowing the world outside. The air smells of damp earth and old coffee. Charles sits hunched at the table, pencil scratching across his psychology homework, his mind locked in quiet focus.

'Hey! What's up, Chuck?' The voice explodes behind him, loud and disturbing, slicing through the silence. Todd's breath hits his ear like a slap. Charles flinches hard, spine stiffening, and whirls to glare over his shoulder. His adoptive brother stands grinning—a smug crescent carved into his face.

Todd looks like a ghost of high school glory, still draped in his letterman's jacket two years after graduation. The fabric hangs relic-dull, but Todd wears it as armor. His hair is slicked, his skin gleaming with borrowed confidence, and the sharp sting of Old Spice rolls off him in waves. Charles sniffs twice, exaggerated, his lip curling in disgust. He turns back to his paper without a word, pencil moving like a polygraph needle.

The flat crack of palm against the back of his skull comes without warning. Pain blooms white-hot. Todd skips sideways, clownish, landing by the fridge with a flourish. He yanks a paper cup from the dispenser, flings the fridge door open so hard the jars rattle like bones in a box. Glass clinks, metal wobbles, chaos spilling into the room. The disruption is malicious and intentional. Todd fills his cup from the spigot protruding low on the glass water jug, slams the door, and hops onto the counter like a king mounting his throne.

He chugs, throat working in greedy gulps, then crushes the cup and whips it with sniper precision. It smacks Charles square in the temple resulting in a sting sharp enough to blur his vision. The cup ricochets, skitters across the table, and dies on the floor. Charles doesn't flinch. Doesn't speak. His pencil moves, but his knuckles whiten. Heat crawls up his neck.

Todd slides down, saunters over, and leans in close, elbows sinking into the table, chin cradled in his hands. His grin is venom. "Hey Up Chuck, buddy ol' pal... I need you to take care of my chores today. I got people to do and places to see."

Charles writes. Breath steady. Pencil scritch-scratching paper.

"Just nod if Charles can hear me—is anybody home?" Todd croons, butchering lyrics and faux-singing Pink Floyd into Charles's ear. His voice drips mockery.

The pencil never falters.

Todd's hand lands soft on the back of Charles's head, stroking like a lover—then clamps hard, fist twisting hair. "I said... Just NOD!" The word detonates as Todd slams Charles's face down hard into his open textbook. Bone meets stacked paper with a sickening thud. Pain bursts behind his eyes. Blood gushes, painting the page in violent strokes. Todd jerks Charles's head back up by the hair, finishing his custom lyric with a hiss: "...so you can hear me."

The book's pages are webbed with crimson lines. Drops splatter like ink. Todd releases him, snatches the textbook, and flips it shut with a brutal clap, inches from Charles's face. He turns and mounts the counter again, thumbing through pages as if rifling a corpse. "Psychology: Its Principles and Applications, huh?" His voice is a blade honed on contempt.

He turns the blood-stained spread toward Charles, grinning wide. The mirrored blotches leer back like twin ghosts.

"Ready for a psychology test, freak? What does this ink blot look like to you, psycho boy?" Todd's laugh is loud, hollow, knee-slapping theater. His own joke slays him.

Charles stares, silent, blood threading down his lip. His eyes burn hate. Todd's grin curdles into a snarl. "Is this the type of shit they teach you in your special school for retards, Up Chuck? You freak of nature." The book sails in a vicious arc, smashing into Charles's face, pages first. Pain flares. The book falls into his hands like dead weight.

Todd lunges, grabs Charles's head, and drives his finger into his temple, stabbing syllables into flesh. 'My chores better get done or I'm going to beat you senseless when I get home. Don't let me down, Devil boy. Never mind taking off all day to wherever it is you go, you freak.' Each jab is a nail hammered into bone.

Charles feels the thin, perfect spear of a pencil in his grip. The thought manifests dark and sudden: drive it deep, blind him, end him. The fantasy ignites. He moves. Fast. The pencil plunges into Todd's eye socket, a wet crunch splitting the air. Todd screams, staggering, but Charles clings, twisting, forcing the shaft deeper, deeper, until the eraser kisses skin. Blood geysers, hot and slick. Todd convulses, spine bowing, good eye rolling white. They slam into the wall together, a grotesque embrace. Charles watches him die, savoring every twitch, every gasp.

A crack explodes against his skull. Reality snaps back. Todd stands whole, grinning, hand retreating from the back of Charles's head. Rain roars through the open door as Todd backs out, finger still stabbing the air in threat. 'You listening to me, Up Chuck?' His voice drips poison. The door shuts. Glass swallows his silhouette. Then he's gone.

Silence fills the void in the wake of Todd's storm, broken only by rain's relentless hiss. Charles sits bleeding, eyes rimmed in shadow, scanning the wreckage. Papers are torn, pages stained, crimson drizzled across white. His gaze drops to his palm. The watch gleams there, gold and warm, its weight a balm against the storm inside him. He rolls it slowly, feeling its heat seep into his bones. The rage ebbs. The world narrows to metal and silence. The watch calms him. It always does.

Charles rockets to his feet. The watch slips from his fingers into his pocket, its weight a secret heat against his thigh. He moves fast, anger yanking tight in his chest. Cabinets bang open, drawers clatter. A backpack is wide open on the table, swallowing a canteen of water, a granola bar, an apple; each item tossed with sharp, jerking motions. Rain beats on the windows, a gray roar that drowns the house in gloom.

He snatches his yellow raincoat from the closet and drags it over his shoulders. Zipper teeth bite shut. The pack bulges, stuffed and ready. Charles storms through the back door into the wet November air, the storm slapping his face with icy fingers. He heads for the river, sneakers battering wet grass, breath steaming in the chill.

———

His sanctuary waits—a labyrinth formed from stone and obsession. Years of work, years of secrets. The old walls still stand, adorned with his silent congregation: skulls grinning from shadow, bones curled like question marks. New walls rise beyond, forming a maze that twists deeper into darkness. Dead beavers, snakes, fish; all trophies of time, their decay etched into the air with a stench that clings like oil. The deer carcass sprawls on its altar of stone, now a skeleton draped in leathery tatters, a relic of violence and ritual.

Charles slips through the maze, fingers grazing cold rock, eyes drinking the macabre beauty. At the center, his cathedral of ruin unfurls wide and tall. He drops his pack on a spiky stone, the same kind that cradles the deer's bones, and begins unloading with reverence. His canteen placed squarely. Food stacks neat. The watch stays in his pocket, pulsing like a second heart.

Hours bleed away. Rain softens to mist. Charles works. He hauls stones, shapes walls, weaves death into design. He fishes, hunts, claims. By dusk, five fish, two frogs, and a river rat join his gallery, their faces pressed into the mortar of memory. Satisfaction flows in his veins. He pulls the watch, pops the ruby latch. A click echoes, low and resonant, like a throat clearing in the void. He stares at its frozen face, then shuts it. The snap of the lid closing retorts off the cliffs, the river and from somewhere deep in his skull.

He gathers trash, zips the pack, and huffs toward the triangle-shaped exit crack in the inner cliff wall. He shoves the pack through, belly scraping earth, shoulders grinding against rock. He remembers when this gap felt vast, when he was small enough to slip through like water. Now it grips him like a fist.

Charles pushes the pack under the vegetation, its bulk sliding toward the river side. He follows, elbows digging mud, breath harsh. The shrubs claw at his raincoat as he wriggles free. His head breaches the green. He freezes solid, every muscle locked as a scent grabs his nostrils. Old Spice.

Fifteen feet away, Todd stands with his back turned, cigarette ember glowing like a demon's eye. Smoke circles around his head as he scans the river, then the cliffs, then the sky. His left hand burrows in his pocket, casual, predatory.

Charles's pulse quickens. He pulls the pack back under the shrubs, inch by inch, every movement a prayer for silence. He lies flat, peering through leaves, watching Todd flick ash into the water. Todd's gaze sweeps the bank, sharp and hungry. He steps forward, sneakers sucking mud, eyes narrowing at the bald patch where Charles's maze hides. He studies the cul-de-sac curve of the cliff, noticing the scarcity of larger rocks here, muttering theories to himself: currents, erosion, nature's tricks. Todd thinks he's clever. Todd thinks he's closing in.

He finds a footprint. His grin spreads like rot. He moves faster, stalking upriver, chasing phantoms. What Todd doesn't know and what he'll never guess is that Charles planned for this. For years, he's run a mile past his sanctum, looping back, leaving false trails like a spider spinning decoys. Every footprint Todd follows is a lie, a breadcrumb leading nowhere.

The pack slowly emerges from the hollow beneath the bushes. Charles quietly and cautiously begins to slither from under the shrubbery. He rises and cranes his neck as if it will help him see further up the river bank. The coast is clear. Like a thief in the night, he snatches up his pack and quietly pads through the sand and gravel toward home.

He runs as fast as his legs will carry him. He is in the center of the bank between the river and the cliff, maybe a quarter of a mile from his special place when he hears it.

"Hey, freak! Where the fuck do you think you're going?" Todd's roar goes straight through his ears, over his nerves and into his pulse, shocking and heavy, echoing off stone like a curse.

Charles skids to a halt, chest heaving, rain-slicked air burning his lungs. Behind him, a shadow tears down the riverbank. It's Todd, a dark blur against the bruised dusk. His voice ricochets off the cliff wall just as sharp and jagged as the stone face itself: "You better beat me home and get those chores done or I'll be beating your ass when I catch you, fucker!"

Charles bolts. His sneakers become drenched as he mashes through mud and splashes through rivulets. His lungs cry for more air, heart overworking in his ribs. The riverbank narrows, hemmed by stone and thorn. Todd's footfalls hammer closer, a savage drumbeat chasing him through the mist. Charles doesn't look back. He doesn't need to. He feels Todd's presence like heat on his spine.

The shear, slick cliff rises ahead, its face etched with familiar scars. Charles lunges, forearm muscles firing, fingers clawing for holds worn smooth by years of escape. His sneakers scrabble, slipping on wet stone, but he climbs, fast and frantic, spidering upward with practiced precision. Rain needles his skin. Gravel spits from under his soles, rattling into the void below.

Todd hits the base with a grunt, hands slapping rock. He climbs, slower but relentless, curses shredding the wind. Charles crests the lip, belly grinding against mud, fingernails clawing for purchase. He drags a knee up, shoving weight onto solid ground. Then, pain detonates in his ankle. Todd's hand clamps like a vise, yanking hard. Charles jerks, spine bowing, breath ripping from his throat. If his whole body doesn't give, that ankle will.

Instinct flares. He kicks: once, twice, sneakers smashing Todd's face. Rubber meets bone with a dull crack. Todd snarls, grip tightening, blood threading from his lip. He claws higher, fingers snagging Charles's pant leg, then the strap of his pack. He yanks. The zipper screams open. Gear vomits out. A canteen spins into the abyss, tackle box clatters down the slope.

Charles thrashes, sliding inch by inch toward the edge. Mud slicks his palms; roots tear free under his grip. He swings the pack like a weapon, hooking straps on stones, desperate for anchor. A metallic glint arcs through the chaos.

It's the gold watch, tumbling free.

Charles lunges, snatches it mid-slide. His thumb hits the ruby latch. A click snaps sharp, a thunderous echo in the storm. The lid lifts, jeweled face flashing in the dying light.

Another savage yank. Pain rips through his ankle. The watch jolts loose, skitters across the mud, spinning out of reach.

Charles claws for it, fingers sliding in the mud, but it lies distant now, gleaming like a fallen star.

Todd climbs higher, using Charles as a rope, his weight dragging them both toward oblivion. Charles scrabbles, nails splitting, until his hand hooks a stone jutting from the earth. It holds, but just barely; halting their slide. Rain pours down in torrents, hissing like serpents. Todd grunts, hauling up, his breath hot against Charles's calf.

Then the stone Charles is anchored to breaks free from the soil. His heart jumps into his throat. He rolls hard, twisting his trapped ankle, pain blazing white-hot. He grips the freed stone, rotates fast, and in one brutal arc brings it down on Todd's wrist. Bone crunches with a wet, splintering crack. Todd's scream rips the sky as his grip explodes open.

For an instant, his fingers claw air and then he's gone. His body vanishes over the edge, swallowed by the darkness.

Charles lies sprawled on the cliff's edge, mud streaking his skin, the watch glinting faintly in the mud, an eye that never blinks.

He doesn't glance over the edge. He jerks his legs inward, scrambling backward on his rear, mud grinding into his palms. Distance is what he needs now. His breath screeches through his throat as he lunges for the scattered gear. Fingers snatch straps, bottles, scraps of food. The pack gapes like a wounded animal, spilling its guts across the ground.

He grabs the pack, jams loose items inside, and bolts into the trees. The watch glints in his muddy hand. It is miraculously clean and unmarred. Charles pauses for a moment to let his heartrate slow and to inspect the watch further for damage. There is none. Perfect. He snaps the lid shut, the click booming sharp as a nail in silence, and slides it into his pocket. Warm metal presses against his thigh, steadying him and his pulse.

Branches whip his raincoat, claws raking vinyl. Roots snag his feet, but he drives forward, lungs burning, feet sloshing through the sodden earth. The woods thin out, bleeding into open field. Charles slows, chest heaving, sweat mingling with rain. He wants calm. He needs it before the house swallows him whole.

Halfway across the clearing, his breath steadies. Night creatures stir; their voices threading the dusk. Crickets trill. Frogs croak from distant pools. Serenity drips into his veins, cool and fragile. He tastes relief.

The yard unfolds ahead, slick grass gleaming under porch light. Charles steps into it, sneakers sinking soft into the saturated earth. One step. Two. Five—

Then comes the impact. A freight train slams his spine. Air explodes from his lungs as the ground rises to meet his face. Dirt fills his mouth, gritty and cold, grinding against his teeth. Pain flares in his nose as bone meets earth. Blood floods his tongue.

Hands claw his hair, wrenching his head back until his neck feels like it will tear open.

Todd's voice rips the night: "You stupid fuck! I am going to kill you!" The words scorch his ear as his face smashes down again, jaw grinding against grass and grit.

Charles chokes on mud and blood, teeth scraping stones. Todd flips him like a rag doll. The universe spins, then slams still. Charles stares up into a face birthed from rage—Todd's face, swollen and slick with blood, eyes blazing like furnace doors.

Impossible. He fell. He should be broken, shattered, gone. But here he is, breathing fire.

Todd's hand clamps Charles's throat, pinning him hard to the earth. The other fist piledrives down, smashing cheek, brow, temple. Each blow erupts in his skull. Stars burst behind his eyes.

Blood spatters his raincoat. The night shrinks to fists and pain and Todd's guttural roar.

Charles teeters on the edge of blackness when a voice cleaves the chaos. From the yard comes a scream sharp enough to slice bone. "Todd! Get off him!" Annie's cry rips through the storm, a sword of sound cutting the dark.

Todd's fists rain down relentlessly, each blow erupting against Charles's skull. Flesh splits. Blood spatters the grass in dark, glistening arcs. Charles's head jerks with every strike, his body limp beneath the storm of violence. The night hums with the sound of bone meeting bone, a rhythm of ruin pounding into the earth.

Annie moves in a blur of desperation. Her scream rips the air as she launches herself onto Todd's back, arms snaking around his neck like steel cables. Her nails dig into his skin, her breath hot and enflamed against his ear. With every ounce of strength, she wrenches sideways, dragging him off Charles in a violent arc.

Bodies collide with the ground in a bone-jarring crash. Annie's skull meets stone with a sharp, sickening crack that splits the night. Immense pain flashes behind her eyes. For a heartbeat, everything is motionless.

Todd groans, rolling to his side, blood slicking his cheeks. Annie pushes up, trembling, her breath coming in shallow gasps. Her gaze flicks to Charles. He lies motionless, sprawled in the dirt, his face a mask of crimson ruin. Her stomach knots, bile clawing at her throat.

She turns to Todd. Their eyes lock. His glare still burns with rage, teeth bared like an animal. Annie's own eyes widen, pupils now black saucers, her expression hollowing into something eerie, something unmoored. A cut blossoms above her brow, splitting flesh. Blood snakes down, pooling in her lashes before spilling over her cheek in a slow, scarlet ribbon.

She does not blink. Does not move. Her stare drills through Todd; or past him, into some void beyond. The night presses close, breathless, as if the world itself holds still, waiting for what comes next.

Chapter 13: June, 1984 – Age 17

Charles moves like a storm contained in flesh: swift, silent, bursting with urgency. His backpack lays open on the counter, swallowing supplies in forced gulps: granola bars, a banana, a serrated knife glinting like a fang. Water sloshes into his canteen from the glass jar in the fridge, the sound sharp against the hush of the kitchen. His left eye still blooms with old violence though the bruise is fading to sickly yellow now. The sclera is still veined in angry red. A reminder of Todd's rage etched into his skin.

The sticky, cold raincoat squeaks synthetically as he drags it from the closet. He shrugs it on, zips it tight, and slings the pack over his shoulder. Outside, the sky crouches low and mean. Clouds boil across the sky, swollen with storm. Mist rolls like breath over the yard, and fat raindrops splatter his hood with hollow ticks. Lightning forks in the distance, a crooked vein pulsing across the horizon. Thunder rolls after, deep and guttural, shaking the marrow of the earth.

Charles strides through the grass of the back yard and plunges into the field. Grain towers around him, a sea of green and gold thrashing under the wind's whip. Lightning ignites the sky again, bleaching the field bone-white for a heartbeat before dusk clamps down again. Thunder answers, closer now, a beast's growl stalking the storm.

The dark, tangled woods rise ahead, dripping shadows. Charles slips beneath their canopy. The air thickens, damp and natural, heavy with the musk of rot and rain. Branches claw his coat; leaves slap his cheeks. His breath steadies, syncing to the rhythm of his shoes pummeling wet earth.

Then, a twig cracks, somewhere unseen; a sharp, brittle bone snapping underfoot.

Charles freezes mid-step, muscles locked. He doesn't turn. Doesn't breathe. The silence crawls wide, swallowing even the whispers of wind. Seconds drip like blood. Another snap—closer this time, slicing through the hush like a machete.

He pivots left, veering off his path, threading through the trees parallel to the cliff's edge. His pulse becomes a barrage in his throat. Shadows writhe at the corners of his vision. Then, he sees a flicker. A flash of color darting between trunks, quick as a deer. White? Or was it orange? Gone before his eyes can cage it.

Charles quickens his pace, sneakers almost floating over moss, breath shredding the quiet. Another crack splinters the air behind him. He halts, listening hard. Nothing. Not even the woodland chorus—no chirp, no rustle. The forest holds its breath.

He moves again, faster now. Another smear of color flies through the underbrush. It is definitely orange this time, sharp against the green gloom. Charles doesn't look back. He runs. Explodes into motion, legs spinning like a turbine, arms slicing air. Trees blur past in lengthened streaks. Roots snatch at his feet, but he leaps, vaulting fallen logs like a creature born for flight.

Heavy, relentless footsteps crash behind him, chewing through leaves and twigs. The sound claws closer, a hunter's rhythm pounding in his ears. Charles darts left, then right, weaving through trunks, his breath an oxidized saw. In the corner of his eye, flashes strobe through the foliage: blue, orange, white. Phantom colors flicker at his flank. Whoever hunts him runs hard, runs smart, hugging his blind spot like a shadow stitched to his spine.

Charles digs deeper, muscles maxed-out, lungs scalding with fire.

This is exactly what he has trained for.

He pours speed into his veins, stretching the gap, creating distance from the thing that stalks him. The forest convulses around him. branches whip, roots lunge, storm light strobing through the canopy. And still, behind him, the chase breathes hot and close, a hunger that will not stop.

Todd's breath rasps like sandpaper through his open mouth, chest heaving as he barrels through the woods. His sneakers chew wet sod, spitting clods behind him. Rain needles his skin, mist curling like steam through the trees. Ahead, he catches flashes of yellow, quick as lightning, darting between trunks. It's Charles. Always just out of reach.

Todd barrels forward, eyes scouring the gloom for another glimpse. There. He snags another flicker of yellow slicing through tangled brush. Gone. He pushes harder, lungs begging for more oxygen, heart erupting against his ribs. The forest convulses around him, branches whipping his jacket, roots clawing at his shoes. He runs blind, chasing ghosts.

For miles they dance this savage ballet of hunter and hunted through shadows stitched to storm light. Then the earth betrays him. Todd skids, sneakers desperately searching for purchase against slick soil, arms windmilling for balance. The ground drops away into a chasm punched into the earth, black and bottomless. Vertigo claws his gut as he teeters on the brink, peering into the abyss.

He crashes to his knees, palms planted in mud, breath shredding the silence. Slowly, he crawls forward, heart palpitating, and peers down. Darkness pools, but something gleams at the bottom. Yellow. A smear of color sprawled across pale sand. Todd squints, vision tunneling. It's a raincoat. Still on a body. Face-down beside a stone altar littered with bones. Deer ribs jut like broken teeth.

"Oh fuck," he whispers, voice splintering. Louder now, frantic: "Oh fuck! Oh fuck!" He scrambles along the rim, searching for angle, for clarity. Lightning forks overhead, bleaching the world ivory-white. The truth slams him like a fist. It's Charles. Motionless. Dead.

Todd staggers upright, disbelief clawing his throat. He stares into the pit, mind unraveling.

A shadow bursts from the trees behind him. Charles. Alive. Eyes burning like emerald coals. The tree limb swings in a brutal crescent and smashes Todd's face. Pain explodes. His body lifts, weightless, then plummets backward into the void.

Air roars past his ears, a hurricane of terror. Todd screams with a cut-off, ferocious, animal sound before the void swallows it whole.

Impact never comes.

His hands hook a root, fingers locking in primal desperation. Bark bites his palms, skin splitting, blood slicking his grip. He dangles above death, legs flailing over emptiness.

Charles stalks to the edge, rain hissing off his uncovered head. He peers down, face chiseled in granite. Todd's eyes claw upward, wide and wild, pupils huge with panic. 'Please, Chuck! Please! Help me up. Take my hand, Chuckie. Please!' His voice fractures, raw with terror.

Charles stares, silent, breath now slow and even. Then his hand moves. He slides into his pocket, curling fingers around gold. He pulls his hand slowly from his pocket. The watch gleams in his palm, warm and perfect. He cradles it like a lover, lips creeping a smile. The lid stays shut. A click never comes. He drops it back into his pocket, sealing fate with silence.

Todd sobs, voice collapsing into whispers. 'Please… Chuckie…' His eyes plead louder than words, drowning in fear.

Charles tips his head to the side in a pose of curiosity, gaze soft as velvet. Then the velvet burns. He lifts the limb high, muscles cocked, and brings it down like judgment. Wood meets flesh with a crack that splits the night. Todd howls, grip shattering. Charles swings again. And again. Each blow detonates bone, pulping fingers into ruin. Blood geysers, painting roots in arterial red.

Todd clings, impossibly, until the final strike obliterates hope. His hands explode open. Gravity claims him. He falls like a ragdoll tumbling through black until stone rises like an iceberg. Impact erupts in carnage. His spine bows, ribs spearing inward. A shard of deer bone punches through his chest, white and vile. His skull meets rock with a wet, concussive pop. The back of his head bursts like rotten fruit, brain matter splashing across sand. Twitching. Then stillness.

Above, Charles exhales a sound more sigh than breath. For the first time in his life, words scrape his throat, gravel and blood tangled in air.

"Chaaaaaaaarles," he whispers, voice alien, guttural, a ghost of language clawing free.

He turns from the abyss, rain rivulets streaming down his face. His hands move with ritual calm as they unzip the pack, drawing out the yellow raincoat. Vinyl slicks across his wet skin as he slides it on, hood rising like a shroud. Without a glance back, Charles melts into the storm, tennis shoes drumming a requiem into the wooded earth.

—

The kitchen hums with the low clink of silverware and the muted patter of rain against the windows. A single bulb casts a low, yellowed glow over the table, pooling light on plates of cooling food. Charles sits rigid, shoulders squared, eating with mechanical precision: bite, chew, swallow, repeat. His fork ticks steady as a metronome, blind to the storm outside or the one inside.

"Todd! Come down and eat!" Annie's voice cuts through the hush, sharp with irritation. It's the third call, pitched high enough to rattle the glass in the cabinet. She waits, head cocked toward the staircase, listening for the shuffle of feet, the grunt of acknowledgment. Nothing. Only the rain's relentless whisper.

Annie hasn't been quite the same since the night of Charles's and Todd's big brawl; the night her head dropped hard against a stone. Since her return from her five-day hospital stay, she seems different. Her voice is a little slower in cadence now. Her eyes never seem to focus with clarity the way they used to. She seems a little more—simple.

She exhales hard, lips thinning. "Oh! Where is that boy?" Her neck cranes, eyes straining up the empty stairs as if sheer will might conjure him. She pivots, gaze landing on Charles. "Have you seen him?"

Charles doesn't lift his eyes. His fork keeps moving, carving neat furrows through mashed potatoes. A silent shake of his head: quick, clipped, final.

David snorts, voice dripping acid. 'You didn't expect Chuckles to be of any help, did you?'

"Stop that!" Annie snaps, her tone cracking like a whip. "Will you go up and see what's keeping him, please?"

David's chair screeches back like teeth on bone. He wipes his mouth with exaggerated force, flings the napkin into his plate in a gesture too violent for linen and mutters as he stomps toward the stairs. "Fucking kids! Trying to put food in their mouths and they won't even just come get it for the takin. Got no problem making sure you don't get your meal, but nooooo... Can't show enough respect to make it to the dinner table on time to eat what you give 'em. God forbid dear ol' dad should have an undisturbed meal once in a while. Nope. It's all about you little fucks!"

His voice curdles into a rant, words slurring under the weight of whiskey and years of brain rot. David has been unraveling for a decade, ever since the agency checks dried up when Charles turned seven. Jobs slipped through his fingers like water. Rage filled the cracks. He drinks now like breathing, each swallow drowning the man who once kissed baby Charles on the forehead. That man is gone. In his place: a husk of bitterness, fists heavy with guilt, a temper that bruises everything it touches.

The stairs groan under his weight as he climbs, still barking venom. "Todd! Get your ass down here and join the family unit for dinner. If I have to hear your mother's screeching voice one more time, I'm going to kill you and then I'm going to kill me and believe me if I could do it the other way around—"

The sentence dies mid-breath. Silence slams down, thick and sudden. Annie freezes, fork hovering over her plate. Charles lifts his eyes for the first time, gaze locking with hers. A long, strained, electric beat passes. Together, they turn toward the staircase, ears grasping for sound.

Seconds drip like molasses. Then, socked feet, pale calves descend the stairs slowly, with hesitation. David bends at the landing, peering under as if the shadows might cough up his son. His face is a mask of confusion, anger curdling into something colder.

"He's not up here," David says at last, voice flat, stripped of bluster. He stares at Annie, thumb jerking toward the void above. "Did anyone see him come in?"

Annie blinks, slow and heavy, her brows knitting. "Well... no. Come to think of it, I haven't seen him since breakfast." Her gaze swivels to Charles. "Have you seen him?"

Charles briefly and rapidly wags his head, almost mechanical, without lifting his eyes from the plate. His fork moves faster now, stabbing silence into the meat, as if the act of eating could erase the weight of what hangs in the air. His plate will be bare in moments. The storm outside rages on, but inside, a deeper storm builds, waiting to break.

Annie and David lock eyes across the dim kitchen, silence stretching like a tightwire. Then, like a starter pistol cracking the air, they move. David lunges for his keys, metal clinking sharp against the wood as he snatches them from the counter. Annie bolts for the phone, chair legs screeching against linoleum. Her breath comes fast, shallow, a staccato rhythm that matches the pounding of her heart.

She rips the beige handset from its cradle, cord slapping cloth as she clamps it between her shoulder and ear. Her fingers claw through the bill drawer, scattering envelopes like startled gulls. The black organizer surfaces like a lifeline in leather. Pages flutter under her frantic touch until the right one stares back. She dials, pulse choking her throat.

Outside, the storm door slams. David's voice detonates in the yard, loud and short: "Todd! Todd!" His shouts ricochet off the siding, swallowed by mist. Annie presses the receiver tight, listening to the hollow ring, praying for an answer.

"Thank you for calling IronWorks Fitness Center. Our regular business hours are Monday through Fri—" The recorded voice drones, tinny and indifferent. Annie slams the receiver switch, breath cutting off as fast as the call, eyes scanning the book again. Another number. Another chance. She dials, fingers trembling.

David bursts back through the door, rain stippling his hair, chest heaving. "He ain't in the yard or the shed. You call the gym?" His voice is a whip crack, laced with panic he can't quite hide.

"I called. No answer. I'm calling Jinny now." Annie's words splinter as the line clicks. "Yes, hello? Jinny? Hi, it's Annie. Hey, did Paul make it home from the gym yet?" Her voice pitches high, brittle as a dry leaf. Then: "He did? Okay… would you mind asking him if Todd was with him today?"

Ten seconds drag like chains. Annie's knuckles bone white around the receiver. Her eyes flick to David, who hovers in the doorway, keys dangling from his fist like a weapon. Finally, Jinny's voice filters through. Annie exhales, a sound more tremor than breath. "Oh. Okay. I guess I just didn't see him. He's got to be around here somewhere. Thank you, Jinny. I'm sorry to have bothered you."

She hangs up slow, the click loud in the vacuumed silence and turns to David. "Paul says Todd never showed at the gym today. Not once." Her words should soothe, but they curdle in the air, thick with unease. Relief flickers, then dies, smothered by something darker.

The house holds its breath. Annie and David freeze, statues fashioned from dread. Seconds drip, heavy and slow. David's jaw works, grinding out muttered curses, but his eyes betray him. They are wide, rimmed in fear. He wants to wait, to believe Todd's just screwing around. But Annie knows better. Her gut twists, a serpent coiling tighter with every beat of her heart. Todd would never skip dinner. Not without a word. Not without a reason.

Images slash through her mind: Todd sprawled in a ditch, Todd face down in water, Todd's face pale and slack under a canopy of leaves. She crushes each vision like roaches underfoot, but they breed faster than she can kill them. Her breath stutters. Her fingers twitch. She wants to tear into the yard, scream his name until the night coughs him up. But she stands rooted, nails biting her palms, forcing calm she doesn't feel.

The storm outside moans against the windows. Inside, a deeper storm, wrapped tight with energy, ready to burst at the seams.

The clink of silverware dies as Charles drops his fork into the empty plate with a sharp, metallic crack. Annie jerks, breath sticking, her mind ripped from its spiral of dark imaginings. Charles twists in his chair, movements fluid, almost ritualistic, and rises without a word. His shadow stretches long across the kitchen tiles as he strides toward the staircase.

His hand curls around the banister, foot poised on the first step when David's voice bellows from the open doorway, frantic and angry at Charles for being the one not missing: "Where you goin', Chuckles?" The syllables drip contempt, thick as tar.

Charles freezes, spine rigid, gaze fixed on the stairwell. He doesn't turn. Doesn't speak. The question hangs, stupid and obvious, until David's own mind catches up. His lip curls, voice snapping like a whip: "Make yourself a useful idiot and run around out there wherever it is you kids go and round up my son."

The weight of that one word, *my*, sits heavy on Charles's heart. It is confirmation that Charles was never accepted into David's heart and that Charles was never and will never be a true member of this family. *my*—such a small, inclusive word; signifying ownership, that carries so much exclusion and rejections with it now as it drools from David's lips.

The pause is long enough for tension to wrap tight, then Charles nods. Once. Twice. Three times. Slow, deliberate, like an oil rig, nodding alone in the desert. He ascends two steps at a time, vanishing into the dim hall above.

David mutters, venom threading his tone. "What the hell is he doing?" His glare knifes toward Annie.

"He's probably putting his shoes on, David. Would you please cut the boy some rope and have a little patience?" Annie's voice strains for calm.

David snorts, words curdling into a sneer. "Yeah, I'd like to cut him some rope, all right."

"David! Please!" Annie stabs, sharp enough to draw blood.

Upstairs, Charles sits on the edge of his bed, staring at his bare feet. The silence envelopes him, but does not comfort. His head lifts, eyes hollow pools of thought. Like a light switch thrown, he jumps into action: swift, precise, calculated. Feet hit the floor. Hands seize the backpack then he crosses to the closet where his raincoat dangles like a flayed skin from its hook. He drags it down, slides it over his shoulders, hood limp against his spine.

He crouches, rummaging through a plastic bin, breath steady, movements surgical. Suede work gloves surface: soft, pliant, smelling faintly of dust and sweat. He tosses them into the pack, zips it shut with a hiss. Then he turns his head, eyes locking on Todd's room across the hall.

The door creaks open, spilling stale air thick with urine and old sweat. Clothes sprawl across the floor like corpses. Charles steps inside, shoeless feet stepping over a minefield of filth, and drops to a crouch in the closet's shadow. His fingers burrow through a mound of fabric, closing around Todd's clean sneakers.

This is not the first pair he's claimed. Every shoe Charles has worn bore Todd's ghost first. This particular pair are too big for Charles. He is acquiring them early. He laces them tight, knots biting into his fingers, and rises, silent as dawn.

Downstairs, David's voice rumbles out a storm cloud of curses before fading into the slam of the storm door. Annie watches with a knotted brow.

Charles descends the staircase. He stops. Turns. Their eyes lock. Hers are wide with fear, his dark and fathomless. He moves to her, hands lifting, palms warm against her trembling fingers. He draws her close, silent. They share a lingering embrace.

Annie's voice, frayed with worry, finds his ear. "Charles, please be careful and come back before dark no matter what. I don't want two missing children to worry about tonight, OK?"

His eyes assure her and he breaks the embrace.

"Wait," Annie blurts, darting to the junk drawer. Metal clinks, plastic rattles, until her hand emerges clutching a small, battered flashlight, haloed in dust. She presses it into his palm, lips brushing his forehead in a kiss that tastes of salt and storm. Their eyes meet one last time. Charles smiles—a curve of lips that holds no light. He turns.

The back door pushes open, spilling him into the bruised dusk. Wind claws his hood, rain stippling vinyl in cold, stinging kisses. The yard stretches wide and empty, grass slick underfoot, horizon bleeding into storm. Charles moves fast, shoes drumming a muted requiem as he cuts toward the fields. Night is coming and he knows he must hurry.

The rusty spring shrieks as the shed door yaws open, a sound like metal screaming in protest. The flashlight beam slices through the gloom, jittering across rust-stained tools and dust-choked corners. Shadows leap and twist like startled animals. He spies a tin can glinting on the workbench, its rim rusty and sharp with age. Inside, the green box cutter waits, mute and gleaming like a relic of violence. Charles snatches it, fingers curling tight around its cold spine, and bolts.

Charles

The spring wails again as the door slams, a hollow bang followed by a smaller, mocking echo. Rain needles his hood as he gallops across the rain-softened field, breath tearing through his throat. The sky crouches low, swollen with storm, clouds bruised purple and black. Lightning forks overhead, flashing the world as though God has just taken a photo.

Charles plunges into the woods, a phantom stitched to shadow. Branches rake across his raincoat, vinyl scraping under their talons. Roots lunge from the earth, slick and treacherous, but he vaults them with the grace of a gazelle. The cliff looms ahead. He drops his pack at its lip, rips it open, flashlight and blade tumbling inside. Gloves surface. He slides them on, zips the pack, straps it tight.

The rope coils at the base of the tree root like a sleeping serpent, knotted thick, scarred by years of use. Charles grips it and begins his descent. The cliff face looms beneath him, slick with rain, stone biting his sneakers. Gravity claws at his spine, but his movements are precise, practiced, born of ritual.

At the bottom, the river roars like a swollen beast thrashing against its banks. It is much higher than usual due to all of this excess rain. Water licks the cliff walls, black and glassy, swallowing the sand. Charles splashes through, the cuffs of his jeans drinking the flood, cold gnawing at his bones. The sky still bleeds orange fire along the treetops, torches guttering against the purple dusk. Darkness hunts him, but he runs faster, lungs scalding, legs motoring through the mire.

The mound; the humped spine of earth veined with roots rises. Charles dives under the shrubs, belly grinding against wet sand. Water pools at the entrance to his lair, sucking at his knees as he crawls through the triangle crack. Vinyl shields his torso, but his jeans cling heavy and sodden.

Inside, the air curdles—rank with rot, thick with the musk of death. Shadows writhe along the stone walls, their surfaces tattooed with skulls and bones, trophies of years steeped in silence. Charles threads the maze, sneakers padding over sand, breath syncing to the pulse of the river beyond. He reaches the inner sanctum; the original chamber, the altar of ruin.

Todd waits. Or what's left of him. The body sprawls across the stone table, grotesque in its stillness. Both legs shattered, splintered bone jutting through denim like ivory tusks. One arm dangles, limp and broken, wrist twisted at an angle that mocks anatomy. His face—oh, his face is a ruin. Eyes, like black windows punched into a corpse, gape wide, glassy and blind as they stare at the hole above. The skull is smashed, the back flattened as if the stone itself had cradled his skull in a pillow. Bone shards spike through wet hair, pale and obscene. Blood fans across the sand in a V-shaped bloom, brain matter clinging in viscous ribbons.

Charles crouches, nostrils flaring. The stench of copper and rot crawls into his lungs, sharp enough to taste. He leans close to the corpse, tongue tasting the air, then recoils, lip curling in disgust.

The pack thuds onto the sand. Charles unzips, fingers fishing for the blade. The box cutter gleams in his gloved grip, its edge whispering promises. For a moment, he just stares as memory flickers like film: Snowflake's soft fur, Todd's laughter slicing the dark. Rage coils tight in his gut. Abruptly, he moves. Todd's hand flops under his touch, fingers cold, joints stiffening with rigor. Charles wipes the handle of the blade on his soaked jeans and then presses the cutter into the palm, rolling it, forcing each fingertip to kiss the weapon. When he's done, he slides it into the sodden pocket of the letterman jacket, now a burial shroud for guilt.

Charles

The raincoat lies crumpled, yellow bright against the sand like a severed sunbeam. Charles snatches it, stuffs it deep into the pack. Jeans follow. They are heavy with grit, coughing sand as he shakes them. He folds them into a tight, obedient roll. Zipper hisses shut.

Then the dance begins. Slow at first with Charles simply circling the stone. His movements swell, spiraling wider, faster, a savage waltz around the corpse. Sand sprays underfoot, footprints multiplying like a lifetime of bruises. His breath comes in pieces, laughter ghosting his lips. Minutes bleed away, swallowed by the rhythm.

And then Todd speaks; or seems to. A single word echoes like a shot in the cavern: "Chuckles." The syllables slithers through the dark and wrap around Charles's spine. He jerks, smile collapsing, body locking in mid-step. Eyes snap to the table. Todd hasn't moved. But his voice lingers like a memory.

Charles stares into those dead eyes, glassy with oblivion. Seconds fall like drops of blood. Then his brows soften. His lips twitch. The smile crawls back. He begins to bounce in tiny, rhythmic pulses, sneakers kicking sand, as if the word were a drumbeat only he can hear.

Charles plunges his hands into the mangled tangle of Todd and deer bones, fingers curling around a femur thick as a club. He wrenches, muscles pulling, until sinew snaps with a wet pop. The bone tears free, slick with stink. He hoists it high, a grotesque trophy, and spins away from the altar in a savage pirouette.

The dance begins again: wild, frenetic. His sneakers tread over the sand as he storms through the maze, leaving uncountable divots; soft and rounded. Shadows leap under the jittering glow of dusk. He lashes the bone against walls, pokes the hollow sockets of beaver skulls, smacks the leathery coil of a snake until it spins and drops in a stinking heap. At the back wall, he halts, breath labored, and reaches into the cubby carved from soft rock. His fingers graze leathery flesh, tufts of dirty white fur barely clinging like ice in springtime. Snowflake. The first. The genesis of this cathedral of ruin. His chest becomes a vacuum, memory clawing at his ribs. Then the moment dies. He spins, bone slicing air, and storms back toward the front.

Bones pile like driftwood on a secondary altar, each armful wrenched from Todd's grotesque cradle. Sand sprays underfoot, sweat rolls down his spine. When the last shard clatters onto the heap, Charles bolts for the triangle crack. Water sucks at his knees as he crawls through, jeans drinking the flood. Vinyl abrases against stone. He bursts into the open, dusk bleeding purple across the sky.

The climb is a gauntlet. At the cliff's lip, he coils the rope and drops to his knees. The pack rips open under his hands. Steel flashes as the serrated kitchen knife emerges in his grip, its teeth glinting like a predator's grin. He hacks at the rope lashed to the tree root, fibers groaning, strands snapping in slow, stubborn surrender. Minutes bleed away. At last, the rope slumps free, limp and defeated. He stuffs the knife into the pack, coils the rope, and slings the coil over his shoulder. He runs with lungs still scalding, heart slamming against his ribs.

The woods convulse around him, shadows clawing at his hood. He bursts into the clearing, storm light strobing through the canopy, and veers toward the hole. Three miles vanish under his sneakers, each stride an action of obsession.

The pit, rimmed in roots and sharp-edged stone gapes ahead. Charles staggers to the nearest tree, knees buckling, and drops the pack. His labored breath assaults his throat, hard and stinging. Fingers fumble with the rope, looping it around the trunk, knotting it tight. He lurches to the edge, shoves the coil into the abyss. It unspools in a serpentine rush until the frayed end dangles fifteen feet above Todd's shattered shrine.

Charles grips the rope in his gloved hands. They lock around it like vices. He drags it hard against the sharp, granite lip. Fibers fray, a dry scream in the hush. He grinds back and forth, tendons straining. Sweat pours down his temples, stinging his eyes. His breath hisses through clenched teeth, chest heaving like a bellows. Minutes stretch. The rope frays, strands surrendering one by one.

Ten minutes. A quarter cut. His arms quake, veins bulging like innertubes ready to pop. He slumps, forehead kissing his sleeve, lungs clawing for air. Frustration erupts in his skull. He tilts his head back, eyes clawing at the bruised sky, and gulps air in swallowed bursts. Mental notes flicker. He needs to do more arm work, less running. He's soft. Weak. This was supposed to be easy.

He rises, fury stitching his spine, and wraps the rope tight around his fists. Granite bites the fibers as he grates harder, faster, savage strokes shredding the silence. His shoulders burn, a furnace of agony. His heart jackhammers, throat raw with breath. Oxygen flees his blood, leaving him hollow, trembling. Still, he works. Still, he grinds. Until the world narrows to rope and stone and pain and nothing else.

A bead of sweat breaks free, sliding down his nose. Time slows. He watches it fall. He sees the droplet swell, stretch, fracture light as it plummets into black. It kisses blood-soaked stone below.

Then darkness blooms behind his eyes.

Charles crumples sideways, cheek grinding grit, arm twisted under his ribs. Semi-conscious, he rolls, body tipping toward the void. The claws of gravity drag him down. The rope jerks taut, biting his wrists. Reflex flares like a primal spark and his fingers cinch tight, locking the rope against his flesh. He dangles, breath shredded, the abyss yawning beneath like a mouth ready to feed.

Dazed, Charles drifts in a fog of pain and panic, his mind clawing for clarity as the world rocks beneath him. A cold rush of air licks his face, and then the truth slams into him. He's dangling, suspended over the gaping mouth of his secret cavern. Below, shadows pool like ink around the stone altar, and sprawled across it, pale and broken, lies his foster brother. The sight punches through the haze, and his stomach knots so violently he almost lets go of the rope.

The rope bites into his wrist, a cruel tether that keeps him from plummeting into that silent grave. He twists and reaches upward with his one free hand. Fingers scrape against the coarse fibers until they latch onto a taut section above his head. The rope complains under his weight, a sound sharp as a shout in the cavern's belly. Then, a sickening snap followed by another. Tiny strands fray and curl like severed veins. Charles freezes solid, breath stuck in his chest. Terror roots him in place. He dangles like a carcass on a butcher's hook, every squeak of the rope a ticking clock counting down to his fall.

Slowly, he forces his eyes upward, afraid that even the weight of his moving orbs will be enough to break the lifeline. His own hands clutch the rope, knuckles bloodless, tendons straining. Beyond that, more rope, stretching into darkness above. He doesn't dare look higher. He focuses on the next grip, the next lifeline. One move at a time. He wants to ease his lower hand free, but the thought of hanging by one hand feels like suicide. His strength is a candle guttering in the wind. Still, he acts. Fingers peel away, trembling, and shoot upward to seize a fresh hold. Fibers snap like tiny twigs as his weight shifts. The rope shivers. His body sways over the abyss, and the cavern craters wider in his mind, hungry for him.

Charles knows the slow climb will kill him. He's too weak, too spent. Desperation claws through his veins, and he hooks a leg around the rope, skin burning as fibers twist and grip against flesh. He kicks, loops the rope around his calf, pinches it tight with his other foot. His legs and arms work in savage rhythm, hauling him upward the way they taught in gym class, but this is no drill. This is survival. Each thrust grinds the rope against the granite lip, shredding it by the tens. The sound is a buzzsaw chewing through his lifeline.

He lunges, grabs just above the fray with his right hand. One last kick, a soundless scream ripped from his throat, and his fingers hook a jagged stone jutting from the rim. He heaves, muscles tearing fire through his limbs, and drags himself over the edge. Solid ground greets him like a lover's embrace, but the rope behind him still hangs in tatters.

Charles sprawls on his back, chest heaving, lungs begging for air as the world moves and steadies beneath him. Rain's drizzle has vanished, leaving the forest slick and glistening like a skin freshly peeled. Above, the canopy parts in broken seams, and through them, stars blink like cold eyes. Some shimmer from oxygen-starved vision, but others burn real and merciless in the bruised evening sky. He stares until the spinning slows, until the pounding in his skull becomes a dull, rhythmic beat; a reminder that time hasn't stopped, even if everything else feels broken.

The thought of time jolts him upright. He forces composure, dragging breath into fragile order. His gaze hooks on the rope, that frayed umbilical cord dangling over the abyss. It's nearly severed now, fibers curling like wires. Luck, he thinks. Or maybe fate. Either way, it's ending. Carefully, deliberately, he grips the rope with both hands and works the last strands loose. Each snap is a firecracker in the silence. When the final thread gives, the rope slithers downward in a silent, limp surrender, landing in a twisted heap across Todd's body. The sight; a deserved gift laid at the altar of revenge.

Charles reaches for his backpack, fingers trembling but sure. He doesn't hesitate. He can't. Charles looks down at his feet; his sneakers. No. Todd's sneakers. He lifts his right foot and views the side of the shoe. He bounces his leg gently to feels its weight, feel the history stitched into every fray. He reaches down and pats the side of the sneaker twice, congratulation on a job well done. Together, he and those sneakers move, pounding the path carved by years of shared footsteps.

He runs. The woods absorb him, shadows clutching at his sleeves, but he doesn't look back. He will never look back. This is the last time, the final breath of a place built from rage and grief. This is no longer Charles's special place. This is now Todd's special place. A shrine of lies and payback. A tomb for innocence and snowflake's ghost.

Charles runs harder, the stars wheeling above like time flying by, and the forest vibrates with the sound of endings. He knows with marrow-deep certainty: he will never return.

—

Charles slips through the back door, the aluminum panel clapping shut behind him. The sound ricochets through the house, and before he can draw a breath, Annie bursts from the living room, her slippers skidding across linoleum. She collides with him in the kitchen, arms wrapping tight, voice breaking into sobs.

"Oh my God, Charles! I was so worried about you!" Her words tumble out, wet and frantic, and then her gaze snags on his face. A gasp slices the air. "What happened?" Her tone softens, trembling on the edge of panic, but Charles offers nothing, just silence.

Annie steers him to the sink, hands fluttering like nervous birds. Water runs, a cloth darkens, and then her touch is on his skin. It is gentle, tender, almost holy. Each dab stings, and Charles flinches. Annie murmurs half-formed prayers under her breath, words meant for comfort but laced with fear.

"Just shake your head, Charles. Did you see Todd?" She asks, filled with hope. He shakes no, the motion stiff, mechanical.

Her voice sharpens, brittle with exhaustion. "It's dark outside, Charles. I should be so mad at you! You scared me half to death!"

Charles always feels such discomfort when she babies him this way, but he allows it. He knows her heart. He would never want to bruise it.

Her hands keep moving, blotting blood and rain, but her eyes glisten. "The sheriff said twenty-four hours. Twenty-four hours before they'll even look for him. Do you know what that does to a mother? Sitting here, helpless, waiting for her children to come home?" Her voice cracks, pleading now. "What happened out there?"

Charles stands mute, an image painted from guilt. He feels her warmth, hears her pain, but inside, the truth spools like barbed wire. He says nothing.

Then the air cracks. "Where the fuck have you been, you little ass wipe?" David's voice slams through the doorway, hate-filled and frustrated. He fills the frame like a storm cloud, arms crossed, eyes drilling holes.

Annie freezes, cloth limp in her hand. Her whisper is urgent, slicing through the tension. "Go upstairs. Get ready for bed." A shove, gentle but firm, sets him moving.

Charles drops his head, feet scraping toward escape. But the hall is barricaded by David, who doesn't budge. He leans, weight anchored, gaze burning like a brand. Charles edges closer, heart building pressure, and squeezes through the narrow gap. David shifts just enough to make it a fight, elbow grinding against Charles's ribs, a silent warning pulsing through the contact.

Charles bursts free, stumbles two steps, then bolts for the stairs. He doesn't look back. He can't. Behind him, voices collide—Annie's tremor, David's thunder, and he climbs, each step a thud of dread. Upstairs, the walls close in, and the truth sits with him like a corpse at the foot of his bed.

—

A focused dot of harsh yellow sunlight crawls across Charles's bedsheet, inching like a second hand over fabric, then tracks down and over his closed left eyelid. The lid flickers. The eye twitches beneath. He squeezes shut harder at first, then snaps it open.

Nothing moves in the room except for his eyes. His room is dark other than the light bleeding in around the window shade and penetrating the constellation of pinholes punched through it. One of those pinholes is the tiny sun that so rudely stabs him awake. This is not how mornings begin for him. What is this? He sits up, crawls his mattress to the window, finds the bottom of the shade, and yanks. The roll springs up six inches. White, blinding sunlight floods in. Pain needles his retinas and he jerks back from it, a reflexive recoil like a vampire from dawn.

Slowly, he raises the shade fully as his eyes adjust. He leans in, forehead nearly against the glass, and peers out. Morning stands in full bloom; the sun is already high. The grass shows no lace of dew. He doesn't know the exact time, but he knows he's late for a habit that used to own him. Normally he's down there, at the place, long before the sky bruises with daylight. He hasn't needed a clock; he never does. His body wakes itself before sunrise, the alarm hardwired into bone. Today, the alarm does not sound. It does not need to, he tells himself. He doesn't have to run to the special place before school anymore. He can run whenever he wants now; or not run at all. Free time spills out before him, strange and weightless. Today is a different kind of day.

Two small gray rabbits nibble clover in the yard, heads dipping in quiet rhythm. A squirrel launches from a limb and lands on the bird feeder with a metallic thud, hanging upside down by its hind feet. The feeder trembles. Seed scrapes into the tray and then vanishes into cheeks already swollen. Charles unlatches the window and lifts it a few inches. Fresh morning air slips in cool and green, carrying the soft tick of the world waking up: leaves rustling, a distant truck downshifting, the feeder's faint clink.

He places the barrel of his Crosman 760 ten-pump pellet gun on the sill of the open window and settles in behind the scope. The world narrows to glass edges and crosshairs. He breathes. The yard drifts across the lens. One rabbit swells into view; its nose twitches as it chews a sweet purple flower. The crosshairs hover, steady at the rabbit's shoulder. He inhales deep, exhales slow, and slides the scope left.

The second rabbit glides into the circle. The sight picture is perfectly clean and centered between the eyes. He counts the breath: in through the nose, out through the mouth. At the keel of his exhale, there is that practiced pause, the pocket of silence where his finger knows what to do. The pellet will punch through. It always does.

But he inhales sharply instead, and swings his viewfinder to the squirrel. The little thief hangs inverted, its spine stretched

135

like a wet rag, back legs hooked at the top. Its hands work fast, scraping seed, stuffing life into its cheeks. Charles has his pick of anatomy. The crosshairs touch the base of the tail. They drift down, pause at the knee. Down again, resting between the shoulders. Down once more until they settle dead center on the head. The shot lives there: simple, honest, certain.

He knows this kill. He has taken this shot hundreds of times and almost never misses. He knows what comes after, too: the careful picking of metal from meat, the surgical prying, the transplanting, the work done in the place, the ritual of making things into other things because he must. Now, he doesn't have to anymore. He holds the perfect picture in the scope, breath measured, heart steady. He hears, beneath the silence, the faint ticking of a clock that exists only inside him. The tick says habit. The tock says choice.

He doesn't need to do this. He tells himself again, and again, more fiercely. Yet wanting rises anyway, a heat that convinces the hands and convinces the bones. He wants to prove it to the animal, to himself: that he is flawless with a rifle, that he can thread a pellet through the smallest door in the world. He wants the certainty of impact, the soft collapse, the quiet after. Desire is louder than reason, as loud as a breeze.

He inhales through his nose. Exhales through his mouth. The pause opens.

It stays open.

Without firing, the crosshairs leap upward into sky. The barrel lifts. The world through the scope becomes blue, bare, forgiving.

He lowers the gun, sets the butt on the mattress. The barrel remains on the sill, aim gone slack. The rabbits keep chewing. The squirrel keeps stealing. They live another day. For the first morning he can remember, Charles lets them.

Charles

Charles steps out of bed, bare feet pressing into carpet that feels colder than it should. His eyes lock on the crumpled pants sprawled like a dead thing on the floor. He snatches them up, fingers clawing through pockets: right front, left front; empty. A jolt punches his chest. The watch isn't there.

He never keeps it in the back pockets. Never. Still, his hands dive in, frantic, scraping seams as if the gold might materialize from denim. Nothing. The room spins. He kicks through clothes, shoes, debris; eyes sweeping the floor in wild brushes. The watch is nowhere. Nowhere. His pulse thrashes against his ribs like fists on a locked door.

He reels backward, mind clawing through memory: last night, bed, darkness, Annie's voice soft and trembling. Before that: homecoming, the sting of cloth on his wounds. He rewinds further, scene by scene, until the reel stops on an image that freezes his blood.

The hole. The rope fraying under his fingers. The ground rushing up. His body slamming face-first into grit, and the watch; tumbling free from his sweatshirt pocket, spinning like a golden second hand in slow motion before kissing sand beside Todd's stillness in Todd's special place. The shrine of lies. The graveyard of innocence. The watch lies there now, gleaming like guilt in the dark.

Charles stands stiff, terror racing through his gut. His plan was ironclad: never return. Never. But the watch; his watch, is out there, screaming its betrayal in silence.

The doorbell rings.

His head snaps toward the bedroom door. Footsteps land heavy downstairs. A hinge groans. Voices: low, male, official, spill in. Words blur, but the tone is unmistakable: authority. Charles pulls into himself and moves like a cartoon robber, creeping to the door, pressing his ear against the wood. He strains, catches fragments, but nothing clear. He peels the door open fast, ripping the squeal like a bandage. The sound is sharp, high-pitched, but no one calls up. No one knows he's listening.

He skirts across the hall into Todd's room, heart still speed-boxing his rib cage. Todd's window frames the front yard like a stage. There, center spotlight, squats the sheriff's car.

Blood drains from his face. A chill floods his skin, ice water pulsing through veins. He should feel ready. He told himself he was ready. He rehearsed this moment until it was muscle memory. But the watch—God, the watch—is out there, glinting like a confession waiting to be found.

Without it, he is naked. Without it, he is nothing. The golden watch is his armor, his proof, his pulse. He must retrieve it. He must.

Charles yanks Todd's closet door open, fingers clawing for the sneakers he wore last night. He sees them, still smudged with dirt and secrets, and snatches them, bolts back to his room, and drags on clean clothes like armor over skin that feels too exposed. The sneakers go on last, their laces stiff. Their soles caked with transgression. He doesn't think about that. He can't.

He darts into the bathroom, splashes water, scrubs teeth, rakes fingers through hair. Every motion is a sprint against time, against the pounding in his chest. He needs out; out before questions starting popping up like weeds; out before eyes start digging.

Downstairs, voices chatter low, a current of tension transmitting through the house. He hits the top of the stairs and freezes. David stands at the open front door, one hand gripping the frame, the other braced on the edge like he owns the threshold. His posture is casual, but the weight in his stance says otherwise. Beyond him, two uniforms cast long shadows into the hall.

Charles descends, head bowed, eyes locked on the banister. He grips it, swings into a tight U-turn toward the kitchen. He catches a flicker of faces as he scoots by. It's Sheriff Dobson, his broad grin gouged into weathered skin, and his deputy, looming like a question mark. Charles doesn't break stride.

"Well, hello, young Mr. Charles, sir!" Dobson's voice booms, jovial and deep enough hit oil.

Charles stops dead in his tracks. Prickly heat floods his neck. He doesn't turn. His head hangs low, eyes drilling into the floorboards as if they might do him the favor of opening up and swallow him whole.

"Oh now, don't you go worrying yourself about your big brother," Dobson rolls on, words warm and heavy like syrup. "I'm sure he's fine. Like I told your dad—if you don't hear from him by dinner, we'll be back to help you take a look around. I'm sure we'll find him safe and sound." A pause, then the hook: "That be alright?" His smile is audible, a curve Charles can feel without seeing.

Charles nods fast, jerky, like a puppet. Then he scurries, short steps snapping him into the kitchen.

Annie rises from her chair like a shot, coffee sloshing in its cup. Her face is a map of sleepless hours, eyes ringed in bruised crescents, skin pale under the kitchen light. She barrels into him, arms wrapping tight, voice spilling caffeine-fueled tremors.

"Oh Charles, my sleepy boy. You poor thing! Your body needed extra rest, didn't it?" She peels him back, palms framing his face, twisting it left, right, inspecting damage like a jeweler appraising flaws. "No shiner, thank God. But that scrape—oh, that looks raw." Her words tumble, frantic, tender. "I thought I'd drive you in late myself, but you can stay home if you're not feeling up to it."

Hope rises in his chest. Stay home. Yes. His eyes flare bright, head bobbing quick in silent agreement.

The kitchen door screams open like a wildcat. "The hell he can!" David's voice roars.

He fills the doorway, a storm in human form. "Three days left in the school year! Kid's too damn stupid to be missing class. We got enough shit on our plate with one kid gone. I don't need to worry about this one too. He's going to school."

The wind dies in Charles's sails. His chest caves inward.

"Get your shit together and get in the truck. I'll run you in myself." David's command cracks; a whip woven of malice.

Charles pivots, legs wooden, and trudges toward his room. The house pulsates behind him with a chorus of worry, anger, and secrets. Every step feels like walking deeper into a trap he built himself.

—

All day, Charles sits in classrooms that feel like cages. Chalk squeals on boards, voices drone, clocks tick—but none of it reaches him. His mind is a spinning reel, looping the same frames: the watch, the hole, the sheriff's car like a phantom outside his house. He sketches plans in silence, not on paper but in the frantic corridors of thought. Step one, step two, step three—each move rehearsed until it hums like muscle memory. He wants confidence, needs it, but the clock inside him keeps screaming: too late, too late. Dammit, why couldn't he stay home today? Why couldn't the world give him that one mercy?

The final bell might as well be a starter pistol for Charles. He bolts for the bus, hoping to get the seat closest to the door. Every mile home is a mile stolen from his plan. When the bus sighs to a stop at the end of his long, dusty drive, he's already moving: feet a blur, lungs accepting all the oxygen they can take, legs eating distance like a freight train. The house looms ahead, small, ordinary and monstrous all at once.

He slams through the front door, floats up the stairs, peels off school clothes, drags on running gear and Todd's dirty sneakers—the same pair.

Down the stairs, fast, faster, fingers hooking the banister in his signature swing. He whips into the kitchen doorway, momentum carrying him like a thrown dagger.

His foster mother, Annie is there, hunched over coffee, eyes sunken by sleepless hours. She looks up, and light floods her face. Light always floods her face when she sees him, no matter how much darkness tries to extinguish it. She rises, joy sparking like a match. "Oh Charles! You're home right on time! I'm so happy to see you!" Her hands clutch his shoulders, her voice a tremor of caffeine and hope. "Well, I'll bet that face feels tight today. You're dressed for your run already, honey? No homework first?"

Charles nods, sheepish, every muscle bribing his brain to bypass her warmth and bolt for the door. He shifts, a single step telegraphing intent.

"You remember Sheriff Dobson, right Charles?" Annie's words hit like a bear trap snapping shut. Charles's body turns to ice. Only his head turns, slowly. He peers over his shoulder, and there he is—Dobson, leaning against the counter, coffee steaming in his fist, grin engraved deep. Two more steps reveal the deputy, Elderkin, propped in the corner like a totem.

"Well, hello, young Mr. Charles, sir!" Dobson booms, voice too big for the room. "Long time no see, huh son?" A chuckle follows, hearty and hollow. "Son, you remember Deputy Elderkin from last night. I'm confident that with his help and the help of Buzzy's hounds…"

Hounds. The word suddenly encases in ice in Charles's skull. It spreads from there and undulates through his veins. He expected a search; even planned for it, but not this soon. Not now. The watch. The golden watch lying in sand, waiting for him. Fingerprints won't be an issue. The watch seems impervious to damage and dirt. There will be questions though. If they find it, it's gone forever. If they find it, everything unravels.

"Pleasure to meet you, Charles," Elderkin says, hand extended, voice smooth as butter. "There are a lot of ways a person can get snagged out there, like wild animals, hunters, traps, pitfalls. It's treacherous terrain. You think you know it, then it jumps up and surprises you. I'm sure your brother's just in a jam. Happens all the time. Folks end up with nothing worse than a bruised ego." His hand waits, dangling like bait.

Charles's eyes flicker: floor, deputy, floor; gaze never landing. He doesn't take the hand. Instead, he turns to Annie, eyes pleading, silent words screaming: let me go. She reads him, sighs, and nods.

"OK, well you run along now, Charles. Get your exercise and calm your mind." Her voice is soft, sacrificing. "Come back quick and join us in the search, honey. We'll be heading out soon."

A horn blares outside—one of those musical 're-mi-do-re' types, piercing the day. Barking erupts a moment later. It's a chorus of hounds. Charles's stomach caves. They said dinner. Dinner! Why now? Why early? The plan shreds in his hands like wet tissue.

He bolts for the back door, legs pushing to full speed with no warm-up, breath ready for mind and body to catch up.

"How's he doing?" Dobson's voice floats behind him, tinged with concern.

"Oh, you never can tell with Charles," Annie answers. Her words chase him into the yard like hounds.

—

Charles rips the shed door open so hard it ricochets against the wall with a crash and a metallic clang. The smell of oil and old wood slams into his nostrils. He dives inside, heart ready to leap from his throat, and drops to his knees before the cabinet. His hands claw through a box buried in dust, fingers scraping metal and splinters until they close around a coil of rope. He yanks it free, the old fibers rough against his palms, and spins toward the workbench. A metal drawer screeches open; gloves on top. He snatches them, jams his hands inside, and bolts from the shed like artillery fired into daylight.

The fields stretch before him, wind combing through tall grass like fingers through hair. He runs, lungs pleading, legs wheeling, the rope slapping against his thigh with every stride. Through the dense woods—almost there. The cliff's edge reveals itself ahead, its edge a blade against the sky. He veers right, plunging into vegetation that claws at his arms, and barrels toward the big tree: the old anchor, the monument of his secret descent.

The tree looms, bark gnarled like ancient bone. A short length of weathered rope still clings to its largest exposed root, gray and frayed, a relic of darker days. Charles loops the newer rope above it, fingers fumbling, knot cinching tight. He yanks hard: once, twice: testing strength, testing fate. Then he hurls the coil over the edge. It unspools in a hiss of fibers, slapping rock, dangling like a lifeline cut short. Two-thirds down. Not enough. Not thick enough. But it will have to do.

He grips the rope, breath held, and swings over the brink. Gravity grabs him, drags him down. His sneakers scrape sand and stone, his gloves bite rope. Every muscle goes to work. He descends fast, too fast, until the rope ends and only air extends beneath him. He clings to rock now, fingers clawing for holds, Todd's shoes skidding on grit. The cliff wall presses cold against his chest, its surface slick with moss and shadow. He drops, knees bending, sand exploding around his feet. The impact drives him into a crouch, breath shoved from his lungs.

He starts to rise but suddenly freezes, still bent double. For a heartbeat he looks broken, a coat slung over a chair back. His face flames red, veins bulging, breath squeezed off tight. Then a smile blooms—impossible to read. Pain or pleasure? Both? Neither? His arm swings down and dangles loose. It hovers a long moment before touching down, fingers closing on something half-buried in sand.

The watch.

Golden. Gleaming like a sun, cast down and condemned to earth. His watch.

A breathy, voiceless laugh emits from his throat. He straightens, arches his back the other way to stretch it out and tilts his head to the sky. Eyes shut; lungs gulp air like water after drought. He exhales slow, opens his eyes, and stares up the cliff—upside down from his angle. He turns, drops the watch into his pocket, and faces the climb.

Rock tears at his gloves as he scrambles upward, muscles imploring. He reaches the rope, grabs it like salvation, and hauls himself higher. Fifteen feet from the top, a sound punches through the silence.

A bark.

Faint, distant, but real. His pulse pumps hard in his arteries. He climbs faster, rope burning his palms through the gloves, shoes gouging stones right out of the wall. Another bark, closer now, sharper, followed by a second voice. There are two dogs, two predators, closing in. He grits his teeth, drags his body up, every muscle a live wire. The cliff's lip looms. He lunges, rolls onto solid ground, chest heaving, vision swimming.

He coils the rope in frantic loops, drops it at the tree's base, and whirls toward the clearing. Then, he stops short. Brush parts only a few yards in front of him. Two dogs prowl into view, shadows with teeth, their coats rippling like liquid night. No handlers. Just hunger and instinct. It doesn't seem right for these dogs to be this close to a bluff without a handler nearby. They sniff, snort, bark in short, staccato bursts. Their noses rake the earth, tracing scent trails like lines on a map. Then, as if summoned by some dark compass, they pivot—toward the hole, toward Todd's special place. Yips slice the air, sharp and urgent, a signal flung into the woods: we've found something. Come.

Charles stands frozen, heart racing, the watch a weight in his pocket, counting down to ruin.

Charles ducks and presses himself into the shadow of the anchor tree, breath locked in his chest, muscles compressed like springs. The clearing settles with silence, broken only by the whisper of wind combing through leaves. He rises and peers through a lattice of branches. One dog breaks from the other, its shape flickering between trunks, then cuts hard and pads back toward the open ground. The hound noses the earth, sweeping toward the cliff's edge. Charles bends his knees, sinking lower, spine curving into bark. He can't see it now, but he feels its presence like heat on skin.

Please. Please go back. Please follow your friend.

A twig snaps. Charles flinches, rolls his body around the tree, scraping bark against his jacket. He slides down until he's seated, back pressed to the trunk, legs drawn tight. The forest stirs: scuffling, a bark, leaves crackling under weight. Another twig fractures. Rustling swells, then dies. Silence floods in again. Charles waits, every nerve standing on end. Another bark?

Nothing. Another shuffle? Nothing. Time stretches, long and cruel.

His hand drifts to his pocket, trembling. Fingers close on his golden talisman, his pulse in metal. He draws it out, rolls it in his palm, feels its warmth kiss against sweat-slick skin. The ruby latch gleams like a drop of blood telling him: press me. He presses. The lid pops with a soft click, contemptible in the hush. **4:23**. The numbers stare back, inhumane. He cranes his neck, peering over his shoulder, around the tree, through a veil of leaves. Nothing moves. No sound. Relief trickles in, thin and fragile. He exhales slow, muscles unclenching, head resting back against the tree.

A single bark erupts inches from his face, a blast of heat and spit. Charles jerks, skull slamming into hard wood. Pain flares behind his eyes, flashing like fireworks. The watch slips from his grip, tumbles into dirt with a muted thud. Stars wheel across his vision, constellations flickering in a black sky. Another bark—muffled, distant, as if underwater. The dog's nose looms, black and wet, filling his vision. Teeth flash, then vanish behind a tongue that lashes his cheek in a slobbering parody of affection.

Sound rushes back all at once, a tidal wave crashing through fog. The hound's bark rips the air, louder, closer, a siren calling doom. Behind every bark is a master. Behind every master is discovery. And discovery is death.

Charles snaps upright, adrenaline flooding his limbs. The anchor tree stands tall at his back; the clearing breathes shallow and mean. The hound's breath is still hot on his cheek, its nose working the air, head tilting, ears pricked for a command that could arrive any second.

He moves fast, hands finding rope by memory. His eyes never leave sight of the dog as his hands slowly retrieve armlengths of the rope that is dangling over the cliffside. A slip loop manifests between his fingers: a quick half-hitch flipped into a noose.

The hound's wet, bewildered eyes catch his. "Sorry," he mouths. Then the loop falls and he drops it over the dog's head in one clean motion. The hound jolts; Charles cinches the loop, then feeds a turn of rope around the trunk, twice, three times. The rough bark bites into the fibers so the tree becomes a brake, a belay. He doesn't have the mass to throw forty pounds ten feet out; physics won't lie for him. But he has leverage, friction, and the cliff.

The dog backs, paws scrabbling, then lunges forward, confused by pressure at its neck. Charles sidesteps, draws the rope tight across his hips, and angles the line toward open air. One more wrap around the trunk; his gloved hands smoke with friction, palms burning. He doesn't heave the animal—he lets momentum choose the path. The hound's forelegs hit loose sand; the ground crumbles; weight shifts; gravity makes its decision.

The dog slides over the lip, nails clawing at nothing, and drops. The rope pays out in a savage hiss, then arrests with a hard, ugly yank. A single, high yelp knifes upward. The body pendulums, smacks stone with a fleshy thud, swings back, and shudders to a stop. Silence follows as if the forest itself inhales.

Charles crouches, rope locked around the trunk, forearms trembling. He listens. Wind combs leaves. His heartbeat counts out seconds. Somewhere below, the line creaks and the hound stutters a small, breathless whine.

"Sandy! C'mon, Sandy! Where you at, girl?" A voice bleeds across the clearing: wide, searching and too close.

"Brandy! Brandy girl!" Another call from deeper in the woods, answered by a distant bark that echoes off stone. It seems old Buzzy has lost a little control over his dogs.

Charles rises just enough to peer through a screen of laurel. Buzzy McLeod steps from the tree line, stocky and sure, hat brim low, orange vest bright against the green. He moves into the clearing, eyes sweeping. "Well, that's Brandy," he says, loud enough to carry. "She's onto something off to the left. Swear I heard Sandy over this way, though." He angles toward Charles's cover, gaze narrowed. "Two strong paths. Real strong."

Sheriff Dobson and Deputy Elderkin break the trees next, shoulders squaring as they stride to meet Buzzy. The three men stand in a wedge, facing the same tangle of brush that hides Charles. Coordination clicks into place—voices low, tones professional, urgency resonating.

"Alright, Elderkin," Dobson says, palm down in a steadying gesture that signifies thoughts collected. "You and Buzzy work this sector. I'll head north with Dave and see what the other hound is onto. I want constant radio contact—no dead zones."

"Copy," Elderkin answers, eyes already mapping the terrain: the clearing, the cliff, the choke points.

David steps out of the trees, swatting pine needles from his shirt. He looks rattled, then clenches his jaw and saunters up beside Dobson.

"Come on with me, Dave," the sheriff adds. "We've got a fork in the road, so to speak."

Charles can't catch every word, but the shape of the plan is clear: split, sweep, tighten the net. He flattens behind the trunk, making himself smaller, shoulders tucked, spine pressed to bark. He hears Buzzy's approach. That man does not move quietly. Twigs snap under heavy steps; brush scours against canvas pants; breath works like a half-plugged bellows. Ten feet, maybe less.

"Everything cool, Buzz?" Elderkin calls from the clearing, voice barely above the whisper of wind.

"Yup!" Buzzy booms, careless with volume. "Nothin' yet!"

The rope sings against bark, a low somber hymn vibrating through the roots. Charles reads its notes in tremors: the weight, the torque, the savage jerks as the hound ricochets off stone. One hand clamps the standing end, the other throttles the brake line, muscles wired for a single fatal choice. Panic flares, then calcifies into simple math.

He's terrified of the dog and more terrified of the men.

He thinks of the watch. He pictures it in the dirt, the lid open; the face is a bright coin waiting to be discovered. He doesn't dare look.

Buzzy stops. Silence closes around him. The handler listens: head cocked, mouth closed, chin lifting as if scent itself could speak. Charles's lungs suffer; he sips air, shallow and silent. If they find him, they'll find the rope around the tree, the freshly cut end that mirrors the length they'll certainly pull from Todd's special place. They'll ask questions he can't answer. He will not survive that.

"Sandy!" Buzzy barks into the brush, concerned and carrying. "Where ya at, girl?"

From below, the line jerks; the hound gives a choked bark, then a whine.

Buzzy may have heard that.

He moves slightly toward the sound, and to Charles. Closer now, five steps, four.

In the clearing, Elderkin moves toward the cliff, scanning edges, crouching to study scuffs in the sand, the fresh abrasion on rock; a struggle dried in mud. He leans, glances over the lip, then straightens, eyes narrowing.

"Got sign," Elderkin murmurs into his radio. "Fresh disturbance at the edge. Could be a slip."

Dobson's reply crackles from the speaker on Buzzy's shoulder. "Copy. Dave and I have vocal on Brandy. She's working left flank. Keep your eyes on that edge, but don't get sloppy."

"Get sloppy—" Elderkin mutters under his breath. An unimpressed smirk pulls into his right cheek. His head shakes in disbelief.

Buzzy pushes through the brush toward Charles, snapping branches as they snag on his vest. He's closing the distance, step by step, drawn by some strange gravity.

Charles's hands sweat inside his gloves. He keeps the rope quiet, the tree wraps tight, the slightest surge from below will light a fuse. Panic flashes hot, then settles into something colder—calculation. If Buzzy breaches the screen, if Elderkin leans one more inch over the cliff, the game is over. He pictures the path out. He could take two steps to the sapling, drop to his knees, feed slack, let the dog swing to the shaded alcove under the lip, then lock again. Buy time in inches.

A heavy, labored breath. A footfall. The brush parts.

Charles holds himself so still he could be a root. The rope thrums faintly, a pulse he feels more than hears. His heart answers in the same rhythm.

Buzzy's face enters the green—a smear of stubble, eyes hard. He stares into the thicket and the thicket stares back.

"Anything?" Elderkin calls, closer now.

Buzzy hesitates, listening, tasting the air. "Maybe," he hollers back. "I got something."

Charles squeezes the brake line and prays the next second belongs to him.

Buzzy takes five more steps. The toe of his boot drops into Charles's peripheral vision with a dull scuff and a puff of dust. Silence clamps down. Buzzy squints, extends just his head forward and scans the scene like a searchlight. The smallest tilt downward of his chin would certainly reveal a set of sneaker-clad feet. Charles holds his breath until his lungs consider betrayal, every joint painfully locked, wishing he could melt into bark. He wants to roll around the tree, vanish deeper into shadow, but he knows: one twitch, one scrape, and it's over.

If Buzzy moves another step, the game ends anyway.

"Sandy! Where the hell are ya, girl? C'mon! C'mon now!" Buzzy's voice thrashes through the brush. Nothing. No bark. No rustle. Just the wind combing leaves like a loving mother tussling her young boy's hair.

Charles counts heartbeats. One. Two. Three. Then Buzzy pivots, boots twisting a divot just inches from him, and walks away. Relief floods Charles's chest in a trembling wave. He exhales, slow, shaky; the air he's hoarded too long.

A sound slices the calm.

A long, high-pitched whine, thin as silk thread, rising from below the cliff's lip.

"Sandy?" Buzzy's voice cracks, disbelief bleeding through syllables. He whirls, stares at the void beyond the edge. "Sandy Girl, that you?"

Three short whines answer, sharp and desperate, echoing off stone like ricochets.

Buzzy drops to his knees so hard the ground shudders. He scrambles forward, palms clawing dirt, then flattens to his belly and slides toward the brink. His vest snags roots; his boots kick up grit. He stretches, torso cantilevered over emptiness, eyes locked on the sound. Charles presses flatter against the anchor tree, heart lodged tightly in his throat. Buzzy's face is inches from the rope cluster, so close Charles can smell the tang of sweat and leather.

"Sandy! Oh, Sandy girl! What the—" The words choke off. His breath grabs with sudden determination. His hand shoots out, fingers groping for the rope that sings tight against the root mass. He hooks it, tugs, grunts. Leverage betrays him. His body is too far over, weight wrong, strength bleeding into air. He curses, lets go, and begins the ugly, unbalanced crawl backward, elbows gouging soil, boots scrabbling for purchase.

Charles uses this noisy distraction to roll from the tree to a small patch of underbrush just feet away. From there he peers through the laurel, still mostly exposed, terror clawing up his spine. One glance. One flick of Buzzy's eyes, and the truth is revealed.

Buzzy hits solid ground, panting, and lunges for the tree's base, closer to where the rope seems to be anchored. His hands flurry over the gnarled roots and find the knot cinched tight around bark of the largest root. "What the fuck is this?" he spits. His knife; a bone-handled fang, rips from its sheath and buries into a root for quick retrieval. He braces, grabs the rope with both fists, and hauls.

The line protests under strain, fibers creaking like ancient bones. Below, the hound yelps—a strangled, broken sound that drills into Charles's skull. Buzzy's arms pull, muscles bunching under canvas, breath tearing out in grunts. His panic is visible in every savage pull, every curse hissed through clenched teeth. He is a man unmade, stripped to raw instinct: save the dog, save the bond.

Charles's world narrows to rope and breath and the pounding of boots in the clearing. Voices flicker: Dobson barking orders, Elderkin's radio crackling, David crashing through brush—but they're nothing compared to the living threat ten feet away. Charles scans the ground for escape routes, for weapons, for miracles. Nothing. Just roots and dirt and the watch burning out of reach like a live coal waiting to start a forest fire.

If Buzzy turns his head, if Elderkin steps closer, if Dobson swings wide; everything unravels. The rope, the knot, the match to Todd's length. The dog. The watch. His life.

Buzzy snarls through another pull, veins bulging, sweat dripping from his jowls. "C'mon, girl! Hang on!" he begs into the void, voice cracking. The hound answers with a thin, pitiful whine that makes Charles flinch harder than any shout.

He prays the next sound isn't his name.

Buzzy hauls with everything left in his arms, rope creaking under strain. Sandy's head breaches the lip, eyes squeezed shut, ribs almost motionless. The root mass claws at her haunches, snagging fur like barbed wire. Buzzy lunges farther out, his center of gravity creeping toward the void. He dips his arms, lowers twelve inches, and the dog jerks free with a violent snap. The sudden release slings weight into his shoulders, nearly ripping him over the edge. His boots skid; his breath expunging in a grunt. He recovers—barely—and begins the last hoist.

The hound flops onto the ledge, limp, sodden with sweat and fear. Buzzy crouches low, knees quaking, fingers clawing for the collar. He hooks it, first one hand, then the other, and drags Sandy up in a savage heave. Her body slaps dirt, dead weight in his arms.

"You'll be OK, Sandy. I'll get you help. Hold on, girl. Hold on." His voice breaks, skinned with panic. The dog exhales a thin whimper.

Buzzy scoops up the limp animal moves backward, slow and shaky, boots testing each root before surrendering weight. His spine bows forward, knees buckling every few steps. He shifts Sandy's mass to his left arm, reaches back with his right, fingers blindly feeling for bark until they find the anchor trunk. Relief flickers across his face as he grips solid wood.

Then he sees it.

Charles.

Standing in the green, just feet away, half-hidden behind a thin weave of brush. Their eyes collide—two worlds smashing in silence. Buzzy gasps, a sound ripped from his gut, and his balance shatters. His boots skid; his torso leans; gravity claws for him. He windmills one arm, clutching the dog with the other, and catches himself by sheer luck. Bark gouges his palm. His breath tears out in a ragged laugh.

"Christ, boy! You scared the bejeezus out of me." His eyes bulge, whites glaring. He shifts Sandy's weight and reaches toward Charles with a trembling hand. "Take my hand, son. Help an old man up, will ya?" His voice pleads, brittle and urgent. He shuffles an inch closer to safety, hand still extended, but something curdles in his gut. The kid's stare. It's flat, unblinking. It feels wrong. Feels lethal.

Shock flips to anger as Buzzy stutters, "Now, now... quit messin' around, you, you little retard. You hear me? I don't know what you're up to but—"

"Hey Buzz! What's the hold up? You good?" Elderkin's voice floats through the air from the clearing.

Buzzy pivots toward the sound, then back to Charles. Their eyes lock one last time. Confusion knots his brow. He turns to answer, inhales—

Air hisses. The branch scythes.

Wood meets meat in cleaver sound; a splinter drills the throat and exits in a red fountain. The heavy spar caves his nose, shattering porcelain bone; teeth skitter in pink foam.

Gravity writes the rest: vertebrae pop down the column, the torso jackknifes backwards. Sandy sails with him, her body a pendulum of fur and rope.

They arc in a perfect, silent parabola; then drop. Two-thirds down, the rope arrests Sandy in a savage jerk. Her spine bows; her ribs creak; she slams the cliff in a wet percussion. Buzzy keeps falling, arms flailing, blood streaming in ribbons that streak the air.

Impact.

Face first. The sound is sickening: a crack, a splat, a thud braided into one. His head whips back, neck snapping like a green branch. Vertebrae explode in sequence; his spine folds, then breaks mid-lumbar with a gunshot pop. His torso jackknifes, belly splitting open in a geyser of viscera. Loops of intestine slither free, slick and glistening, as his lower half slaps earth with a meaty smack. Blood pools fast, dark and syrupy, spreading like ink.

Above, Charles stares over the edge, breath locked, pupils black saucers. Below, Buzzy lies face down, a ruin of bone and pulp. The dog dangles limp against stone, rope trembling under its weight.

The watch glints in the dirt behind Charles, lid still open. Waiting.

A branch snaps behind Charles with a sharp crack that ruptures the hush. He whirls, pulse spiking, and sees Deputy Elderkin gliding through the trees, radio hissing faint static. The man is close. Too close. Did he hear the scuffle and fall? Charles drops low, spine curling, and scuttles toward the cliff's lip. No way out but down. He grips roots slick with moss, fingers clawing for purchase, and lowers himself inch by inch until the bulb of the anchor tree's roots, protruding from the lip of the cliff, shields him. He clings there, half-hidden, eyes tracking Elderkin's boots as they crunch nearer.

The radio spits a burst of static. Sheriff Dobson's voice grinds through: "Tim… How's about a sit-rep?"

"Nah, nothing yet," Elderkin mutters into his mic, tone lazy, oblivious. "Been pretty quiet. Too quiet, really. Buzzy and his dog done run off on me or something. I dunno. You got anything going on?"

Charles dips a few inches lower as Elderkin drifts closer. He's only about five feet away now, maybe less. The deputy's voice carries casual, but his boots speak intent, edging toward the anchor tree like fate on rails.

Dobson's reply crackles: "Ten-four. Hold your position and wait for Buzz. If the trail goes cold, head this way and join us. This hound is excited about something."

"Roger that, boss. Holding," Elderkin answers, and holsters the mic with a flick.

He steps to the brink, hands on hips, and breathes deep. The river sprawls below, liquid silver under a bruised sky. He exhales slow, nodding like a man baptized in beauty. For a heartbeat, the world feels airy, absurdly calm.

Then he sidesteps to the anchor tree, fingers fumbling at his zipper. His smile curdles into mild frustration. Silence stretches. He shifts, wiggles shoulders, exhales hard—and then a fart pops like a cork. A laugh bubbles from his throat as urine arcs in a golden stream, splattering bark in a hiss. "Ahhhlways gladder when the bladder is flatter," he croons, chuckling at his own joke. Rivulets of pee make their way toward the cliff's edge, trickling down the smaller roots.

Charles lowers himself further below the knot of roots, using the rope to gain valuable inches, and continues watching through a web of roots, terror coiling tighter with every second.

Elderkin's gaze drifts down the trunk, tracing the rivulets of piss. There, at the roots, it catches on rope. Two ropes: one thick, old, freshly cut; the other thin, taut, rigid with tension. His smile dies. He zips up slow, eyes locked on the knot. He crouches, fingers grazing hemp, and gives a tug. The line thrums like a live wire. Something's on the other end. Something heavy.

Dark, inevitable thoughts flicker across his face. Missing kid. Suicide. Happens all the time. His jaw muscles flex. He creeps toward the edge, spine bowed like a question mark. He wants backup. He wants certainty. He wants neither. Inch by inch, he shuffles onto the exposed root mass, fear etched in every tendon.

Then he sees it.

Hair.

A pale crown spilling over shadow. His breath detonates in a gasp. "Oh fuck, kid. Fuck!"

Dobson's voice rides atop the first thought that enters his head. He has just pissed on a scene— "sloppy."

He drops to hands and knees, scuttles forward, rope gripped tight. He peers over—and freezes.

Eyes.

Charles's eyes, emerald and bottomless, staring up from the void.

Shock slams Elderkin backward. His grip on the rope dies; his hands claw roots in a frantic scramble. For a heartbeat, his brain stutters, gears grinding. That's not a suicide. That's not even Todd. That's the quiet one. The foster kid. The wrong kid in more way than one.

"Christ, kid! You okay? You scared the shit out of me!" His voice cracks as he lunges forward, arm outstretched. "What'd ya do, try to climb down there? Jesus! Take my hand!"

Charles doesn't move. His stare drills through the deputy like an auger.

Elderkin mutters, scooting closer. "What the hell did you see down there that'd drive you to a stunt like this?" He hooks his hands under Charles's arms, grunting. "Jesus Christ. That's right—you don't talk. You hurt? Hold on, let me get a grip." He shifts, muscles bunching. "What's wrong with your other arm? Can you grab my jacket?"

Then his face drains white. His eyes flick past Charles; down, into the abyss, and lock on ruin. Buzzy. The dog. A tableau of meat and rope and silence.

Charles moves.

His dangling arm arcs upward, metal flashes. The bone-handled knife punches Elderkin's eye socket with a wet crunch. The blade tunnels through orbital bone, ruptures the globe, and spears deep into brain tissue. Elderkin convulses, jaw yawning in a soundless scream. Charles twists hard; the knife grates against sphenoid, then rips free in a gout of vitreous and blood.

Before breath can return, Charles pulls himself a few roots higher and the blade slams home again—same socket, deeper, splitting dura, shredding frontal lobe. Elderkin's hands still clamp under Charles's arms, frozen in grotesque embrace.

Charles wrenches the knife loose, pivots, pulls himself upward on the roots a little more and drives it straight up into the deputy's crotch. Steel carves through scrotal sac, shears spermatic cords, and plunges into pelvic cavity, hitting ligament, tendon and then bone. He yanks, levering up, and feels the edge kiss pubic symphysis before tearing free in a spray of arterial blood.

Elderkin's body tilts forward on his knees, balance murdered. Gravity takes him. For a breath, he hangs—a crouched manikin frozen in time—then drops.

The impact is apocalyptic: a crack of skull on stone, a splatter of brain and blood, a thud that shakes roots. Limbs sprawl, twitch, then go still. Silence swallows the gorge, broken only by the rope's low hum and the river speaking softly far below.

Charles clings to bark, chest heaving, knife dripping rubies into the dirt. Behind him, the watch lies open, a witness to it all.

Charles climbs the root mass. His hands and feet spike into knotted wood, hands clawing for grip-sized roots. He pops up to solid ground, drops to his knees, and scrabbles around the anchor tree to the shadowed patch where he hid before. There; half-buried in grit, at a tilt on its hinge; lies the prize he came for. The golden watch.

He snatches it from the soil, blows hard; no dust. The face gleams, perfect, unmarred. **4:23**.

He feels the hinge tension under his thumb. The lid snaps shut with a clean metallic kiss. It is a Sound that no longer booms in his head. For a heartbeat, the woods seem to hold their breath. Then sound rushes back: wind fingers leaves, somewhere a dog yips, far off a radio hisses static.

Charles palms the watch, drops it into his pocket, and bolts. His young legs spring like a yearling cut loose. He tears through the green wall, bursts into the small clearing, and sprints for the opposite woods where the trail carves on. He hits the path the sheriff and David took, turns his shoulders sideways to weave through alder and birch, and pours on speed. His lungs and heart find a machine rhythm; adrenaline spools into clean power. Feet place themselves. He becomes motion.

———

Twilight thickens under the canopy. The sky holds light, but the woods drink it; turning browns to slate, greens to bruised purples. Air cools. Damp loam climbs the back of his throat. He clears a fallen trunk, skims a boulder's shoulder, slides between saplings whose leaves brush his cheeks with wet whispers.

Ahead, a bark cracks the hush. Another joins, closer, but from behind him. He's moving faster than the little search party; their beams waggle now, pale cones slicing the dark. Voices bleed through. Sheriff Dobson's breaks first, bright with a hunter's edge.

"This hound is excited about something!"

Static and radio chatter stutter; the main hound barks, sharp and insistent.

"I don't know exactly what we're onto here, Dave," Dobson says, a clipped urgency in his words, "but I think we're warm. Let's move."

Charles transports tree to tree, shadowing the party from a distance—close enough to track, far enough to vanish if they turn. Light strobes through leaves: white on bark, black again, white on his knuckles. The dog's voice is a metronome for dread.

Then, from behind him—a bark answers. He freezes, weight sinking, shoulders tight. Another bark rolls up from the rear, nearer now; a stretched howl follows, long and rising, and the front hound replies in a stitched duet across the timber. Pressure builds in his skull. Run or duck? Left, or right? The trees have too many sides and none at all.

Brandy pivots in a sudden decision; wheels and blasts past Dobson and David, tearing back the way they came.

"Well now what the hell's gotten into that hound?" Dobson barks, baffled.

David and the sheriff trade a quick, sharp look then swing around and head for the chorus building behind them. Brush thrashes. Leaves crackle. The search takes a turn, and with it, the path of danger.

Charles sees the dog spear through thicket gaps, its blocky head a moving knot of shadow. He sees the bobbing lamps of Dobson and David above the lower vegetation; closing, unknowingly, right toward him. Another howl swells from behind, and the rustle becomes everywhere: twigs snapping left, leaves whispering right, breath of panting hounds in stereo. He has nowhere to hide.

All at once, he rises from his crouch. He jogs forward toward the two beams; a calm mask over a sprinting heart. Brandy reaches him first, a living siren: barking, howling, nose blitzing over his shoes, then up his legs as he moves.

Dobson and David stop dead, listening. Heavy footsteps drum toward them. Barking spikes. Leaves cut light into slices; something flickers in the breaks. Both men snap to alert. Dobson's thumb pops his holster; his hand settles on the revolver's grip. Two flashlights spear the dark.

Light finds Charles's face with a white splash across eyes, nose, cheek. Another beam skitters down his chest.

David's palm lands on Dobson's gun hand. "Shit," he growls. "It's just Annie's idiot foster kid." Then, to Charles—controlled, edged: "Damnit, kid! You could've gotten yourself shot, running up on us like that. What are you doing?"

Charles jogs in place, wrist angled like he's checking his pulse—a snarky disguise for an answer to a silly question. David eyes him, lips pursed, expression flat as a badge.

"Well," David drawls, voice edged with sarcasm, "you might as well come along with us, Chuckles—though I'm tempted to send you running home, see if you can get yourself accidentally shot by the deputy." His tone sharpens. "Just keep out of the way."

Charles shifts his fake jog into forward motion, trailing behind the two men as they push deeper into the timber. Brandy ghosts at his heels, nose glued to Todd's sneakers like they're gospel.

"What, you got nasty feet, Chuckles?" David snorts, then snaps at the dog: "Get! Get on up there! Go!"

Brandy peels off, tail flagging, and rockets ahead, nose to the ground, pulling the hunt back on track.

Minutes bleed into twenty. Boots cover distance. The woods have thickened into a cathedral of shadow now, the air becoming moist and dense. Radios crackle now and then.

David huffs, voice riding fatigue. "Sheriff, how far we planning to hump it before we call it and regroup? We still have to walk all this back. How far you figure we've come?"

Dobson answers in clipped bursts, breath replenishing between words. "You're right. We could turn back and regroup, but the dog's hot. Don't want to lose the scent to wind or dew." He pauses, chest heaving. "On the other hand—we've logged about three miles already, and I'm not thrilled about the return trip."

He stops dead, boots planting firm, and thumbs his radio mic. The handset pops static as he keys up.

"Dispatch, this is Unit One. Mary Lou, copy?"

A beat. Then a woman's voice, bright and steady: "Go ahead, Sheriff."

Dobson leans into the mic, voice firm. "Mary Lou, have Jack and Randy gas up the ATVs, hook up the utility wagons, and stand by for coordinates. We're going to need mechanized support." He cuts a glance at David, adds dryly, "I think we've earned wheels."

He releases the key. Static hisses, then Mary Lou's voice snaps back: "10-4, Sheriff. Copy that. I'll get 'em mounted up."

Dobson adjusts his duty belt, nods at David, and pushes forward, beam slicing the black. Charles shadows behind, heart ticking like a metronome.

The woods have gone full night now; flashlights the only stars. Radios chirp, then spit static. A male voice punches through: "Unit One, Jack here. All units mounted and fueled. What's your location?"

Dobson keys up without breaking stride. "10-4, Jack. Cut through the James farm back field, then straight through the timber to the river. Keep it slow. The last thing we need is you playing Evel Knievel off a bluff. Once you near the edge, cut left and run parallel. We're about three and a half clicks in."

Jack's voice fires back, crisp: "10-4, Sheriff. En route."

Dobson adds, tone hardening: "You'll likely run into Buzzy and Elderkin before you hit us. Don't literally run into 'em. Eyes up, radios hot. No accidents tonight."

The ether fills with affirmations:

"10-4, Sheriff."

"Roger that, Boss."

Flashlights swing like pendulums. Somewhere ahead, Brandy bays—a long, hollow note that threads through the timber.

Charles feels the shift in his bones. The hunt isn't over. It's just changing shape.

David's lips curl; his nose wrinkles like scorched paper. The stench hits him in a wave that is thick, oily, alive.

"What the fuck is that smell?" His voice blurts, gag riding shotgun. His throat works like it wants to spit but can't.

Dobson halts mid-stride, nostrils flaring. "Jesus Christ! I don't know! Just caught a whiff myself. Smells like a big dead animal!"

The words hang, wrong and heavy. Dobson's eyes flick to David, remorse flooding fast. "Oh Jesus, David. I'm sorry. I don't know what that smell is."

Silence mushrooms—ugly, awkward, as the three men trade looks, each searching for a sentence that doesn't exist. None comes. They walk on.

The dog's voice grows louder—barks stitched with howls now, urgent and fixed. No more running ahead. Stationary now. Waiting. The smell thickens with every yard, a miasma that crawls into sinuses and coats the tongue. Sweet rot braided with copper tang. It clings to sweat, seeps into cloth.

"Christ!" David gags, palm clamping his mouth and nose. "I don't think I can stomach this another minute! I'm gonna puke!"

Dobson's voice grinds low, grim. "Look—if you want to turn back, now's the time. You may not like what's up ahead anyway. But we all know why we're here. Wait or go. It's your call. I'm going on."

He pushes forward, beam cleaving black. David stalls, hand welded to his face. Charles hovers a beat, then bolts. legs roll-fast and he spirits up beside Dobson, matching stride and leaving David behind.

David stands alone, the stink wrapping him like wet cloth. He knows this smell. Knows it in marrow. Death. Decay. Rotting flesh liquefying in its own heat. His gut knots; bile climbs. Behind him, a dog barks in the distance, far, then near. It is answered by the lead hound's howl, sharp and near. David runs.

The woods have him. Flashlight beams vanish; voices die. Only the dog's cry guides his way. A flicker of light winks through leaves—there, then gone. He lunges toward it. Another flash, farther on. He pounds earth. He's not fit for this. His lungs protest, but he runs; until a white spear blinds him.

Dobson erupts from shadow, Maglite glare drilling David's eyes, arm slamming his chest. "Whoa! Stop, David! Don't go over there!" His voice spikes—half bark, half plea. He shoves and hugs in one motion, dragging David back from the brink.

"It's Todd, David. It's Todd." The sheriff's breath saws in and out. "He's had an accident. He didn't make it. And it isn't pretty. I'm sorry, David. Please—take that kid and go home."

The words gut him. David folds, vomit ripping free in a wet roar. Acid scorches his throat; tears sting his eyes. He wipes his mouth with a trembling sleeve.

Charles stands, eyes dark hollows, face emotionless.

Dobson keys his radio, voice flat as a poor man's grave marker. "Dispatch, Unit One. Mary Lou, copy?"

Static spits. Then: "Go ahead, Sheriff."

"Call the state. We've got a 10-54. I say again, 10-54."

The speaker crackles, then a pause long enough to feel like prayer. "My God, Dobbs. Copy. I'm on it. Jesus."

They move as one toward the sound—the dog circling a hole gouged in earth, pausing to sniff, to howl, to stare into black. Flashlights jitter as boots crunch tiny twigs and seed shells. The smell is a living thing now, crawling into lungs, slicking the back of the throat.

They reach the edge. Beams spear downward, slicing the abyss into rings of ghost-light.

And there he is.

Todd.

Sprawled on stone like a broken offering, limbs splayed at wrong angles, skin waxen and split. His face—oh God, his face is a ruin of pallor and shadow, lips peeled back from teeth in a rictus grin that mocks breath. Eyes gape wide, dry, staring at nothing. Fluids pool beneath him, black and viscous, haloing his corpse in a crown of filth. Around him, the cavern sprawls—a cathedral of rot so big, its entirety cannot be viewed from this earthen portal. The stench surges up like a fist, thick with sweet decay and something older, something untamed.

The beams dance, jittering circles on flesh that should never see light again. Silence swallows words. Even the dog whimpers now, tail tucked, voice strangled to a low, mournful keen.

Death has a sound. It's the sound of breath stopping in three throats at once.

—

Halogen white explodes over the clearing—blinding cones that turn trunks to ivory and faces to masks. Engines roar, echoing off the lip of the hole, then cut in unison. Darkness drops like a curtain. In the sudden hush, the smell seems louder.

Jack and Randy swing off their ATVs, helmets in hand.

Jack staggers a half step, gag stuttering behind his teeth. "Christ almighty, what is that stench?"

Dobson is on him in two strides, voice low and hard. "That stench, Mr. Sensitivity, is David James's dead son." He jerks open the rear toolbox, steel clacking. "And I'm only letting that slide because I did the same thing thirty minutes ago." Harness webbing hisses over aluminum as he drags it free. "He can't be more than a day gone. We picked up the scent half a mile out."

Randy peels his helmet, eyes squinting into the pit. "That ain't no one-day-dead smell. You got bigger problems down there."

Dobson nods once, curt. "That's what I'm thinking." He steps into the full-body harness, legs threading, buckles snapping home. "Back that rig to the evergreen tree. Tie in and give me slack off the winch."

He fishes out a lightweight helmet with a lamp mounted at the front. The strap bites under his chin as he cinches it. He moves toward the hole, the smell thickening to a taste: sweet rot, wet copper, swamp.

Jack thumbs the starter; the ATV coughs, then growls. Tires spit dirt as he half-pivots the machine and nests it between the tree and the pit. He kills the motor, hops off, and hustles to tether the machine. He jogs to the front, pops the winch clutch, and pulls cable—three, four, five arm-lengths, until the hook kisses the edge.

"All set, Sheriff," Jack reports, breathing fast.

Dobson clips the hook into the harness's front ring, palms the metal. "I'm going first. You lower on my call. Keep it slow."

He drops to hands and knees, peers over the edge and twists the lamp bezel. The light pierces into the pit—pale smeared on stone. He turns to position himself and slides backward, belly down, toes searching for the void. They find it. Inch by inch he scoots backward until he bends at the waist— feet dangling and thighs pressing hard into twisted root and stone. He pauses for a moment. The cable slackens. Using that slack, a shove of his hands and a thrust of his thighs against the rugged side, he pushes his full weight off and away from the edge. The harness takes him. The cable comes alive with tension and vibrates against his sternum like a metal heartbeat.

"Ease it out," he orders. "Slow."

The winch whirs, steady and mechanical, a small motor against a huge dark. Beams from above rake downward, spiderwebbing shadows. Dobson's lamp smears a circle on the cavern wall, then the floor—sand, rock, and something that moves only because the light makes it look like it might.

He clicks on his handheld auxiliary and throws both beams wide. "It's huge!" he yells up. The words come back twice, softer, like the pit is mocking him childishly.

The stink wraps him entirely now. He can taste the film of decay greasing his teeth.

The cavern swallows the light ravenously, yielding only what Dobson forces from it: body, ground, wall. Shadows drink the light in greedy gulps, walls slick with secrets that refuse to shine.

The ground below resolves into shape: sand sloping into a maze of low stone walls; their courses set by hand, tight joints, intentional turns. Not talus. Not cave fall. Built.

"This can't be natural!" he calls.

Randy's voice floats down, baffled: "What can't?"

"Stone work. Constructed. Somebody put this here." His words echo into the maze.

Up at the rim, Charles can't help it—pride warms him from the sternum out. The darkness keeps his face his own, but the word *built* rings in his skull like a bell.

"Stop!" Dobson barks into the void.

His descent comes to a sudden halt. His weight bounces heavy in the harness, face flashing a brief grimace of pain as straps dig into both sides of his groin. Before he can even inhale through his clenched teeth, small rock and sand debris rains down, clattering off his polymer helmet like a handful of spare change. His head instinctively tries to pull itself into his chest for cover, much like a startled turtle. He waits with rigid neck muscles for the bigger stuff to land—nothing.

Dobson slowly rotates in the pitch; feet hovering just a few feet above the sandy floor. He collects himself, inhales deeply and is about to release a barrage of admonishment when from above, a voice sends a single word echoing through the cavern:

"Sorry!"

He releases the frustrated breath—pent-up tension denied parole. There's a scene to investigate. Can't get distracted.

He aims both lights downward. Beneath his dangling legs, the sand's surface is a battlefield; completely littered with little craters. These are obviously predominantly man-made. They are footprints, but they lack any useful detail. They are simply divots in sand. After a few moments of assessment, he determines that his own prints will not contaminate the scene if he is careful.

"Lower me!" He shouts upward. "Slowly!"

A small bounce and the cable vibrates in his grip. Dobson's boots hit sand. "Stop." The command snaps out sharp. The cable settles with a click. He thumbs the latch, unhooks, drops the steel onto grit, and turns straight for the body.

His beam finds Todd and hovers there. No pulse checks necessary; the geometry of limbs and the gloss of skin answer the question before it's asked. He looks up into the ragged circle of night where faces hover. "I'm sorry, David!" he calls.

David turns away, ten paces, shoulders hunching as his gut betrays him. Randy breaks from the perimeter, hand on David's back, murmuring something that disappears into the trees.

Dobson swings his lamp in fast half-moon motions, mapping danger. Black swallows back. Then something catches his eyes—three silhouettes against the wall. A trio of decayed monstrosities.

He approaches, cautiously. The light reveals what the brain refuses: a beaver carcass, tail splayed like a waffle iron, topped with the skull of a bass; a bloated duck sewn under a rabbit's head; a rabbit body wearing a duck's mask. He mutters without meaning to: "What in the wild world of..."

Suddenly, feeling watched, he widens the sweep.

Suspicions confirmed. In the rock's honeycomb gaps, hundreds of fish are wired in place: each granted a beak and two bird feet, each staring out of dried sockets that hold no eye, but pretend to. They stare blindly and in unison toward—something.

He raises his voice toward the hole. "You're not going to belive this."

"Believe what?" someone echoes.

"I'll brief you topside," he calls back, realizing he'll never be able to express the ghastly nature of this place in short bursts through a hole in the ground. The radio has become intermittent and unreliable since he breached the cavern. There's a little piece of him that knows he calls up to quell the suffocating feeling of being alone in this crypt of decomposition.

Charles watches the descent like a coronation. The praise is a crown he'll never get to wear. He keeps his pride small, folded like the watch in his pocket, and lets the scene devour him.

Dobson resumes the walk. His beam ravages over hybrid grotesques. A turtle shell sprouts a squirrel tail, turtle legs jutting, crowned by a fish skull. The deeper he moves, the more the dark behind him feels like the breath of something following. He turns and sweeps the lamp—nothing. He sweeps the wall again. Nothing moves, nothing lives, everything rots. He takes a few more steps deeper into the lair with head, eyes and flashlight still focused on his six.

He feels it before he sees it—a cold kiss at the back of his head, slick and putrid. He whips his head and light around, and lunges forward—straight into a curtain of serpents. Snakes, dozens of them, dangling like rotting vines, their bodies in every stage of ruin: some bloated and split, others shriveled to leather cords, many dripping filth. The stench grabs firm hold in his sinuses, a cocktail of ammonia and death.

He plows through the tangle, serpents dragging like tendrils against his jacket. Something wet slaps his cheek—a gelatinous wipe that crawls toward his jaw. He smears it away, fingers trembling from disgust. The stench grows teeth in his sinuses. His gut convulses; bile surges like a tide.

He swallows it down and pushes on.

The maze tightens, walls pressing closer. Dobson rounds the last corner, lamp beam leaping ahead. He halts. The light paints a picture that should not exist: a stone slab, altar-like, bearing the skeletal remains of a deer—but not a deer anymore. Its bones have been re-scripted into nightmare geometry: leg bone segments splayed into eight grotesque limbs, ribs arched like mandibles, skull grinning at the void. A spider made of deer, crowned with antlers like a god of all dead things.

"God almighty!" The words rip from him, echoing off stone, chased by silence.

Then—movement at his ankles, subtle as breath. His pant legs flutter. A draft snakes low, cool and clean, threading through the rot. Fresh air. He tastes it: thin, sweet, a phantom of salvation riding the foul tide. He lowers his beam, hunts the source, and finds it: a triangle of black cut into the wall, edges sharp as a cutlass.

Dobson moves closer and drops to his knees, lamp probing the fissure. Sand glitters wet inside, dark as coal. The smooth, wet sand fans out into the room until it meets the still dry sand. He scans the area for any detailed footprints. Nothing of use scrolls by his circle of light. The soft divots in sand turn into tiny pools, rimmed with smooth mounds and fade away into the smooth black. There is nothing of use here.

He approaches the vent and aims his light inside. For as far as he can see, it appears tight, but traversable. The fresh air and the murmur of the river emanating from the fissure conspire to convince him that the tiny tunnel is not a dead end. As much as he really doesn't want to, Dobson crawls on hands and knees into the dark wetness. Shoulders scrape stone, harness creaks. The crack narrows. The air fattens with claustrophobia. Every inch feels like a dare. The cliff seems to lean, ready to crush him flat. His breath is loud in his own ears.

The wet sand turns to sedimentary mud, sucking at his palms. Water beads, then pools; an inch deep, cold as death. He flattens, belly to grit. The water is freezing cold. He can feel it through the vinyl of his rain gear and he can feel it uncomfortably seeping in through entries sealed against showers, not deep-sea diving. His lamp jitters as he worms forward. The smell mutates—rot thinning, ozone rising. Then it hits: clean air, sharp and wild, flooding his lungs like grace.

His head breaches first, then shoulders, then hips. He spills out onto open night, gasping like a man reborn. He stands, boots sinking in black water, and drags in buckets of oxygen that taste like heaven.

A shrub-covered crescent of sand humps around him like an island. On the other side, the current mutters low, swollen high over its banks. Behind him, the cliff rears—a monolith of shadow, its crown lost in stars. A half-wall of stone crouches at his waist, its courses neat, deliberate; man-made, like the maze inside. He palms it, feeling the chill of sculpted intent.

He rounds the wall and climbs the mound, knees sink-sliding in wet sand. He belly-crawls under a snarl of shrubs. Branches rake his helmet; leaves spit dew into his mouth. He bursts through, chest heaving, and rises into a world rimmed with silver. The river babbles close now, swollen and black, licking at the little island like a hungry tongue.

He looks like a sugar cookie.

He keys his mic, voice spent. "Jack—Dobson here. I'm outside the cavern, riverbank side. Found an exit."

He swings his lamp toward the cliff face, beam jittering skyward like a distress flare. He shakes it side to side, semaphore in the dark. Seconds stretch, then light answers—one, two, three beams diving over the rim, stabbing down like spears.

His radios crackles then comes to life. "Jack here. What's the plan?"

Dobson replies, "Stand down for a few minutes and I'll let you know.

He switches channels and keys up again, tone iron. "Dispatch, Unit One. Mary Lou—copy?"

Static spits, then her voice, tight and thin: "Go ahead, Sheriff."

"Patch me into the state," he says, eyes on the cliff, on the hole that birthed him into night. "We've got a scene."

—

It takes a few minutes, but Dobson finds himself patched into the state police; reporting the severity of the crime scene and some brief details. He requests assistance. The static-laden reply through the radio's speaker is quick and to the point. He'll get a callback in fifteen to twenty minutes.

Dobson knows the process: command will evaluate the request, confirm jurisdiction and determine the resources that will be needed; most likely crime scene techs and air support being at the top of that list.

Static is silenced with a click as Dobson switches frequencies again and keys the mic. "We've got some time on our hands here, gents, I don't much care to crawl back through this cliff wall and I'm freezing my fanny off, so go ahead and rig a line over the edge for me."

Static hisses then cracks. "Coming right up, Dobbs."

After ten minutes, Dobson finds himself topside again, gathered with the others around an ATV; now tied off closer to the cliff's edge. He takes a moment to collect himself before attempting to relay to the other the horrors he's seen below.

"I've never seen anything like it in all my years." He starts, but his thought is cut short by loud static and a pop followed by Mary Lou's voice. "Dispatch to Unit One. Sheriff. You there?"

"Unit One, Dispatch. Go ahead." Dobson responds.

Mary Lou gets right to the point, "The state is mobilizing for this. They're sending detectives and forensic teams from regional HQ. Also, they've authorized air support. You're looking at about one to two hours for them to start showing up on scene."

"Thank you, Mary Lou," responds, Dobson. "Keep me posted of any updates, please. Out."

The reply is quick and professional: "Ten-four, Sheriff. Will do. Out."

———

Almost two hours later, the clearing mutates into a war zone of light and sound. Twenty men swarm the site, radios spitting static like angry hornets. Off-road rigs crouch under the trees, engines ticking as they cool. Flashlight beams jitter through the timber, slicing faces into masks. Overhead, the helicopter hovers—a steel dragon shredding the night with rotor thunder. Its spotlight drills into the hole, turning the pit into a stage and painting every man in harsh silver. Heat radiates down, baking sweat into skin.

The air is chaos: rotor chop, shouted commands, exhaust fumes braided with the sweet-sick stench of rot. Voices strain against the mechanical roar.

"What's the plan, Sheriff?" Randy bellows, palms cupped around his mouth.

Dobson turns to him. "Two techs are going to document before we move the body. I'm going back in with them. I need you and Jack to—"

A sudden eruption cuts him off. Two hounds burst from the dark like cannon fire, tails flagging, teeth flashing. They whirl around Dobson's legs, barking sharp, howling in manic duet. One is leaner, rangier, its coat matted with burrs; the other heavier, its voice a deep, throaty bay that punches through the rotor noise. They circle like they own the ground.

Dobson's boots slam mud. "Alright! Can we get these dogs out of here? Where the hell is Buzzy?" His voice cracks like a whip, fury surfing fatigue.

Randy scans the melee, eyes flicking past a knot of men near the rigs. "I just seen him with one of the groups over there." His tone carries a shrug, but his glance lingers. "I think."

Dobson spits heat into the night. "Well, please! Find him! Round these mutts up and get 'em gone! We don't need 'em anymore!" The dogs ignore the order, snapping at each other in play, their shadows leaping like demons under the halogens.

Randy bolts, weaving through men and lamps. Dobson turns back to Jack, voice dropping to a growl. "Cripes! We got enough chaos without fur in the mix. I need you and Randy to take Mr. James and his boy home. Clear 'em out. Give 'em your helmets and go slow. They've had enough for one lifetime and trust me, neither needs a close-up of what's left of that kid." His jaw knots. "It ain't pretty."

Jack nods, solemn. "We'll take good care of 'em, Sheriff. Don't worry."

Dobson claps his shoulder twice—hard, punctuation in flesh. "Good man."

From above, the yellow rescue basket dips lower, dangling from the chopper's belly like a wasp nest. Cable hums under tension; rotor wash lashes the treetops. Men cluster at the rim, helmets gleaming, gloves flexing. Radios crackle with clipped codes: 10-4, copy, stand by, as the plan locks into motion.

The stink surges again, punching through jet wash and pine sap. Dobson tastes it on his tongue, bitter and revolting, but somehow, he's become accustomed to it. He stiffens his shoulders, eyes on the hole, and feels the weight of the night press down like a punishment.

Behind him, the dogs wheel once more, their voices braiding into a wild harmony. Somewhere beyond the rigs, a man's voice calls out: "Brandy! Sandy! Let's go girls!"

Dobson doesn't turn. He grips the cable, fingers closing like an oath, and breathes once, deep and slow, before the descent begins.

Chapter 14: October 1986 – Age 19

It is noon, and the old shed is alive with the low frequency of memory and metal. Charles sits on an overturned milk crate, spine curved, elbows braced on knees, a ratchet clutched in his fist like a weapon. The air tastes of fuel, oil and rust, thick with the ghosts of machines long dead. From a battered radio on the workbench, Led Zeppelin's "Good Times Bad Times" bleeds through static—a gritty hymn to boys becoming men, beginnings and ends. The riff drives him. The words, especially the first ten lyrical measures, wrap around him, a soundtrack for resurrection.

Before him sprawls the beast: a 1955 Harley-Davidson Panhead, reborn from ruin. Two years ago, it was nothing but a carcass—a rust-scabbed frame, a dented tank, two fenders pitted like old teeth, and a cardboard coffin of engine parts. A basket case, they called it. Hopeless. But Charles saw marrow in the bones. He saw what could rise from wreckage. Piece by piece, bolt by bolt, he has stitched this corpse into something that breathes.

The ratchet clicks—a metronome for obsession. Each turn tightens more than steel; it cinches the distance between who he was and who he means to be. Building beauty from ruin. Forging grace from grit. The bike is more than metal—it's a gospel of control, a sermon in chrome. He wipes a smear of grease from the tank, and the reflection stares back: nineteen now, jaw harder, eyes darker, a man grown from the boy who once dangled over a hole with death licking at his heels.

His mind drifts as his hands work. Two years since the accident. Two years since Todd's secret place vomited its truth into daylight. The official report was poetry—every line a stanza Charles wrote in silence. Open and shut, they called it. A tragic misstep. Evidence sang the chorus: years of Todd's footprints to and from the site; the freshest of which too big to have been created by Charles, years of stonework, grotesque taxidermy stitched in shadows. They found the box cutter. They found Snowflake—poor, broken Snowflake; entombed in Todd's cathedral of rot.

The rope was the only discordant note. Fresh cut, no long-term wear on the anchor tree outside the hole. Questions fluttered like moths, but the light of logic burned them quick. Investigators traced the rope's origin, mapped the river's swollen veins, and wrote the ending Charles had planned: Todd, driven by floodwater to seek another way in, trusted an old rope too short for salvation. He dangled, he fought, he lost. Gravity wrote the last verse. The fray against ragged stone explained the snap. Case closed.

David and Annie swallowed the ruling whole. Deep down, they knew the flavor of truth: Todd was wrong inside. Twisted. They'd seen the shadows in his eyes, felt the chill in his silences. Shock came, yes—but not surprise.

Grief sprouted like mold, slow and choking. David drowned in whiskey and rage, storming the basement like a man hunting demons. Annie poured her love into Charles like water into a cracked vase—lavish gifts, soft words, desperate clutches. No more hand-me-downs. No more Todd's ghost stitched into fabric. She dressed Charles in absolution, hoping silk and denim could keep him from vanishing the way Todd did.

For every ounce she gave him, she stole from David. Their words became knives, their silences worse. Nights ended with Annie sobbing on linoleum and David stomping into the dark below, bottle in hand, secrets in tow.

Charles tightens the last bolt. The ratchet falls silent. He exhales, slow, tasting the bitter tang of memory and the sweet oil of triumph. Two years of labor crouch before him on two wheels—a resurrection in chrome and steel. An ode to time freed and habits killed. He palms the tank, feels the cold promise under his skin. Today, the beast breathes.

Finished, Charles rises and kicks the milk crate backward with a sharp heel strike. The shed exhales heat and oil fumes as he strides to the door, shoves it open, and props it wide with a scarred length of two-by-four. Sunlight knifes in, turning dust motes into sparks. He pivots back to the beast.

Slowly, the tail of the Harley edges out—black and brutal; like a panther sniffing daylight. Charles walks beside it, hands firm on the grips, guiding its weight down the ramp with reverence. Outside, the bike unfurls in full glory: a resurrection in steel and sweat. The rear fender chopped short, thick tire bared like muscle under skin. Flat-black paint drinks the sun, swallowing glare. Wheel rims echo the same matte darkness. A sprung solo seat crouches low, leather taut and mean. Exhaust pipes, stubby and wrapped in black manifold tape, coil like twin vipers ready to spit fire. Ape-hanger bars spear the sky; a Springer front end gleams like a relic from war. It's not just a motorcycle. It's a manifesto.

He kills the motion, folds the kickstand down with a flick of his boot, and palms a square of plywood from his pocket. He drops it in the grass, sets the stand on its tiny altar, and lets the Harley lean into rest. Then he steps back—ten paces, twenty, and stares. It's beautiful. He beams with pride. Slowly, so as to enjoy the full sight picture for as long as possible, he approaches it again, lays his palm on the tank. The warmth that the paint has already drawn from the sun mixes with his beaming pride and sparks a memory: Annie's hand on his fevered brow—warm, soap-sweet, a hush that made the house gentle. He smooths the steel the way she once smoothed his hair. The machine breathes; for a moment, so does he. He understands.

His eyes drink it in, slow and greedy. He circles, orbiting his own creation, letting his gaze appreciate every curve and weld. For two years, this machine was a dream in rust and ruin. Now it crouches in sunlight, black and beautiful. His chest tightens with something fierce and wordless. Pride. Hunger. Freedom waiting to happen.

He can't stand it anymore.

Charles swings in close, fingers steady as they twist the key. The headlight flares; the tail lamp glows red like a warning. He thumbs the fuel petcock open, waits, then pulls the choke knob. His leg arcs over the saddle—slow, ceremonial, and he settles into the leather like a king claiming his throne. Kickstand snaps up under his heel. Three twists of throttle prime the beast. His pulse intensifies. Will it start? Did he earn this moment? Questions snarl in his skull as he folds out the kicker and taps for a high tooth. He drives his weight down—hard. The pedal plunges; the engine spins, coughs, dies. Ratchet whines back up. He resets, breath sharp, sweat beading his lip.

Another kick. Steel groans. A gunshot pop detonates from the pipes, and the kicker slams back like a mule, smashing into the bottom of his boot, jolting him into a stutter-step dance. He grins—primal, unbroken, and lines up again. This time he throws his whole body into it, lifting off the seat, leg dropping, gravity obliterated. The pedal dives—and hell wakes up.

The Harley roars to life, a thunderclap in black. Sound floods the yard—inflamed, animalistic, a throat ripped open to scream. The idle spikes high, choke choking, engine shaking the frame like rage in a cage. Heat rolls off the heads; the pipes spit breath hot enough to blister paint. Charles lets it scream, oil surging through veins of steel, then feathers the throttle—tiny blips, teasing the beast. He drops the choke slow, coaxing the idle down, each twist a whisper of control. Backfires crack like distant gunfire, then fade as he tunes the carb with a lover's touch: a graze to the idle screw, a kiss to the mixture—rich to lean and back again—finding the point where pop becomes purr.

He sits with it, listening. Not just hearing—the kind of listening that feels with guts and bones. The idle steadies, imperfect then better, wobble smoothing into heartbeat. In the lope there's a lesson: patience first, then adjustment, then restraint. He knows the bike exists because he had hours to give—hours he once spent sharpening himself into a weapon. Revenge was a clock that owned him; now, those minutes became tools, became paint, became quiet mornings in a shed with metal and intent. From everything he didn't have to do, he built everything he wanted.

He straddles his iron horse, palms easing over grips, clutch lever biting under fingers. Left boot presses the shifter— CLUNK—and the bike jerks, alive and eager. He eases the clutch, rolls forward, tires crushing grass. The sound ricochets off the house, a basso growl that crawls up his spine and ignites behind his eyes. First gear hums like a vow. He slides onto the dirt drive, shifts to second—silk. He feels the world stretch.

The road unfurls ahead, straight and empty, a ribbon of escape. He checks left, right, then guns it. Throttle twists; the Harley answers with a roar that shakes the marrow. Third gear. Fourth. Speed rips the breath from his lungs; wind slaps his face raw. The bars quiver under his grip, but the bike holds true—a black bullet screaming through farm country. No plate. No helmet. No fear. Just Charles and the machine he built from bones, tearing a hole through the quiet world.

Now the ritual begins: the dangerous art of getting better while moving forward. He wedges a short-tipped screwdriver between seat and thigh, crosses his left arm over to hold the throttle, and frees his right hand. It feels alien—control flipped and fragile—but necessary. The straightaway runs arrow-true. He lifts the brim of air with his chin, tastes dust and heat, then slides the screwdriver out, steel warm from his pocket.

A quarter turn on the carburetor's mixture screw; just a breath, and the lope changes, smoothing the beat without killing the growl. He listens over the wind, over the road, to the motor's language: what the engine wants versus what it will tolerate. He richens the mixture a hair to damp the faint pop on deceleration, then leans it back to sharpen throttle response. Each tweak is a gamble, a prayer, a promise; each movement demands trust from a machine that owes him nothing.

His left arm cramps under this crossed grip; his right shoulder burns as the road blurs by. He steadies. He breathes. He tunes. The bike answers: the blub becomes a clean, rolling thrum, the throttle snaps back without complaint, the pipes bark then settle. The Panhead sings a different song now—one Charles wrote with sweat and listening and risk.

He lets the screwdriver bite the seat again, reclaims the throttle with his right hand, and flexes the fingers of his left to flush the ache. The wind is louder than thought. Fields run green to the horizon, each stalk bowing as he passes like the world acknowledging a new king.

He backs off, tests the brakes. Front lever firms under his fingers; rear pedal bites low, softer than he wants. He notes it— a mental chalk mark on a board only he reads. Then he rolls on again, not as fast now, letting the machine find its rhythm with the road.

This is simple, complicated, and true. Power becomes obedience when asked the right way. The carb becomes conversation: lean here, rich there, listen, answer. He smiles, small but honest. He knows he built this thing not from obsession but from the absence of it—space where fury used to live now filled with bolts, bearings, and the long patience of a man adjusting until he feels it is right.

At a crossroads with no signs, he idles down, listens again, and feels the motor want a touch more air. He gives it, small. The idle drops lower, steadies.

He sits a moment, listening to the idling engine, or more feeling it. He ponders his choice of direction.

For now, he must turn around at the crossroads and roll back toward home.

———

At the end of the driveway, he downshifts, coasts, and lets the bike breathe. The shed waits; open-mouthed, like a stage after the applause. As he slowly rolls past the house, toward the shed in the back yard, he can hear the heartbeat of the motor echoing off the siding. Blub, blub, blub, blub. The sound brings a calming peace over him. The smell of hot paint and fuel and grass settles into one new thing: the smell of beginnings.

Charles releases the grips, brings the engine to a low, throaty idle, finds neutral and swings off the saddle. Heat rolls off the Harley's heads, shimmering the air like a mirage. The smell of hot oil and raw fuel clings to the yard. He folds the kickstand down onto its plywood square, lets the bike lean like a beast at rest, and jogs up the ramp into the shed. His hands move quick: shop rag, two wrenches, tools bundled tight. He's grinning, content, pulse light, a bounce in his step. Sunlight slants through the open door, painting the floor in fiery stripes. Today feels like victory.

Until he turns and sees David.

The sight stops him cold on the ramp. David circles the bike like a vulture orbiting fresh kill. His hair hangs in greasy ropes, clotted with sweat. His cheeks bristle with days of neglect. The white tank top clinging to his frame is a map of stains: beer, grease, old meals, yellow sweat bleeding through cotton. His bare arms gleam with grime. In one fist, an amber bottle sweats down his knuckles.

Charles freezes, tools limp in his grip, eyes locked on the orbit. Every step David takes feels wrong—too close, too casual, like a trespass dressed as curiosity.

David swigs deep, throat working, then wipes his mouth with the back of his hand. He burps, loud and wet, before turning his head just enough to throw words over his shoulder. His voice rides the rumble of the Harley's idle.

"All done, huh?" He doesn't look at Charles. His eyes stay on the bike, crawling over black paint and chrome like slimy little fingers. "Looks good."

Charles says nothing. The tools bite his palm. His chest knots.

David flicks his eyes to Charles, slow, grin curdling into something sharp. "Say, listen, pal. Do me a favor?" His tone drips sugar, fake and slick.

Charles feels the warning coil in his gut. He knows what's coming.

"Would you mind not running this thing next to the house when people are trying to SLEEP?"

The last word explodes—spit riding the consonants. And with it, David moves. The bottle arcs from his hand in a blur of brown glass and malice.

Time fractures. Charles watches the spin in slow motion—the hollow whistle, the spray of beer flinging off in golden ribbons. His heart caves as the bottom of the bottle slams the tank's flank with a sound like a heart breaking. Metal dents deep, a cruel crater punched into perfection. The bottle ricochets, spewing foam, and lands whole in the grass like a smug survivor.

Charles

The Harley shudders under impact, pipes barking a startled cough. Beer streaks the black paint in sticky trails, dripping like spit down a chin.

Charles can't breathe. Rage boils behind his eyes, white and blinding. For a heartbeat, he sees murder—David's throat under his thumbs, his skull cracking against the ramp. His muscles retract, ready to spring.

But David's back is already turned. Filthy cotton, hunched shoulders, shambling gait. He's halfway to the house, halfway to bed, leaving ruin in his wake. The door creaks open, swallows him whole and slams shut, unhindered.

Stillness crashes down, broken only by the Harley's uneven idle—a wounded animal panting in the sun.

Charles steps off the ramp like a man walking into a funeral. He drops to his knees beside the bike, fingers trembling as they trace the dent. The metal feels warm, violated. He whispers nothing, but the apology lives in his touch. His hand slides from tank to seat, a slow caress, like soothing a lover after violence.

He straightens, teeth clenched, eyes burning holes through the house. Hate wraps tight in his throat, black and slick, but he swallows it down like poison he means to keep.

The tools are squeezed in his grip now. He straddles the Harley and pulls in the clutch. The shifter clunks; the bike lurches forward, wounded but obedient. He rolls up the ramp, back into the shed's shadow, and kills the engine dead.

The silence feels heavier than the roar. Charles sets the wrenches down, breath labored, and reaches for the tank bolts. His fingers move with precision, without mercy. If David wanted war, he'll get it. But first, Charles will heal his machine.

—

The kitchen feels like a trap tonight. The walls are too close, air too heavy. Charles sits at the table, fork moving in mechanical rhythm, mandibles grinding through bites he barely tastes. Across from him, Annie hunches small, her body folded like a question mark. Her hair clings in greasy ropes, scalp shining where strands part. A small scar at the top of her forehead catches the light a little differently than surrounding skin. No makeup masks the bruised crescents under her eyes. She lifts her wine glass with trembling fingers, drains it in one long swallow, and sets it down so gently it barely clicks. Her fork drifts over the plate, pushing food like debris on water. The silence between them is thick, broken only by the wet sounds of chewing and the brittle scrape of silverware against glass plates.

Fifteen minutes crawl by before the stairs creak and David staggers into the kitchen. He's a ruin in motion—white tank top sagging under stains of sweat and sauce, briefs yellowed at the seams, hair a tangled snarl. His face looks to be molded from grease and anger. He scratches his scalp, palms his cheeks, muttering curses that slither through the room.

"Goddamn headache," he growls, voice gravel and venom. He yanks the fridge open; cold light paints his silhouette in sickly blue. "Can't even get any fucking sleep around here. Fucking kid running a goddamned Harley Davidson outside my bedroom window all day." Bottles clink. He snatches a beer, slams the door, and lurches to the table. The chair screeches in protest as he drags it, then collapses into it like a sack of bones. "What are we eating, crazies?"

Annie flinches like a struck dog. Her fork clatters into her plate. She springs up, snatches his empty dish, and scurries to the stove. Her movements are frantic, servile—a choreography of fear. She heaps food high, returns quick, and sets the plate before him as if laying an offering at an altar. Then the napkin—snapped open, draped across his lap with trembling precision. She retreats to her chair, eyes locked on his face, waiting for judgment like a prisoner for sentence.

David scans the table, lip curling. His nostrils flare with each breath, animal and sharp. "What? You couldn't have the common courtesy to wait until I got here to eat?" His voice cracks like a whip.

"I'm sorry," Annie whispers, words thin as a moth's wing. "We thought we'd let you sleep a little longer."

"Sleep a little longer?" His laugh is a bark, humorless and poisonous. "Christ! It's dinner time!"

The blame lashes her skin, though the guilt is his own.

Charles keeps eating, slow and steady, eyes nailed to his plate. Every fiber in him screams to leave, to vanish before the next blow lands. But he stays, joints locked, rage simmering in his gut.

David reaches for his fork. It lies just beyond his lazy sprawl. He huffs, belly heaving, then lunges forward with a grunt to snag it. Metal scrapes ceramic as he spears a steak tip, lifts it to his face. He sniffs, nose wrinkling, then shoves the meat between his teeth. He chews. Pauses. His expression curdles into disgust.

The explosion comes fast. A deep inhale through his nose, then a violent blast—chewed meat spraying from his mouth in a wet volley that splatters Annie's cheek. She jerks, gasps, but the assault isn't done. David surges upright, plate in hand, and slams it across the table. Porcelain sails, food flies, and the wall behind Annie spatters with impact—meat and gravy painting it in indecent strokes.

"This shit is cold!" His roar shakes the air.

Annie sits frozen, peppered with scraps, wine glass trembling in her grip. David is already at the fridge, yanking another beer, muttering filth. He cracks. swigs deep, foam slicking his lip, and shambles toward the hall. His back is a map of stains, his gait a sneer.

Charles watches him go; fork suspended midair. His pulse rages, bile clawing up his throat like fire. For a breath, he sees it—David's skull cracking against tile, his blood pooling like spilled wine. His fingers twitch around the fork, white-knuckled, ready.

As Charles watches David, Annie watches Charles. His eyes catch hers. Wide, wet, pleading—and afraid. Not of David. Of him. She sees the shadow in his stare, the pledge of violence wound tight. And somewhere deep, a secret flicker: fear braided with hope.

Charles drops his gaze and shoves another bite past teeth that would rather grind bone. The room murmurs with silence, broken only by the fridge's low drone and the sound of Annie's breath wheezing like a broken hinge.

—

It is pitch black. Hours have passed since Charles drifted into sleep—a sleep hard-won after the storm of the day. His body lies heavy, but his mind floats free, untethered. Dreams cradle him like warm water. For once, reality loosens its claws. No ropes. No holes. No rage. Just quiet.

Then—motion. His eyes flicker beneath their lids, rapid as bat wings. The dream blossoms: he is airborne, weightless, soaring high above a quilt of earth stitched with rivers and roads. The peace of night has fallen over this land. His hand is clasped in another—a hand soft, warm, alive. Beside him drifts a woman in white, her dress a flowing banner that ripples like silk in moonlight. Her hair spills dark and lustrous down her back, a waterfall of shadow. Her skin glows porcelain-pale, kissed by silver light. Lips gleam ruby, curved in a smile that feels like home.

And her eyes—God, her eyes. Emerald novas, green so vivid it seemed to pull color from everything else, lit from within by the moon's cold fire. They hold him, pin him, melt him. In those eyes lives a love so pure it burns. He doesn't know her name. Doesn't need to. Her gaze is enough. Her touch is life. In this sky, she is gravity and grace, and Charles is hers without question.

They glide together, hand in hand, over a miniature world—cities shrunk to toys, lakes glinting coins, mountains crouched asleep.

Charles feels untouchable, a god over insects. He is not down there in the mud and blood. He is here, aloft, with her. Safe. Whole. Loved.

He turns to her, face split by a smile that feels drawn from sunlight. She meets it with her own—a smile steeped in love, wordless and infinite. For a breath, time stops.

Then her expression falls flat.

It happens like glass breaking: serenity shatters into terror. Her lips part, trembling. Her fingers tighten on his hand, pulse pounding through skin. Charles feels the fear before he sees its source. He whips his gaze downward, following the invisible line of her stare.

And there he is.

David.

Small as a figurine yet clear as crystal, standing in the backyard by the shed. A shotgun juts from his fists, barrel pointing skyward. One eye squints shut in a permanent wink; the other glares down the sight, cold and merciless. His grin is a crooked wound, teeth glinting like broken ceramic shards. The muzzle tracks them as they drift, slow and helpless, across the black vault of night.

"No!" Charles screams, sound refusing his plea. He thrusts his free hand downward, as if he could pluck David from the earth and hurl him into oblivion.

The blast comes like a god's fist.

A boom splits the dreamscape, echoing throughout the land. The woman jerks—a violent spasm, and her white dress erupts in a bloom of red at the belly. Crimson petals whirl in the wind, staining silk like transgression. Her eyes find his one last time, drowning in pain. He watches the green bleed out, color washing away like paint in rain. They pale, clouding to milky white—then stranger still: a film slides over them, cataract-thick, with a whisper of hazel ghosting one iris. Her skin dries and prunes as though the moisture is being sucked out of it.

Her grip loosens. Fingers slip. And she falls.

Charles lunges for her, but the sky betrays him. His power dies; his body drops. He plummets after her, wind shrieking like a jet engine in his ears. The roar swells, devours thought, becomes everything. Below, the earth craters—a canyon carved from nightmare. The hole above Todd's special place gapes wide, then warps, mutates, becomes a mouth. David's mouth. Lips peel back in a grin of meat and teeth. Tonsils quiver in the throat's red cavern as the roar bellows out, a sound like worlds ending.

Charles spears downward, a javelin of flesh, screaming a silent scream until his throat splits. The mouth rushes up, swallowing sky, swallowing him. He sees the uvula swing like a pendulum—feels breath scorch like furnace fire.

Then impact—wet, crushing.

He snaps into wakefulness and jerks upright in his own bed, lungs dragging air like water, skin slick with sweat. The scream still claws his throat, fighting to get out. His heart pummels his chest form within, a fist punching ribs. For a long time, he just sits; shaking, silent; while the dream's ghosts curl around him like smoke.

The roar still lives in his skull—a beast's bellow pounding against gray matter. Darkness crowds the room. For a breath, he thinks he's still falling, still plummeting into David's gaping, roaring mouth. Then the sound sharpens, grows teeth. Not dream. Not monster.

Reality.

The roar is real.

Charles lunges for the window shade, fists clenching vinyl. One savage yank—and dim, white light washes the room. Moonlight floods the glass just as the shed door explodes outward. Wood slams against siding, hinges shriek, the steel spring cries. A white beam knifes through the dark—the Harley's headlight, savage and blinding. The bike bursts from the shed like a bullet from a barrel, ramp barely touched by its weight. Dirt spits as tires hit earth.

David is on it, wearing nothing but his filthy tank top, sagging, stained briefs and an untied pair of worn-out work boots.

First gear screams under strain, throttle pinned to hell. The tail kicks sideways, fishtailing like a hooked shark as the rear wheel claws mud. Pipes rip the night open, a metallic howl shredding silence. David whoops—a drunken war cry; his voice riding the engine's fury. He jerks the bars, leans hard, and slings the bike into a wide crescent at the yard's edge. Mud geysers under the spinning tire, spraying black rain across the grass.

Charles stares, frozen in the window's frame, breath locked. His machine: his blood, his hours, his salvation, thrashes under David like a beast in chains.

The Harley straightens. David guns it. The headlight carves a white wound through the dark, jittering like a blade on bone. The motor's shriek spirals higher, a cyclone of steel and rage. Sod erupts in twin geysers under the rear tire, spraying grit like shrapnel. The beam slashes his window, branding his face in white glare.

David slams the brakes. Tires slide through grass and scar dirt. The bike skids sideways, halts inches from the siding. Engine snarls, pipes popping like gunfire. David throws his head back and howls.

"HEY, CHUCKLES! YOU UP?!" His voice is a cleaver, hacking through the roar. "WHAT'S UP, BUDDY? TRYING TO SLEEP IN THERE, PAL? HELLOOO!"

He jerks the throttle—WHAM—pipes spit flame, engine roars in manic bursts. Then the clutch dumps. The rear wheel spins free, ripping sod into birdshot. Mud and grass lash the window in wet fists as David swings the rear of the bike around in a half donut. Charles ducks, arms shielding his face as clods hammer glass.

Panic escapes its cage in his chest. He needs to stop this—kill it—before something worse happens. His gaze snags on the pellet rifle propped in the corner. Useless. A sting, nothing more. He vaults off the bed, snatches his jeans, jams legs through denim. His fingers dive into the pocket, claw out the golden watch. Lid pops. 3:00 a.m. Christ. The drunk sleeps all day and burns the night like gasoline.

Charles flings the watch onto the bed, drags a sweatshirt over his head, and grabs the rifle anyway—habit, not hope. He scrambles back onto the mattress, eyes slicing through the glass.

And sees her.

His foster mother, Annie.

She bursts from the porch, barefoot, nightgown whipping like a torn flag in the wind. Her arms flail, waving frantic signals in the dark. Her voice rips the air—thin, shrill, desperate. "STOP! DAVID, STOP!"

The headlight strobes her in brief flashes—white, then gone, then white again—her face a mask of terror, eyes wide and wet. She runs straight into the yard, straight into the storm.

David doesn't hear. Or doesn't care. His grin is a wound, teeth gleaming as he spins tight donuts, throttle welded open. The Harley shrieks, engine clawing for mercy as mud fans out in black halos. David leans, drags a boot, spits laughter into the wind. He's not angry now. He's exultant. Drunk on speed, drunk on power, drunk on ruin.

Just plain drunk.

Then the circle breaks.

The bike snaps upright, headlight lunging forward like an angry cyclops. David guns it—full bore, no breath, no brake. The beam slices the yard, hunts the house.

And finds her.

Annie freezes in its glare, arms outstretched as if flesh could halt steel. Her nightgown billows, a ghost in the white blaze. Her mouth opens, a scream swallowed by the engine's roar. Her eyes lock on David—and in that instant, time dies.

Impact.

The front tire slams her knee. Bone snaps like dry kindling, a crack that punches the night. Her leg folds backward, grotesque, wrong. The wheel climbs, smashes into her hip, and Annie's body slams to earth with a sound like a sack of grain dropped from a tailgate. Her body whips, limp and boneless. Her skull ricochets off sod. The front tire misses her head by inches, but the rear kicks wide, catches her chin, rakes her throat. Skin splits. Blood spatters black onto the lawn.

Charles screams—a raw, breathy animal sound that tears his throat. "NO!"

David's howl curdles into horror. "FUCK!" He wrenches the bars, stomps the brake. Wheels lock; the bike skids sideways, headlight jittering like a dying star. It freezes on Charles's face in the window—washed white, eyes molten with hate. For a heartbeat, David sees it: the look that swears something worse than death.

He knows what flashed in that beam. He knows what he did.

David turns the bike around. The beam slices through darkness and lands, lighting Annie's broken body in a ghastly glow. Crimson blooms across her nightgown like spilled paint, soaking cotton until it clings to her ribs. Her cheek is a ruin, torn open to the hinge of her jaw; molars gleam through flesh like pearls in blood. Arterial spurts pulse weakly from her neck—tiny fountains marking time.

"Annie?" David croaks, voice strangled. He stares, slack-jawed, beer-stale breath fogging in the cold. "Annie?" Louder now, panic cracking through the booze haze. His hands tremble on the grips; the throttle twitches like a live wire.

Then motion—a blur of rage.

Charles bounds from shadow, pellet rifle swinging like a war club. The wooden stock reaches high, then crashes down. The crack of impact is revolting—a sound like splitting timber. David's head snaps sideways; his body sloughs off the bike in a boneless spill. Steel and flesh hit earth together, a tangle of limbs and chrome. The Harley coughs, snarls, then settles into a guttural idle: blub… blub… blub… a carnivore purring over its kill.

—

Charles

Darkness swallows minutes. Then stars bloom in David's eyes—tiny pinpricks scattered across black. He blinks, groggy, skull ringing like a struck bell. The world pulsates and spins, rights itself, spins again. He tastes iron. Feels soil grinding his teeth. Slowly, sound filters in like a bull emerging from a foggy pasture—a low, rhythmic throb, deep as a heartbeat. Blub... blub... blub...

He turns his head. Pain detonates down his neck and the top half of his spine. Vision flares white, then clears—and the light hits him again. A headlight this time, glaring like a ruling, drills into his pupils. He squints, tries to raise a hand, but his arm lies dead at his side. Panic races through him, cold and slick as he realizes he has no sensation in his arms or legs.

The sound swells. The idle becomes a growl. Then a roar.

Blub-blub-blub—WHAM! Charles blips the throttle, and the pipes bark like gunfire. The bike lunges, then checks, front tire kissing dirt inches from David's skull. Heat rolls off the heads, warming his face. Gas fumes sting his nostrils. He can feel the vibration in his skull—a savage rhythm pounding through earth into marrow.

David's breath comes in shards. His eyes lock on the tire tread, black and brutal, close enough to taste rubber. Beyond it, boots—two black guards bracketing the wheel. Charles stands over him, a silhouette chiseled from fury, face a mask of shadow and hellfire. His hands clutch the bars like strangling throats.

"Hey... Chuck." David's voice is a dry, thin and broken. "I'm sorry, man. I was just... messing around and—"

WHAM! The throttle snaps open. The Harley screams, pipes spitting sparks. The sound slams into David's skull like a hammer. He flinches, teeth rattling.

"Listen, man—" Another rev, sharper, meaner. The bike barks *shut up* in a language older than words.

David swallows terror like razor blades. His gaze crawls to Charles's boot—the left one lifting, slow, deliberate, then stomping down on the shifter. CLUNK. The gear bites. The bike shivers, frame ready as a drawn bow.

Charles leans forward, eyes burning emerald, lips peeled in something that isn't a smile. His chest heaves; his breath fogs the night. Rage boils off him in waves, thick enough to taste. The Harley snarls under him, hungry, impatient.

David feels it—the moment stretching, thinning, ready to snap. Fear floods his veins, hot and choking. He knows what's coming. He knows he deserves it. And he knows, in some twisted corner of his mind, that this is how men like him should end: under the wheels of the thing they mocked.

The throttle twists. The pipes erupt. And the night holds its breath.

David stops trying to talk and just stares at the tire— knobby rubber slick with wet grass and dust, each block a black tooth waiting to bite. The engine pulses. Blub, blub, blub. The idle stutters like a clock that refuses to die.

Charles revs. A thick, raw note cuts the air. David can feel his own pulse answer it, fear building in his chest like a second engine. His throat tightens. He tastes hot metal and old gasoline.

Charles blips the throttle and pops the clutch. The front tire snaps off the ground in a mini wheelie—twelve inches of lift, a clean arc. He pulls the clutch and taps the rear brake; the tire slams down with a thud and hiss of compressed forks. The bike lands an inch closer to David's head. Heat rolls off the cylinders and crawls over David's skin.

"Jesus, Charles! What are you—" David's words vanish in the bark of the engine. Charles gooses it again, clutch out, throttle wide. The front tire climbs higher, an ugly rearing horse. David emits a high, broken scream—child-bright and helpless, as the wheel rises over him. He squeezes his eyes shut, torn between prayer and disbelief. He wonders, for a sliver, if he'll feel it when his skull gives.

Clutch in. Rear brake taps. The tire comes down hard, a fraction of an inch from his face, crushing grass into the dirt. Dust sprays. The fork tubes judder, seals whining.

David's face knots. Teeth grit, eyes screwed tight. He isn't dead. He drags air between his teeth, quick, shallow, wet. He doesn't dare open his eyes, but the engine keeps pattering— blub, blub, blub—each pop a tick he can feel in his jaw.

He peels one eyelid open. White shows. Charles snaps the throttle at the sight, clutch out in the same heartbeat. The engine backfires—a gunshot—then roars alive. The front wheel darts to the sky, even higher. David's eyes bulge; the tire crests directly over him, eclipsing the sky. He cannot move. The bike slams down. The full weight—steel, fuel, a five-hundred-pound animal—slams earth on the far side of his skull. The shocks groan and compress. Dirt grinds into skin.

Now he's under it. The bike straddles him; the crankcase breathes heat onto his left cheek, almost burning. Charles feathers throttle. The rear tire breaks traction, a quick screech of rubber skittering on sod. The bike lurches forward an inch, then two. The bottom of the frame clips David's chin, forces his head to turn, pins it between packed soil and sump.

A recessed bolt head finds flesh, gouging open his cheek. Gravel and dirt engrave themselves into the wound, becoming part of him. Something overhead drips—oil from a breather, slick and boiling-hot—mixing with grit and blood. It bites. Thermal sting overlays the blunt shove of weight. The pain is huge, but the claustrophobia is worse: a smothering machine pressing him into earth. He can't expand his chest. Every breath is a fight against steel.

The engine barks and the bike crawls forward. The exhaust header drops to within an inch of his cheek. Heat becomes a presence, palpable; he can feel hairs singe. Then Charles leans the bike hard right, balancing the mass without letting it tip. The pipe lowers until it kisses David's left temple.

For a fraction of a second, the burn feels cold—the paradox of nerve endings overwhelmed—then sensation returns true. Flesh sizzles. The smell is unmistakable: collagen denaturing, hair searing, grease and skin together. David's temple and upper cheek stick to the steel; proteins glue him there.

Charles holds it, steady as a surgeon, for a long count— ten, twelve, fifteen. The world narrows to sound and pain. The engine ticks. Something inside David's head hisses. The bloody, gurgling shrieks being emitted by David bring great satisfaction to Charles.

When he peels the exhaust away, the skin comes with it— charred epidermis and dermis, cooked through, leaving a raw, white-yellow plate of exposed tissue. David's eyelid is gone; the cornea of the left eye clouds in the heat, blistered, the sclera marbling, aqueous humor hissing off as vapor. David screams again—a full-body scream that strips the air of oxygen and doesn't stop.

Charles feeds throttle and creeps forward until the frame no longer pins David's skull. Now the head lies between engine and rear wheel.

David wrenches his head upright and then to the left. The relief is short-lived. He is staring at the knobby rear tire. Charles looks down at the geometry, precise, patient, and inches the bike forward, touching David's chin and pinning his face to the ground again. Charles creeps forward again, as slow as the minute hand on a clock, until the tire forces David's chin toward the starboard side of the bike. Finally, the tire kisses the soft of David's neck.

"Oh Jesus, c'mon, Chuckie. Don't do it!" David gurgles. Blood from his ruined cheek spatters with each word, flecking the case, painting the tread. He tries to swallow and chokes; the airway is filling.

Charles revs to drown him, then lets the idle settle, the engine ticking time again.

"Listen, kid... I promise... I'll never—"

Another blip, louder.

Desperation spits out as rage: "You let me up right now, you little— you let me up or I swear to Christ, Chuckles, I'm going to—"

Charles opens the throttle and dumps the clutch.

The rear tire flashes to life, torque ripping at rubber, at earth, at whatever it touches. The knobby blocks bite skin and hair and the thin strap of muscle along the jawline, and then comes the degloving—cheek torn free from bone, sliding under tread like a tablecloth yanked clean. Teeth clack and scatter; the mandible fractures at the symphysis and both condyles, a sickening crack. The tongue jerks loose, mangled, gagging him as blood floods his mouth.

The tire chews across the anterior neck. Knobs tear the platysma, then the delicate anatomy beneath: the thyroid cartilage, cricoid ring. Rubber grinds the trachea flat. The chain catches wisps of hair and a scrap of shirt collar and drags, adding a lateral wrench. Carotid arteries shear open and spray. Blood is everywhere—hot, pressurized, bright. For a second, the spray arcs in rhythm with the wheel.

Torque drives his upper body left. His shoulders are pinned; the rest cannot move. The forces dump into the cervical spine. There is a close, internal sound—like green wood cracking, when C2 goes. A hangman's fracture: the pars interarticularis snapping under hyperextension and distraction. The skull and spine separate in one brutal, invisible motion. The lights go out behind his eyes even as the wheel still spins.

Soft tissue hangs, then tears. The tire keeps eating, and the remaining attachments—skin, fascia, a strip of posterior musculature, fail. The head frees and rolls, not thrown but urged away by tread, gaining speed downhill, leaving a comet tail of blood and mud. The body stays, twitching in spinal silence, painting the dirt with pulses that slow.

Charles never touches the brakes. He holds throttle until he's almost at the house, engine bellowing, rear tire flinging clotted red. At the walkway he chops the ignition; the motor dies in a single, decisive beat. He flips down the kickstand, leans the bike, lets the mass settle.

The air shivers in the sudden quiet. In the kitchen window, glass throws back a thin reflection of Charles—helmetless, jaw hardened, eyes flat. Somewhere beyond the walls, time feels wrong, stretched. The engine's last echo circles the yard like a second hand that refuses to stop ticking.

He swings off the bike, boots twisting gravel, and strides into the house without looking back. The hallway waits quietly, every shadow stretched long like the years he's leaving behind. His room waits—walls still tattooed with the ghosts of posters, corners heavy with the smell of oil and sweat and something older, something that clings to childhood like dust.

Charles throws his backpack onto the bed. The springs reply with a short squeal, a tired sound, as if the mattress knows this is the last time. He moves fast, hands sweeping across surfaces, grabbing fragments of a life: a knife, a shirt, a photograph folded too many times. Each item lands in the bag with a dull thud, a punctuation mark in a sentence that ends tonight.

He yanks the zipper closed, straps the weight to his back. His eyes fall to the watch—the golden watch lying open on the bedspread like a wound that never healed. Its lid gapes, the face glinting faintly in the lamplight. He does not touch it yet. He leaves it open, leaves it breathing.

Charles steps into the hallway. The air feels heavier now, thick with ghosts. He passes Todd's door. It's cracked open. The rooms sits undisturbed, exactly as it was the day Todd died; step parents unable to initiate the task of clearing it. The closet is visible in a sliver of moonlight. Sneakers sit inside, toes pointed, waiting for feet that will never come. The sight hits him like a fist. A flash—Todd's laughter, sharp and cruel, the sting of a belt across his back, the taste of copper and acid in his mouth as he bit down to keep from screaming. It's gone in an instant, but it leaves a shadow that clings to his ribs.

He moves on, legs stiff, breath shallow. His step parents' door looms next. Another flash—David's voice, low and venomous, the smell of whiskey thick in the air, the slam of a fist into the wall inches from his head. The memory slices quick and clean, then vanishes, leaving only the echo of rage.

He glances to the side of the bed his step mother sleeps on. A softer ghost waits there. A flash—her hands cupping his face after a fever, cool cloth against his brow, her whisper like a prayer: "You're my boy, Charles." It grows warm for a heartbeat, then fades, swallowed by the dark. His focus shifts to the closet.

With intention in his grip, he yanks the closet door open and drops to his knees at its threshold. He immediately starts tossing items from the floor of the right side of the closet to the floor of the bedroom. Shoe boxes, a shoe rack, a plastic bag full of old sweaters, all ejected from the closet in a flurry. Charles is a man on a mission to find something not lost. Something that he has always known the location of.

The safe.

He punches in the code, numbers he has known for years, since he first started learning new tricks and making new plans. A beep of success sounds and with a clunk, Charles wrenches the handle. With a heavy thud and a breath of give, the door swings open silently. Inside, there is no money. There are no gems or items of precious metal. Instead, all that resides in this safe are some important documents. A large folder is on top. It is labelled *mortgage documents*. Charles flings it to the floor of the bedroom. Next in the meager offerings is a stack of papers that are stapled together. It's an old loan document for David's truck, long ago paid off. It flutters to the floor of the bedroom.

There it is. The prize. A thick manilla envelope with a single name written on the face. ***Charles***.

He snatches the package, bolts and heads quickly back to his own room as if trying to move away from the memories. There he stuffs the newly acquired envelope into his pack. He snatches the open-faced watch from the bed, bolts out of his room, down the stairs and out of his home for the last time. The lightweight kitchen door slams with finality behind him.

Outside, the bike crouches where he left it, chrome catching stray shards of moonlight.

He swings a leg over, kicks hard once and the engine turns over. He is the only person for miles that could possibly hear the roar now. The motor coughs, then bellows, alive and angry. Headlight flares, cutting the backyard open. Two shapes lie in the grass—dark, broken silhouettes that were once voices, once faces. He stares at them, motionless, the idle thudding beneath him like a heartbeat that isn't his. Blub, blub, blub. Time pools in the spaces between those sounds.

Charles

It is goodbye. Not the kind spoken, but the kind carved deep, the kind that bleeds years. He looks back at the yard one last time, at the bodies sprawled like discarded chapters. Then his gaze drops to the watch in his hand—the lid still open, the face still shining in the moonlight.

He breathes once, sharp and final, and snaps the lid shut. The click is precise, clean, a sound that feels like cutting the cord on everything behind him. He slides the watch into his pocket, the weight settling against his thigh like a signed contract.

First gear clicks in. The bike noses forward, slow, deliberate. He rounds the house, the headlight sweeping walls that once held laughter and lies. The motor's echo slaps back from the siding—one last voice from a place that will never speak to him again. Blub, blub, blub, blub.

The dirt drive stretches ahead. He feeds speed into the machine, gravel spitting like salt bouncing from a plate. At the end of the drive, he turns right. The throttle twists open. The bike rockets into the dark, a streak of steel and fury. Behind him, the house shrinks, then vanishes. He does not look back. He will never return to this house.

Chapter 15: Summer 1994 – Age 26

The night opens wide as Charles barrels down the isolated road like a force of nature. The engine roars beneath him, a savage symphony of compression and fire, echoing through the summer heat. Dust kicks up in his wake, curling into phantom ribbons that chase his taillight.

Wind tears at his long, wavy hair—dirty blonde strands whipping like banners of rebellion. His face is carved in shadow and moonlight: strong jaw, high cheekbones, and that perfectly stubbled beard that looks accidental but isn't. At the base of his throat, just visible above the collar of his worn leather jacket, a number of neck adornments hang. Black leather tubing with various trinkets. There's a silver circle that looks like a hieroglyphic symbol, a shark tooth hangs from another black leather thread. There is a pewter feather dangling from a brown leather strip. The largest is a half-dollar-size emblem, solid and engraved with the face of a clock.

And there is the scar.

It catches the streetlight's reach—a pale, upside-down cross etched into his skin like a brand from another life, peeking from under that clock emblem as it heaves in the wind.

He wears the road as a second skin, shoulders broad, hands gripping as if born to it. Seven years have hardened him, sharpened him. He is not the boy who left this town—broken, angry and rudderless. He is a man now, riding back into this town—rugged, dangerous, beautiful—and the night seems to know it.

With the help of the contents of the envelope, looted from David's safe seven years ago, he is legally no longer Charles James, the boy whom few in this town knew. He is now Charles Belial Watkins again, the man nobody in this town knows.

Charles

—

His motor winds down as he downshifts, loose pavement popping under the tires. A wide dirt lot sprawls open to his left, littered with chrome and steel—rows of Harleys and custom choppers crouched like beasts of prey at rest. He backs his bike into the end of the line, kills the ignition, and swings off. The sudden silence feels dense, broken only by the tick of cooling metal.

The building squats at the far edge of the lot, its roof crowned with neon: a massive motorcycle engine and rear wheel glowing electric blue and white. The lights flicker in sequence so the wheel seems to spin, and every few seconds a bright orange flame spits from the tailpipes—a cheap illusion that somehow feels alive in the dark. Below the flaming wheel, letter by letter, the words THE DUSTY SPOKE spell out in neon orange. Behind the building looms a wall of corrugated steel, so shaded that the details blur. The neon lights gleaming directly into Charles's eyes certainly don't help his night vision.

On the entrance door, a white, hand-painted sign screams in blood-red letters: NO COLORS. The wood is scarred, the screws sunk deep, like a warning nailed to bone.

Charles, six-foot-two and not a man to be messed with, ascends the steps, grips the handle, pulls and confidently steps inside. Heat and sound hit him like a wave—music grinding low, laughter sharp, the smell of beer and sweat braided with cigarette smoke. He doesn't pause to gawk at the décor or size up the crowd. He moves straight for the bar, boots landing loud and hollow against warped planks, and claims a stool like he belongs there.

"What can I get you, baby?" The voice is warm honey with a steel edge. Charles looks up—and stops. The bartender is a contradiction: too clean for this place, too bright for the shadows. Her hair is thick and wavy, chestnut brown that catches the dim light like polished wood. Big eyes, deep chocolate, framed by lashes that don't need mascara. Her smile is a weapon—white, perfect, and effortless. She's built like a promise: curves that speak of strength, not fragility, and skin that glows against the grit of the room.

Charles points toward the Jack Daniels behind her. She follows his gesture, then swivels back, one brow arched like a question mark. "Jack Daniels?" Her grin widens, teasing. "What's the matter, hon? Cat got your tongue?"

He smiles and nods, silent. He gently slides his clock medallion aside and taps his scar twice with the tip of his index finger. He moves the same finger to his lips and smiling, he expels *shhhh...* He winks. The smirk softens into pity. "Oh, I'm sorry, you poor thing." Her tone dips, gentle now. "Well, I'm Mandy. Pleased to meet you—and I guess I'm gonna need some ID to get your name then, huh?" She drops an empty shot glass in front of him, palm out, waiting. One brow lifts, that practiced arch that says she knows exactly how it lands.

Charles smiles back, slowly, with half his mouth, and fishes his wallet from his back pocket. He slides his license free with a flick, magician-smooth, and slides it into her hand. Her fingertips linger—just long enough to make him wonder if it's an accident. Her eyes hold his, steady, even after the card is hers. Something unspoken briefly flashes between them in that gaze and then she breaks it. She looks down and reads aloud, voice curling around the syllables like smoke.

"Eh hem! —Charles Belial Watkins," she says, mock-serious, like she's cross-examining him. "Born November tenth, nineteen sixty-seven." Her gaze flicks up, playful now. "Well, that makes you legal then. Doesn't it, sweetie?" She hands the card back, nails grazing his skin. "Can I call you Charlie?"

His instinct is to say no, but the name sounds different coming from her mouth—softened, warmed. He would love nothing more than to hear her say that name again.

Still, he shakes his head no, smiling, and it feels like a friendly line drawn in sand.

She shrugs, grin intact. "Charles it is." The bottle tips, amber spilling into glass. She slides the shot toward him, fingertips barely kissing the rim, eyes locked on his like a dare. There's a spark there—something not uttered, something that oscillates louder than the jukebox. In the black mirrors of her pupils, he sees himself, a silhouette without detail. Then another featureless figure materializes into view behind him.

A hand drops heavy on his shoulder. A voice booms near his ear: "You hittin' on my old lady?"

Charles doesn't turn. He just continues looking into those doe-like eyes. He's still grinning. He knows whose hand has just landed on his shoulder.

"Charles, my good man! Glad you could make it!" The laugh that follows is big enough to fill the room. Charles turns, already grinning, and clasps the hand of Steve Mack—a man built like a brick wall with a smile that could sell sin. His beard is a riot of copper and black, his eyes sharp with mischief. "Come on," Steve says, clapping him hard enough to rattle teeth. "First drink's on me—unless Mandy's already got you hooked."

Mandy smirks, tossing her rag onto the counter. "Hooked? Please. He's still deciding if he even likes me." Her tone is teasing, but her eyes say otherwise.

Steve laughs, booming again, and leans in conspiratorial. "Don't let her fool you, Charles. She's trouble wrapped in sugar."

Mandy fires back without missing a beat: "And you're cholesterol wrapped in leather."

The exchange sparks laughter from a couple of nearby patrons. It's a ripple of humor in a room thick with stone dust and testosterone. For the first time tonight, Charles feels something loosen in his chest. Maybe this place isn't all knives and shadows after all.

Steve grabs the stool next to Charles and drops a black plastic grocery bag onto the bar like it owes him money. "Jesus, man! I didn't even see you come in! What are you, a ninja? I was sitting right there!" His voice booms over the jukebox, drawing a glance from two bikers down the line.

He's still grinning, pumping Charles's hand like he's trying to start a lawnmower when he swivels toward Mandy. "Hey, baby. Pour us a couple more shots of the same, will ya?"

Mandy doesn't waste words. She lines up three shot glasses with the precision of a pool shark, fills them to the brim, and leaves the bottle like a peace offering. Then, without a glance back, she glides down the bar and disappears through a doorway draped in a curtain of beer bottle caps stitched together with fishing line. The caps clink softly, like coins in a gambler's pocket.

"Oh, she's a good girl," Steve says, eyes tracking her sway like a man watching a miracle. Charles watches too—maybe a beat too long. When he looks back, Steve's smirk is waiting for him like a cocked and loaded gun.

"Heh. Yeah, she's a looker. Hard not to stare, ain't it?" Steve chuckles, then drops the bomb with a grin sharp enough to cut leather. "That's why I wrapped her up and took her home with me, bro." He punctuates it with a friendly jab to Charles's forearm.

Charles grips the edge of the bar, steadying himself against the nudge, and answers with a chin lift—a silent nod that says he's cool, even if his pulse just tripped over itself. Steve's not-so-subtle hint is taken.

Steve leans in, voice dropping like a dime. "Anyway, I'm glad you gave it some thought. This is gonna be a good match. I can feel it. The old man's gonna love you. Just be your regular cool self and everything'll be golden."

He refills two of the glasses, raises his like a preacher with a gospel. "To the future."

Charles picks up his glass, their eyes locking in a silent pact. A simultaneous nod and they shoot the whiskey together. Steve slams his glass down hard enough to rattle the bottle and exhales like he just outran the devil. "Woo! That's good stuff!" He shakes his head, grinning, and reaches for the bottle again.

Charles sets his empty glass down with calm precision, watching Steve pour like a man possessed. Steve's energy radiates—too bright, too sharp. Either he's wired on adrenaline or riding a chemical wave. Hard to tell. He lines up three more glasses, but when he tips the bottle toward the fourth, Charles covers it with his hand.

"Oh… Alright, bro." Steve backs off with a shrug, bottle clunking onto the bar. "Suit yourself."

Charles raises his fresh pour. Steve snatches his own so fast it splashes onto the bar and his lap. He doesn't care. He grins, eyes locking on Charles. They nod once, shoot again. Steve slams his glass down like he's trying to break the bar in half. Charles just smiles, slow and steady, and sets his glass beside the other—two empty contracts lined up in the dim light.

Mandy slips out from the back room like smoke curling through neon. She heads straight for Steve and Charles, her voice pitched low, almost secretive: "Go on back now." The words land soft, but they carry weight. She glances around the room from under her brow, turns, slides the bottle onto the shelf, pivots like a soldier, and vanishes into the crowd, leaving the air charged and buzzing.

Steve pops up from his stool so fast it screeches against the floorboards. He grabs his last shot, downs it hard, and exhales like he's spitting out nerves. The empty glass hits the bar with a crack. "C'mon! Let's go!" His hand smacks Charles's arm: a quick jolt of urgency.

Charles rises, silent as a spirit, but his presence feels heavy, magnetic. Steve hooks his sleeve and steers him toward the back. "Follow me and don't say nothin'. Let me do all the talking." Four steps in, Steve winces at his own words and glances back. Charles's amused look says everything—no need to rephrase. Steve chuckles under his breath and keeps moving.

—

They slip through the bottle-cap curtain, the clinking sounds of tokens tumbling into the return cup of a slot machine— except this jackpot feels dangerous. Beyond the curtain, the air changes. Cooler, thicker, tinged with oil and old secrets. The hallway stretches ahead, narrow and dim, painted in deep burgundy that swallows light. The walls are alive with history— frames packed tight, each one a window into decades of asphalt and blood.

The first frames whisper from another time: black-and-white faces hard as iron, men with eyes like gun barrels and women with smiles sharp enough to cut. Sepia tones bleed into brittle newsprint—headlines about turf wars, charity rides, funerals. Some frames cradle clippings with ink faded but still legible: words like "shootout," "brotherhood," "vengeance."

As they walk, time accelerates on the walls. Black-and-white gives way to washed-out color: Polaroids curling at the edges, snapshots of grinning men astride chrome beasts, arms slung over shoulders, beer bottles raised like trophies. Every photo shares a common thread: leather, steel, and the primal pride of men who live by their own scripture. Motorcycles crouch in the background like altar pieces. In some shots, the bikes take center stage, gleaming like idols under sun or neon.

Between the photos, relics punctuate the story: a framed club charter, its ink bold and defiant; a glass case holding a founder's patch, frayed at the edges like a battle flag; memorial plaques etched with names and dates, candles burned down to stubs beneath them. A banner droops from the ceiling, its letters faded but legible: 'Ride Free or Die Trying.'

The air smells of old varnish and sweat baked into wood. A low frequency vibrates through the floor—music from somewhere deeper, bass notes like a heartbeat under concrete. Charles moves in silence, eyes scanning the ghosts on the walls. He feels them watching back.

At the end of the hall squats a door that doesn't belong— a slab of steel thick enough to stop time. It looks armored, industrial, a relic ripped from a warship. Tarnished plates overlap like scales, rivets punched in precise rows. Above it, a camera pivots like a Praying Mantis spotting its next meal, servos whirring as its glass eye locks onto them. Charles feels the weight of unseen eyes behind that lens, measuring him, peeling him open.

They wait. The silence is surgical. Then—CLACK. A latch disengages with a sound like a rifle bolt ejecting a casing. The door slides open, smooth and soundless, defying its own mass. Filling the gap is a man who looks chiseled from iron and bad intentions. Six-five, easy. Black leather vest over a shirt that's seen too many miles. Jeans faded to ghost blue, cinched by a belt thick as a tow strap. The brass buckle gleams—a Harley etched in relief, worn by years of fists and friction.

His boots are black anvils, scarred and heavy. Grey hair spills down his back in ropes, tamed by a bandana black as midnight. His beard is a storm cloud, long and tangled, swallowing his mouth beneath a mustache that could hide a knife. His arms are a gallery of ink—flames licking bone, skulls grinning through time, pinup girls frozen in jailhouse lines. Webs snare his elbows; spiders crouch in the crooks. Most tattoos blur into the haze of decades, but one stands out on his right bicep: the earth cradled by an anchor, rope knotted thick, an eagle perched atop the globe with wings spread wide like protection. Below it, a banner screams U.S.M.C. and above, Semper Fidelis.

Ink crawls up his throat, spilling past the collar. One piece owns the space beneath his jaw: a switchblade rendered in crude detail; its tip buried in the hollow of his throat. Blood drips in red ink from the wound, and across the blade, etched like law, one word: SILENCE.

Steve leans close, voice low and tight. "That's the Sergeant-at-Arms. Don't blink." The man jerks his chin toward the inner sanctum—a signal sharp as a command. Steve steps first. Charles follows, shadow and steel.

Inside, the air feels different—moving, charged. Steve slides the door shut, the latch dropping with a weighty finality. Ahead, the giant moves, his vest a banner of menace. Charles catches the patch sprawled across its back: a white rocker arched upward, letters black and brutal—WICKED ONES. Below it, a gargoyle-winged number one bleeds red lines from its center bottom making the numeral resemble an inverted cross. NOMAD grins from the bottom rocker, and a smaller, square patch broadcasts MC in blood-red thread. The emblem glows under dim light like a sigil, an oath, a threat.

Charles knows what he is here: not a prospect, not even close. Just a potential hang-around: a name whispered by Steve, a gamble walking on two legs. And now, the house of wolves is watching and he is delving deeper into their den.

The hallway spills them into an L-shaped expanse that feels like another world. Charles slows for half a beat, eyes sweeping the space. The front bar façade was a lie—this place is massive; a hidden kingdom behind neon and smoke. The corridor stretches long and clean, lined with closed doors every fifteen feet, each one a vault of secrecy. Burgundy walls rise high, broken only by brass sconces glowing like golden coins between doors. The light is warm, rich, almost regal, and it throws shadows that dance across the oriental carpet underfoot. The rug runs wall-to-wall, a river of burgundy threaded with gold and black, its patterns curling like ancient script. The ceilings soar, hinting at two-story construction, steel ribs masked by elegance. It's aged but proud, a strange castle of power tucked behind a dive bar's skin.

Steve moves with purpose, but Charles catches the twitch in his eye, the way his fingers fuss with the black plastic bag he's been carrying. Without breaking stride, Steve reaches in and pulls out a rolled leather bundle. It unfurls in his grip like a Black Rat Snake—his vest. He slides it on with practiced ease, the patches flashing under the sconces: WICKED ONES, NOMAD, the gargoyle-winged number one glaring like a war standard. The grocery bag disappears into an inside pocket like a cuttlefish. Charles notes the symmetry—the same colors as the giant who led them here, the same silent declaration of belonging.

They round the corner and the mood changes. Ahead looms a set of steel double doors, industrial gray and unapologetic, a blunt interruption in all this burgundy finery. A small red sign screams AUTHORIZED PERSONNEL ONLY, its letters stark against the metal. Banks; the Sergeant-at-Arms, waits like a garrison, arms folded, eyes flat. Up close, Charles reads the patch over his breast: SGT AT ARMS. The title fits like a custom weapon.

Steve's vest reveals its own rank when Charles glances sideways: SECRETARY. The hierarchy clear as the air, invisible but heavy. Charles feels it pressing down, reminding him what he is—just a hang-around, a name Steve floated like a wish. No patch. No rank. Just a man walking ever deeper into the wolves' den.

Banks moves without wasted motion. A card swipes through a reader mounted on the wall. A buzz splits the silence, sharp and sterile. The steel door floats open, smooth and soundless, and the world beyond hits like a revelation.

The space is enormous—an aircraft hangar masquerading as a garage. Light floods from high fixtures, glinting off painted steel and polished chrome. At the far end, a roll-up door towers like a fortress gate, thirty feet high and at least fifty feet wide, its center painted with the club's insignia in screaming color. Spotlights crown it like a halo, making the patch glow: WICKED ONES, the gargoyle wings, the inverted cross bleeding through the number one. It's not decoration. It's doctrine.

A thirty-foot long RV crouches near the enormous door, dwarfed by its scale. Against the right wall, four motorcycle lifts stand like altars. One cradles a bike stripped to its bones—no seat, no tank, just the skeleton of speed. Toolboxes and stainless tables flank each station, cluttered with wrenches, oil cans, and the detritus of creation. Down both sides, closer to the center, vehicle lifts rise like giant robots—two standard, two heavy-duty for trucks. There's room to turn a semi in here, and still space to breathe.

The opposite wall is a mosaic of utility: a coffee station with a cube fridge and powdered creamer; a tire changer hulking like a beast; a state inspection rig blinking green; a pamphlet table and water cooler standing guard before a set of glass doors leading to a waiting area. This isn't a backroom hustle. It's an empire with torque and teeth.

Men move through the space like currents—three, maybe four, each vested in the same colors, patches blazing. One unboxes a leather seat at a steel table, fingers working with reverence. Two wrestle RV furniture through a narrow door, their curses ricocheting off metal walls. "For Christ's sake, turn it and take some of the weight off me, will you?" one bellows, voice booming like a loudspeaker at a stadium. Muted grumbling answers from inside the RV.

A young man appears from somewhere and pushes a broom across the floor, head down, vest bare of pride. No flying one, no Wicked Ones rocker—just a bottom patch that reads PROSPECT.

Banks' voice cracks the air like a whip: "Prospect!" The kid freezes, straightens, hustles over.

"Yeah, Banks. What do you need?"

"Get out of here. Go help Mandy out front." The grunt is final. The kid vanishes through the steel doors, gone like a breeze.

The trio halts at an office door set flush in the wall, plain but heavy. Banks knocks twice—two dull thuds that sound like a gavel. A voice answers from beyond, deep and clipped: "Come." Banks swings the door open and gestures inside, silent and sharp, like a father sending sons to penance.

Charles steps through first, Steve at his shoulder. The office breathes authority—leather and steel, wood polished to a dark gleam. Banks follows, shuts the door, locks it with a click that feels like a sentence. He plants himself before the exit, feet braced, hands clasped behind his back, eyes fixed on nothing. He stares through the far wall, a monument carved from muscle and ink. The air is saturated with silence and power, and somewhere in that silence, Charles feels the weight of Dusty—the man behind the voice; waiting like a storm about to break.

The very large man rises from behind an antique desk carved like a cathedral door. The wood gleams dark under the light, its edges etched with scrollwork that whispers of old money and older power. He moves slowly, but the room seems to move with him, gravity bending toward his bulk. At first glance, he looks like a leather-clad Santa Claus—white hair, rosy cheeks, a belly that strains his vest, a smile wide enough to warm winter. If only he had a beard.

His voice rolls out deep and jovial, rich as bourbon: "Mack! Come in! Thank you, Banks. …And you must be this Charlie Watkins I've been hearing about."

His hand extends across the desk, big enough to crush bone, palm open in welcome. Charles doesn't move. The silence stretches, a thin string, ready to snap. His eyes drop to the patch stitched over the man's heart: VICE PRESIDENT. The title gongs like a warning bell.

Steve fills the gap, words tumbling fast: "He likes to be called Charles and he doesn't—"

The smile dies like a light snuffed out. Dusty's eyes harden, blue ice under heavy lids. His voice cuts, sharp and sudden: "What? Can't Charles speak for himself?" The question hangs like a pendulum. For a breath, the room feels smaller, the air compressed, as if the walls lean in to listen.

Steve swallows, his tone dropping to something careful, almost reverent: "Actually, no. He can't talk. He's a mute. Sorry. I thought I told you that. Guess I forgot."

Dusty's hand doesn't waver. His face shifts again—storm clouds breaking to let the sun through. The grin blooms back, big and bright, as if the darkness never happened. "Can't talk, huh?

Perfect! Just the kind of guy we're looking for around here! Loose lips sink ships, my daddy always said! Pleased to meet you, Charles. I'm Dusty Kane."

Charles steps forward, grip firm, eyes locked. He smiles, nods—a silent greeting etched in steel. Dusty meets it with equal weight, his shake solid, his gaze probing like a miner's light searching for gold.

"Please, have a seat." Dusty releases Charles and snags Steve's hand mid-motion, catching him in a half-crouch. Steve fumbles the shake, cheeks coloring as he drops into the chair.

Dusty lowers himself back into his throne of leather, the chair groaning under his mass. He exhales like a man settling in, hands folding over his belly. "So... Charles." His voice softens, almost purring. "No talking, huh? Well, we'll see if that's a blessing or a curse." He leans back, eyes narrowing with a glint that could be humor—or hunger. "I suppose as long as you're as good as Mack says you are, you don't really need to say anything at all, do you? Actions speak louder than words."

Charles smiles, shakes his head no.

"Mack here tells me you're looking for work. Says you helped him out a few times and you've got a good head on your shoulders. You get shit done. Is that true?"

Charles shrugs, nods—humble but sure.

"He says you've got an uncanny knack for getting in and out of places without being seen." Dusty's grin widens, teeth flashing like ivory dice. "That sounds like a talent I could put to some real good use around here. You seriously interested in hanging around and maybe seeing what happens?"

Charles nods once, slow and deliberate.

"Alright then." Dusty leans forward, his bulk rising like a tide. He grunts as he stands, breath hissing through clenched teeth. "Oh, Jesus Mary and Joseph!" His cheeks flare crimson, his chest heaves, but he powers through, looming tall again. "Why don't you hang around out front for as long as you like tonight. Relax. Drinks are on the house. Meet some of the guys and get a feel for the whole thing. You're welcome back any time. Hang around for a few months. See if you can make a few bucks and help us out at the same time. No strings attached. We can part ways whenever it's just not fun anymore. That sound OK to you?"

Charles smiles, nods, and steps forward with his hand outstretched. Dusty clasps it, grip iron, then turns to Banks with a voice that booms friendly but lands like law: "Banks, see Charles to the front and make sure everyone knows he's going to be hanging around for a while. Show him around. Make him feel at home."

Steve rises halfway before Dusty's gaze pins him. "Mack, you stay here a minute, will you please?" The words are velvet, but the weight behind them is granite. Steve lowers himself back into his seat.

"No problem, Dusty," rumbles Banks, already on the other side of the threshold. Charles turns to follow, but not before giving Dusty one last nod—silent respect, eyes steady. Then he moves, shadow trailing Banks, the door closing behind him with a click that feels like a decree.

Steve watches the door click shut; the sound sharp as a slide cocking. For a beat, the room brims with silence, broken only by the faint tick of a clock and the complaints of Dusty's leather chair as he shifts his weight.

Dusty speaks first, voice low and deliberate, like a man testing the ground before he steps: "You sure about this kid?"

Steve leans forward, elbows on his knees, eyes bright with conviction. "Yeah, bro. He's solid. I'm telling you; the dude can get you pretty much anything you want—fast and for dirt cheap. I've built damn near my whole FXDX from parts he scored me. Cost me a tenth of what it would've run any other way." His words tumble out quick, eager, like cards slapped on a table.

Dusty's gaze doesn't flicker. "How'd you meet him?" The question lands heavy, a weight dropped in the middle of the room.

Steve grins, nostalgia flashing in his eyes. "Just like that, man. Hanging down at The Tank a few months ago, smoking a J out by the bikes, you know? Regular stuff. Just a few guys talking chrome and horsepower. This guy was one of them. Needless to say, he didn't do much talking. He was already there long before I even showed up. I start bitching about how I need a new EVO for my Dyna rebuild—just shooting the shit. Next week, same spot, same time, same vibe, and he drags me over to his van. Pops the door and boom—brand spanking new EVO, still in the crate sitting right there. Kid sold it to me for seven hundred bucks. Seven hundred! I got his number that night. Called him for more, and every damn time he comes through." Steve's voice sharpens with excitement, hands slicing the air like punctuation. "I'm telling you, Dusty. This guy's the real deal."

Dusty leans back, chair groaning under his bulk. His fingers drum slow on the desk, each tap a warning shot. "You ever seen him do it?" His tone is calm, but the edge is there—a dagger under velvet.

Steve hesitates, the grin faltering. "Well… not exactly. I mean—" He stammers, scrambling for footing.

Dusty's face ignites, cheeks blazing red, eyes narrowing to sapphire slits. His voice snaps, sudden and savage: "How in the fuck do you know he's not a cop with access to warehouses full of impounded shit if you've never seen how he does it?" The words slam into the air like fists, and for a second, the room feels like a cage

Steve throws his hands up, palms out, voice rushing to fill the fire. "No, listen, bro! I've been in on a few shenanigans with him. Pulled watch while he slipped in, took care of business. Either comes out with what we need or opens the place up and lets me in to shop for myself. He's good. No alarms, no heat, no bullshit. He hasn't let me down once. There's no way he's a cop. He's done way too much dirt with me already to be law. I'm telling you, Dusty—give him a shot." His words spill fast, desperate but fierce. "Hell, put him to the test. Have the guys make some light requests, see how he handles it. Don't burn him out, but check him out for yourself."

Dusty's glare softens by degrees, the storm pulling back but leaving heat lightning and thunder in its wake. He leans forward, forearms sinking into the desk, voice dropping to a growl that feels like sand under boots. "I got a better idea. We put in some requests and you tag along. You watch him work. You see it with your own eyes."

Steve nods hard, relief flickering across his face. "Alright, Dusty. That's cool. We'll do it like that. Just… give him a few weeks to settle in, yeah? Let him get comfortable, then we'll put him to the test." His tone pleads but holds steady, like a man betting his last chip.

Dusty exhales slow, a lasting hiss that empties the room. He clasps his hands, pointer fingers pressed to his lips, eyes drilling into the desk as if answers might rise from the grain. The silence stretches, thin and tense, before he looks up, gaze cold and clear. "Sounds good. Keep a sharp eye on him. Keep me posted." The words are iron, final. Then the edge of his mouth quirks, almost a smile, as he waves Steve off like a bad smell. "Now fuck off and let me get back to my shit."

Dusty shifts in his chair, attention already gone, fingers curling around the phone receiver. The dial tone buzzes like a bee as Steve rises slow and quiet, a man leaving church after confession. He slips out without another word, the door closing behind him with a click that feels like relief.

Out front, the bar buzzes like a living engine—music grinding low, laughter ricocheting off wood and steel. Charles sits in a booth crowded with leather and attitude, the air thick with beer breath and exhaust talk. He's already made rounds outside, comparing bikes under the fiery glow of security lights, nodding approval at chrome and horsepower. Now, inside, the conversation rolls like thunder.

"Steve-O!" Mark Wheeler's voice cracks the din, sharp and bright. He's tall and wiry, a scarecrow in denim and leather, his black hair braided into ropes that hang past his chest. A goatee juts from his chin like a dagger. He can't be a day older than Charles, but his beard, sideburns and temples are speckled in gray already. His eyes gleam with mischief—the kind that promises trouble and laughs in equal measure. He slaps the table with a palm scarred from years of wrench work, grinning wide enough to show teeth stained by smoke and whiskey. He lives his life the way he rides—fast and hard.

Banks rises slow, deliberate, like a glacier rolling over. His handshake swallows Steve's, grip iron, eyes flat and measuring. "Welcome back, Mack," he says, voice low and gravy-thick. He steps aside, making room for Steve to slide in, but his gaze never leaves Charles. It's not curiosity—it's scrutiny, sharp as a blade. Banks doesn't blink. Doesn't smile. He's the kind of man who counts exits before he sits down.

Steve drops into the booth, easy grin plastered on his face, and pats Charles's arm like sealing a deal. "I see you've met my friend Charles," he says, voice pitched to carry. "Good man.

Good man right here." The words land like a stamp of approval meant for every ear at the table. He tosses the black plastic bag onto the scarred wood, the leather inside bearing the symbols of rank and belonging.

"We were just working through our language barriers," drawls Jake 'JJ' Jardini, his voice syrupy and smug. JJ is a slab of flesh stuffed into faded denim, tall but bloated, his chin melting into a stubble-covered waddle that jiggles with every word. His hair is cropped short, his eyes small and shiny like wet pebbles. He grins, lips slick with beer, and lets loose a laugh that shakes his gut. "Beer, bikes, and titties seems to be the international language of brotherly love!" He punctuates it with a guffaw that rattles glasses.

Steve chuckles, easy and loud. Charles exhales a small huff through his nose, chin lifting in silent amusement. Wheeler smirks, tapping ash into an empty bottle. But Banks? Banks doesn't move. His stare pins Charles like a nail through wood, cold and unyielding. He's listening, cataloging every twitch, every glance. Skepticism pre-loads in his posture like a snake ready to strike.

The night stretches, stitched together with laughter and liquor. Stories spill like oil—rides gone wrong, fights gone right, engines rebuilt from rust and prayer. JJ roars at his own jokes, Wheeler spins tales with hands carving the air, and Steve plays maestro, keeping the rhythm alive. But Charles drifts. His focus slides, drawn by gravity to the bar.

Mandy moves to music only she hears—hips swaying, hair catching light like chestnut fire. She pours, wipes, smiles, her hands quick and sure. Every so often, her eyes flick toward the booth, and Charles is there, watching. At first, he looks away fast, heat crawling his neck. But later, when her gaze hooks his again, he holds it—just long enough to feel the spark snap between them. Her smile curves slow, secret, before she turns back to her work. Charles tracks her like a compass to true north, his silence louder than words.

Banks notices. Of course he does. His eyes cut from Charles to Mandy and back, a flicker of tension in his face muscles. He leans back, arms folding like gates closing, and watches—silent, inquisitive, questions burning behind his stare. The kind of questions that don't need words: Who the hell is this guy, and why does he look so damn comfortable in my house?

Chapter 16: November 10th, 1994 – Age 27

Charles has become a fixture at the Dusty Spoke. Months have passed since his first night and the place feels less a bar, more a second skin now. He drops in twice a week—sometimes Tuesdays when business crawls, sometimes Fridays when the joint throbs with bodies and bass. Other times, he shows up unannounced, slipping in during daylight to tinker in the garage, grease under his nails and laughter in his ears. He helps with bikes, swaps stories, and always, somehow, Mandy is behind the bar when he's around. Coincidence? Maybe. But Charles doesn't believe in coincidence anymore.

Tonight is Thursday. Cold air clings to the lot outside, but inside the Spoke, heat radiates from neon and whiskey. Charles pushes through the door carrying a bottle of Jack Daniels like a peace offering. It's his birthday—not that anyone knows. He moves with quiet confidence now, eyes sweeping the room without fear, nodding at faces that once felt like threats. This place is home. The leather, the laughter, the low undertones of outlaw life—it all fits.

Steve spots him first. "Hey! Charles! Good to see you, bro." His voice booms warm, genuine, as he claps Charles's hand and hauls him into a half hug, punctuating it with three hard pats on the back. His grin widens when he sees the bottle. "Oh, what'd you do? What is this, a bottle? Man, you didn't need to trouble yourself."

Charles hands him the Jack, then flicks his gaze toward the door—a quick jerk of his chin, sharp as a signal. No words, just motion. He turns abruptly and strides for the exit. Steve blinks, confused, then hustles after him.

Outside, the night bites. Gravel rolls under boots as Charles leads Steve toward a white box truck squatting near the building, its bulk almost blocking half the lot. No logos, no markings; just steel and silence. Steve's brows knot. "What's this? Where's your bike?"

Charles doesn't answer verbally. He saunters to the back of the truck, turns toward Steve, looks him straight in the eyes and smirks. Without breaking his gaze, he reaches out, precisely grips the latch, flips it, and yanks the handle toward the heavens. The door rockets upward with a roar like thunder after a nearby bolt strikes. Light spills into the cavernous belly of the truck. Steve's jaw goes slack. Cases. Stacked high, row after row. Beer, wine, whiskey, vodka. Enough to drown an army.

Charles, with smirk still gracing his face, continues watching Steve's face even though Steve's gaze has long ago pulled away and his attention is focused elsewhere.

"What the fuck?" The words skyrocket from Steve's depths, half laugh, half disbelief. His eyes dart over the haul, pupils widening like a man staring at treasure.

Charles just smiles bigger—a slow, wolfish curve, and in a swift single motion, high-steps onto the bumper and grabs the canvas strap. He pulls down and then hops from the bumper, strap still wrapped around his wrist. The door slams shut behind him with a crash that echoes off steel and stone. He lazily slaps the latch into place, motions Steve toward the garage, then swings into the cab like he owns the night.

By the time Steve hits the overhead button, Charles is rolling up, the truck's engine growling low. The overhead door climbs, rattling like chains, and the Spoke's inner sanctum unfurls wide. Charles eases the beast inside. The rattle of the diesel motor pings off the walls of the cavernous space. He kills the motor, and hops out. He moves swiftly to the back, pops the latch, and throws the door high. Cold air rolls out, carrying the scent of cardboard and booze.

He grabs the nearest case—Grey Goose, the box heavy and waxy, and drops it into Steve's arms. Steve staggers, laughing like a maniac, head shaking in disbelief. "Jesus Christ in a cradle, Charles!" he barks, voice cracking with boyish glee. "You're out of your gut-damn mind!"

The noise draws eyes. Wrenches pause mid-turn. Heads swivel. One by one, the garage crew drifts closer, heavy boots drumming on concrete. When they see the extent of the stash, grins split faces like cracks in stone. Hands dive in to help. A ramp is pulled from a hidden slot just under the floor of the truck box. It sounds like a backward storm with thunder rolls first followed by the crash of the ramp being dropped to concrete. The men begin hauling cases like loot from a raid. Voices rise: shouts, curses, laughter ricocheting off steel walls. The air thickens with sweat and celebration.

A quick step onto the bumper and Charles seamlessly reaches for a grab handle. He swings into the truck like a primate, muscles flexing under leather but movements fluid. He unhooks the dolly that is mounted to the wall. Metal clinks as he frees it, rubber-coated wheels squeal as they hit the steel floor. He loads cases with swift precision, his movements clean, controlled—a man who knows how to work in chaos.

Steve bolts for the bar, yelling before he's even through the door. His words blur into the din, but the tone is pure triumph.

Inside, the Spoke erupts. Boots pound. A dozen men spill out like floodwater—Dusty among them, his bulk leading the charge. They burst into the garage as if a dam has broken and swarm the truck, arms bulging, laughter booming like artillery. In minutes, the beast is gutted, its belly stripped bare.

And then—stillness. The crowd melts back inside, voices fading to a low rumble. Only Banks remains, a totem of ink, shadow carving his face. He stands with his back to the wall, arms folded, eyes locked on Charles. No grin. No word. Just that stare: cold, clinical, peeling layers Charles doesn't show anyone. For a long beat, silence stretches between them, a tight, live wire. Then Banks turns, boots pivoting sharply on dusty cement, and vanishes into the dark.

Charles exhales slow, the weight of that look clinging like cigar smoke to a wool sweater. He drops the last two cases—tequila, and puts them on the floor. He jumps up onto the bumper, grabs the strap, and slams the door shut. The sound cracks the quiet like a grenade. He hefts the boxes, crosses the expanse of the garage and strides toward the bar.

The bar pulses electric. Most of the haul is already stashed, hidden like treasure. A few open boxes sprawl across the counter, bottles gleaming under neon. Mandy moves among them, her hands quick, her smile easy, pouring new product into old bottles. Her hair catches the light, a chestnut halo that makes Charles's pulse hitch.

Steve is waiting, grin wide enough to dissect his face. "Nice snag, bro!" he crows, voice thick with awe. "Way to score points! How the fuck did you pull that off?"

Charles just shrugs, lips curling in a hint of a smile. He drops his boxes on the bar, the clanking thud swallowed by music and laughter.

Steve flags Mandy down, two shot glasses already waiting. "Mandy, baby—pour us a couple shots, will you?" he calls, voice riding high on adrenaline.

Mandy spins, unopened bottle in one hand, just in time to catch Charles's gesture—palm flat, sweeping over the glass like a metronome. No. He fishes the truck keys from his jacket, metal glinting under neon, and jingles them in front of Steve. A silent message: duty calls.

He grips Steve's shoulder, firm and friendly, then slides the empty glass toward him—a gift, an offering of celebration without him. His nod is sharp, respectful. Then he turns, boots hitting heavy across worn wood as he heads for the door.

On his way out, he lifts two fingers to his brow in a salute—small, clean, enough to speak volumes.

The night swallows him as he climbs into the cab, slams the door, and fires the engine. The truck growls, hungry and loud, as Charles rolls out of the garage and into the dark, leaving behind a bar buzzing with questions and admiration.

"Mack… Wheeler… Take the Suburban and follow him." Banks' voice slices through the celebratory tone of the bar, low and cold, his silhouette framed by the window's neon OPEN sign bleeding red across his face. He watches the box truck's tail lights crawl into the dark like embers fading in ash.

Steve and Wheeler move fast. They shove through the door. The night slaps them with cold air sharp enough to bite. The Suburban waits in the lot, black and hulking under a flickering security lamp. Doors slam, engine growls awake—a beast roused from slumber.

They roll out, tires pinging small pebbles of asphalt into the wheel well, headlights dead to keep their shadow game clean. They glide from streetlamp glow to streetlamp glow seeking the tiny, fiery eyes of the box truck's taillights.

It doesn't take long to catch the glow ahead—two red eyes blinking through the dark. They hang back, wraiths in the rearview, close enough to taste the exhaust, far enough to stay unseen. The road winds like a mythological dragon, curling through the boondocks, trees scratching at the sky. The Suburban hugs the curves, rubber singing a soft tone against asphalt.

At the edge of town, the truck veers left, slipping into the industrial zone—a graveyard of brick and rust. Mill buildings loom like dead giants, their windows black. Alleys swallow darkness like throats. Charles drives deep, deeper, until the box truck crawls past a slit of an alley.

Steve squints. That alley is a dead end. Chain-link fence at the far end glinting under a sick moon. The truck noses in and disappears.

"Keep rolling," Steve mutters. Wheeler obeys, creeping fifty feet before swinging a U-turn, tires whimpering against damp asphalt. They park behind a rust-bitten Volkswagen Beetle, twenty feet from the alley mouth. Windows down. Engine off. Silence swells, thick and tense. The alley squats ahead, black as a coffin, the box truck parked in it nose-first like a square peg properly placed in the square hole.

Shadows swallow them like an oil slick. They wait. They watch. They listen.

The driver's door of the box truck creaks open. A figure spills out—Charles, leather jacket catching moonlight. His boots kiss pavement soft, soundless. He shuts the door, glances down at something in his hand. Small. Gold glints faintly before vanishing into his pocket. Keys? A lighter? They can't tell. He rounds the truck's snout and melts into darkness.

Minutes drag like chains. The alley stays mute. Steve shifts, restless. "What is he, taking a piss or something?"

"More like a shit," Wheeler grumbles, fingers drumming the wheel. "How long does it take to drain the tank?"

Two minutes. Three. Silence thickens, pressing against their ears. Wheeler huffs, grabs the handle. "Fuck this. I'm going to see what's up." He shoves his elbow against the door—

ROAR.

Harley pipes explode like thunder, ripping the night apart. The blast detonates inches from the Suburban's partially opened door, a streak of chrome and fury screaming past so close Wheeler jerks back like he's been shot. The door slams shut under its own recoil.

"The fuck?" Wheeler's voice cracks, heart clawing at his throat. "I almost shit myself! Was that him?"

"Yeah, it was," Steve fires back, adrenaline spiking. "There's gotta be a back way out. Go! Follow him!"

Wheeler twists the ignition key. The Suburban lunges forward, tires spitting small pills of rubber as they tear after the phantom roar. Headlights stay dark, the chase running blind through blacktop veins. Ahead, the Harley flickers in and out of sight—a comet burning through curves, taillight winking like a dare.

The road unravels into wilderness, trees crowding close, their limbs reaching over the road like claws ready to pluck prey. Charles veers hard, peeling off into the tree line, swallowed by shadows. Moments later, the Suburban approaches the approximate spot, skids, fishtails, then jerks onto a narrow trail, branches whipping against steel. Headlights go on. They push as far as the beast will fit, tires grinding roots, headlights blowing tunnels through black.

Then—nothing. The roar fades, dwindles to silence. The woods stand still, breathless, holding secrets in their clutches.

Steve kills the engine and the lights. Darkness floods in, thick and absolute. They sit, listening—straining for a growl, a cough, a clue. Nothing. Just the wind threading through pines like a ghost's fingers.

"He's gone," Wheeler mutters, voice flat, defeat bleeding through. He starts the truck again, pulls the light switch, drops the shifter into reverse and backs the Suburban down the scar they carved, tires crunching slow, retreating from the black maw of the forest.

Behind them, the woods swallow the trail whole. Ahead, the road stretches empty, slick with moonlight. They drive back to the Spoke in silence, the question hanging like smoke: Where the hell did he go?

—

The office breathes wealth. Leather and old money linger in the air like a quiet warning. A massive desk, carved with intricate patterns, gleams under the soft glow of a brass lamp. Behind it, a high-backed executive chair faces away from the room, angled toward a wall of glass that overlooks the town center below. Beyond the glass, winter sunlight scatters across parked cars and bundled pedestrians, oblivious to the power sitting in this room.

A pigtail telephone cord snakes across the desk and disappears behind the chair's imposing silhouette. The voice that emerges from that hidden space is sharp, clipped—authority wrapped in irritation.

"Check into it and get back to me." A pause, then harder, like a blade pressed to skin: "Run the plates. Check the paper. Watch the news. I don't care how—figure out how he snatched a truckload of booze, undetected."

The chair pivots just enough for movement to register— a slow, deliberate turn, but not enough to reveal the man's face to the room. Only a hand emerges from behind the padded leather shroud, slamming the handset onto its cradle with a crack. The hand is immaculate, nails trimmed, skin smooth. A Panerai watch glints beneath a cuff of white cotton, anchored by carved onyx cufflinks. The jacket sleeve is sharkskin black, whispering wealth and menace with every shift. Whoever he is, he doesn't need to raise his voice to remind the world he owns it.

Across town, Dusty hangs the handset up with a little more force than necessary. He sits hunched at his own desk for a moment before sloppily slapping his hand down and sliding a sheet of paper from the desk to his eye level. The sheet of paper is pulled tight in his hands now, like a shield of answers against a lobby of questions.

Burns stands in front of him, silent, waiting. All he sees is the crown of Dusty's cotton-white hair above the paper. The room feels heavy with expectation. Dusty lowers the paper slowly, lays it flat, and stares off into space as if the words he just read are still rearranging themselves in his mind. Burns doesn't move. He knows better than to interrupt when Dusty's gears are turning.

Finally, Dusty speaks from behind his folded hands, voice low, almost to himself.

"So… looks like they're blaming the driver for the booze truck heist. Inside job, they say." His eyes flick over the sheet, scanning for something he might have missed. "Driver swears it wasn't him. Says he watched the truck get loaded, locked the door himself, jumped straight into the driver's seat. First stop, same alley he always uses. Unlocks the cargo door, grabs the cases, locks up again and rolls the order inside. Comes back out, unlocks, puts the dolly back in—booze is all there. Shuts and locks the door. Next stop's fifteen minutes away. Shows up, unlocks the truck right in front of the store owner and—" Dusty exhales sharply through his nose. "—the fucking thing is empty."

He leans back, chair creaking under his weight, eyes narrowing as he chews on the impossibility.

"Driver's dumbfounded. Store owner swears he took no longer than usual, but convinced he unloaded the booze somewhere." Dusty shakes his head slowly. "But why? Why show up empty and stick around to take the rap with nothing but a fairy tale to defend himself?"

Burns finally breaks the silence. "Sounds like a pretty clear case of the driver did it." He shrugs. "So, what—he was working with the kid? No… that doesn't make sense. Why would he show up with an empty truck and hang around to get burned?"

Dusty's eyes snap to him, sharp. "No. There's no way they were working together." His voice hardens, conviction settling in. "The kid hijacked the truck somehow. But here's what gets me—" He leans forward, elbows on the desk, fingers steepled. "—the whole thing was done in broad daylight. Middle of the afternoon. No cover, no shadows. You think he knocked the driver out? Drugged him?"

Burns slowly leans his head, considering. Dusty barrels on before he can answer.

"They don't mention injuries. No blackout, no memory lapse. Driver never says he came to from anything." Dusty's jaw works as he stares at the paper like it might confess if he glares hard enough.

He looks up suddenly. "That alley where the kid parked yesterday… same alley the driver used at his first stop?"

"Yeah," Burns says without hesitation.

Dusty grunts, a sound that carries weight. His mind is a storm now, possibilities colliding like billiard balls.

"Fifteen minutes," he mutters. "Fifteen minutes to make a truck vanish. No forced locks. No broken seals. No one saw a damn thing. Either this kid's a ghost, or he's got something we've never seen before."

The room feels smaller, tighter, as Dusty's voice drops to a near whisper. "Well… we either need to get on this kid, or get this kid on board. He's got something going on." His eyes lock on Burns, cold and certain. "Keep an eye on him. Try to bring him closer."

Burns meets his gaze, nods once, solid. No words needed. The game just changed.

Chapter 17: June, 1995 – Age 27

Charles has become a welcomed, familiar face at the Dusty Spoke. He still drifts in only once or twice a week, but over the past six months, he's proven himself—loyal, helpful, never a burden. No grand gestures like the truckload of booze since that day, but enough quiet favors and steady presence that everyone enjoys having him around.

Tonight, he shares a booth with Steve, voices low over the din of conversation.

"Okay then. I understand. That's cool, but the offer stands whenever you're ready," Steve says, leaning in with a grin that's half-guilty, half-hopeful. "The club likes you, and the prospect period ain't that bad, man." He chuckles, knowing full well it's hell.

Charles smiles, shakes his head. No again. He reaches across the table, grips Steve's hand—a gesture of respect, not rejection.

The front door bangs open, and a blast of dusty wind sweeps through like an uninvited guest. Heads turn.

Standing in the doorway is a man dressed like a neon billboard for bad decisions. Blue and white leather from neck to toe, boots climbing three-quarters up his calves, chunky white latches like ski gear. On his back, a BMW logo sprawls across the jacket like a corporate tattoo.

He steps inside, removes his matching helmet with a flourish, and beams at the room like he's stepping onto a stage.

"Afternoon, boys!" His voice effeminate and dripping with privilege, too loud, too cheerful—like a politician kissing babies.

The room freezes for a beat. Then, without a word, heads swivel back to beers and conversations. A few sighs, a grunt. Silence swallows his greeting whole.

Unfazed—or pretending to be; he strides to the bar with the swagger of a man who thinks every eye is still on him. He pulls up a stool, leans in toward Mandy with a grin that's meant to charm but lands somewhere between smug and creepy.

"Hi hon. Can I have a Bartles & Jaymes original, please?" His eyes dart everywhere but hers, scanning the room for admiration that isn't coming.

Mandy doesn't miss a beat. "Um. No, ma'am," she fires back, voice dripping sarcasm. "We still only have beer in bottles or the hard stuff since last you inquired."

"Well, it doesn't hurt to keep checking now, does it?" His tone sharpens, defensive under the fake cheer. "Maybe someday you'll start listening to your customers' desires and learn how to fulfill their needs. It's the simple law of supply and demand. We demand, you supply, and everyone's happy, right? Works for me!"

Mandy stares at him like he's a bug on her windshield.

"Uh huh." Her lips purse, eyebrows arch—both of them this time, which is nowhere near as cute as when she raises just one. "Is there something I can supply you with then, sir?"

Charles watches the exchange, amused, then taps Steve's hand, nodding toward the blue-and-white spectacle with a silent question: Who the hell is this clown?

Steve leans in, voice low.

"That's Blake Kerrington. His great-granddaddy pretty much owned this town back in the day, then his granddaddy, then his daddy. Never lifted a finger to earn a cent on his own. Just had it handed to him on a platter and still expects everyone to treat him like royalty. He's a real piece of work. A real piece of shitty work."

Charles turns back to watch Blake, who now raises his light beer like a royal decree.

"To the customer!" he shouts, bottle held aloft like a scepter, waiting for applause that never comes.

Mandy turns away without a word, polishing bottles with deliberate indifference. A few groans ripple through the room before dying back into the rattle of conversation.

Blake, standing alone in his self-made spotlight, takes a long swig of beer and exhales like he's just conquered Everest.

"That's good stuff right there!" he announces, stabbing a finger at the bottle and trying to sound more manly. "That is some cold beer right there!" He pauses, then adds, "Hey, is Dusty around?"

Mandy vanishes behind the curtain of bottle caps without answering. Blake sips his beer, oblivious to the wall of silence pressing in on him.

Three minutes later, Mandy reappears with Dusty in tow. Dusty pokes his head through the curtain, motions Blake to come on back. Blake leaves his helmet and drink on the bar like a man expecting his throne to be waiting in the next room.

Charles watches him disappear, then looks at Steve for answers.

"No clue, buddy," Steve says. "They must have some kind of business, and it ain't mine or yours." He leans back, voice dropping. "Kerrington's some kind of importer. Does a lot of buying, selling, trading. He acquires things for people." Steve makes air quotes around *acquires*. "There's no telling what kind of deal they're cooking up in there."

Charles just stares at the curtain, nodding slowly, thoughts turning dark.

Chapter 18: June 10th, 1995 – Age 27

A frog croaks once from the mossy edge of the watering hole, then leaps into the green stillness. The algae swallows the ripples almost instantly, erasing the evidence of movement like the forest keeps its own secrets. Dusk settles in slow layers, and the air is alive with life—crickets chirping their endless rhythm, peepers punctuating the silence with sharp, cheerful notes. Together, they weave a symphony that belongs only to the woods.

A black water moccasin glides across the surface, its body carving a perfect S through the algae blanket. The snake moves like a shadow, silent and certain, a killer in a world that doesn't need witnesses.

A mosquito whines near Charles's ear, the sound swelling like a warning. He smacks his neck hard, feels the sting, then pulls his hand around to inspect the flattened speck of life—black and red, legs curled inward. He wipes his palm on his jeans and returns to the task at hand. The screwdriver bites into the tail light lens as he tightens the last screw.

He straightens, steps to the front of the bike, and flicks the ignition. The headlight bursts to life, slicing through the dimness and throwing pale light across the watering hole. Shadows scatter. Something unseen stirs in the brush. Charles squeezes the brake lever—the tail light glows bright red. Releases it—dims again. He presses the foot brake. Bright again. A small smile tugs at his mouth. It all still works.

His fingers find the new switch he just installed on the left handlebar. He flips it. Darkness swallows the bike. Flips it again—light floods back. Back and forth, testing, confirming. Perfect. He reaches for the license plate, pushes it upward, feels the spring-loaded resistance. It locks in place. He presses the button near the grip—the plate snaps down like a steel jaw. Fast. Hard. Invisible now. He resets it manually, presses again. Snap. He grins, satisfied.

Ignition off. The voice of the woods returns, bustling and alive.

Charles grips the handlebars, leans into the bike, and gives it a shove. Tires crunch over dry leaves and brittle twigs as he rolls it toward the house—a squat, one-room structure crouched in the trees like it grew there. Its walls are boulders stacked with stubborn permanence, roof heavy with slate shingles weathered by decades of storms. A chimney juts from one side, built from the same stone, blackened at the mouth like it remembers fire.

Charles didn't build this place. It was here long before him, maybe a century or more. He calls it The Lincoln House. No driveway, no path—just earth and secrecy. Even now, he's careful, leaving the main trail from a different point each time so no pattern betrays him. No ruts. No signs.

He stops in a thicket and props the bike on a flat slab of slate waiting like an altar. A brown tarp slides over the machine, followed by a camouflage net tangled with silk leaves—a camouflage shroud for steel.

The mosquitoes are relentless now, whining in his ears, biting at his skin. Time to go in. He steps onto the porch—just a slab of stone before a single door of heavy timber. Pushes it open.

Inside, the air is cool, stale with the scent of dust, stone and centuries. Empty space breathes around him. No furniture. No carpet. Just a crude concrete floor and a pop-up tent pitched before a massive fireplace. A few bottles of water, some snack wrappers scattered like breadcrumbs of survival.

Above the hearth hangs a portrait of Abraham Lincoln, its wooden frame rough-cut and splintered, the glass filmed with age. Lincoln stares down, solemn and eternal, as if judging every soul that crosses this threshold. On the mantle, a rusted kerosene lantern waits, unlit. Beside the hearth, fresh-cut wood stacked like bones. A hatchet leans against the stone chase, edge nicked from work.

Charles closes the door. Silence presses in, thick as velvet. Then—a sound. Faint, distant, but wrong. He freezes. Listens.

A motorcycle.

He yanks the door open, bolts outside, rounds the corner fast and low. His hand finds the pistol at his waistband, slides it free. He crouches at the back corner, breath steady, eyes locked on the trees. The sound grows—a headlight flickers through the branches like a ghost lantern. Charles pulls back, hiding everything but one eye behind the stone wall. He will not let his face catch the light.

The bike skids to a stop in front of the stone structure, pine needles spitting under its tires before settling into silence. The engine cuts out, leaving only the chirps of crickets and the distant whisper of wind through the trees. Lights die, and the rider swings a leg over, boots crunching against forest earth. A voice breaks the stillness, warm and familiar.

"Charles! Hey Charles! You in there?" calls Steve, his tone carrying easy confidence, like he knows he's welcome here.

It's been a few weeks since Steve fessed up and relayed to Charles that he was asked to keep an eye on him. He admitted that he followed Charles from the industrial park that night and inquired about where Charles had vanished to in those woods.

Charles, knowing he was in a tough spot, showed Steve the place, welcomed him to visit any time and asked him to keep the location to himself as much as loyalty would allow. He elaborated, in his own way, that he wasn't keeping a secret from the guys as much as he was keeping a secret from everyone in general, admitting he was squatting illegally there.

Charles tucks his pistol away, the metal cool against his belly before disappearing beneath his waistband. He moves like a shadow, rounding the corner without a sound until he's inches behind Steve.

Steve startles hard, spinning with wide eyes. "Oh Jesus! Why do you do that to me?" he blurts, clutching his chest in a mock display of cardiac arrest. His laugh follows, rough and genuine, echoing off the stone walls.

Charles grins, the kind of grin that says he enjoys the game but means no harm. He extends a hand, and Steve clasps it tight, their shake firm—more than greeting, it's a promise of trust.

"I brought dinner!" Steve declares triumphantly, diving into a saddlebag and producing a bottle of whiskey like a found treasure. He lifts it high, amber liquid catching the last scraps of dusk's light.

Together, they step inside the cabin. The air is cool, tinged with stone and old wood. Steve claims the hearth like it's his own, dropping onto the edge with a sigh that speaks of comfort. From his jacket, he pulls a pack of Marlboros, taps one free, and sets it between his lips. A flick of his chrome Zippo, and fire manifests. He draws deep, smoke curling toward the ceiling before he exhales slow, savoring the moment.

The whiskey bottle cracks open, its seal surrendering with a twist. Steve offers it first, arm extended in silent respect. Charles takes it, tilts it back, and lets the burn stream a path down his throat. He hands it over, and Steve follows suit, their shared silence saying more than words.

Charles sparks the kerosene lamp with a black Bic lighter, adjusting the flame until the room glows in soft orange, shadows dancing against stone. Twilight filters through warped leaded glass windows, painting the edges in purple dusk. Steve lifts the bottle again, toasting the emptiness, the peace, the strange sanctuary they share.

"You know, there's a part of me that sees why you do this," Steve says, voice almost reverent. "It's peaceful. Tranquil. I've been here three minutes and I'm more relaxed than I've been in months. Go figure."

He drinks deep, then offers the bottle again. Charles accepts, raises it toward the room, then toward Steve—a silent salute, and takes a double shot before crouching to coax flame into the waiting wood.

Steve watches him, words tumbling out with smoke. "Don't you ever want more though, bro? I mean, don't you ever want something of your own? This is nice if you're camping, but it ain't even yours. Don't you want a bed? A woman? Hell, a life? You're a loner, yeah, but you like people. You're not a freak." He laughs, punctuating it with a friendly smack to Charles's arm.

The fire catches, crackling to life, and Charles settles beside him. He takes the bottle, drains a swallow that takes two gulps, then meets Steve's gaze.

Steve leans forward, sincerity etched in every line of his face. "Man, I ain't trying to be offensive. You know that. I'm saying you could have it better. Hell, you could have this exact thing, only yours. No squatting. No worrying about getting run off. Maybe you buy this place. Maybe you build more. You could have brothers. A woman. Money. Don't let them tell you it can't buy happiness, 'cause brother, it can."

He pauses, realizing he's drifting, then reels himself back. "Listen, bro. The point is this—I can help you, but you gotta want it. I can't force it. I can only offer it as your friend."

His hand hovers for the bottle, and Charles passes it without hesitation, calm as ever, letting Steve speak his truth.

"Here's the thing," Steve says, voice dropping to a conspiratorial tone. "I got another job offer for you. Something simple. If it goes smooth, we all end up in better places. You interested?"

Charles's brows dip, a mischievous half-smile carving across his face. He nods once, slow and certain. Interest confirmed.

To seal the deal, Charles reaches into his inside jacket pocket and pulls out a pack of Marlboros. His fingers move with deliberate calm as he slides out a joint—a slender promise of escape. The Bic flicks, flame kissing paper, and smoke curls upward like a secret. He takes a few short starter hits, then a deep inhale that he holds, eyes half-lidded, before passing the doob across the glow of the kerosene lamp.

Steve accepts it with a grin that borders on impatience. He draws in slow, savoring the fine-smelling blend, lungs ballooning with the weight of it. For ten seconds, silence reigns—two men holding their breath, holding their thoughts. Charles exhales first, a slow ribbon of smoke unfurling into the dim orange light. Steve follows, coughing out a laugh as he hands the joint back.

"Wow. Good shit, man. Can you get more of that?" Steve asks, voice roughened by smoke but tinged with awe.

Charles nods, wets his fingertips with spit, tamps the canoeing ember, then takes another drag deep enough to hollow his cheeks. He passes it back, and Steve devours his second hit like a starving man at a feast. Charles watches him through a haze, noting the gratitude in Steve's eyes—a small twinkle that says more than words.

Steve tries to speak mid-hit, but all that escapes is a strangled "Dude..." before the smoke bellows from his lungs in a coughing fit. He hacks so hard his face flames crimson, but he's laughing, eyes watering, as he thrusts the roach back toward Charles.

"Holy fuck! Good fucking shit, man! Damn!" Steve wheezes, voice shredded and intermittent but joyous.

Charles inhales again, slow and steady, then snuffs the roach on the hearth. The room settles into a warm, narcotic hush. Outside, night has claimed the woods, and the creatures of darkness begin their shift—crickets sawing, owls asking, the forest alive with secrets.

For long minutes, they sit in companionable silence, buzz wrapping them like a blanket. Finally, Steve breaks it, words dragging like heavy boots. "So, ya, man. What's up? You interested in that job or what, bro?" He turns, squinting through the fog of his own high.

Charles meets his gaze, nods once—and in that instant, both men register the other's squinty-eyed state. Steve erupts in laughter, a raw, unfiltered bark that ricochets off stone. Charles blows air through his lips, laughter sputtering like a backfire. For half a minute, they're kids again, drunk on nothing but smoke and trust.

Steve wipes his eyes, sobers enough to speak. "So, cool then, bro. You're in if you want it. There's just one catch." He leans forward, voice dropping to a conspiratorial rumble. "I can't get you involved if you're not at least prospecting for the club. You gotta be on the inside for this one, my brother. No other way. Believe me—I tried."

Charles stares at his boots, thoughts pooling in the quiet. When he looks up, his eyes search Steve's for truth—and find it there, steady and unflinching.

Steve presses on, tone softening. "Listen, man. I'd never feed you bullshit just to rope you in. I'm offering this as your friend. Sleep on it. Think it over. If you want in, come down to the bar by Wednesday night. It's happening this weekend. Fair enough?"

Charles nods, slow and deliberate. Decision deferred, but interest undeniable.

"Good man!" Steve barks, smacking Charles's knee before levering himself upright with a groan. "Alright, bro. I'm gonna ride my drunken, stoned ass down this dark, leaf-covered slope now. Wish me luck!"

They clasp hands, pull into a shoulder-to-shoulder embrace, backs slapped hard in the language of men who trust.

"Take it easy, bro," Steve calls as he steps into the night.

Charles lingers in the doorway, tossing a lazy salute as Steve mounts up. The bike snarls to life. Charles raises a thumb; Steve answers with a wave before dropping the clutch and spinning a half donut, tail light bleeding red into the dark until it fades, then vanishes. Silence swallows the sound.

From behind him, inside the cabin, something shuffles— a long zip, a shadow peeling from deeper shadow. Mandy emerges from the tent, barefoot, wrapped in nothing but a blanket, her hair spilling like a waterfall over her shoulders. She steps into the doorway behind Charles, eyes on the woods where Steve disappeared. For a breath, they stand like stone, then retreat together into the glow of the kerosene lamp. The door closes, sealing the secret in.

Chapter 19: June 14th, 1995 – Age 27

It's Wednesday night—a night that should feel slow, quiet, uneventful. But tonight, the Dusty Spoke sparkles with life. The parking lot glitters under the neon glow, chrome catching the light like teeth in the dark. Rows of bikes stand like gravestones, engines ticking as they cool, their presence a silent promise of brotherhood and rules.

Charles rolls in, his tires crunching tiny chunks of loose asphalt, the low rumble of his engine fading as he kills the ignition. He swings off the bike, boots hitting earth with a weight that feels heavier than usual. This isn't just another night. This is a turning point. He knows it.

Inside, the air is thick with smoke and laughter, the scent of beer and leather mingling in a cocktail of grit and comfort. Heads turn as he steps through the door, and for a beat, the room greets him like family: cheers, nods, a few raised bottles. It's not just noise; it's acceptance.

Steve is on his feet before Charles can take another step. His grin is wide, his energy electric. He closes the gap fast, hand outstretched, pulling Charles into a shake that morphs into a half-hug; the kind that speaks of trust earned over time.

"So?" Steve's voice is tight with hope, words tumbling out like he can't hold them back. "What's up, bro? You in?" He's still gripping Charles's hand, eyes locked, searching for the answer like its oxygen.

Charles meets his gaze, and the world narrows to this moment. Seconds stretch. He replays every thought, every doubt, every reason to walk away—and every reason to stay.

Then, a smile. A nod. Yes.

Steve explodes like a kid who just scored a keg for the party of the year. "Ya, buddy! Alright, bro!" His voice cracks with excitement as he slaps Charles on the shoulder. "C'mon, man. Let's go see Dusty."

They move through the room, Steve detouring just long enough to snatch a black plastic bag from his table. "Be right back, fuckers. Don't drink my beer," he fires over his shoulder.

Banks lifts Steve's glass in mock salute, grin sharp. "I'll guard it with my life!" He takes a long, deliberate gulp. "I'll store this away for you." Another gulp between jabs. "Might give it back later—if you're interested." Another swig.

"Asshole!" Steve shoots back, middle finger raised as laughter detonates around them. Banks calls after him, voice booming: "It might be a little warmer when you get it back!" The room roars, and for a moment, it feels like home.

Charles chuckles, but inside, something shifts. Banks— the hardest nut to crack: laughing, joking, treating him like one of their own. If Banks is warm, the rest are lava. This is the time. No second-guessing now.

He's played hard-to-get long enough.

—

Steve swings his cut from the bag, the leather vest cutting through the air before landing on his shoulders like it belongs there. He tucks the bag away as they approach the keypad. No secrets—Steve punches in the code without shielding it. The door buzzes, heavy and final. He pulls it open, gestures for Charles to step through.

"Alright. Listen, bro. Just be cool. Dusty's expecting us. This is all set, but hang-around time? It's over. You good?"

Charles nods, pats Steve's back. His pulse thrums like a drumline as they stop at Dusty's office.

"Come!" The bark is all they need to hear before Steve grabs the knob and the door swings open.

Dusty looks up, his face breaking into a grin that feels like sunrise.

"Come in! Come in!" His voice booms as he pushes to his feet, belly shifting papers like a tide. His hand extends, big and calloused, the kind that's built empires of asphalt and iron.

Charles grips it first, firm, eyes locked. Intent burns in the silence between them. Steve follows, their handshake a ritual of brothers: knuckles, palms, a squeeze that seals loyalty.

The men take their seats.

Dusty settles back, gaze steady. "So… Mack says you might be interested in joining our merry band of brothers. That a fact?"

Charles nods, no hesitation now,

Dusty's smile deepens. "Excellent. You've been solid. Earned trust. You're good at what you do, and we'd be proud to have you. Probation first, of course—six, maybe eight months. But if things stay smooth, I see no reason you won't be official."

He extends his hand again, and Charles rises, grip iron, eyes locked like tractor beams. No smile—just resolve stamped into his face.

Dusty presses a button on the phone, voice calm but commanding. "Have the men congregate in church." He hangs up, steps around the desk, taps Charles on the arm. "C'mon. Let's make this official."

Steve's fist bumps Charles's forearm, quick and sharp, his whisper slicing through the high of adrenaline: "Yes!"

And just like that, the air changes. The weight of brotherhood settles on Charles's shoulders, heavy and holy. This isn't just a choice. It's a vow.

The two men fall in behind Dusty, the weight of the moment pressing down like the humid air inside the cavernous hall. Footsteps echo in the vast space where laughter and music usually reign. Tonight, it feels different—quieter, heavier, like the walls themselves are holding their breath.

The men pass a rack stacked with tall water bottles, blue plastic gleaming under fluorescent light. Dusty points without slowing, his voice flat, commanding: "Grab a bottle each and follow me." No explanation. No room for questions. Charles obeys, fingers curling around the cool cylinder, the simple act feeling like part of some unspoken ritual.

Ahead looms the steel roll-up door, massive and imposing, its surface painted with the Wicked Ones logo. The snarling emblem seems to watch them approach. Dusty stops, his bulk framed against the metal like a sculpture. His hand hovers over two buttons: one green, one red. He presses green.

The silence shatters into clatter as the chain drive jerks to life, rattling like bones in a steel grave. The door shudders, then begins its ascent, each panel groaning as it folds into the next. The sound ricochets through the hall, a mechanical roar that feels like the prelude to something irreversible. Charles feels it in his chest, a vibration that rubs against his ribs.

When the gap is high enough for passage, Dusty slams the red button. The door halts with a thunderous boom, panels settling like a beast curling back into slumber. Dusty strides forward without a glance, and the men follow, stepping into the night air thick with the scent of oil and dust.

Thirty feet out, under the jaundiced glow of a security lamp, waits a sea-land container. Rust bleeds down its corrugated sides. Dusty reaches into his pocket and produces a key that catches the light before sliding into the padlock. A click and the shackle pops free.

He grips the long handle of the door and with a small grunt, cranks it in a half-circle. Metal protests, hinges scream before surrendering. The right-side door creaks open, darkness spilling out like ink. Dusty swings it wider, revealing a hollow throat of steel that smells of rust and secrets.

"Put those bottles right over there near those other empty ones," Dusty instructs, his finger stabbing toward two lonely bottles resting just inside the threshold. His tone is casual, but the air isn't. It's charged, brimming with something Charles can't name yet. It's a sense that every step forward is a step deeper into trust, and into something far bigger than he imagined.

The men comply, setting the bottles down with heavy, liquid thuds that echo in the steel throat of the container. Charles straightens, eyes sweeping the dim space just as a sudden glow startles the shadows into corners.

A single naked bulb flickers to life overhead, its light caged in a steel dome like a bird trapped behind bars. Charles turns, catching Dusty's hand retreating from a switch near the entrance. Then Dusty grips the door and hauls it shut with a grunt, sealing all three men inside. The clang reverberates like a cannon shot.

Unease grows in Charles's gut. He pivots toward Steve, searching for answers, but Steve only stands there grinning, arms folded, posture loose as if this is all routine. The smile doesn't soothe him—it sharpens the edge of uncertainty.

Charles's gaze darts around, cataloging exits, weapons, anything. A shelf stacked with motor oil. An old tire slumped against rusted steel. Two wooden crates crouch near the far end, their contents hidden except for a single tool handle jutting like a bone. Across from him, a floor jack squats near the wall, its pipe handle screwed tight. Beside it, another shelf sagging under dusty tools: a tire iron, coffee cans brimming with bolts, relics of work long abandoned. His eyes shift back to the tire iron, briefly enough for no one to notice.

Dusty moves deeper into the container, boots grinding sand into steel with reverberating steps.

Charles shifts sideways, giving space but angling closer to that tire iron—just in case. His pulse pounds, a primal drumbeat whispering fight or flight.

Then—a metallic clank detonates behind him. The door screeches open again, spilling in Banks, Jardini, Wheeler, and another face Charles can't see because its owner is still wearing a black, full-faced helmet and no cut. Boots pound and scrape, voices low, and then the last man swings the welded bar across the locking mechanism. Steel bites steel with a brutal finality. The lock drops into its catch, punctuated by a sharp, echoing clank.

Charles freezes. Why would a shipping container lock from the inside? And why is he standing in one with six armed men whose cuts gleam like badges of judgment? His throat tightens. Is this trust—or his casket?

Banks closes the distance, his bulk blotting out the light. Charles edges back, feigning trying to simply get out of Banks' way, until his spine kisses cold metal. The shelf digs into him, coffee cans rattling. His fingers hover inches from the tire iron, every nerve screaming to grab it.

Banks stops close enough for breath to mingle, eyes drilling into Charles's like augers. Seconds stretch into eternity. Then Banks lowers his gaze—not to Charles, but to the tire iron. His hand moves, slow and deliberate, claiming the tool. He straightens, grip firm, stare unbroken. For a heartbeat, Charles braces internally for the swing.

Instead, Banks side-steps left and reaches around behind Charles. His fist clamps the jack handle, yanking the device aside with a screech of metal on metal. A small hole is punched in the steel floor where the jack once squatted, its edges rough-cut with a torch, slag still present. Banks slides the tire iron into the void. It drops halfway, then catches. A twist. A click. The bar sinks deeper, locking into some unseen mechanism.

Banks cranks hard. The sound erupts: thunderous, mechanical, alive. The floor slams downward a solid inch. Charles's knees buckle; his hand snatches the shelf edge to keep from sprawling. His heart jumps against his ribs. What the hell is happening?

The others don't flinch. They smile. They knew. They wanted this.

A groan shivers through the walls as the roof begins to rise, stretching skyward like a steel beast waking from slumber. The container elongates, walls growing tall, shadows warping as the lone bulb shrinks smaller and smaller. It is as though a giant has grabbed the container and it pulling it from the ground. Charles's mind scrambles for logic, but instinct beats it to the punch: he's in an elevator. A massive, hidden elevator containing six armed men who hold his fate in their hands—and he's definitely going down.

The elevator slows, its deep vibration fading into a low mechanical sigh. Then—light erupts. From the far end of the container where the door once stood, brilliance floods upward like a tide, washing the steel walls in stark white. It pours in from below, climbing from the floor to their boots, then to their knees, until the entire space is brightly illuminated.

Charles squints, heart thudding as the descent ends with a smooth, almost elegant stop. He glances up the shaft, craning his neck to trace the steel throat they've traveled. Thirty feet, maybe more. Enough to bury secrets deep.

No words pass between the men. Dusty steps first, onto the polished floor beyond. Steve follows, casual as ever, and Charles moves in their wake, pulse tapping in his ears.

Charles

The hall stretches before him: long, sterile, white as sun-bleached bone. Fluorescent tubes march across the ceiling in perfect rows, their cold light buzzing like electric bees. The air smells faintly of ozone and concrete, clean but lifeless. Their footsteps echo, sharp and hollow, swallowed by the corridor's endless stretch.

At the far end looms a steel sliding door, heavy and industrial, its surface scarred by years of use. The concealed man, that Charles still doesn't know, grips the handle, muscles bunching under leather as he yanks hard. Metal bangs and groans, then yields. The door screeches open to reveal a void of darkness.

They file in, boots silent on the polished floor. Banks reaches for a switch. An audible, industrial solenoid click engages in the silence, followed by a staccato chorus as gymnasium-style gas lights flare to life overhead. Shadows scatter like roaches.

The space is massive—an underground cathedral of steel and concrete. It stretches nearly the size of the hangar above, though the ceiling hovers lower, maybe fifteen feet. No offices line these walls. No toolboxes hum with work. Just raw, open floor, broken by clusters of mystery. Burlap-covered wooden crates crouch like sleeping refugees. Pallets draped in canvas hint at shapes too large to guess.

Vehicles punctuate the emptiness: a dune buggy gleams jewel-bright, pickups squat like predators, motorcycles poised as chrome stallions. Beyond them, the carcasses of machines lie in disarray: a red Porsche gutted of its heart, a silver Mercedes stripped to an empty carcass, its interior a hollow ribcage, its paint pristine.

Against the right wall, a blue rack bristles with motorcycle frames, skeletal silhouettes dangling like trophies.

Beside it, a steel shelf glitters with chrome engines, their polished curves catching the harsh light. Other shelves sag under the weight of parts: seats, tanks, fenders, primaries, handlebars, rims, headlights—a kingdom of speed dismantled and waiting.

The men move deeper. At the far end, double doors rise from the wall: wooden, massive, scarred by time. Banks grips both handles, twists, and wrenches them open in one fluid motion. Beyond lies another darkness.

They vanish inside A switch snaps, and light spills over a conference table vast enough to seat kings, ringed by high-back leather chairs that gleam like thrones. Charles steps forward, instinct pulling him toward the glow; but a hand bars his chest.

The stranger stands firm, arm outstretched like a gate. "Wait here a minute, man," he says, voice calm but edged with command.

Wheeler swings the doors shut, their weight sealing the room with a muffled thud. Silence swallows everything. Charles strains for sound, for whispers, for clues, but the wood is thick, and the secrets thicker.

He glances at the man beside him, who stares outward like a robotic soldier on post, unreadable. Charles follows his eyeless gaze into the vast chamber, eyes climbing the steel staircase that claws up the wall at an angle. It ends at a lone door and a catwalk that runs the length of the room; a spine of steel suspended in air. At the far end, a spiral staircase corkscrews down like a drill into the earth.

The walls are steel plates, cold and gray. No doubt there is poured concrete behind them. The concrete ceiling rides on girders thick as tree trunks. Charles wonders how deep this bunker runs, how long it's been here, and what kind of men build sanctuaries like this. It feels like a fortress. Or a tomb.

The double doors burst open. Banks fills the frame, voice barking like a Pitbull: "Come in!"

The stranger's hand softens, patting Charles's shoulder. "C'mon, man," he says, guiding him forward into the unknown.

Charles stands behind the nearest empty chair, the weight of the moment pressing against his shoulders like a physical force. The room is drenched with silence, thick and expectant. The men sit in a semicircle of authority, their cuts draped across broad backs, patches glaring like silent judges.

Charles lets his gaze sweep the table: a battlefield of decisions, a stage for vows. The stranger slides into the last open seat, posture rigid, masked face forward. All others turn toward Charles, their faces carved from granite, waiting.

Dusty leans forward, forearms braced on the table, voice low but carrying the weight of command. "Charles, we've got a job, and we'd like to enlist your help. It pays well if we can pull it off, but we need skills like yours to do it. We want to know if you're interested in working with us."

Charles nods slowly, absorbing every syllable, the gravity sinking deep.

Dusty's tone hardens, words sharpening like steel. "Now—we've shown you some pretty big secrets tonight. We're already out on the limb of trust with you, and here's the thing: we can't go further unless you're one of us. So, with that being said…" His sentence trails into silence as his hand dips beneath the table.

When it rises, it carries a black leather vest like a relic from some sacred order. Dusty flips it, revealing the back—bare except for a single lower rocker, white background stitched with stark black letters: PROSPECT. No logo. No name. Just the promise of belonging—and the burden of proving it.

Dusty lays the vest on the table with a soft thud that sounds louder than a bottle rocket in the hush. His eyes lock on Charles as he speaks. "We'd like to invite you to prospect for the club. This doesn't mean you're chained to us for life or owe us your firstborn—yet." A ripple of laughter floats through the room, thin but real. "It means you're official on a trial basis. If you decide it's not for you, walk away. If we decide you're not right, we cut ties—no harm, no foul. If you want to give it a shot, put that on and take a seat."

The silence that follows is a living thing, crawling across Charles's skin. He stares at the vest, its leather gleaming like wet paint, and feels the weight of every mile that brought him here. He knows what this means. Brotherhood. Obligation. Blood, maybe. He doesn't want to hesitate too long—hesitation smells like fear. But eagerness reeks of desperation. Balance is everything.

Seconds stretch into lifetimes before his hand moves. Fingers curl around the leather, cool and supple, carrying the scent of oil and newness. He lifts it, the weight heavier than expected, and stands motionless, cut dangling like the condemned.

One by one, his eyes meet theirs. Banks. Jardini. Wheeler. Steve. Dusty and then the stranger, whose eyes he still cannot see. Charles can see his own gaze staring back in the reflection of the visor. Each gaze returns his, steady and unblinking, faces blank but throbbing with something deeper— hope, maybe; or judgment. The room feels frozen, breathless, as if even the air waits for his choice.

Then—motion. Swift, decisive. Charles swings the vest around, arms spearing through the holes, leather sliding across his shoulders like a second skin. It settles with a whisper, and the room exhales as if a dam just broke. Smiles crack stone faces. Steve's grin awakens like sunlight.

Charles drops into the chair, the scrape of rubber wheels on concrete loud in the hush. Steve's hand slams his shoulder, a pat that's half congratulation, half claim. Dusty leans back, satisfaction curling his mouth.

"Alright then! Welcome to the club, Charles." His voice booms, shattering the last shards of tension. "Let's get down to business—because it goes down Friday night."

Chapter 20: June 16th, 1995 – Age 27

It is a gorgeous day, the kind that feels almost staged: sky painted in flawless blue, trees shimmering in lush green whispers.

Sunlight glints off a van's windshield. An arm extends from the driver's side window. Gloved fingers begin punching the digits on a pedestal keypad. A buzzer slices through the calm, sharp and metallic. Ahead, a black iron gate, bars thick as prison steel, groans as it pulls inward. Beyond lies a white concrete driveway, straight and flawless, cutting through a sea of manicured emerald lawn. The grass gleams, freshly cut, blades standing in rigid formation. At the far end, a Victorian mansion rises, pale and proud, its yellow facade glowing like old ivory under the noon sun. Even from here, its size is staggering—a monument to wealth and secrets.

The van glides forward, tires whispering over concrete, until it halts at the walkway leading to the front door. The engine dies. A door creaks open, and a heavy work boot thuds onto the drive, followed by its twin. A rawhide tool belt cinches tight around a waist clad in khaki slacks. The man steps clear, slamming the door shut with a hollow clap that echoes off the mansion's bones.

His shirt is light brown, crisp, stamped with a bold blue C above the word CableCast. A name tag gleams over the right pocket: Floyd. He is perfectly branded as company property. A brown cap shadows his face, its brim embroidered with the same blue insignia. Even the van behind him wears the uniform— brown and tan with a blue logo.

Floyd ascends the steps and presses the doorbell. The chime sings, rich and deep, like notes struck on cathedral brass. Seconds later, the door slowly opens, revealing a man fashioned from etiquette—a tall figure in a tuxedo, skin pale as parchment, eyes cool and distant. His voice drips civility. "Hello. How may I help you?"

The answer is violence. Floyd's arm whips up from his thigh, a spring-loaded lever of flesh and bone driving a flat-tipped screwdriver under the man's chin. The steel bites deep, punching through soft tissue, rupturing vessels in a crimson bloom. It pierces the floor and then the roof of the mouth, shattering bone, then tunnels into the brain with obscene ease.

The man's eyes balloon, pupils expanding in primal terror. Floyd grunts, twisting hard, the handle grinding like a gear as gray matter yields in wet, fibrous chunks. Blood geysers from nostrils, cascading over lips, drools down Floyd's forearm in steaming ribbons. Charles feels the chrome shaft vibrating inside the man's throat, glimpses its gleam through the gaping mouth—a grotesque tongue of steel.

Floyd shoves forward, steering his meat puppet into the foyer. Boots skid on polished marble as he kicks the door shut behind him, heel cracking wood. The man convulses, legs jerking like severed live wires, but Floyd pins him to the wall, muscles corded, breath steady. He wrenches the screwdriver side to side, sawing through cerebrum like carving a roast. The skull's inner sanctum collapses under the assault, and the tuxedoed keeper crumples, sliding boneless down the wall.

Floyd eases the twitching heap to the floor, calm as a coroner laying out a cadaver. He yanks the tool free with a wet pop, gray slurry clinging to the tip, and wipes it on the man's silk lapel. No time to admire the ruin. He rockets toward the kitchen door.

A square window punctuates the door, framing a slice of domestic calm—a chef in immaculate whites, hands dancing over sushi like an artist at canvas. The man hums softly, oblivious, blade flashing in rhythmic cuts. Floyd hesitates, weighing mercy against mission. His gaze flicks to the staircase curling upward like a question mark, then back to the kitchen.

The chef's face fills the glass. Close. Staring. Eyes black and bottomless.

He's been seen. The realization fires off in Floyd's mind like a flare. He clamps his own bloody wrist, feigning agony, and barrels through the swinging door shoulder-first. Stainless steel tables shudder as he ricochets off their edges, his boots skidding, barely clinging to the polished tile.

The kitchen blinds with sterile brightness, the scent of raw fish and vinegar sharp in the air. Floyd staggers toward the sink, breath rapid, water hissing from the faucet as he thrusts his hands beneath the stream. Blood swirls in ribbons, thick and dark, painting the basin in crimson spirals. His sleeves cling to his forearms, sodden and heavy, dripping gore like rain.

He glances back, eyes slicing toward the chef. The man stands frozen, cleaver dangling from his grip, whites immaculate against the bloom of violence. His face is a mask of shock, eyes wide and bulging, lips parted as if words might crawl out but die before birth.

Floyd turns fully, letting the chef drink in the sight of his mangled arms. Their gazes lock—a silent exchange of dread and deception. Then the chef moves, sudden and desperate, charging forward. The cleaver glints—

—Then clatters onto the counter, steel ringing. He seizes Floyd's wrists, his touch gentle, almost tender, guiding them under the torrent.

Blood rinses away in thick ropes, revealing skin inch by inch. The chef's fingers probe, searching for the rupture that spilled such rivers. He finds none. His brows knot, confusion digging trenches across his face. He unbuttons the cuff, peels back the sleeve, eyes scouring for the truth. Nothing. No gash. No puncture. Just flesh, pale and whole beneath the gore.

The chef looks up, and Floyd meets his stare. In that instant, realization blooms in the chef's eyes—a terrible flower of dread. His mouth opens, but no sound escapes.

Floyd's left hand flies up and back down like a guillotine. The cleaver's tip kisses the chef's temple and drives inward with a sickening crunch. Bone splinters, the blade carving through orbital ridge and eye socket, splitting the globe in a gush of vitreous jelly. The heel of the cleaver buries in the bridge of his nose, cleaving cartilage, exposing ivory skull beneath.

Blood erupts, a crimson curtain cascading down his face, pooling at his collar. The chef reels, clawing at the handle now fused with his anatomy. He stumbles, collides with the counter, then lurches forward, a puppet tangled in its own strings.

Floyd snatches the back of his head by the hair, yanks back hard, and slams him face-first onto the steel prep table. The impact drives the blade deeper, metal shrieking against steel and bone. The chef thrashes, strength surging in a final spasm, shoving the table until it skates across the tile with a screech.

Floyd hooks a boot around his ankles, sweeping them out. The man crashes forward, skull meeting floor with a wet, concussive thud. Floyd rides him down, weight crushing, hammering the cleaver deeper into the cranial vault. Blood geysers, thick and plentiful, spreading in a dark halo.

The fight gutters out, leaving only tremors. Floyd rises, breath dragging, and lifts his boot high. It comes down like a piledriver onto the back of the chef's head. Once. Twice. A third time. On the fourth, steel kisses sole—the cleaver's edge severing the skull in a diagonal snap.

The sound is vulgar, a brittle crack followed by the slop of surrender. The cranium splits, halves cleaving apart like broken fruit. Brain matter spills in gelatinous clumps, plopping into the warm, viscous pool spreading across the tile. One half of the skull rocks gently before settling, an empty bowl rimmed in hair and ruin.

Floyd slips from the kitchen like a shadow, boots silently rolling across marble as he cuts through the foyer. The air tastes metallic, thick with the ghost of blood. He mounts the staircase, each step groaning under his weight, and then from somewhere—faint, distant; a tune slithers through the silence.

Mack the Knife. Its jaunty rhythm drips from unseen speakers, a cruel soundtrack to the carnage below. The melody embraces him as he ascends.

Upstairs, the corridor unfurls long and dim, doors punctuating its length like untold stories waiting to be read. Floyd moves slow, deliberate, peering into rooms one by one. Empty. Empty.

There it is. The last door, alone on its own wall. The master bedroom. The door stands slightly ajar, a voyeur's invitation. Steamy fingers curl down the hall, beckoning him closer.

Through the slit, he glimpses a bed dressed in pristine folds; a white house-dress sprawled across the comforter like a discarded soul. He nudges the door wider, head sliding through for a full view. A small, shaded lamp on the nightstand burns low and alone. Silence, save for the music bleeding from beyond.

The door to the master bathroom is half open, light spilling in harsh rectangles across the polished wood of the bedroom floor. Steam boils from the upper frame, carrying the scent of soap, fresh and clean. Water rains against porcelain, a steady percussion beneath the tune. And then—a voice. Soft, lilting, threading through the mist as it hums and sings along, butchering the lyrics.

"Hm hmmm… Sneaking 'round the corner. Could that someone hm hmmm, be Mack the Knife?"

Floyd glides forward and peers through into the misty space. Frosted glass obscures the figure within, but the outline is unmistakable: a woman, curves etched in condensation, hips swaying to the beat.

When her back it turned to him, he slips inside the water closet, lowering onto the commode lid like a silent gargoyle, cloaked in blood.

She moves like memory—hands skating over slick skin, loofah tracing paths across her body. She bends, and the glass fogs deeper, teasing glimpses of flesh that stir ghosts in Floyd's mind. The boy in him aches to look; the man in him wrestles for restraint. He steals fragments—a smooth slice of thigh, the pendulum sway of breasts, then tears his gaze away, shame gnawing at his gut.

Steam thickens, curling around him like smoke from a pyre. The song lilts on, cruel in its cheer. She rinses, arms lifting, silhouette full against the glass. Floyd's chest knots, memory colliding with reality in battle.

The water dies. The door slides open, and time cracks like a mirror. She stands frozen, eyes wide, mouth a cavern of horror. Her scream never comes—only a gasp, thin and brittle, as Clarence "Frog Man" Henry croons from the radio, his famous hit, *I Ain't Got No Home*.

Floyd catches a side-eyed glimpse as the door is slid open. He can't help but to hold it just a moment too long before shame drives his eyes back to the floor in front of him. The woman he once revered, the beacon of grace from the agency, now looms naked and trembling, her body a map of years etched in sagging lines and purple veins. Skin hangs in tired folds, breasts flattened against a ribcage knotted with age. Her hair, stringy and gray, clings to her skull like seaweed. Her face is creased, hollowed, lips worm-thin.

Shame detonates in Floyd's gut. The boy who peeked is dead; the man now sits on a toilet seat, drenched in blood. He turns his head and raises his eyes to meet hers. Emerald brilliance explodes through the mist. Two spirits tangle in a moment that feels endless. She suddenly quivers under the weight of recognition. The song mocks them, jaunty and cruel: Woo-woo-woo-woo-woo-woo-woo-woo.

Like a child, the song taunts Charles with overly joyful lyrics about having a voice and loving to sing.

She moves first. Slowly, trembling, she slides the glass shut with a silent glide, never breaking his gaze until the door fully divides them. Silence dwells.

Then, a voice from behind the glass, frail and splintered: "What do you want, Charles?"

Seconds bleed away.

"What do you want from me?" she pleads, words quivering.

Still, nothing. The radio croons on, merciless.

Finally, defiance sparks. The glass door slides open and her head thrusts through, eyes blazing with brittle courage. "What the hell do you want? Look—take what you want and go! Just get out!"

Charles rises, slow as dawn. She recoils, spine kissing tile. He grips the door, slides it wide in a single, violent motion. She squeezes her eyes shut, teeth grinding, braced for oblivion. Seconds stretch, cruel and compassionless. Nothing comes.

When she dares to look, death wears a strange face—a towel, clean and white, extended like a truce in front of her. Her gaze flickers from cloth to man, confusion rippling through fear.

Charles

The man's head is turned away, eyes averted. She takes the towel, trembling, wraps herself in its cotton hush.

Charles turns his head to lock eyes and steps back, hand still outstretched—a bridge across the gulf of years. She stares, torn between fight and surrender, sanity and madness.

The woman fears she has spent too much time pondering such simple options and reluctantly reaches out to take Charles by the hand. She allows him to assist her as she steps over the edge of the tub. His eyes hold no frenzy, only something deeper, darker, unreadable. He takes her by the arm and puts his other hand on her back to gently nudge her in the direction he would like her to go. They move from the bathroom to the bedroom.

Inside the bedroom, Charles guides the old woman toward the king-sized bed. The silk comforter gleams clean under the lamplight, brown streaked with burgundy threads like dried blood woven into luxury. Above the headboard looms a painting. It is massive, framed in dark wood, its surface a chaos of swirls and strokes. Nothing defined, yet everything suggestive.

Charles pauses, gaze dwelling on the canvas. Earth tones writhe across it, tangled with flesh hues that whisper of bodies, limbs, mouths. The brushwork winds like lovers locked in eternal motion, yin and yang devouring each other.

The woman follows his eyes, turns to look. Her breath catches. Does he want her? Is this the prelude? Her pulse raps against her ribs as Charles steps closer, his shadow swallowing hers. Then—a shove. Gentle, but firm. The backs of her thighs graze the mattress edge. She freezes. He nudges again. Her thighs press harder into silk. She can't move further. His chin dips, eyes narrowing toward the bed. The message is clear.

So, it's not murder. It's rape. Or rape first, then murder. Her stomach knots, bile clawing at her throat. She doesn't fight.

What's the point? She crawls onto the bed, knees sinking into the plush spread, and turns to face him, trembling.

Charles points toward the headboard, expressionless. She looks at it, understands and obeys, crawling like a penitent to the altar, until pillows mound against her chest. He gestures again, insistent. She stretches, spine arching, fingers clutching the top rail. Her mind screams, but her body moves, arranging itself in the posture she imagines he wants. Arms outstretched, head bowed, ready for desecration.

Charles approaches from the side, thighs pressing into the mattress edge near the pillows. His eyes rake her form, lingering on the awkward sprawl of limbs, the towel clinging to her like a last defense. And then—his face changes. Not hunger. Not malice. Something else. His brows lift, lips twitch, and for a heartbeat he looks almost… amused. The kind of look that says: Oh, bless your heart, you delusional little thing, you.

A laugh puffs through his nose—soft, incredulous. His hands shoot upward. In one swift motion, he lifts and yanks the painting from the wall. He stands it on edge between himself and the mattress and with a snap, whips and points his finger to the space where the painting once hung. The woman flinches at the snap, heart stopping, until her gaze settles on the wall in front of her.

A safe. Steel-faced, glaring from its hollow like a fox. The truth slams into her chest. This isn't lust. It's larceny. Relief floods her veins, dizzying, chased by fresh dread.

"I can't believe he would send someone here like this," she mutters, voice brittle, more to herself than to him.

Charles points at the dial, silent as death itself.

"Oh, I can't open that. I don't have the—" Her protest dies as steel whispers free. Charles lifts the box cutter from his belt, blade sliding out with a hiss like a serpent's tongue. He turns it in his hand, studying the edge with unsettling reverence. Light skates along the razor, painting his knuckles in silver. He doesn't look at her. Not once. Just the blade.

Her breath stutters. Moments ago, she welcomed death. Now, absurdly, hope flickers: fragile, trembling. Compliance might buy survival. She spins the dial, fingers jerking in frantic rhythm. Right. Left. Right. Thirty-seven. Twenty-five. Thirty-six. The numbers fall into place like dice on a table. She grips the handle, twists. Metal groans, then yields. The heavy door opens wide, baring its soul.

Stacks of cash leer from the shadows, fat and green. Keys glint. Papers sprawl—wills, bonds, deeds, the architecture of power.

"Take the cash. All of it. Please—just take it and go," she begs, voice cracking under the weight of terror and relief.

Charles doesn't move. His eyes comb the hoard, cold and methodical, until they lock onto a single prize—a padded envelope half buried in the corner. He plucks it free, tears it open, and slides out a black VHS tape, its matte surface swallowing the dim light.

Without a word, he turns from the bed, the tape dangling from his fingers, and strides to the dresser. The portable television squats there, its plastic shell shiny and spotless. Beneath the glass screen of this combination unit is a slot that looks hungry. He powers the unit with a short twist of the knob, the click of contact sharp in the hush. The screen comes to life, slowly fading from black to a square of ghostly light that paints his blood-streaked silhouette in flickering silver.

The tape slides home with a mechanical gulp. Whirring spools devour magnetic ribbon, and the image stutters, then steadies. A thick band of static rolls slowly from top to bottom, mangling any part of the picture it touches.

Shadows dance around Charles's back, his frame rigid, shoulders squared like a soldier awaiting orders. Abigail can't see the screen. His body is a wall, but the glow spills around him, licking the edges of the room in pale fire. She doesn't need to look. She knows what's on that tape.

Her breath falters. Shame drags her gaze to the comforter. Tears well, fat and trembling, clinging to lashes before surrendering to gravity. Her voice crawls out, brittle and raw: "You know what Caleb will do if he gets that back." The words fracture, splintering into silence as sobs threaten to come.

Charles doesn't turn. The tape rolls softly, a serpent whispering secrets into the room. Abigail's pulse rockets, each beat a countdown to ruin. She swallows hard, desperation clawing up her throat. She has to speak. Has to make him understand.

"I, I swear—please—you have to believe me. Listen to me." Her voice spikes, stoked with panic, then crumbles into pleading. "I didn't want this. I didn't ask for any of it." Her fingers clutch the silk like talons, twisting fabric until her knuckles go white.

She drags in air, chest heaving, and words spill in a torrent, frantic and uneven: "I was the one who found Clinton in the study that day—the day he was shot." The confession hangs, vibrating in the charged silence.

The television continues to flicker, casting fractured light across Charles's jaw, hard and unyielding. He doesn't move. He just watches, while behind him Abigail trembles—a woman shackled by guilt, clawing for absolution before the blade of judgment falls.

As Abigail's voice trembles in the present, Charles drifts into the world she conjures—a tableau painted in heat and wealth.

Charles

—

A black limousine glides up a driveway shimmering like obsidian under the morning sun. The asphalt breathes vapor, thin mist curling from its surface as dew surrenders to the rising heat. On either side, lawns stretch in flawless symmetry—bright green seas clipped to military precision, their blades glittering with the last jewels of dawn.

At the crest of the hill, the manor looms—a citadel of opulence willed to existence from stone and pride. Its pale facade blazes against a sky scrubbed clean, a perfect canvas of light blue unmarred by clouds. Columns rise like towers, their shadows slicing across marble steps. The air buzzes with cicadas, their chorus weaving through the hush of privilege.

The limousine exhales to a stop beneath the stone carport, tires whispering against the polished drive. Heat shimmers around its glossy flanks, distorting the world into liquid mirage. Inside, Abigail Kerrington sits poised, draped in sunlight and silk. Her hair is sculpted to perfection, a pale-yellow crochet beret slouched artfully, pinned into waves that gleam like spun gold. A white silk daisy blooms above her ear, a whisper of innocence against the sharp geometry of her style.

Her dress—a secretary's cut in canary yellow, clings with tailored grace, peppered in black polka dots that dance like notes on a score. While the world still stretches in bed, Abigail has been awake for hours, armored in elegance, ready for war disguised as business.

"Is that Caleb's bike?" Her voice cuts the hush, curiosity laced with unease. From the back seat, her eyes spear the silhouette crouched near the steps—a motorcycle, chrome fangs glinting in the sun.

"I do believe so, ma'am," the chauffeur replies, his tone lacquered in deference. He has been awake as long as she— perhaps longer—his face a bust of stoic service.

Abigail's lips purse, thoughts flickering like moths against a lit bulb. "Well… I wonder what brings him here so early." The words drift, half to him, half to the possibilities gathering in her mind.

The chauffeur slips from the car, movements crisp, and circles to the rear door. It swings open with a sigh, and his hand extends a lifeline of etiquette. Abigail accepts, her fingers grazing his glove as she steps into the furnace of morning. Heat licks her calves, silk whispering against her thighs. Still clasping his arm, she pivots as he shuts the door, the thud echoing like perfection in craftsmanship. Together they ascend toward the entrance, dark marble steps radiating warmth through the soles of her shoes.

Her foot kisses the first step—and the world blows up in her face. The door bursts wide, and Caleb erupts from its frame like a shot. Three strides devour the landing; he vaults the remaining stairs in a single leap. Boots slam stone, knees buckling, absorbing shock with predatory grace.

Abigail freezes, breath snagging in her throat. Caleb doesn't glance at her. He doesn't glance at anyone. His trajectory is pure velocity, a storm wrapped in leather. He races toward the bike, sweat stippling his brow. His face—a blanket of mania; gleams with heat and something darker. She knows that look. Has seen it before in him, in his father, in Blake. Rage distilled to its purest form.

"Caleb!?" Her voice cracks, half scold, half plea, ricocheting off stone. He doesn't flinch. Doesn't blink.

He straddles the machine, fingers dancing over chrome, coaxing it awake. His eyes spear hers, fiery and merciless, as his boot hammers the kick starter. The bike wakes into sound—thunder caged in steel, ricocheting through the carport. The air convulses, compression slamming into Abigail's chest with every ignition spark. Heat and noise swallow the morning.

"Caleb! What's going on?" Her words shred against the roar, ribbons lost in the maelstrom.

His scowl doesn't waver. His lips peel back, teeth flashing like a wolf's. He jerks the clutch, slams the gear, and leans into her gaze.

"Call the police." The command is sharp and final.

Then he twists the throttle. The rear tire screams, spitting black rubber pellets as the bike whips in a savage arc. Smoke billows from the rear tire, curling like spirits as Caleb rockets down the drive. The sound: deep, guttural; shreds the morning calm, echoing off manicured walls as he vanishes into the horizon.

Abigail stands frozen in ice, fingers trembling against her chest, lips parted in mute horror. Her eyes claw at the empty road, chasing the phantom of her son. Slowly, mechanically, she pivots toward the chauffeur, seeking confirmation, absolution, anything. His stare mirrors hers: wide, hollow, stunned.

The door remains open behind them, a mouth waiting to spill secrets. Abigail spins, skirts flaring, and bolts for the threshold. The chauffeur jolts, then lunges after her. Together they storm the stairs, shadows snapping at their heels.

The foyer engulfs them, its silence a cathedral of dread. Marble sprawls beneath their feet, polished to a mirror sheen that throws back fractured reflections of their movements. Twin staircases coil upward on either side—curved spines of stone crowned with oak rails thick as tree trunks.

Directly ahead, a copper-plated elevator gleams, its surface sterile against the warm opulence of carved wood and silk draperies. Abigail cuts right, eyes combing the main hall that spears into darkness. The chauffeur mirrors her, scanning left, his posture stiff as steel. They trade glances, necks craning in opposite arcs, confirming what their guts refuse to believe: everything looks normal. Too normal.

"Clinton?" Her voice fractures the stillness, ricocheting off marble and echoing into the void. "Clinton, dear! Are you home?" The words flutter like startled birds, swallowed by the cavernous space. She presses on, tone brittle, desperate to stitch normalcy into the air. "I'm home early. Beatrice fell ill and we had to cancel. Clinton?"

Her heels click like drumsticks as she strides toward the elevator, fingers stabbing the glowing button. A pause. A mechanical sigh. Then the doors part with a whisper, smooth as silk sliding off skin. They step inside, the hush thickening, and ascend into the bosom of privilege.

The doors spread open again, spilling them into a sanctum of wealth—a study dressed in antiquity and arrogance. The ceiling vaults high, cradling twin alabaster chandeliers that drip light like molten pearls. Walls silently complain under the weight of books, their spines cracked with centuries, flanked by busts of forgotten titans glaring from shadowed perches.

At the far end, a portrait looms—a shrine to power rendered in oil and gilt. Abigail and Clinton Kerrington, immortalized in pigment: she seated, he standing rigid behind her, hands resting on her shoulders like manacles disguised as tenderness. Their faces—youthful, flawless, are devoid of joy. Abigail stares at the painting, memory clawing at her ribs, dragging up ghosts of triumphs that taste like ash. What good is empire when love is a myth?

Her gaze sinks, snagging on the mahogany leviathan crouched beneath the painting. The desk sprawls like a beast, its flanks carved in snarling scrollwork, its hide stitched in Italian leather. A brass lamp crowns it, jade shade bleeding green light across a manila envelope. Behind it, a chair looms—high-backed, predatory, turned away like a conspirator shielding plans.

Something primal stirs in her marrow. The hairs on her neck bristle, a silent alarm screaming through her veins. She lunges, skirts threshing, and grips the chair's crown. One savage twist—and the universe implodes.

Clinton spills into view, slumped like a discarded rag doll. His shirt—once white, now a butcher's canvas, clings to rivers of blood flowing from chest to lap. Crimson pools in the leather seat, fat droplets plummeting to the Persian rug below.

Abigail's scream shreds the air, inflamed and serrated, a sound that doesn't belong to language. The chauffeur vaults forward, his breath a gasp, eyes locking on the ruin of Clinton's torso. He wrenches Abigail aside with brutal gentleness, fingers clawing at the shirtfront. Buttons explode like shrapnel, skittering across the desk as silk tears under his assault. Flesh is exposed, pale and slick, a single wound grinning in the sternum—a black mouth vomiting blood.

He shreds the tie from Clinton's throat, hands moving with surgical ferocity. The top button arcs skyward, a tiny comet, before vanishing into shadow. The chauffeur balls the tie, slams it against the wound, crimson soaking through in an instant.

"He's been shot!" The words crack like a whip. "Here—hold this! Press hard! Keep pressure!"

Abigail obeys, fingers trembling as they clamp the sodden silk, her nails carving crescents into her own palms. The chauffeur leans in, teeth clenched, and slides his fingertips to Clinton's neck, just beneath the ear—searching for the fragile drumbeat of life in a house gone silent.

"He's still alive!" The chauffeur's shout ignites in the hush, hopeful and urgent. His fingers clamp the pulse point beneath Clinton's ear, knuckles blanching as he leans in, breath slicing through the tension. His gaze flicks to his wristwatch, lips peeling back in a grimace. "Pulse is weak... blood pressure dropping..." The words spill in clipped fragments, chopped down to save seconds that bleed like lifeblood.

He lunges for the phone, snatching the receiver with a violence born of desperation. His finger crashes hard into the chrome stop as he dials, each rotary spin a scream in the silence. "Nine-one-one," he snaps, when the line clicks alive, voice serious and short. "Gunshot wound. Male. Mid-fifties. Massive blood loss. Send help—now!"

Behind him, Abigail floats in a fog of shock, her body present but her mind splintering into shards of memory. Caleb's face ignites behind her eyes—sweat stippling his brow, panic carved into every line. She sees details now, grotesque in their clarity: the full-fingered leather gloves strangling his hands, the oversized black knit cap slouched on his head like a mask of intent. Summer heat blistered the air, yet he wore winter's armor. Her stomach knots, bile clawing at her throat.

She jerks free of the trance, eyes ricocheting across the study in frantic sweeps. The desk menaces, a battlefield strewn with currency and ink. Stacks of cash leer from the lamplight, flanked by checks sprawled like folded poker hands. An open checkbook speaks, its pages uttering secrets. Documents litter a tray, their faces naked to the world. Vulnerable. Dangerous.

Instinct grabs hold of her. She lunges, fingers clawing at paper, sweeping bills and bonds into her arms with protective urgency. Pages crumple, edges bite her skin, but she doesn't stop. Her breath comes in short bursts, chest heaving as she scours the surface—until her gaze falls on the anomaly.

The envelope. Manila, mute, crouched beneath the jade glow of the antique lamp like a suspect being interrogated. It doesn't belong here; not now. Its silence screams louder than the chaos. Abigail pauses, dread rampaging through her veins. What is this? Why does it feel like a land mine disguised in paper?

She hesitates—a heartbeat, no more; then snatches it, shoving it into the crook of her arm where cash and checks huddle like prisoners of war. Her heels pivot, silk brushing against her calves as she bolts across the study. The clack of her heels against marble echoes. Shadows claw at her skirts, the chandelier's light splintering across her path like shattered glass.

Behind her, the chauffeur's voice ricochets off marble, barking coordinates into the phone, summoning salvation that may already be too late. Abigail doesn't look back. Can't. The weight of secrets drags at her arms, but she clutches harder, fleeing into the labyrinth of hallways as the study exhales its last breath of silence.

—

Charles presses the eject button, the machine exhaling as the tape slides free with a mechanical sigh. He slips it back into the yellow envelope, fingers folding the flap with care. The glow of the television dies, leaving the room steeped in amber lamplight and tension thick enough to taste.

He turns. Abigail is still kneeling at the head of the bed, towel clutched like a shield, her eyes twin pools of terror and pleading. Charles steps toward her, the envelope dangling from his hand like a prognosis. Their gazes lock—hers frantic, his fathomless.

"I didn't know what was on the tape when I found it. I had no part of it, I swear!" Her voice cracks, splintering into the silence.

Charles doesn't speak. His quiet is a hatchet, chipping panic into her bones. Words tumble from her lips, desperate, disjointed, clawing for absolution. She spills secrets like blood, confessions pooling at her knees. Her eyes glisten, her breath stutters, but Charles remains a monolith: listening, absorbing, judging without decree.

When her voice gutters out, the hush swells. Charles moves; not with violence, but with grace, bounding onto the bed in a single fluid motion. She flinches, a strangled gasp lodging in her throat, but he doesn't strike. He slides the envelope into the safe, closes the heavy door and spins the dial, sealing history behind steel. Hi lifts the heavy frame and drops the painting into place, just as he found it. He drops to the floor and without looking back, strides to the door.

"You won't tell anyone, will you?" Her voice is a whimper flayed thin, trembling on the edge of hope. "It's my business... my name."

Charles halts, shadow stretching long across the hall rug. Silence blankets, thick and suffocating. Slowly, he pivots, and the look he gives her is not wrath—it's something softer, sadder. His lips curve into a smile, warm and genuine, a benediction formed in flesh. He lifts a hand, beckoning.

She hesitates, terror shackling her limbs to the mattress, but compliance wins. One knee unfolds, then the other, her feet touch the floor, body trembling as she rises. Each step toward him is a prayer, her fingers strangling the towel tighter with every inch.

When she reaches him, Charles closes the gap, his presence a tide swallowing hers. His hands rise—not fists, but open palms, settling on her shoulders with a tenderness that steals her breath. His eyes hold hers, deep, vivid emerald and steady, and in their depths, she sees no malice. She only sees mercy.

He cradles her face, thumbs brushing the parchment of her cheeks. A tear escapes, silvering down her skin, and he wipes it away with infinite care. His smile lingers, soft as dusk. He leans in, lips grazing her forehead—a kiss that feels like absolution. When he pulls back, his gaze is a promise: peace.

His hand slides to her chin, thumb tracing the fragile seam of her lips. She doesn't resist. Doesn't yield. She simply exists in his grasp, suspended between dread and strange serenity. His other hand ascends, fingertips combing through the wet tangle of her hair, massaging her scalp with a lover's grace. Warmth floods her veins, drowning fear. Her muscles uncoil, breath evening as calm seeps into her marrow. She believes him—not in words, but in touch. Believes that this man, this blood-soaked phantom, means her no harm. Her eyes soften, gratitude flickering like a dying candle.

Charles twists. A single, savage motion cloaked in mercy. Bone snaps—a brittle crack swallowed by silence. Her body folds, collapsing into a heap of towel and flesh at his feet. His face doesn't so much as flinch—until he drops his gaze to the crumple of flesh and towel at his feet. His lips purse and his head wags.

He doesn't linger. He bolts. Doesn't look back as he strides through the doorway, and vanishes into the hush of the house, leaving behind only the echo of tenderness and the chill of inevitability.

Sunlight drenches the estate in molten gold as Charles steps out through the doorway, the silence of the house collapsing behind him like a dying breath. The air outside is warm. It hums with cicadas and is thick with the scent of distant honeysuckle. His boots silently glide across the polished drive, each step deliberate, putting distance between himself and the mansion of mayhem—closing distance between himself and his destiny.

The van crouches at the edge of the circular drive, its brown-and-tan flanks shimmering under the glare. Chrome winks like a signal mirror as Charles grips the handle and swings the door wide. Heat billows from the interior, carrying the faint tang of oil and something darker—something metallic that clings to the back of the throat.

He climbs in, movements smooth, unhurried, and drops into the driver's seat. The vinyl sighs and expels hot air under his weight. His fingers find the ignition; the engine coughs, then settles into a low, throaty hum. Sunlight splashes across the windshield, parting his face into planes of shadow and fire.

Charles reaches for the gearshift, shifts it to reverse then rotates in his seat, twisting at the waist to glance through the rear window as he begins to back down the drive. That's when the familiar tableau sprawls into his view. Floyd lies naked on the steel floor, a hideous still life painted in arterial red. His throat gapes wide, gash sliced deep, blood has flowed into the corrugated grooves and now they brim like gutters after a storm. The van's ridges cradle the gore in neat, glistening channels, sunlight skating across the crimson like stained glass.

Charles faces front again and reaches up to adjust the rearview mirror. The golden watch sways there, its lid gaping open, catching shards of daylight; hypnotic rotations, scattering flecks of brilliance across Charles's face. The chain trembles with each vibration of the idling engine, a pendulum marking time's fragile lines.

Charles doesn't stare too long. His gaze flicks to the road ahead, hands steady on the wheel as the van glides down the serpentine drive, tires whispering over sunbaked concrete. No rush. No panic.

—

Charles

Miles bleed away beneath the wheels, black ribbons curling through fields scorched in summer light. At last, he noses the van to the shoulder before a white colonial home huddled in the heat haze. A ladder leans against a telephone pole, emaciated against the cobalt sky. He kills the engine; silence drops like a stage curtain.

Methodically, he strips away the costume: button-down peeled, boots landing against steel, khakis slithering down his legs. Fabric flutters onto Floyd's contorted mask, veiling death in cotton anonymity. From the passenger seat, jeans wait like a prediction. He slides into them, stiff denim scuffing against skin, then cinches his own boots tight.

Charles swings the door wide, steps into the blaze of daylight, and walks—slow, deliberate, down the road where shadows travel short and sharp, and the summer air holds its tongue. Slowly but surely, the van that entombs Floyd, shrinks out of sight.

His hand rises, fingers curling around the watch's chain. It sways once, twice, before stilling in the palm of his other hand. He studies it, eyes hooded, expression formed by appreciation. Then, with a motion soft as breath, he snaps it shut. The click is a whisper, a guillotine, a door slamming on unseen things.

—

The golden watch sways from the rearview mirror, its lid splayed open, catching shards of halogen, neon and moonlight as the vehicle prowls through the dark. The headlights bore tunnels through blackness, their beams wiping across rusted fences and graffiti-scrawled walls.

A flash of green erupts in the glow—a street sign, glowing like a beacon in the void. Hale Street. Charles flicks the wheel, tires quietly protesting as he turns right. The van glides past boney shadows, and then the warning flares into view:

DEAD END. The letters scream in reflective white, haloed in the high-beam glare of his lamps.

He presses on, slow and deliberate, the narrow street strangled between brick monoliths stacked like blocks. One-story hulks crouch beside five-story giants, their windows boarded in steel and plywood, their faces tattooed in graffiti—angry splashes of color bleeding under the sickly orange glow of sparse streetlights.

Chain-link fences stitch the alleys shut, their diamond claws biting into rusted posts. Gates sag under the weight of padlocks and chains, fat with corrosion, guarding dirt lots littered with hollowed-out machinery and oil stains. The air tastes of iron, earth and old rain, syrupy with the flavor of gasoline.

Charles hooks a left, nosing into an alley that cuts between two brick carcasses. The van's beams rake the walls, igniting shards of broken glass embedded in mortar like monster teeth. He rolls to a stop before a gate, chained tight. He kills the engine, steps out and moves to the lock. It hangs open, a frown carved in iron. He slips it free, lets the chain slither to the ground like a shed serpent skin.

The gate moans as he heaves it wide, hinges shrieking into the night. He slides back into the van, door ajar, and eases through without fully closing it. Once inside the lot, he kills the momentum, hops out, and darts back to drape the chain, loose, restoring the illusion of security.

Ahead, the earth tilts downward, funneling him toward a cement wall that looms like a fortress. Water snarls beyond it, a river gnashing at its chains, its voice a low, eternal growl. Charles cuts the wheel hard, hugging the wall's spine, the van crawling past cadaverous lots and the hunched backs of industrial husks.

Then—the tunnel. A black maw threatening ahead, its throat gagged by another gate. His high beams spear the void, but the darkness swallows them whole, a beast that devours light. He angles the van perpendicular, the sliding door kissing the gate, and kills the engine. It is quiet now, but not silent. The river rages behind the wall with a low rumble, heavy and endlessly rolling.

Charles steps out and moves to the gate. The lock frowns open here too, mocking caution. He unhooks it, drags the gate wide enough to slip himself through, then seals it behind with a lover's care.

The tunnel gulps him down into darkness. After a dozen paces, the last smear of evening light dies, and the black becomes absolute—a void that eats sound and sight. He fishes a flashlight from his vest, thumb flicking the switch. A spear of light stabs forward, but the gloom swallows it, leaving only a pale sword slicing inches ahead. The beam feels finite, its tip blunt and piercing nothing.

The air is damp, rank with mildew and the copper tang of rust. Beneath it slithers another scent—gasoline, faint at first, then swelling with every step. Shadows writhe at the edge of his vision, graffiti ghosts climbing the walls. His boots scuff damp concrete, the sound a muffled echo, strangled by the weight of silence.

Then—the darkness explodes. A light erupts, savage and white-hot, blasting his face in a furnace glare. Heat licks his skin, sears his retinas. He reels, arms snapping up to shield his eyes, breath ripping from his throat.

"Fuck! Good! It's you!" The voice ricochets through the tunnel, short and slapping, riding the echo like a whip crack.

The beam dips, igniting brilliance across the concrete, and shapes congeal from shadow. Charles blinks through the afterimage, vision clawing its way back. Steve materializes, grinning like a wolf in the dark.

"You're a little early," Steve mutters, voice pinging off the tunnel walls like a pebble tossed into a well. His silhouette leans against the chrome spine of his bike, cigarette ember winking in the gloom. He pushes off, boots grabbing traction on the sandy concrete, and strides toward Charles with a grin that doesn't quite mask the tension in his brow. Their handshake snaps like a cap gun, followed by a half-hug that feels more like armor than affection.

Charles fishes a battered cigarette pack from his vest, thumb flicking it open to reveal not tobacco but decompression—a joint, slender and fragrant. He sparks it, flame licking paper, and without tasting the smoke, extends it toward Steve. A peace offering. A ritual. Steve snatches it like a drowning man clutching driftwood, lips sealing around the tip as he drags deep. The ember flares, painting his face in hellfire hues.

He hands the doob back to Charles and exhales slow, a ribbon of gray unraveling into the black, and a sigh hitchhikes on the smoke. "Oh yeah, man..." The words bleed relief. Charles holds the joint out again, and Steve takes it with less urgency this time, greed tempered by calm. Another drag, longer, deeper, his cheeks hollowing as if he's trying to inhale oblivion. He clamps the smoke inside until his eyes bulge, veins crawling his temples, then exhales in a shudder that sounds like surrender.

He passes the stick and his driving thought finally escapes his mouth. "So, you really think you can do this, bro?" His voice is a cheese grater now, sandpapered by doubt and smoke. "You really think you can crack one of those things?"

Charles answers with nothing first, then a slow, deliberate smile, curling like the weed smoke. His hand clamps Steve's shoulder, weighty and warm, a gesture that says more than words: trust me. He passes the joint back, and Steve accepts, reading the message in the motion. Stop thinking. Start breathing.

"It's cool. It's cool, bro. I know you got this." Steve's tone softens, but the tremor lingers. "It's just—the president's in on this one. He's watching close. I just hope it all goes right."

Charles nods, smoke sneaking out and rising from his lips. He knows the stakes. Knows the weight of failure would crush more than bones.

Then the rumble comes. Low at first, a growl slithering through the tunnel's throat. It swells, mutates into thunder, until the concrete vibrates under their boots. Light flickers at the far end, strobing like a heartbeat. Steve snatches his mega-light, thumb stabbing the switch. A blade of brilliance carves the dark, catching motes of dust that whirl like ash in a furnace.

The beast arrives—a Harley, black as midnight sin, its headlamp vomiting fire. The rider kills the engine, but the light lingers, a cyclopean eye glaring through the gloom. He dismounts, boots kissing concrete with steady grace. His helmet—a full-faced monolith, hides everything but menace, mirrored visor swallowing everything. The cut on his back screams allegiance: Wicked Ones. Above the vest pocket, a patch shouts power: PRESIDENT.

He closes the gap, movements fluid, wrapped with authority.

Charles recognizes the helmet, the build, the walk. It's the unknown helmeted man from church.

Then the helmet lifts, and Blake Kerrington exhales into the night—a grin slicing his face, teeth gleaming like ivory knives. The insufferable BMW Blue Man reborn in black steel and leather.

His hand spears forward, clasping Charles's in a grip that feels like a contract signed in blood.

"Hi, Charles. Pleasure to finally officially make your acquaintance." His voice is velvet wrapped around razors. "Heard a lot about you. Glad to have you on the team. Sorry for all the cloak-and-dagger bullshit, but we had to make sure you were solid. You get that, right?"

Charles nods, grip firm, eyes steady. No words needed. Blake's grin widens, animalistic and electric.

"Alright—let's do this."

They turn without question and without hesitation, almost in unison, boots devouring wet grit as they march toward the tunnel's mouth. Their voices braid with the echo, low and lethal.

"If we do this quiet, nobody gets hurt. No matter what—don't touch the old lady. If she gets hurt, someone else bleeds. That's all I'm saying." Blake's tone is an iron crowbar.

Steve grunts. "What about Belvedere and the chink?"

Blake's eyes glitter in the half-light. "Chef doesn't clock in till five. Butler should be dead to the world. We slip in, grab it, fade out. Clean. Simple. Got it?"

"Yeah, bro. Got it." Steve's voice is steadier now, tempered by smoke and resolve.

Charles answers with a nod, thumb stabbing skyward—a silent oath.

Flashlights die as they near the exit, darkness reclaiming its throne. Outside, the van lies in wait. Charles sweeps around the front to the driver's door, metal sighing as locks click free. Blake slides into the passenger seat, spins, and yanks the side door latch for Steve, who's busy chaining the gate with lazy precision.

Steve vaults in, the door still open when Charles guns the engine. The van lunges, tires spitting dust, and Steve stumbles toward the back of the van, laughter barking from his throat. "Easy there, killer."

They tear along the cement spine, the river snarling beyond the wall, then turn sharply into the alley's throat. Steve bails before the van fully halts, boots anchoring into pavement as he wrestles the gate wide. Metal shrieks, chains slither, and the van slides through like a rifle bolt chambering a round. The van comes to a halt. Steve seals the breach, padlock clipping shut with metallic bite, then dives back inside. The door slams, the brake lights wink out, and the van exhales fire from its tailpipe as it rockets up Hale Street.

—

The van ghosts to a halt in the darkest pocket between two streetlights, their sickly halos sputtering against the stone wall that girds Abigail Kerrington's estate. The engine idles low, then dies, leaving silence thick enough to choke on. Heat from the hood bleeds into the night as Charles kills the lights, plunging them into shadow.

Inside, breath feels louder than words. Blake twists in his seat. His voice breaks the hush: "Take this." A transmitter pack and mic dangle from his fist like a lifeline. Steve snatches it, fingers fumbling through the snarl of wires.

"You're not coming in with us?" Steve whispers. The question drips with dread more than curiosity.

Blake's laugh is a short, stubby knife. "Of course not. This is my mother's house. I can't take that kind of chance. I'm here to monitor, make sure nothing burns down—and watch our boy Charles work his magic. I can hear everything. You can't hear me. Whisper if you need to. Got it?"

Steve nods. "Yeah, Blake. We got this. Right, Charles?" His hand claps Charles's shoulder, a gesture that feels like both faith and plea.

Charles answers with a thumb stabbing skyward, his face covered in calm. Steve exhales, drags the mic from his pocket, and tests it with a hissed, "Hello. Hello—"

"Jesus, yes!" Blake snaps, voice cracking through his own earpiece. "Don't eat the mic. Just leave it. It'll pick up fine."

Steve grins sheepishly, nerves fizzing under his skin. "Alright. We good?"

Blake's reply is steel wrapped in resolve: "Do it."

That's all they need. Charles slides into the back, Steve shadowing him. The side door unlatches with a tiny click, gliding open slow, deliberate. They spill into the night, backs pressed to the van's flank, swallowed by the stone wall's shadow. Blake's last command still hums in their ears like a phantom heartbeat. "Do it."

"Okay, bro, here we go," Steve breathes, words barely stirring the air. "Fast walk. No running. Act like you own it. You good?"

Charles nods, eyes steady, and Steve reads the steel in them. "Let's move."

They glide toward the gate, two silhouettes stitched to the dark. Light sand on the almost spotless sidewalk crunches almost silently under their boots, but loud as fireworks in their skulls. The keypad for the gate looms, its buttons glowing faintly. Steve punches the code for the smaller gate, designed for pedestrian traffic—two, five, six, one—each press a sonic siren in the silence. A metallic clank startles, then the hum of magnets surrendering. The latch spits free.

The gate swings open slightly, iron ribs groaning. They slip through, Steve sealing it behind them with a click that sounds like a coffin lid closing. The driveway stretches ahead, pale under the moon, flanked by hedges crouching like chess pieces. Halfway up, the world ignites like a solar flare—security floods erupt, bleaching the yard in brutal white. Shadows flee, leaving them naked and exposed under the glare.

Steve's pulse doubles. Charles doesn't break stride. They walk like kings returning to their castle, eyes scanning windows for ghosts in glass. The house looms, a monolith of stone and secrets, its panes black and blind. Relief trickles in as they mount the steps, swallowed by the porch's shadow.

Steve grips the knob. Locked. His fingers dive into his pocket, fishing out a lone key. It slides into the lower lock like silk, turns with a lover's ease. The knob yields—but the door doesn't. A deadbolt winks above, newer, meaner, its chrome sneering in the porch light. Steve jams the key, metal struggling, noise scraping nerves. He twists left. Nothing. Right. Nothing.

"What the fuck!" His whisper cracks the quiet, sharp enough to make Blake flinch in the van.

Charles taps Steve's arm, calm as midnight. He grips the knob, pulls while twisting the key. It spins left, smooth as oil. A click sighs through the wood. The door gives an inch. Their eyes lock—then they slip inside, shadows melting into deeper dark.

The door seals behind them with a kiss of silence. Security lights die, plunging the foyer into black so thick it feels alive. They flatten against the door. Seconds stretch, long and painful. Then—breath returns, labored and slow. They're in. Undetected.

Charles rolls right, Steve left, eyes slicing through the gloom to the glass slits flanking the door. Outside, the world sleeps under a quilt of shadow. Inside, the house holds its breath, waiting to see what demons have come to call.

They turn slowly, light-starved pupils wide, breathing shallow, their eyes now adjusted to the dim glow spilling from the chandelier above the open foyer. It isn't as pitch black as their floodlight-accosted eyes had thought. The house stretches before them like a sleeping giant, silent except for the relentless ticking of the grandfather clock; each tick a nail driven into their nerves. Beneath it hums the low mechanical breath of the house itself: refrigerators murmuring, vents exhaling warmth, unseen systems pulsing like veins beneath plaster and wood. It sounds normal. Too normal. And yet every squeak of their boots on polished floors feels like a mortar round.

Steve tucks his chin close to his right shoulder, voice barely a thread of sound. "We're inside. Everything's cool," he whispers for Blake's benefit, though his own pulse beats like a speedbag. He taps Charles on the thigh, a quick signal, and motions him forward.

They move toward the kitchen door on the far side of the foyer, steps slow, deliberate, like men crossing a frozen lake. Halfway across, the silence shatters into a million little pieces. A single high-pitched beep slices through the air from a small panel near the front door. Both men whip around, horror plastered across their faces as a red light begins to flash like a warning eye. An alarm system. The realization slams into Steve's skull like a brick.

Another shrieking beep emits before they can react, louder this time, urgent. Steve lunges toward the panel, heart ricocheting against his ribs. The display glows, cold and clinical, counting down seconds like a fuse burning toward obliteration. Twenty. Nineteen.

"What the fuck?" Steve whisper-yells, voice saturated with panic. "Nobody said anything about any goddamned alarm system!"

Inside the van, Blake's voice erupts. "What the fuck?" His scream feels like it could wake the dead. Nobody but Blake hears it—his own voice returning from the inner walls of the van and slamming his eardrums.

288

Charles doesn't hesitate. He shoves Steve aside, muscles flexed tight, and plants himself before the panel. His fingers fly, punching in digits—two, five, six, one. The machine answers with another shrill beep and a merciless subtraction of five seconds. Thirteen now. The red light pulses like a heartbeat gone berserk.

Charles snarls under his breath, stabs the asterisk key. The speaker emits a longer, piercing tone that seems to turn the remaining silence into confetti. When it dies, the red light surrenders to green. The display blinks: DISARMED.

Both men exhale elated breaths, relief flooding their limbs like morphine. They spin, scanning the room, ears straining for footsteps, voices, anything. The house holds its breath. They wait. They listen.

Blake waits too, alone in the van, every nerve wired to the silence.

Grandfather's ticking resumes its tyranny. The hum of the house returns, steady and indifferent, but Charles and Steve remain statues, frozen in an expanse of dread. Seconds crawl. Their heart rates decelerate by degrees, though adrenaline still flows in their veins. One minute. Two. Finally, they move, slow as shadows at dusk, toward the staircase. The kitchen is forgotten now—irrelevant. The stairs loom now like a ladder to doom.

At the foot of the steps, Charles veers off, curiosity victorious over fear. He peers into the family room, its vastness sprawling like a museum after midnight. Antique furniture hunkers in pits of shadow, glass cabinets glint with relics that whisper of wealth and age. No movement. No sound. He returns, and together they climb.

Each step groans faintly beneath their weight, a treacherous confession. At the landing, Charles halts, indecision flickering across his face. Left, or right? Steve gestures sharply, a silent command, and cuts left. Charles let's Steve lead and feigns being unfamiliar with the layout.

"Blake says it's in the master bedroom at the end," Steve breathes, voice barely audible.

Charles nods, falls in behind him. They float across the carpeted landing, the great foyer unrolling below like a black ocean. Calm begins to seep back into their bones.

—until the grandfather clock erupts.

The chime rings out like a church bell, flooding the house with sound, rolling up walls and crashing against the ceiling. Not one chime, but the full Westminster melody, each note a mallet blow. Steve freezes mid-step, nostrils flaring, head sagging and shaking in disbelief and defeat. Charles touches his shoulder, urgency blazing in his eyes. One hand signals forward, the other toggles between cupping his ear and stabbing a finger toward the foyer, toward the sonic storm.

Steve understands. They move, swift and silent, using the clock's thunder as cover, masking the treacherous whispers of the floor beneath their boots. The hallway stretches like a freight car toward the master bedroom door, shut tight, holding secrets behind its skin.

The two men huddle outside Abigail's door, shadows pressed against the wall. Steve reaches into his vest pocket, fingers brushing metal, and withdraws a black bandana and a silver whiskey flask. The cap loosens with a metallic whisper. Charles flinches. Even that tiny scrape feels deafening here. The grandfather clock tolls its first chime, a low bronze moan that rolls down the hallway like distant thunder.

Steve bundles the bandana and flask in his left hand, turns the knob with his right, slow as molasses. The second chime strikes, vibrating through the bones of the house. Charles catches a sudden whiff—sweet, pungent, almost floral yet sickly, from the flask. His stomach knots. He jerks his head aside, expelling air through nose and mouth in a sharp huff, as if the odor itself could betray them. Steve notices, eyes widening, and lowers the flask with a silent apology, mouthed in the dim glow. Charles waves him on, urgency drawn in every line of his posture. The hallway feels tighter now, air thick with that syrupy scent. The third chime lands like a hammer blow, reverberating until the silence returns.

Steve cracks the door. Darkness feeds beyond, swallowing the sliver of light. He pushes farther, head and shoulder slipping through. Inside, the blackness is almost tactile, pressing against his skin. A faint green glow leaks from a nightstand clock, painting part of the bed in alien-light. A hump under the comforter protrudes like a shallow grave. Steve slides into the room, Charles close behind, leaving the door ajar to sip what little light the hall offers.

—

Outside, Blake sits cocooned in the van's darkness, the world outside muffled. His ears catch fragments: wind fingering the side panels, the occasional tick of cooling metal, but mostly, there is silence. His mind drifts, restless, until something gleams in the corner of his vision: the ornate golden watch dangling from the rearview mirror.

He reaches up, fingers brushing the cool chain, and lifts it free. The weight surprises him—dense, deliberate, like it carries more than gears and springs. He cradles it in his palm, the metal warm from the van's breath, and tilts it toward the faint streetlight glow. The craftsmanship is exquisite: filigree etched in curling patterns, a case that whispers of centuries past. The lid gapes open, revealing a face frozen in perfection. Both hands point to twelve, locked in eternal midnight. They do not move.

Blake frowns, instinctively glancing at his own wristwatch. The times clash like dueling truths. He flips the golden piece over, hunting for a winding stem, a battery hatch—anything. Nothing. Just seamless gold.

"Nah," he mutters to himself, voice rough in the hush. "Looks too old to use batteries." He turns it again, studying every curve, every tiny groove, as if the metal might whisper its secrets.

On impulse, he closes the lid. The click is soft, intimate, like the closing of an eye, yet it seems to reverberate with an inexplicable volume in this van. In his hand, the watch feels different now: complete, solid, almost alive. It fits his palm like it belongs there, like it knows him. Desire flickers in his chest, sharp and guilty. He wants this thing. Wants it bad. But he won't steal from a brother. He can't. He tells himself that twice, maybe three times, gripping the watch as if the thought alone might brand him.

His thumb grazes the casing, searching, pressing, until it finds a subtle notch—a hidden latch triggered by a tiny inlaid gem. He squeezes. The lid springs open with a delicate snap, and Blake's breath catches. The hands have moved. No longer at twelve. They now stand at two minutes past three.

"Oh wow," he whispers, awe threading through the words. Then louder, a laugh edged with disbelief: "Well I'll be a pig in shit. Would you look at that?"

He stares, mind spinning like the watch's gears must have. How? He closes it again, waits, then pops it open. Still 3:02. The hands have stopped once more, frozen like before. He hangs it back on the mirror, leaving it open, and watches it sway—gold catching faint light, spinning lazy circles like a pendulum of mystery.

Minutes drip by. Blake studies the stillness of the watch's hands, brain clawing for logic. Near as he can figure, the watch hides its motion, conserving energy, winding itself when the lid shuts. Maybe it tracks real time in its guts, revealing truth only when summoned. Maybe the hands stop to save strength. Or maybe it's magic. He almost laughs at that, but the sound dies in his throat. At this hour, with nerves frayed and shadows thick, magic doesn't feel impossible.

Eventually, he settles on a theory—half-baked, but good enough, and lets the watch dangle, hypnotic in its slow spin. Outside, the night presses close, and Blake sits alone with the deafening silence, the weight of gold, and a question that stirs like static in his skull.

—

Inside the room, the air feels heavier, as if the walls themselves are squeezing in and compressing it. Charles and Steve creep toward the bed. The mound beneath the comforter crests like a sleeping form, and for a heartbeat, both men brace for movement. But when they draw close, the truth is revealed. The hump is nothing but tangled fabric, a comforter thrown in careless abandon. The bed is unmade, chaotic, as though someone rose in haste and never returned.

Their eyes sweep the room, adjusting to the gloom. Shadows cling to corners, stretching long fingers across the floor. The bathroom door stands open, black as a cave, its light dead. Steve moves toward it. He slips inside, breath shallow, and flicks his gaze across porcelain and tile. Empty. No steam, no scent of soap—just sterile silence. He retreats, tension yanking tighter in his gut.

The closet door stands shut. Steve hesitates, instincts prickling. Before he acts, he drops to one knee, pressing his cheek to the carpet, peering into the darkness beneath the bed. Nothing but dust and darkness. He rises, jaw clenched, and grips the closet knob. Metal chills his palm. He's about to twist when

Charles lifts a single finger—a silent command telegraphed through the quiet.

Charles leans over the bed, fingers grazing the exposed sheet. Cold. Lifeless. No lingering warmth of a body. He flashes a thumbs-up, and Steve exhales, tension bleeding out in a sigh. Still, his eyes linger on the knob, suspicion gnawing. He turns it slow, the mechanism smooth and silent, then yanks the door wide in a sudden burst.

Nothing moves.

Light explodes as Steve finds the switch, flooding the walk-in closet with fluorescent brilliance. Racks of clothes hang in rigid rows, shoes aligned like cars in a showroom. No movement. No sound. Just the hollow echo of their own breathing. He leaves the door ajar, letting the glow spill into the bedroom, a light shield against the dark. They dare not touch the main light—too risky, too visible from outside.

Steve vaults, dirty boots grinding against fine linens as he climbs onto the bed without ceremony. The mattress dips under his weight, fibers groaning in protest. He plants himself before the wall, where a framed picture is mounted like a guardian. With deliberate care, he lifts it free, muscles mildly taxed by the weight of the piece, and props it against the headboard. Behind it, the safe waits, a square of steel embedded in plaster like a cold, dead heart.

"She's not here," Steve mutters, voice low but firm, feeding Blake's ear through the mic.

He glances back at Charles, grin flickering like a match in the dark. "What's up, bro? You ready to do your thing or what?" His whisper carries a charge, a dare. He gestures toward the safe with a flourish, game-show grandiose, like Vanna White unveiling fortune.

Charles steps up, boots sinking deep into the mattress, and slides a hand into his vest pocket. When it emerges, steel glints—a stethoscope, coiled like a centipede. Steve's brows lift, amusement tugging at his mouth. He hops down, arms folding across his chest, posture loose but eyes sharp, ready to watch the performance.

"There he goes," Steve murmurs into the mic, voice a thread of sound. "He's gonna try to crack it."

In the van, Blake hears every syllable, the words dripping into his ears like essential oil.

Charles stands on the mattress before the wall safe, its steel face glaring back like a challenge. The air feels electric now, charged with expectation. He spins the dial to the right, fast at first, then slows to a crawl, each tick a tiny heartbeat in the silence. The stethoscope's cold metal kisses the safe, its twin earpieces feeding him nothing but hollow jargon. He tilts his head, feigning concentration, eyes narrowing as though deciphering foreign language buried in the tumblers.

He drags the dial forward, a digit at a time, milking the moment for all it's worth. Sweat beads at his temple, though not from effort—from performance. He doesn't know how long a real pro would take, but too quick would raise questions. Better to look clumsy than clairvoyant. Click. The dial lands on thirty-seven. He freezes, releases the knob, and flicks a glance at Steve. Steve answers with a sharp nod, brows lifted in silent query. Charles flashes a thumb, then wipes his fingertips on his pant legs. He wiggles his fingers theatrically before gripping the dial again, turning left now, slow as cold maple syrup. Each tick mark clicks under his touch. He wonders—what would he even listen for if he were legit? The stethoscope resounds with nothing but the hollow throb of his own pulse. He stops at twenty-five, ears straining, hearing nothing but the blood in his head. Another glance at Steve, then back to the dial. No time to linger. He spins right again, the wheel groaning softly as numbers blur past. The distance feels endless, a desert of digits stretching toward thirty-six.

Finally, he halts, breath pausing. His hand slides to the handle and he looks at Steve, eyes locking. He twists hard. The handle refuses, rigid as bone. Charles rattles it, metal clapping back in protest. Nothing.

"Fuck!" Steve hisses, cracking the hush. "The fuck, bro? I thought you said you could crack this shit!"

In the van, Blake explodes, words spitting like sparks: "Fuck! I knew this was too good to be true!"

Charles lifts a finger—wait. Then presses it to his lips—silence. His other hand floats, palm down, soothing the air like ripples on water. Calm down. Give me a minute. He resets, spinning the dial twice to the right, faster now, urgency clawing at his spine. He lands on thirty-seven without flourish, no theatrics this time. Left to twenty-five, smooth and sure. Then right again, the final stretch, numbers ticking like a countdown in his skull. Thirty-five. He stops. His hand clamps the handle, knuckles whitening. He stares at it, willing steel to surrender.

For a breath, he holds, milking suspense like blood from a stone. Then he twists, hard, every tendon firing at once. The handle gives—a sudden, glorious yield, and the door cracks open with a sigh like a tomb unsealed.

Steve exhales a laugh, relief filling in his chest. "Fuckin' A, man! Holy shit!" His whisper bursts into a grin, eyes wide, teeth flashing. "You actually cracked that shit, bro!" He chuckles, giddy, the sound bubbling up like champagne. "I mean, I knew you could do this kind of shit and shit, bro, but... Wow! Nice fuckin' work!"

In the van, Blake slumps low, breath spilling out in a long, shaky stream. For now, the night feels merciful.

Charles walks across the bed to its foot and hops down. He leaves the safe door cracked, granting Steve the honor of unveiling its contents. Steve doesn't hesitate. He springs up, muscles excited, and swings the door wide with a metallic groan. Inside, shadows cling to stacks of wealth—bundles of cash, glittering jewelry, papers curled like scrolls. But Steve's eyes lock on the prize: a manila envelope, dull and unassuming, yet pulsing with promise.

His hand darts in, fingers grazing cold steel before clutching the envelope. He tears it open just enough to glimpse the contents—a video cassette. Relief floods in his chest. "We got it," he breathes, voice trembling with victory, feeding Blake's ear through the mic like a lifeline.

The tape vanishes into the waistband at his back, snug against his spine like contraband. No time to savor the win. Steve snatches a pillow, rips its case free and begins sweeping the safe clean. Cash rains into the sack, crisp bills falling like dry leaves. Jewelry clinks. Documents slide in, their edges biting his knuckles as they topple. He works fast, feverish, until the safe is gutted, hollow as a corpse. He spins the bag's heavy bottom, twisting it shut like a tourniquet, then slams the safe door and spins the dial, erasing their fingerprints from fate.

He hops down, breath barely controlled, adrenaline clawing at his ribs. "Can you put that back up, bro?" he mutters, jerking his chin toward the painting. Charles complies, lifting the frame with reverent care, restoring the illusion of untouched wealth. Together, they slip from the room, shadows gliding through the hall. The landing calls ahead, carpet muffling their steps as they descend the staircase, each creak a brain-punch in their skulls.

At the bottom, freedom, in the form of a front door, approaches. Charles halts abruptly, fingers clamping Steve's arm like a vise. His chin tilts toward the kitchen. Through the small square window, a dim glow bleeds like a dying ember.

"That wasn't on when we came in," Steve whispers, voice as squeezed and airless as possible. His mind races, gears grind. "Butler's quarters are off the kitchen. He's probably just up getting a late-night snack or something."

They trade a glance, heavy with dread. Every instinct screams to bolt, to vanish into the night, but loose ends can strangle. Steve creeps forward, Charles shadowing him. The window looms, glass slick with reflections. A flicker. A flash of movement slashes across the pane. A figure glides past, pale and silent, heading toward the butler's quarters.

They surge forward, closing the gap. Steve peers in just as the figure reaches the switch. A hand flicks. Darkness swallows the kitchen. The door to the quarters clicks shut, sealing answers behind its grain. Steve stares, eyes wide, seeing only his own ghost in the glass now. But in that last sliver of light, he swears he saw a white nightgown trailing like mist.

"No," he mutters, voice cracking. "Couldn't be."

Charles taps his shoulder, silent inquiry etched in the lift of his chin. Steve scratches his head, words tumbling like stones. "I dunno, bro. I think the butler wears ladies' clothes." His gaze drops, thoughts grinding like gears stripped round. "It's either that or..." He chokes the rest, dread curdling in his gut.

They lock eyes, a silent pact; for Blake's sake, for their own, they turn away, feet dragging toward the front door.

—

Outside, the night air welcomes them back, grass slick with dew under their boots as they move. Twenty paces in, security lights erupt. Shadows leap like startled beasts. They don't flinch or falter. They march on, Steve hurling the bulging pillowcase over the wall with a grunt. It lands with a dull thud next to the van, hidden from view of anyone not standing right there.

The gate waits, iron ribs gleaming. No code, no barrier— just a knob. Charles twists. Freedom sings open. They slip through, casual as deed holders, and pad toward the van.

At the curb, Steve snatches the loot while Charles slides the side door open, its rails gliding silently on oiled ball bearings. They climb in. Charles eases the door almost shut, leaving the latch undone, a promise of quick escape.

No words. None needed. Charles crawls between the seats, fingers curling around the wheel like talons. The keys wait, halfway into the ignition. He finishes the insert and twists. The engine coughs, then purrs. Gear engages with a muted clunk. The van rolls, slow and spectral, headlights flaring only after they've drifted a dozen feet into oblivion.

They glide through the sleeping neighborhood, eyes raking windows for signs of life. Curtains hang limp. Lawns sprawl in innocence. Peace hums like a lullaby, mocking the chaos in their veins. At last, Steve slides the door open a tad, air knifing in, then slams it shut hard.

It isn't until the van has swallowed a mile of darkness that Blake finally moves. Silent as a shark, he pivots in his seat and snatches the pillowcase from the floor. His fingers claw into the fabric, rifling through its swollen belly with frantic urgency. Jewelry clinks like brittle bones. Paper rasps against paper. Cash whispers in hollow promises. But the weight he seeks—the sacred prize, is absent.

"Where's the tape?" His voice disturbs the calm that has just begun to settle in, panic threading every syllable.

Steve jerks, eyes wide, then slaps his own waistband with a curse. "Oh shit, bro." His hand dives behind him, fishing out the manila envelope like a magician pulling salvation from a hat. "Here you go."

Blake seizes it, clutching the envelope to his chest as though it were a newborn torn from fire. His chin drops hard, locking the package against his sternum. Relief blasts through his veins, flooding him with heat. Nothing else matters—not the cash, not the jewels, not the paper wealth rattling in the sack. This is the heartbeat of the night. This is everything.

He exhales a laugh, maniacal and genuinely joyous, breaking the ice like a chisel through glass. "Christ almighty," he blurts, voice pitching high with giddy disbelief. "I really didn't think this was going to work out, but I'll be dipped if you didn't pull it off, you sons of bitches!"

For a moment, silence hangs. Then Steve erupts, laughter spilling like shrapnel, words tumbling in a fevered rush. He rehashes every beat of the heist, voice crackling with adrenaline, painting the air with snapshots of chaos and triumph. Charles grins in the rearview, lips twitching as tension bleeds out like poison drained from a wound. The van becomes a cocoon of victory, laughter ricocheting off steel walls, their relief a living thing clawing for space.

Outside, the night sprawls in velvet silence and the drone of tires devouring asphalt. Streetlights flicker past like dying stars. Shadows hide between houses, watching, waiting. But inside, the men ride high on the aftershock, nerves jangling like struck wires.

—

Back on Hale Street, the mill looms—brick ribs jutting against the sky, windows black, blind eyes. Charles noses the van toward the alley gate. This time, Blake leaps out before the wheels stop turning, boots pounding pavement, hands gripping cold iron. He heaves the gate wide, metal shrieking. The van crawls through, passenger door wide open. Blake slams the gate shut, loose and lazy, then vaults back inside.

They descend the incline, tires crunching. The sound bounces back off the river wall. The tunnel awaits ahead. Charles steers slow, deliberate, until the van kisses the same patch of shadow it claimed hours before. Engine idle fades to a purr and then silence. Doors snap open—Steve sliding the side door with an oiled, metallic quickness, Blake flinging his own wide. Both men spill out like wolves freed from a cage.

"Alright," Blake barks through the still open door, voice sharp with command yet warm with triumph. "Get this thing back to wherever you got it, and we'll meet you at the clubhouse." He leans in, eyes locking on Charles, gloved hand smacking the van's flank twice. "You done good, Charles. I appreciate it. It won't go unrewarded, and I want you to know that. Thank you."

Charles absorbs the words in silence, humility etched in the slope of his shoulders. He lifts a thumb, a gesture small yet heavy with meaning. No speeches. No bravado. Just acknowledgment.

Steve and Blake vanish into the tunnel's gaping maw, shadows swallowing their forms. Charles watches until they vanish, then twists the key. He rolls the van in a tight semi-circle, tires almost kissing the river wall, and creeps toward the alley mouth.

Then—a sound. Tiny. Alien. A high-pitched chatter threading through the quilt of silence. Charles stiffens, ears straining. It's not metal squeaking or tires whispering. It's something else. Something unusual.

He brakes, the van sighing to stillness. The noise persists, faint and intermittent, like voices too small for human throats. He kills the engine. The hush slams down, heavy as a coffin lid—except for that sound. That damned sound.

Charles leans right, following the tiny phantom with his ears. It dances, elusive, teasing him with fragments. He gropes the floor, blind fingers sweeping cold steel and grit, until they snag something. It's the headset; Blake's headphones. The receiver pack clings to them like a parasite. He pulls the tangle from beneath the passenger seat.

Charles lifts the earpiece, presses it to his ear. Static crackles, then a voice bleeds through—Steve's voice, distant yet sharp, riding the invisible highway of radio waves. The chatter wasn't tiny aliens. It was men. It was the echo of their own sins whispering back from the dark. Steve still has the transmitter.

"…Stand-up guy," is all Charles catches at first, Steve's voice bleeding through the static as he presses the headset tight against his ear. The words crackle like embers, followed by the low thrum of footsteps echoing in the tunnel. He adjusts the earpiece, leaning forward instinctively, as if proximity could sharpen sound. The stethoscope is tucked away, but now the night has given him a new instrument—a wire into their world.

"I'm telling you," Steve continues, breath catching up with feet, vest fabric rasping against the mic with every stride. "I stood right there and watched him do it. No tricks. No help from anyone. He cracked it old school, stethoscope and everything. It was legit."

Charles exhales slow, nostrils flaring, the compliment sliding into his ears like warm liquor down a throat. Through the headset, the tunnel breathes; swallowing voices, amplifying every scuff of boots, every scrape of leather. He can hear their lungs working, the rhythm of exertion, the faint metallic clink of gear shifting against zippers.

"Well, he definitely did us a solid," Blake's voice cuts in, deeper, edged with authority. "And I can't deny the results. I don't know where you found this kid, but he's good. I have to admit it."

Charles smirks in the dark, lips widening as pride grows in his chest.

"Yeah, bro," Steve fires back, excitement sparking like flint. "I think he's gonna be great for the club. We should think about patching him in a little early—secure our goldmine."

Charles chuckles under his breath, a puff of air escaping like steam. Goldmine. If only they knew.

Blake ignores the bait, his tone turning sharp. "So, the old lady wasn't home?"

"I dunno, bro." Steve's voice wavers, a tremor threading through bravado. "I didn't look in the garage—probably should have. All I'm saying is she wasn't in her bed when we got there, and I didn't need to use the juice on her." A pause, then a stammer: "Does she ever... sometimes sleep downstairs in the butler's quarters? You know, like when he's not there and shit?"

Blake's reply pops like a balloon. "Why? What do you mean? Did you see something?" His words tumble fast, sharp, like a man cornered.

"Naw, naw, naw, man!" Steve blurts, panic fraying his edges. "I didn't see nothin'. I'm just trying to figure out where she might've been if not in her own bed, you know?"

Silence floods the channel like wet concrete. Charles can feel it pressing against his skull, the weight of unspoken thoughts grinding like gears.

Steve claws for escape, voice pitching high. "So, what's in the package that's so important anyway? I mean, you passed up a bag of cash, jewelry, and valuable documents to single out that package. What's in it, if you don't mind me asking?"

Blake's tone drops to ice. "I do mind you asking. Let's just say it's a very sentimental home video and leave it at that."

Charles huffs through his nose, a single sharp exhale. Sentimental. Sure.

Steve presses on, desperation bleeding through. "So, what was this, like another test or something? I mean, couldn't you just call your mother and ask her for the home video? Were you just making sure of Charles?"

The reply doesn't come from Blake. It doesn't come from Steve. It slithers through the static like a razorblade through silk—a new voice, venomous and cold—a snarky mimic.

"NO! Blakey COULDN'T just call and ask for his home video because he was too ashamed to just call and ask for his precious home video. Weren't you, Blakey?"

Charles stiffens, pulse louder in his ears than the transmission. He cups the headset tighter, pressing it hard, as if force could drag clarity from chaos. That voice—alien, sharp, dripping malice, doesn't belong to either man he left behind. He leans forward more, breath shallow, every nerve strung tight.

"Why don't you go ahead and toss that bag over here, Blakey," the stranger purrs, menace embroiled in every syllable. "Thanks for picking it up for me—and thanks for not hurting Mom in the process, you stupid fuck."

A beat of silence. Then a thud reverberates through the channel—the pillowcase hitting concrete, a sack of sins surrendered.

"Go pick that up," the voice commands, tone snapping like a whip.

Footsteps shuffle, boots grinding sand. Charles strains, muscles locked, as the drama unfolds in his ear like a play staged in hell.

Blake's voice erupts, brittle with defiance. "What are you going to do now, Caleb? Kill me?"

Caleb. The name slams into Charles like a brick.

A laugh answers: low, serrated, crawling with contempt. "Fuck no, I'm not going to kill you, Blakey. That'd be too easy." A pause, then venom drips slow: "I'm just going to kill your entire charmed fucking life. Show the world what pieces of shit you and Dad are, and let karma take care of your stupid asses for me."

"You know Mom's going to hate you for this," Blake spits.

Caleb snorts, derision thick as tar. "Yeah, well, Mom always did like you best anyway, so no big loss there. You're lucky she found the tape before the cops did."

"Well, maybe if you didn't try to kill Dad and let the cat out of the bag…" Blake starts, words edged.

Caleb slices him off mid-sentence, voice a machete. "Dad is a sick man. And the nut didn't fall far from the tree with you. He deserves worse than what he got. He got off lucky. I fucked up. It won't happen again. I promise you."

Blake fires back, venom for venom. "You're just as sick—and you were all about the family business until you got all wet and tender like a vagina on us and walked away."

Caleb's snarl rips through the static. "No! I grew up and realized what we were doing is wrong. I didn't know when I was a kid, but I grew up, you piece of shit."

"Oh, bullshit!" Blake roars, rage boiling over. "You were nineteen fucking years old when you left—and it wasn't until right after Dad put me in charge. You just couldn't stand that I was running the show. You acted like a jealous baby and stormed off. I know it and you know it, so don't go acting all righteous on me now. You know what you've done."

Silence waits, deep and dangerous. Then Caleb's voice snaps, sharp as applause. "Why am I wasting time trading snide remarks with you anyway? You're in charge of two things right now, bucko—Jack and shit. And Jack just left town." A pause, just long enough for Caleb to appreciate his own humor. "We're going to do things a little differently this time, brother. You and Father Dearest are both going to get what you have coming."

Charles hears grinding sounds, boots shifting on concrete, and then Caleb's voice rips through the static like Velcro. "Vaccaro, Calnan! —" The words crackle, sharp and commanding. "—Take this to Local Twenty-Two. Keep it under the limit and make sure it gets there. Put it directly in the hands of a reporter. Have them make a copy for themselves—and I want this original back. Understood?"

Responses tumble in, clipped and obedient.

"Got it, boss," Calnan barks.

"No problem. On it, bro," Vaccaro adds, voices fading into the hollow echo of the tunnel.

"Go now," Caleb snaps, final and absolute.

Charles listens as footsteps scatter like marbles across concrete, then fade into distance. Silence creeps in again, long and torturous—until Blake's voice fractures it. "So now what?"

Caleb's reply drips acid. "So now you idiots should probably head on down the tunnel and tend to your disabled bikes while we walk the fuck out of here. And maybe while you're doing it, you should each thank your lucky fucking stars you haven't taken a slug to the back of your head yet."

Charles doesn't wait for more. His pulse rockets. He slams the shifter into drive, tires spitting asphalt and rubber pills as the van lunges forward. Hale Street unspools in a blur of shadow and sodium glow. The van leans hard, tires shrieking as he rips the corner onto the main drag. He floors it. The transmission downshifts with a guttural snarl, and the van rockets ahead, pinning him against the seat like a fist.

———

The cargo van devours twenty minutes of blacktop, its engine howling through the serpentine road. Trees loom like mythological monsters, their crooked arms clawing at the night sky. Wind lashes the mirrors, carrying whispers of leaves. Charles grips the wheel, knuckles whitening, eyes slicing through darkness as paranoia gnaws at his spine. Every bend feels like a trap. Every shadow, a reaper.

Finally, floodlights bloom ahead—a lonely outpost perched atop the hill, glowing like a campfire in the wilderness. Chain-link fencing girdles the small building, its crown bristling with barbed wire. Satellite dishes jut from the roof and the nearby tower, their faces tilted toward the void. A news van is parked beside a hulking broadcast bus, flanked by a lone sedan. Above the door, a sign declares in stark black letters: LOCAL TV 22.

The compound is dead with silence. No voices. No movement. Just the sterile glare of halogens painting the asphalt in harsh yellow scars. Charles creeps past, cresting the hill, then stomps the accelerator. The van surges, plunging down the far side into a throat of darkness.

A mile later, he veers off, tires snapping twigs and munching dried leaves before sinking into brush. Branches claw at steel as he buries the van deep in wooded shadow. He kills the engine, breath still not fully under control, and snatches the golden watch from the mirror. Its lid gapes like a book, waiting for the story to unfold. He snaps it shut, tucks it into his vest, and bolts.

The night shrouds him. He darts across the road, boots barely audible against asphalt, then vanishes into the woods on the other side. Blackness presses close. Twigs snap underfoot. The air reeks of damp earth and pine sap. His lungs burn, heartbeat motivating the charge as he threads through the labyrinth of trees. At age twenty-seven, he's still a gazelle in the woods.

Steel glints ahead. Another fence, tall and perilous, dissecting the forest like a scar. Beyond it, rows of hulking silhouettes hunch under floodlights—military vehicles, their armor absorbing light like earth-toned velvet. The reserve guard motor pool. Charles scans for movement. Nothing. Just the frequency of high-voltage lamps and the mutterings of wind.

He pads forward to the fence and then walks its perimeter until he is positioned behind an M35 deuce-and-a-half.

There should be a guard here, but there never is. Charles grips the chain-link. No barbed wire at the top. Ironic. He scales it like a ninja, fingers clawing steel, boots biting metal. At the crest, he swings a leg over, followed quickly by the other, drops, and rolls—a fluid tumble that kisses the ground without sound. He rises in one breath and sprints toward the nearest giant: a six-wheeled troop carrier, its bulk blotting out the light.

The passenger door yields with a muted click. He slips inside and seals the world out. The cab reeks of diesel and old canvas. His fingers find the green lever on the dash—an invitation waiting to be accepted. No keys required. He twists and holds the lever to the right and waits for a yellow dash light to go out, thumb pressing hard, then releases the lever, which settles to the ON position. A second lever, just to the side of the first, twists under his grip.

The entire machine rocks as the engine detonates—a huge, mechanical, guttural roar that shreds the silence, reverberating through the compound like a monster unchained. Charles clamps the clutch, jams the stick into gear. He revs once, twice, the cab flinching like a living thing. Then he floors it, clutch snapping free. The truck bucks and bounces, snarling, tires clawing at concrete. He slams the clutch again, breath barely contained, muscles screaming as he wrestles the beast into submission. Second gear bites. The carrier lunges, hunger in its bones.

The gate approaches. Charles doesn't brake. Doesn't blink. He guns it, engine howling, and the truck smashes through in an explosion of shrieks and splintering metal. The gate crumples, folding like tin under the wrath of the six wheels. Shards scatter, sparks spitting into the night as the monster barrels free, leaving ruin in its wake.

Charles barrels down the winding road, the truck's massive frame shuddering with every curve. He grips the wheel like a vice, muscles still wrenched, eyes burning holes through the darkness. The headlights on this thing are weak and shaky and he's outdriving them now—speed bleeding into recklessness. The diesel growls like a caged beast, gears snarling as he pushes harder, faster. His pulse syncs with the engine's roar, a savage rhythm pounding in his skull.

He reaches into his vest pocket, fingers brushing warm metal—the golden watch. He flips it open, its face gleaming faintly in the cab's dim glow, then loops the chain over the sun visor, sliding it across until the chain drops neatly on the visor's mount. It swings gently, catching stray beams and spinning them around like a pendulum of fate.

The road straightens, a long, black tongue unfurling into oblivion. Charles stomps the pedal. The truck lunges, tires raging against asphalt. Ahead, a pinprick of orange glows—a cigarette ember? No. A tunnel peeks open, its mouth rimmed in shadow.

And then—headlights. Two blazing eyes hurtling toward him, splitting into twin beams. Motorcycles. Sleek, fast, outlaws on steel steeds.

They burst from the tunnel, engines shrieking, exhaust spitting fire. One rider tucks in tight behind the other, their silhouettes slicing through the night like fins. Charles feels something primal ignite—a cold, surgical rage. His hands twitch. His jaw locks. He jerks the wheel hard, the truck veering into their lane like a juggernaut unleashed. He braces.

Impact—a cataclysm of steel and flesh.

Plastic shatters, chrome splinters, bones snap like dry twigs. The sound is obscene, a symphony of destruction: grinding metal, popping joints, the wet slap of meat against steel. Charles slams the air brakes, the truck screaming in protest as tires gouge the pavement in jumpy chirps. Speed is reduced abruptly.

Through the windshield, chaos sprawls. A bike cartwheels, rider welded to its frame, then both slam earthward onto the road in a grotesque pirouette. Sparks geyser from torn metal, showering the asphalt in fiery confetti. The wreck skids twenty feet, carving a scar of blood and rubber before collapsing into stillness. The truck fishtails, then lurches to a halt, hissing steam like a wounded dragon that has just crashed to earth.

The only sound that survives is the truck's sinister hiss of escaping steam.

Charles kicks the door open. A boot thuds onto the step, then another. He descends into a fog of smoke and vapor, the single surviving headlight painting him in a halo of pale fire. The beam doesn't pierce the mist—it churns it into a glowing wall, a spectral curtain framing the dark figure stalking forward.

Charles

He walks slow, deliberate, tire iron dangling from his fist like an executioner's axe. The road is a spill of wreckage—amber shards, a chrome eye staring from gravel.

Gasoline fumes sting his nostrils, mingling with the copper tang of blood. He passes a leather seat, a twisted horn cover, fragments of shattered dreams.

Then—the trail. A black ribbon snakes through the headlight fog; he knows its true color. Red.

It begins where leather surrendered to friction, where flesh travelled pavement. He tracks it, boot soles printing into gore, the line leading like an artery toward the ruin.

A wristwatch lies in the center, face cracked, hands frozen in eternal rest. Nearby, a wallet splays open, bleeding photographs. A Motorola phone sprawls in pieces. Charles ignores them all. He hunts bigger prey.

The first mound looms—a heap of meat and cloth, unnerving in its stillness. The rider lies on his right side, body curled like a sleeping child. Almost peaceful—except for the grotesque inward fold of the left shoulder, bone jutting like a snapped wing. Charles crouches, tire iron glinting, and peels back the jacket flap. Leather wrinkles under his gloves, shiny with blood. He pats down the torso, fingers skating over limp flesh. Nothing.

He hooks the iron under the man's shoulder and heaves. The body rolls, joints crackling like brittle ice. Ribs grind, splintered ends grating against each other as the chest cavity collapses inward, then flops open with a wet thud. The legs remain eerily inert, meat sacks tethered to ruin. Charles stares.

The face is a horror show—a cheek sanded to bone; eye socket cratered deep. The lid is gone, but the eyeball clings stubbornly, staring glassy and grotesque.

The mouth gapes, teeth shattered, gums flowing crimson. Through the ragged cheek, molars gleam like tombstones. He scans the left arm—what's left of it. Forearm stripped to pink ivory, tendons dangling like frayed rope. Two fingers gone, stumps jutting bare. Upper arm flayed; muscle peeled back to marrow. Shoulder sanded an inch into bone, white glistening under gore.

He hooks the knees, rolling them aside. Denim and flesh slough away in tatters, revealing a thigh chewed to pulp, muscle shredded into ribbons. The ass cheek is a ruin, fat and flesh smeared like butcher's scraps. No pocket. No prize.

Charles lingers, breath hot, eyes tracing the arterial smear back to the wreck. Steam coils like phantom serpents. He turns back to the pulsating mass at hand—and freezes.

The biker's eye flickers and his gaze of torment shoots directly to Charles. His chest spasms. A scream rips free, unearthly and animalistic, clawing at the night. Fingers clamp Charles's arm, slick with blood, vise-tight.

Instinct takes over. Charles swings. The tire iron arcs, crunching into the man's face with a sound like a melon splitting. Bone caves, remaining teeth scatter like shrapnel. The grip holds. The scream climbs, a banshee wail shredding the dark.

Charles roars, smashing down again—forehead this time. Skull splinters, fragments spraying like porcelain shards. Again. Again. The iron rises and falls, motor-fast, until flesh liquefies and bone becomes paste. The scream dies, replaced by the dull metallic clink of iron kissing pavement where a head used to be.

Charles claws for oxygen, chest heaving, breath desperate. Blood freckles his gloves, his jacket, his soul. He stares at the ruin—a smear where a man once lived. Then, with a guttural snarl, he wrenches upright and storms toward the twisted carcass of the motorcycle, boots crunching through gore, mist swirling like ghosts in his wake.

Charles rips through the leather saddlebag dangling from the twisted Harley, fingers clawing at buckles slick with blood. The bag lies open, spilling shadows. He digs deep, rubber gloves dragging against torn leather, and finds only a pair of gloves. He flings them into the street, their limp fingers spreading like broken bones. The stench hits him then—alcohol, sharp and acrid, riding the heavier reek of gasoline that saturates the night air. His nostrils burn. His stomach knots.

Shards glitter inside the bag—jagged teeth of glass, remnants of a Jack Daniels bottle shattered by impact. They glint like ice, edges hungry for flesh. Charles hesitates, wary of slicing through glove and skin. Nothing else lurks within. He mouths a curse, voiceless, the expelled air swallowed by the fog of steam curling from the truck's wounded radiator.

He pivots, boots digging in with intent, and stalks toward the road's edge. His pace quickens, urgency clawing at his spine. Time is bleeding out. Even on this lonely stretch, even at this hour, he's been here too long. Ahead, another saddlebag crouches by the shoulder, black and bloated like carrion. He lunges, rips it open, and upends its guts onto the asphalt. A punctured quart of oil sloshes free, slick and viscous. A rag, stiff with grime, flutters down like a dead moth. Sunglasses clatter, lenses spiderwebbed. A bag of weed sprawls like a green corpse wrapped in a shroud. Useless. All of it.

Rage boils up. Charles boots the empty bag, sending it skittering into darkness. He storms past the truck, breath hissing through clenched teeth, and zeroes in on the second bike—a mangled carcass sprawled fifty yards back. His eyes rake the pavement, scanning for debris, but the road lies eerily clean, as if the violence scrubbed itself from existence.

The Harley rests in ruin, chrome twisted into unimagined angles, frame buckled like broken ribs. Only one small pouch clings to the handlebars, stubborn and silent—a survivor in a shipwreck. He tears it open. Hand tools spill out—wrenches slick with grime, a screwdriver bent like a snapped femur. Nothing. No salvation here.

Charles pauses to collect himself. His gaze drifts, slow and sinister, to the truck hulking under its halo of steam. He knows now. The prize isn't on the asphalt. It's entombed in steel.

He stalks back, boots crackling tiny shards of glass, and mounts the fender step of each side, one at a time. Rubber clasps yield under his grip with a wet snap. He heaves the hood upward, hinges groaning like tired joints. Heat slams him—a wave of scorched air thick with copper and char. The engine bay gapes like a furnace, and within its maw lies horror.

The second rider is fused to the truck's anatomy, a grotesque sculpture of flesh and metal. He came through the grill like a bullet, skull first, crushing the radiator before folding inward upon himself. His head is gone—obliterated, pulped into a crimson coagulant tucked deep into the chest cavity. Vertebrae protrude like ivory plates through the ruin of muscle. The torso arches grotesquely over the steaming radiator, leather vest stretched taut across a back split by impact.

Hellfire & Brimstone MC screams from the patch, letters warped by blood and heat.

The left leg spears straight out, thigh propped against the radiator's crown, knee bent backward in a sick parody of anatomy. From that hinge, the shin dangles, flesh sloughing in ribbons, boot hanging by threads of tendon. The right leg snakes upward, grotesque and traumatic, knee jammed where the head should be, foot perched on the intake like a trophy. Both arms droop at the sides, fingers curled inward, nails torn and blackened. Steam coils around him, seeping through gaps where organs used to be. The smell is hell itself—burning flesh sizzling on the exhaust manifold, fat popping like grease in a skillet.

Charles gags, bile clawing his throat, but forces it down. He reaches for the vest, fingers feeling over leather slick with blood and coolant. The right flap yields, coughing up a flask sticky with gore. He tosses it aside, metal clanging against steel inside the engine bay. The left flap resists, pinned under the corpse's weight, hooked on something unseen. He snarls, snatching the tire iron, and wedges its tip between shoulder and radiator. Muscle tears with a wet rip. Bone grinds. He levers hard, the body creaking like a felled tree, and frees the flap in a gush of steam and blood.

His hand plunges into the pocket. Fingers close around salvation—a padded manila envelope, slick and warm, its surface tattooed with arterial stains. He drags it free, heart palpitating, and stares. String binds it tight, looping twin clasps like shackles. Blood stains and freckles its face, dark and glistening. But it's whole. It's here.

Relief settles in his chest, savage and sweet. He slides the envelope into his own vest, tucking it close like a newborn swaddled in sin. A smile curls his lips—devilish, fleeting. Then he climbs down, boots slamming asphalt, and vanishes into the fog bleeding from the truck's wounds.

Headlights suddenly appear, far ahead, twin spears piercing the tunnel's throat. Charles stiffens, instincts flaring. He scurries to the truck and ducks behind its hulking frame. Steam swirls skyward, veiling him in a shroud of spirit-light. He crouches low, breath shallow, eyes locked on the approaching glow.

The car slows near the sprawled wreckage of man and motorcycle, its beams sweeping over the two dark mounds bleeding into the road. A silhouette spills from the driver's side—a slim figure, hesitant yet urgent. She darts toward the smaller heap, kneels, her movements frantic in the halo of headlights. A pause. Then she bolts back to the car, door slamming like a gunshot. The engine winds up, tires grab pavement, and the vehicle creeps forward, nosing toward the truck.

Using the cover of the truck, Charles runs up the road, melting into shadow, and collapses beside the mangled bike, many yards behind the truck. He lies on the pavement next to the wreck, rigid, one eye slitted, watching the car crawl closer. Its beams slice through mist, painting his boots in filtered light. Fifteen feet. Ten. Brakes squeal—a brief, nervous whine.

A door creaks open. Footsteps scuff pavement, soft and tentative. Then—a voice. Female. Young. Fragile. "Sir? Are you okay?"

Charles clamps his lungs shut, strangling breath. Pressure builds in his skull, veins throbbing like struck cables. He counts heartbeats, each one a hammer blow. The footsteps draw nearer, soles whispering against grit. Another call, closer now, trembling with concern: "Sir? Are you—"

A hand alights on his shoulder, warm and feather-light.

Charles ignites. He rolls, muscles cocked, and swings in one savage blow. The tire iron whistles, then connects with a sickening crunch. Bone caves, skull folding inward like wet plaster. The girl collapses, limbs flailing, then still. Her head hits the road. Her eyes lock on his, wide and glassy, pupils growing like ink stains. Blood geysers from the temple, streaming down her face in black rivulets, drowning lashes, pooling beneath the hollow of her throat. They lay there for a moment, locked in the stare.

Charles rises, breath reaching frantically for the air it is owed, and stares. She's young—too young. Skin pale as porcelain, lips parted in a frozen plea. Her hair fans across the asphalt, strands clinging to gore. Innocence radiates from her even in death, a cruel echo of life snuffed out. For a flicker, something twists in his gut—not guilt, not quite. A shadow of thought, fleeting as smoke.

He steps over her, boots traipsing through the crimson halo spreading like spilled innocence. Calm settles on him, cold and calculated. He mounts the truck's step, fingers curling around the rearview mirror. The golden watch dangles there, lid open like an ear waiting to hear. He slides it free, its chain whispering against vinyl as it slides over the visor, and drops to his palm.

The car waits, door open like a welcome sign. He slides in, leather sighing under his weight, and grips the wheel. The seat is way too close. He reaches down, between his legs and eases the seat back. Headlights spear the darkness ahead, tunneling toward escape. For a moment, he glances down at the watch, its face glimmering faintly in the dash glow. His thumb flicks. The lid snaps shut with a soft, surgical click—a sound that radiates through the night.

He pockets it, presses the accelerator, and vanishes into the tunnel, leaving behind steam, silence, and a girl whose story just ended—at least for now.

———

Charles crests the hill, headlights dueling with the predawn gloom, and the manor looms into view—a titan of stone and shadow crouched against the bruised sky. Sterling Heights. Its silhouette rises like a cathedral of wealth, windows black as spider eyes, rooflines peak like a mountain range against the stars. He kills the engine, silence falling down like liquid lead, and exhales slow, steady, as if bleeding tension into the cold air.

He retrieves the envelope from his vest, fingers brushing its blood-stained face. The name Clinton Kerrington glares back in stark black ink—a brand he scrawled moments ago with a Sharpie dredged from the glove box's cluttered guts. Napkins, straws, brittle CDs—all swept aside in his frantic hunt for that marker. The compartment still hangs open, its contents disheveled, a silent witness to urgency. He slaps it shut; the sound sharp in the hush.

The watch waits heavy in his pocket, the weight of fate. He draws it out, pops the lid open, and stares at its frozen truth: 4:30 A.M. Time bleeding toward reckoning. The face of the watch stares back at him, motionless, waiting to know how the story unfolds. He snaps it shut, the click slicing through the stillness, and tucks it close. Then he grips the envelope, swings the door wide, and steps into the night. The dome light flares, painting his face in a dim, orange glow before the darkness outside takes him.

The manor looms larger with every stride, its bones etched in moonlight. Columns rear like marble giants, their fluted spines clawing skyward. The front walk gleams faintly, dew-slick and serpentine, leading him to a door that resides beneath an arch of hand-carved stone. Only one light pierces the void—a pinprick of orange bleeding from the doorbell's eye. He fixates on it, a beacon in the black, and mounts the steps.

The handle resists. Locked. His fingertip hovers, then presses the glowing button. Westminster chimes erupt beyond the door, their melody cascading through unseen halls like liquid silver. Silence follows. He waits. One minute. Two. Nothing. He stabs the button again. The chimes peal, slicing the evening's tranquility.

Charles

Light flares to his right—three windows igniting in unison, washing shrubs and grass in incandescent glare. Charles pivots, eyes narrowing as illumination claws at the dark.

Inside, a monitor flickers to life, spilling black-and-white information: Charles's image, grainy yet damning, splashed across glass. The PROSPECT patch screams from his back, a brand burned into brotherhood.

A hand—gnarled, blotched with age, descends upon a console. A button clicks. Then the voice comes, gravel ground through rust, booming from a speaker hidden in the wall behind Charles.

"Who's there? What do you want?"

The sound stabs through the quiet, jolting him. He whirls, eyes raking the wall, then spears upward to the camera's cyclopean gaze.

Inside, his face glows on the monitor, stark and spectral. Another click. Another lash of sound.

"It's not even the ass-crack of dawn yet. What the fuck do you want?"

Charles lifts the envelope, angling it toward the lens. Ink glints under the camera's unblinking stare: Clinton Kerrington. A pause stretches—long, heavy, pregnant with unease. Then the arthritic finger stabs a different button.

Buzz. Loud, grating, vibrating through the door like a growl. Charles flinches, then steadies, shoving against the panel. It swings inward, sighing like a reluctant accomplice.

He slips inside, darkness engulfing him. The door clicks shut, sealing silence behind him. The air is cool, tinged with polish and old money. Moonlight slants through paned windows, sketching pale ribs across the marble floor. The foyer expands vast—a cavern of opulence. Wings sprawl left and right, their mouths gaping into shadow. Twin curved staircases bow upward like alabaster serpents, their spines gleaming faintly. Balconies wrap the void in tiers, curling toward a domed ceiling where a chandelier hangs like a frozen explosion of crystal. Above it, skylights slice the darkness into eight perfect shards, piecing the night into geometry.

Charles lowers his gaze. Steel rails gleam on the right-side staircase, running from the top balcony to the marble below, terminating at a small block just after the handrail. Between the winding staircases, an elevator gapes—its door wide open, a night-light bleeding amber from its bowels. It waits, patient, hungry.

"I'll be with you in a few minutes," the voice booms again, cannon-loud from another unseen speaker. Charles flinches, jaw clenching as if readying for a strike. He hates that voice—its weight, its arrogance, its echo of power.

He moves, swift and silent, to the elevator. Inside, his eyes rake the control panel—and there it is. The key. Nestled in the service lock, just as he knew it would be. He plucks it free and stabs the top button marked R. Quickly he exits before the door exhales shut, slicing the amber glow. The indicator above the frame begins its ascent, a crimson pulse climbing floor by floor until it halts at the summit—the rooftop atrium.

Charles exhales, slow and even. He slots the key into the lock on the wall to the right of the door, twists hard left. A click answers—a sound small yet seismic. He palms the key, drops it into his pocket, and turns away toward the center of the lobby, eyes flicking toward the twin staircases spiraling into shadow. The stage is set. The trap is primed. And somewhere above, an old man waits, oblivious to the dark storm clawing up his walls.

Charles paces across the vast foyer, hands clasped behind his back, posture formed from calm steel. His boots almost silent against marble as he circles the space, eyes grazing the opulent details with indifferent detachment. Brass pots cradle manicured trees, their leaves trembling faintly in the draft of a vent like nervous fingers. Plush Queen Anne chairs huddle around a marble-topped table, their curves decadent, their silence accusatory. Moonlight drips through tall windows, choking colors into ghostly shades, rendering wealth into pallor.

He drifts toward the front door, where a console table crouches beneath a towering pane of glass. Mahogany bones gleam under gold-leaf skin, its surface littered with pamphlets fanned like a gambler's hand. A brass vase rises from the center, orchids arching in frozen elegance, their petals pale as bone, washed in moonlight. Charles plucks a pamphlet, its glossy face grinning with manufactured joy—a child sandwiched between two perfect parents, teeth blazing like porcelain tombstones. Above them, the word *Kerrington* screams in bold white letters against a sky too blue to be real. *Foster Care & Adoption Agency*. Below, a Bernard Shaw quote drips saccharine poison: "A Happy Family is but an Earlier Heaven."

Charles exhales through his nose, a sharp huff of derision. His lips twitch—not in humor, but in something darker. He tosses the pamphlet lazily onto the neat fan it came from and picks up another. In bold white lettering, outlined in red, one word above the other reads—*Kerrington Kickstart*. The lettering covers the top third of the fold. Beneath that, a water-color painting, meant to look as though done by a child, portrays four little friends, in a row, all holding hands. The two on the end wave. They all have stick-figure smiles. At the bottom, the catchphrase makes him want to lurch.

Prepare For Life.

Light suddenly blazes, flooding the foyer in crystal brilliance. A voice lashes out, rusty and wet:

"Hello, son. Did Blake send you?"

Charles turns around, eyes spearing the source. An old man crouches at the foot of the right staircase. He is in a motorized wheelchair, still attached to the rail, his silhouette hunched and brittle. One arm is still raised from flicking the switch. Skin maps of age blotch his knuckles, veins worming beneath crepe paper flesh. His eyes gleam—sharp, suspicious, predatory even in their rheumy haze. Charles never heard him arrive. That chairlift is quiet.

"I don't recognize you. Are you a new one?" The question drips casual, but the undertow reeks of scrutiny.

Charles nods, slow, deliberate. He turns just enough to bare his back, fingers sliding to the rocker patch stitched in black and white. PROSPECT. His thumb strokes the letters, back and forth, a silent sermon. Read it. Believe it.

He replaces the pamphlet, with surgical precision this time, aligning edges like a man restoring order before chaos. Then he advances, boots silently rolling over marble, shadow clinging tight across the marble floor.

With the click of a magnetic solenoid, the chair is released from the rail. The old man silently rolls forward just a few feet.

"Did he finally get it back for me?" The old man's voice trembles—not with fear, but with hunger.

Charles's hand dives into his vest. The wheelchair jerks backward, motors whining as Clinton retreats, suspicion flaring in his cataract-clouded eyes. Another nudge, wheels squealing, until Charles's hand emerges—not with steel, but with salvation. A package. Padded, blood-stained, branded with a name that burns like guilt.

Relief falls across the old man's face, shame flickering in its wake. He rolls forward, hand outstretched, fingers crooked like talons softened by greed. Charles surrenders the envelope.

Clinton cradles it, staring as if it were a newborn wrapped in redemption. He doesn't open it. He doesn't need to. The weight tells its truth. His lips part, breath erratic.

"That son of a bitch actually did it," he croaks, voice cracking under the strain of disbelief. "He got it back. I never thought I'd see the day."

His gaze sinks into the paper, pupils dilating, mind spiraling into some private abyss. For a heartbeat, Charles swears the old man might cry. Then the trance shatters. Eyebrows vault, eyes blaze.

"Did they kill the bitch, I hope?" The words spit like acid, eager, vile.

Charles nods once, slow as a sword sliding home. He's not lying. He never lies.

"You don't say much, do you, son?" Clinton sneers, brittle humor rattling in his throat. Silence answers, heavy and deliberate. He fills it with arrogance. "Well, I want to thank you for getting here so fast, so early. Blake—he's efficient. Ruthless. That's why I put him in charge. Always makes me proud."

Charles drifts behind the chair, movements liquid, resolved. Fingers wrap over the controls, then clamp. A twist, a click—the Bendix drive dies, severing the chair's electric soul. Manual now. Helpless now.

"What's this?" Clinton hacks, neck craning left then right, joints creaking like rusted hinges. His voice curdles with unease.

Silence is always his answer. He grips the handles tighter and rolls the chair toward the chairlift at the base of the spiral. Wheels squeak, a sound thin and petrified.

"Young man," Clinton stammers, words tripping over dread, "I think it's time I got my old bones back to bed."

Charles locks the chair in place, fingers dancing over levers with surgical grace. Three buttons leer from the panel. He presses the top one. Green. Go. The lift hums, gears silently meshing, and begins its slow, merciless ascent. Charles walks beside it, smile chiseled in calm granite. He looks down at Clinton, eyes meeting eyes. His thumb jerks upward, head tilting, Cheshire grin springing onto his face—a pantomime of reassurance that drips menace.

Balconies coil around them like porcelain ribs as they climb. Shadows writhe. Clinton babbles, desperation frothing into false warmth. "What's your name, son?"

The lift slows to a halt outside the library, smooth. Everything in this place just screams quality. Clinton pitches forward, fingers clawing the armrests. Charles steps around and crouches until his face hovers inches from the old man's. Their eyes lock—soap-water pupils drowning in emerald fire.

His lips peel back. The sound that spills forth is not human. It gurgles from some abyssal pit, wet and monstrous, vibrating the air like a death knell.

"Chaaaaarrrrlllles!"

As Charles utters his own name for only the second time in his life, he raises his chin and finishes the drawn-out word as though he were a wolf, howling at the moon. The old man immediately recognizes the cross-shaped scar on Charles's throat. His eyes widen in horror as he realizes who Charles is.

Charles straightens slowly, his shadow stretching long across the marble floor like a dagger unsheathed. His movements are deliberate, as he glides to the back of the chair. The old man's voice rattles on—a brittle stream of words, looping and stammering, desperate to stitch a veil of ignorance over the truth they both know. He knows who Charles is. And Charles knows he knows.

Charles

From behind, Charles studies the crown of the old man's head. Hair thinned to a fragile canopy, lacquered stiff with hairspray, each strand brittle as straw. No bald spot—just a uniform erosion, a slow surrender to time. Beneath the starched silver, age spots stain like bruises on a white apple, sun-scorched relics of a life steeped in indulgence. The sight curdles something deep inside Charles, a sour taste rising in his throat.

The chair creaks and squeaks as Charles pushes forward. With the sound as dry as dead leaves, the old man chuckles and his voice scrapes the silence. "Thank you again for working so late tonight. I know it's unusual, but I hope you feel it was worth your while."

Charles's nostrils flare, a subtle twitch of disdain. The name that follows slithers into his ears like rusted nails dragged across slate. "You've been there for me and I thank you, Chuck."

The syllable claws at his skull, sour and acidic. His nose crinkles as if the air itself has soured. He rolls the chair onward, toward the elevator—a closed steel mouth waiting for an offering. The key slides from his pocket and kisses the wall lock with a metallic click. He twists hard left, leaving the key impaled in its socket, and stabs the button. A muted hum answers, gears spinning somewhere in the dark.

Behind him, Clinton cranes his neck, joints creaking like a rusty gate. His eyes glint with a feverish gleam as he spews honeyed poison. "Thank you, Chuck. I'm sure you know you will be well rewarded. Your loyalty will not be forgotten. You have saved this family from ruin by bringing me this package and we won't forget it."

Charles moves like a statue come alive—silent, immutable. His shadow looms, swallowing the old man's frail silhouette.

"Hell, I'm ready to cut you a check right now, son! How much do you need?" Clinton is still trying to mentally maintain some semblance of power over the situation.

The elevator doors sigh open. But behind their polished lips there is no car, no salvation. Just a shaft, black and seemingly bottomless, its steel ribs glinting like the teeth of some mechanical beast.

Charles's hand darts forward, snatching the envelope from Clinton's lap in a single, surgical strike. Before the old man can gasp, the chair lunges under Charles's shove.

The front wheels breach the void. Gravity hooks its claws. Clinton pitches forward, head snapping toward the abyss. His eyes widen, veins writhing under paper skin as terror erupts in his chest. His arms jerk wide, faster than they've moved in decades, fingers clawing at the frame, tendons straining like frayed rope. Muscles scream, sinew tearing as he locks his elbows, dragging his carcass back from the brink.

For a moment, he fights fate—old sinew burning, joints grinding like rusted gears. His face burns crimson, veins bulging like cables, tendons standing out in stark relief. Breath sucks through clenched teeth, each gasp a blade tearing at his throat.

"Help me, Chuckie! Help me!" The plea rips from his lungs, ragged, strangled by panic.

Charles stands still, a totem chiseled from malice, watching the grotesque ballet of desperation. Clinton's body trembles, muscles quivering under the weight of doom. Inch by inch, he begins to right himself, dragging his chair back from the jaws of hell.

The silence thickens, pulsing with dread as Clinton reserves his remaining strength not for pleas or groans, but for a final pull to save his soul.

Then Charles moves—one step, quick and explosive. His boot lifts, thigh muscles cocking, and slams into the chair's spine. The impact reverberates like a bomb. Clinton's grip liquefies. Fingers shear free, popping from the frame as though buttered. The chair rockets forward, gravity shrieking as it drags its prey into the abyss.

The scream that follows is inhuman—a sound blackened by an inferno of terror, echoing up the shaft like a banshee's wail. Steel devours flesh as the chair vanishes into the black, and the old man's voice ruptures into silence.

Charles stares down into the elevator shaft for a few moments. As he studies the mangled heap of metal and man below, he starts to notice a thick, shiny pool forming around the man's head. It looks like black crude oil bubbling up from the earth.

He sniffs deep, pulling whatever phlegm he can from the back of his throat and spits into the elevator shaft. He leers at the crumpled body at the bottom of the shaft and snarls in disgust as he cranks the service key to the right again. The elevator door slides closed. He presses the call button and after a few seconds, the door opens again. This time the car is there.

He calmly steps inside, turns to face front and scans the elevator buttons. He needs to get out on the first floor at the foyer. He sees the button labeled 1 and gently touches it with his finger tip, but he does not press it. Instead, he lowers his finger tip and presses the button below. It is marked with the letter B. The door closes in front of him. The indicator shows the elevator's decent from floor three… Two… One… There is a loud crushing sound and the indicator stops on B. There it pauses with a shudder for a few moments. The indicator suddenly reverses direction. It stops at the number one. A small bell sound rings out in the foyer and the door opens. With dark intent in his eyes, Charles steps quickly from the car as though his feet were already moving him in that direction before the door even opened.

—

Charles glides through the sleeping town, the stolen sedan whispering over rain-slick streets. Darkness drapes every storefront like funeral cloth, windows gleaming black and bottomless. Streetlamps flicker weakly, their halos laying pale gold onto the asphalt, pooling like stagnant water. The air brims with silence, broken only by the soft hiss of tires slicing through puddles.

The center of town sleeps in stillness. Stores hunker behind glass panes polished into obsidian mirrors, each one birthing a phantom world. As Charles creeps past, reflections come into view—ghostly images of the sedan pacing him like a shadow tethered to his soul. Each new pane becomes a stage, curtains parting to reveal a car that is his, yet not his.

He watches, breath shallow, as the phantom image sharpens. Chrome gleams like diamonds under the fluorescent glow of a store's lit overhead sign, contours warped by ripples in the glass. And then—eyes. A face. His face, but hollowed, stripped to stark geometry. Skin clings to bone like wet cloth, jawline carved sharp as an axe. The scalp gleams bare, shaven, skull shining under spectral light. Eyes burn from deep sockets, black fire drowning their whites. They lock on him, and the world deforms, two realities grinding like tectonic plates.

The mirror ends, severed by brick. Darkness swallows the phantom. Charles exhales, slow and forced, fingers flexing against the wheel. But then—a new pane unfurls, black, glossy and merciless. The ghost car crawls back from the void, hood first, then windshield, bleeding into existence like a revenant. Charles leans forward, pulse hammering, waiting for the eyes— the abyssal eyes that strip him bare.

They come. But not alone.

The passenger seat gushes with horror. She sits there—the girl. The innocent he slaughtered for this car. Her face is a ruin, swollen and blood-slick, one eye a crater of pulp, the other glaring with vitreous hate. Her lips peel back in a rictus grin, teeth shattered, gums black with clotted gore. She leans toward him, neck twisted, vertebrae jutting like broken glass. Her breath chills his neck, a smear of death's condensation.

Charles's heart bursts. He jerks, neck snapping right, arm flinging up in primal defense. The sedan swerves, tires shrieking as rubber kisses curb. Steel trash cans erupt in a cacophony of clangs, their bodies cartwheeling across the sidewalk. The bumper gouges metal, sparks geyser into the night. Charles stomps the brake. The car skids ten inches, and halts with a chirp that finally slays the clatter.

He sits rigid, lungs strangled, pulse slamming against his ribs. The passenger seat is empty now, a void where horror appeared only a moment ago. He drags air into his chest, long and deep, and forces his trembling hands to the wheel. He exhales with a lengthy blow. Reverse. Tires crunch debris. Drive. The car crawls forward, still crunching, slow as a hearse.

Another dark mirror looms, black and bottomless. The ghost car slithers back into being, its driver's eyes molten with malice. No passenger this time. Relief trickles through Charles's veins, thin and bitter. But the next pane stretches wide, glossy as oil, and dread builds anew. Hood. Windshield. The phantom Charles leans closer now, scalp gleaming, now strangled by a leather strap harness, lips peeled in a death-row snarl. His eyes bore through the glass, drilling into marrow, whispering of volts and vengeance.

Charles stares back, breath held, as the mirror terminates in clapboard gray. The reflection dies. But its echo lingers—in the twitch of his lip, in the tremor of his hands.

—

The next window is not black. It glows faintly from within, a square of amber bleeding into the night—the lights of Rangle's Family Pharmacy & Convenience Store. The sudden brightness slices through the darkness like a katana, and Charles feels it stab into his nerves. His phantom twin, the spectral driver haunting the glass panes behind him, cannot breach this illuminated sanctuary; or maybe he's already there. The thought unsettles him, leaving a hollow ache in his chest. Vulnerability prickles his skin like static.

He idles past slowly, eyes flicking like searchlights across the aisles visible through the glass. Shelves aligned in rigid rows, their shadows long and eerie under the sporadic fluorescent glow. It's too late for business, yet the lights buzz on—a reminder that the Rangles live above their empire, that life stirs even when the town sleeps. Charles feels the weight of unseen eyes pressing against his back.

Fifty yards ahead, he veers left into a narrow drive that hides between two buildings. The sedan glides into its gullet, tires chirping over wet asphalt, until the passage chokes at a chain-link fence. A green dumpster squats at the terminus, hulking and rank. Charles kills the engine, steps out, and inhales the alley's breath—damp concrete, sour rot, the metallic tang of rain.

He scales the dumpster in one fluid motion, boots slick on wet steel. Fingers hook the fence's top rail, muscles straining as he vaults over. He lands cat-soft on the other side, knees bending to drink the shock, then springs upright, shadow melting into deeper shadow. The alley unrolls before him, a corridor of brick, black and silence. He moves quickly to the opposing end and turns left around the corner there. He moves briskly, hugging the backs of the stores, until the rear of Rangle's Convenience looms like a castle wall.

The reenforced back door resists his grip—locked, cold, indifferent. Charles moves on, gliding along the building's flank. Another fence rises, twin to the first, crowned with sharpened wire teeth. Just beyond it, another dumpster crouches under the dim cone of a single bulb. The light drips sickly orange, pooling on slick pavement, painting the alley in hues of rust and ruin.

Charles removes his leather cut and takes it in his teeth. He scales the barrier and at the top, tosses his vest over the barbs. Pressing down on the protection, he straddles over the top. Once over, he carefully pulls his cut from the barbs and descends the chain link, landing quietly atop the dumpster.

Stillness grabs him and locks him in place for a moment. He listens—heart pounding like a muted snare. The alley suffocates with quiet, broken only by the low purr of an air-conditioning unit vibrating in its window cage a few feet away. Water beads along its metal ribs, dripping into a puddle below with soft, rhythmic plinks. The sound echoes between brick walls, a metronome ticking in the dark.

Then—a flicker of motion. A shadow leaps, silent as smoke. A black cat lands beside him, its body a ripple of silk. It sits, tail curling like a question mark, and stares down the alley as if it knows the script. Charles exhales, tension bleeding from his shoulders, and drops from the dumpster.

The crunch of sand under his boots abrades like a cheese grater in his skull. Every sound ricochets off the alley walls, amplified into accusation. He glances upward. Blackened windows threaten from above—dark portals rimmed in moonlight, some cracked open to sip the night air. They leer like blind eyes, watching without sight. Charles imagines ears pricking in the dark, Rangles stirring in their beds as echoes slither through the cracks.

He moves, slow and silent. A stack of brittle milk crates sits nearby, waiting. He seizes one, flips it, and plants it. Boots mount the plastic perch. Fingers twist the bulb from its socket, unwinding light from the alley's throat. The glass sphere wobbles, scorching hot, and Charles juggles it like a live grenade before tossing it onto a bundle of newspapers tied in twine.

He reclaims the crate, readjusts it beneath the window, stacks another on top and takes a lunging step up. The air conditioner thrums like a mechanical heart, its breath damp and fetid. Charles tugs at the accordion folds of the weather seal on one side. Plastic crackles and complains, peeling back to reveal a slit of shadow. He snakes an arm inside, fingers groping for the cord. Nothing. He pries wider, plastic creaking, and plunges deeper. His fingertips graze a cord, then trace it downward to the socket. A sharp tug severs the current. The hum dies, leaving silence heavy and telling.

The window slides upward with a dry hiss, smooth as silk. Charles grips the unit, muscles flexed, leans it toward himself and eases it free. Metal kisses his jeans, cold, wet and slick. He squats and lowers the unit onto one knee. His other leg quickly drops and braces on solid ground. With a small heave, he lifts the unit from his knee and lowers his foot from the crates before lowing the unit to the ground like a priest laying down an offering. He mounts the crate again, palms to the sill. A short hop, and his torso spears through the frame. He tips inward, folding like a serpent, and drips to the floor without a sound.

Inside, darkness strangles—a black ocean entombing him. As his eyes adjust, the pantry gathers around him. From his crouched position, squeezed by darkness, it all looks gargantuan.

Rows of shelves span a mile high, hovering over him like apartment balconies. Charles exhales, slow and lethal, and melts deeper into the shadows. He allows himself time to settle down. He waits for the pantry to shrink to normal size again.

Inside, the air is thick with the scent of cold metal and stale bread. Charles slides a hand into his sweatshirt pocket and retrieves a small flashlight. Its head disappears into his palm, swallowed whole, before he clicks it on. A muted red glow seeps through his fingers, bleeding like a wound. He peels the edge of his hand back just enough to let a sliver of raw light escape.

The pantry is normal size now, a claustrophobic cell lined with shelves that climb from floor to ceiling. Dry goods hunker in neat ranks, their labels ghostly in the dim glow. Cans glint like dull coins. Charles smothers the light again, palm clamping down. Feeling a little calmer now, he eases the glass-paned door open. Hinges sigh, soft as breath.

Beyond; the kitchen sprawls. Silence hums. Power indicators wink like distant stars on the hulking refrigerators. A digital wall clock bleeds green numerals into the gloom: 5:15. The hour feels wrong, too early for life, too late for mercy.

Sweat beads along Charles's hairline, sliding down his temple in icy rivulets. He slips from the pantry. Every step feels amplified, ricocheting through the hollow belly of the kitchen. He drifts toward the nearest door, its small window a black mirror. He leans in, peering through the glass, but darkness stares back, uncaring. His own reflection reveals instead: face drenched from above in sickly green light, eyes ringed with bruised crescents. He lifts trembling fingers, grazing his cheek as if to confirm the ruin staring back.

Then—a sound. Sharp, metallic. His heart blows up, a grenade in his chest. He drops and tucks behind a stainless-steel prep table. Breath lodges in his throat. The clatter of glass bottles rattles the silence, followed by a shower of light—soft, buttery, spilling across steel. Shadows dance along the walls as the refrigerator hangs open.

Shuffling. A dull thud. Then darkness swallows the glow again. Drawers whisper open, their ball-bearing rollers singing in muted tones. A soft slam punctuates the hush. Another clink of glass, another flare of light. Charles dares a glance, eyes cresting the table's edge.

A heavy, old man stands framed in the glow of the open refrigerator, his body a grotesque silhouette of flesh and hair. Off-white briefs sag around his hips, fabric yellowed by time. His belly droops, pale and pendulous, glistening under the fridge's light. Hair dye clings like black mold to the edges of the bald spot on the back of his head.

It's Mr. Rangle, a man not to be toyed with. He has a reputation for being a no-nonsense kind of guy. He was a medic in the military many years ago. He got himself dishonorably discharged for stealing medical supplies and selling them on the open market. Morphine shots were his product of choice. From there, he struggled to find work, due to his military record and ended up landing a job as the prison doctor, here in town. He's been here ever since. He grew his family here. He grew his pharmacy business here. He is as much a staple in this town as the Kerringtons. He stepped down at the prison to focus solely on his own business when the prison's owner was shot and changes were made. Rangle could see the writing on the wall, so he retired a number of years back.

He plucks a quart of milk from the shelf, deposits it on the counter with ritualistic care. Cabinet doors yaw open; a glass emerges, catching the glow like crystalized moonlight. Milk cascades in a white ribbon, pooling in the vessel with a muted splash.

Charles watches, saliva pooling thick on his tongue. When was the last time he ate? Hunger gnaws at his gut, sharp and unexpected. The old man moves with sluggish grace, assembling a sandwich—a symphony of textures. Ham folds in pink layers, lettuce crackles fresh and crisp, tomato slices bleed juice onto the cutting board. A smear of dressing glistens like oil on canvas. Charles's vision tunnels, locking on the sandwich as if it were salvation.

The old man pivots, arm stretching toward the block bristling with blades. Steel hisses as it slides free. Charles collapses behind the table, breath strangled, muscles rigid. Silence swells, pressurized and engulfing. He counts heartbeats, each one a foot stomp.

A pause. Then motion. Charles lifts his gaze, slow as a vampire from behind a cape. The knife dances across bread, severing halves with skilled grace. Layers gape: ham, lettuce, tomato; an anatomy of hunger dissected before his eyes. His stomach revolts, growling loud, a gurgling snarl that shreds the hush. Panic arises like a spring. He ducks, spine curling, breath clamped tight. The sound fades, but its echo lingers like guilt.

Did he hear? Charles waits, seconds stretching into eternities. Then he risks a glance.

The counter area is empty. The old man is gone.

But the sandwich remains; gleaming under the kitchen's pallid light.

"Who the fuck are you?" The voice detonates from Charles's right like a backfire in the silence.

He whirls, muscles knotting, and freezes cold. The old man stands only feet away, knife glinting in his fist, knees bent in a stance that reeks of discipline. His free hand hovers forward, palm open, a shield of flesh and bone. The posture screams training—military, and Charles's instincts flare. This isn't some soft civilian. Underestimation could kill him.

Charles lifts his hands, slow and deliberate, surrender bleeding from every gesture. He rises from his crouch and takes a single step back. The old man lunges forward a fraction, blade slicing the air in a vicious jab.

"Don't you move, cocksucker!" His voice gouges like iron dragged on asphalt. The knife swipes again, cutting menace into the dim light.

Charles raises his hands higher, fingers splayed, expression melting into defeat. His breath hitches, chest rising and falling in shallow tides. The old man's eyes bore into him, pupils black pits rimmed with fire.

"The fuck you doing here, boy?" The words sizzle in the hush.

Charles shifts just his gaze, slow as death, toward the counter. The sandwich gleams under the mild glow. The old man tracks the glance, lips curling into a grin sharp enough to cut.

"You want my sandwich?" His tone tilts, mockery dripping. "You're hungry?" A chuckle slithers free, provoking and cruel. "You broke in here for food, you poor bastard?"

The laugh erupts; harsh barking, ricocheting off steel and tile. Too much laugh for so little humor. Then—silence. His face hardens, grin calcifying into a mask of rage.

"Fuck you and your sandwich too, boy!" His voice spikes, spit frothing. "I'll go you one better. How's three hots and a cot sound to you, son? Courtesy of the state!"

He turns and lunges sideways toward the phone. The old man's fingers claw for the receiver, dialing nine with blind confidence.

That single step; a sliver of distance, is all Charles needs.

He seizes the moment. His arms scythe downward, ripping free from their pantomime of surrender. Right hand plunges into his sweatshirt pocket, fingers locking around cold steel. Left hand pinches fabric, yanking wide as the pistol births from shadow. The muzzle reveals, black and hungry, and rises like a serpent striking.

Three strides. The floor quakes under his boots. The gun's barrel drilling the space between the old man's eyes. Two feet. One breath. The world narrows to a tunnel of iron and intent.

The old man freezes, pupils dilating, breath tangled in his throat. Without turning, without daring a glance, his hand fumbles backward, receiver dangling like a severed limb. Plastic clacks against the cradle. His other hand trembles, lowering the knife to the counter with a muted clink. Fingers peel away, slow and careful, surrender bleeding from every joint.

Two men are locked in a stare of violence, the air vibrating with the frequency of death waiting to speak.

Before the old man can spit another syllable, Charles lunges forward, closing the already small gap like a lion pinning prey. The pistol in his right hand jams into the man's ribs, pressing through a heavy layer of fat and grinding against cartilage and bone. His left hand snatches an unopened soup can from the stainless-steel prep table—a blunt instrument of desperation, and swings it through the dim light.

The can lands, flat steel to orbit with a crunch like green bone. The zygoma caves; the eye balloons and leaks jelly as the socket buckles.

The man shrieks with raw wire in the throat as he claws his own ruin.

He crumples, knees buckling, and slams to the tile. Fingers claw at his ruined face, nails raking skin as agony starts fires through his nervous system. Bare heels skid on the blood-slick tile as he crab-scrapes backwards toward the door, sound serrated with terror. His voice bursts into shrieks, each one serrated with terror.

Blood pressure builds in Charles's head, sweat streams down his temples, stinging his eyes. Panic claws at his throat. He needs silence. He needs it now. The door flaps, a pendulum of vinyl and aluminum, before settling shut with a hollow thud. Beyond it, the old man thrashes, clawing at a shelf of canned goods. Metal clatters, cylinders raining down like spent shells as he hauls himself upright.

Charles charges, vision tunneling on the quarry. The man wobbles, fingers hooked into shelving, tendons straining like frayed rope. Charles swings the same dented can, now a weapon slick with blood, and crushes it into the man's face. The blow smashes against the maxilla, fracturing bone, teeth shearing free in a spray of enamel and spit. He collapses again, spine folding, limbs jerking like severed live wires.

On the floor, he curls, hands cradling his mangled visage. Charles looms over him, breath short and deep, and brings the can down hard on those trembling fingers. Phalanges snap like brittle twigs, metacarpals splintering under the force. The man howls, jerking his hands away, revealing the ruin beneath. One eye sealed shut by swelling, the other gaping wide, sclera spiderwebbed with hemorrhage. Blood pulses from the supraorbital wound in rhythmic gushes, pooling beneath his head.

Charles's stomach knots, saliva thickening as rage eclipses reason. He drops the pistol, grips the can with both hands, and hoists it high. Muscles focus their energy, veins bulging, before gravity conspires with fury. The can plummets, smashing into the man's mouth. A wet crunch erupts as partial dentures shear free, tearing from the alveolar ridge and jamming into the oropharynx. The airway is blocked. He convulses, choking, blood pumping in frothy arcs as he gurgles and gasps.

Charles feels the spray kiss his face—a fine mist stippled with viscous droplets. Copper floods his nostrils, metallic and nauseating. He swings again, the can hammering the temporal bone. A sharp crack ricochets through the room as the thin plate fractures, shards piercing the middle meningeal artery. Blood erupts, dark and arterial, painting the tile in crimson.

Another strike caves the orbit, crushing the delicate sphenoid wing. The eye ruptures, vitreous fluid oozing like jelly across the cheek. Charles roars; a sound untamed, guttural, as he slams the can into the mandible. The jaw dislocates, condyles snapping free, the chin sagging grotesquely as ligaments tear. He pounds again, and again, each blow liquefying structure into pulp.

The man's screaming finally dies—or maybe it never was the old man screaming at all. Charles freezes, chest heaving, realization slithering cold down his spine. His own voice echoes in the void, torn and monstrous. Below him sprawls a ruin—a mixture of bone shards, teeth, brain tissue, and blood congealing into a malformed mosaic. Hair clings to the gore like seaweed in a crimson tide.

Charles staggers back, breath uneven, eyes bulging. The can slips from his grip, clanging against tile slick with viscera. Silence returns, warm and welcoming this time.

He snatches up the pistol, shoving it deep into the right pocket of his sweatshirt, the weight dragging against his hip bone like a guilty anchor. His breath labors, quick and shallow, as his eyes rake the room in a frenzy. Shelves leer back at him, stacked with silent witnesses: cans, boxes, plastic-wrapped goods.

He bolts down the aisle, hands clawing through clutter. Products rain to the floor in chaotic avalanches, clattering like bones. A solution gleams. Lighter fluid. Two bottles, sinister partners, crouching on a lower shelf. He seizes them, fingers weak and trembling from the onslaught, and twists the caps with savage urgency. Plastic threads snap and squeal as they surrender. The acrid stench of petroleum breathes into the air, sharp and chemical, coating his nostrils.

Charles drenches the corpse, torrents of oily liquid pouring over shattered flesh. It pools in the hollows of brokenness, slicking the ruin of muscle and bone. The old man's body glistens under the dim light, an unsightly effigy lacquered in accelerant. Charles's pulse spikes. He will not leave DNA behind—not sweat, not blood, not a single smudge of a fingerprint.

He sprints to the front of the store. His hand snatches a Bic lighter from a display rack, its plastic shell smooth and warm from the overhead lamps. On the return, he raids a shelf for paper towels, ripping the plastic wrap as he moves. Sheets spill like an avalanche as he uncoils the first roll in his grip.

Back at the body, the air reeks of fuel and blood. Charles crouches and plunges the paper towels into the viscous slurry of blood, lighter fluid, and the liquefied remnants of a man. The paper drinks deep, fibers saturating with gore and oil. He yanks another roll from the torn, sagging plastic and stirs the end in the stew. His thumb flicks the wheel of the lighter. Sparks spit. Flame blossoms on the end of the roll in his hand, orange and hungry, licking the soaked pulp until it roars alive.

He hurls the ignited mass onto the corpse. Fire crawls at first, serpentine and deliberate, tracing oily veins across the ruin. Then it flares, a flower of flame unfurling in violent petals. Heat lashes his face, painting his skin in sudden amber. Shadows writhe along the walls, grotesque demons dancing to the crackle of combustion.

Charles

Charles watches, breath steadying, as the inferno devours. Flesh puckers, blistering under the onslaught. The stench rises—a fetid symphony of burning fat and seared protein. It is nothing like the savory perfume of grilled meat once served here. This is death rendered in smoke and char.

His gaze hooks on the hands—those shattered instruments of defiance. Rings gleam in the firelight: a slab of onyx on the right, heavy gold bands on the left. Jewels of vanity, now worthless in the pyre. Flames lick upward, caressing a forearm inked with a panther and a yin-yang sigil. The tattoos writhe as skin blackens, their outlines melting into oblivion. The elbow is wrapped in a spider web tattoo. It rises, then the dermis splits, fissures cracking open to reveal the glistening pink of muscle beneath. Heat sears deeper, unraveling fibers into curling ribbons.

The glow bathes Charles's face, sculpting it in flickering hues. His pupils dilate, twin abysses drinking firelight. For a heartbeat, he feels almost sanctified.

Then—a voice cleaves the silence, short and thunderous, erupting from the front of the store.

"FREEZE!"

Charles stands frozen, a gravestone in firelight, the inferno painting his face in increasingly brighter light. Orange tongues lick the air, their glow pulsing against his skin, chiseling him in flickering chiaroscuro. Smoke billows upward, a phantom dragon writhing toward the ceiling, its acrid breath clawing at his nostrils. How long has he been here? How long has he let the flames mesmerize him, their heat kissing his cheeks, their light drowning his thoughts?

He doesn't respond to the voice behind him. He doesn't move. Doesn't breathe. His hands remain buried in the cavernous pockets of his sweatshirt, fingers curled around steel like a secret handshake.

"Put your hands in the air—Now!" The command bellows from behind him, nervous but thunderous. Charles doesn't flinch.

The voice lashes again, sharper, slicing through the crackle of fire: "Three Tango Niner requesting backup, fire and ambulance at Rangle's Pharmacy. Possible two-seventeen and code fifty-two. Suspect at gunpoint."

Another bark—serious, louder: "Don't you move!"

Footsteps scuff tile, their rhythm quickening, a staccato drumbeat of urgency. Charles tilts his gaze, slowly, eyes sliding left without betraying motion elsewhere. A silhouette bleeds into his peripheral vision—a uniformed officer, pistol leveled. The cop's focus breaks, torn between the motionless figure and inferno before him and the fire extinguisher waiting five feet away like a solution.

"I said take your fucking hands out of your pockets and put them where I can see them—Now!" The officer's voice trembles under its own weight, cracking like ice under strain. He skirts forward, boots sweeping through debris, head jerking in frantic arcs as he tries to command chaos. His fingers twitch toward the extinguisher, desperation bleeding from every gesture.

Flash.

Charles moves without moving. The .38 has been waiting, muzzle angled across his own belly, hidden in the folds of cotton. His trigger finger contracts, a viper striking from shadow. The first shot erupts, muffled by fabric, a dull cough of death. Then another. And another. Fire blossoms from his pocket, strobing in bursts of orange fury.

Charles

Metal screams. One round punches the extinguisher, rupturing its pressurized gut. An eruption of white powder vomits into the air, a blizzard of chemicals swallowing the room. Visibility collapses into chaos. Charles fires blind into the storm, each report a thunderclap swallowed by the hiss of escaping gas. Click. Click. The hammer falls on emptiness.

He turns sharply and dives left, boots skidding across tile slick with soot and fluid. Shelves lurch over him—a barricade of canned goods, and he melts behind them, crouching low as the chemical fog thickens. His lungs wheeze, throat clawed by acrid dust. Silence swells, punctuated by the fizz of settling powder.

Shapes bleed through the haze. Crimson smears bloom on the wall—four black stars punched into plaster, a zodiac sign of violence. Charles lowers his gaze. Sheriff Dobson sprawls in a grotesque sprawl, limbs splayed like a discarded doll. A neat hole crowns his forehead, a third eye drilled into bone. Blood pools beneath his skull, thick and glistening, painting the tile in arterial designs. Sheriff Dobson is fully retired, seven days earlier than scheduled.

Charles goes forward, boots padding through the powder, and crouches beside the corpse. He rests his empty pistol on Dobson's chest like a benediction. He studies the wound, the frozen rictus etched across the sheriff's face. Time slows, seconds bleeding into eternities as Charles drinks in the beauty of it all.

A peripheral glance. The sheriff's sidearm lies three feet away. Charles stretches, fingers grazing steel—

—and a voice explodes from the front of the store, booming like judgment.

"FREEZE! PUT YOUR HANDS IN THE AIR!"

Charles kneels in the haze, smoke curling around him like Satan's fingers, the inferno behind painting his silhouette in boiling orange. His skin prickles under the furnace glow, sweat burrowing rivulets through soot on his face. For a moment, time feels tangible, dripping in slow motion as the world narrows to the crackle of flames and the sound of his own breath.

Headlights spear through the front windows, carving harsh white corridors into the gloom. Red and blue strobes pulse like arterial blood, splashing color across the smoke-choked air. Exhaust fumes rise in billowy spirals, mingling with the acrid tang of burning flesh. A Maglite beam cleaves the darkness, its glare a long white arm, the hand at the end grabbing Charles by the face. He squints, lids trembling against the assault, pupils shrinking to pinpricks.

"Get on the ground! Face down!" The command barks, robotic and merciless. Instead, Charles put his hands into the pockets of his sweatshirt. His muscles lock, a monument built from defiance and firelight. Behind him, the blaze roars, a living beast gnawing at the bones of the building. In front of him, a barrage of bullets waiting for a reason to fly.

He knows the script. He's read this ending before—death by fire or death by cop, a bullet for punctuation. He even welcomed it once. But not tonight. Not like this. Something deep, original, cries that this is wrong, that fate has miscast the final act. He is twenty-seven. Too young for the grave. Too hungry for the life he's yet to build. His pulse builds, heart pounding against the cage of his ribs.

Slowly, Charles rises and turns, smoke wreathing his frame in hell's glow. His back faces the officer now, his shadow stretching long across the scorched tiles. He feels the weight of inevitability pressing down, cold and absolute. Fire in front. Bullets behind. No exits. No mercy.

"Hands out of your pockets! On your head—NOW!" The voice lashes again, fear frothing at its edges.

Charles obeys—partially. His left hand slides free, slow as time itself, fingers unfurling like petals. And there it is. The watch. Golden. Perfect. Its surface glows under the fire's manic pulse. The officer's breath catches. The watch pirouettes between Charles's fingers, spinning in hypnotic twists, catching shards of firelight and fractured neon. Each rotation births a constellation of gleam, a galaxy orbiting in his palm.

The officer stares, transfixed, pupils dilating as the dance unfolds. The world seems to hush, sound strangled by awe. Even the flames falter, their crackle dimming under the watch's silent sermon. Charles flips it, rolls it, lets it tumble across his knuckles like liquid gold. Time feels elastic, stretching thin as the lid glints in the half-light.

Then—stillness. Charles halts the motion, cradling the watch flat in his palm, its lid turned to face the officer like an icon raised for worship. The officer's voice fractures, brittle with tension: "Raise your other hand!"

Charles closes his eyes. Smoke scalds his lungs as he drags in a breath steeped in ash and inevitability. His thumb hovers, touches, then presses the release. A click cleaves the silence—a sound small yet seismic, explosive in the marrow of the moment.

The startled officer flinches, nerves strung tighter than a guitar string. Fear translates into reflex. The trigger jerks. The report booms, deafening, a thunderclap that obliterates the hush. Heat punches the back of Charles's skull, bone splintering under the bullet's kiss. His body folds forward, puppet strings severed, and he crashes face-first to the tile.

He lands face-down on the floor. One arm remains in its raised position, frozen in morbid benediction. The other lies buried in his pocket; fingers curled around absence. The watch tumbles free, spinning in the air before kissing the floor with a muted chime. Its lid gapes, golden and calling, as smoke coils around it like a shroud.

Outside, sirens wail—a requiem for a man now finally at rest.

Elderkin's boots scuff against tile as he storms forward, adrenaline spiking like electricity in his veins. His voice crackles through the radio, pointed and urgent: backup requested, fire and ambulance inbound. The words spill out in a rush, but his eyes are locked on the ruin sprawled before him.

Charles is a motionless silhouette against the flickering glow. Smoke rolls upward, veiling the corpse in spectral ribbons. Elderkin approaches, kicks ribs once and waits. Kicks again— hard, the thud reverberating through the hollow store. No response. He hooks his boot under the shoulder, thigh muscles pulling, and heaves. The body rolls, limp as fallen laundry. Then he sees the exit wound gaping in the forehead, a crater punched clean through bone. Brain matter freckles the shelves above, vile graffiti splattered across canned goods. The suspect is gone. Dead. Final.

Elderkin turns, bolts toward Dobson. One glance seals the verdict: the sheriff is beyond saving; his skull a shattered reliquary. Rage claws at Elderkin's throat, but duty drags him onward. He snatches the extinguisher, fingers fumbling against the steel. A squeeze—nothing. Dead. Empty. He curses, sprints for the kitchen, and wrenches another from its cradle. Foam erupts in a white geyser, hissing as it devours flame. The inferno shrinks, coughing embers, until only a charred husk remains where Rangle once stood. Smoke lingers, bitter and harsh, clawing at Elderkin's lungs.

Then—stillness. His gaze hooks on something gleaming near Charles's outstretched hand. A watch. Golden. Perfect. Its lid waits open, welcoming like a portal that sees beyond time.

Elderkin approaches and crouches, fingers trembling as they close around the artifact. It is warm—almost alive. Its surface, which should be slick with soot and blood, is clean and unmarred. He tilts it, light skittering across its polished skin, and feels the cosmos constrict to this single, hypnotic point.

He lifts it to his ear. Silence. No tick, no heartbeat. The hands rest askew, frozen in defiance of chronology. He shakes it gently, thumb grazing the filigree, and for a breathless instant, the chaos around him dissolves. Sirens wail in the distance, their banshee cries threading through smoke, but Elderkin barely hears. The watch hums in his mind, a siren song of gold and shadow.

It calls to him.

He turns toward the doorway, headlights spearing through the haze, strobes painting the air in arterial reds and blues. Backup is coming. This nightmare is almost over. Almost. Elderkin glances down one last time, pupils dilating as the watch glimmers like a relic dredged from eternity. His breath hitches. A shrug. Then—click.

The lid snaps shut, a sound that should be small, but is huge in this space, bellowing through the hush like a ripple. Elderkin slips the watch into his pocket, its warm weight settling against his thigh like a living thing.

He turns and reaches toward the corpse to frisk it, to find and retrieve the firearm that is surely still grasped in the suspects hand in that sweatshirt pocket—the firearm that will make this a justified kill.

But the floor lays bare before him—empty.

The body is gone.

Elderkin's blood ices. His head whips left and right; eyes carving franticly through smoke. Nothing. Silence. He spins, heart pumping icy blood, and freezes. His eyes cross.

A pistol stares back, its barrel a black tunnel boring into his soul. Elderkin's breath catches short in his throat, a gasp stealing the air. His pupils balloon wide, swallowing light. He has only enough time to inhale, sharp and shallow, before his world ends in black thunder.

Charles stands over Deputy Elderkin's body. The deputy's eyes stare skyward, glassy and vacant, a neat hole drilled dead-center between them. Blood pools beneath his skull, dark and thick.

Sirens wail in the distance, their tortured cries threading through smoke, growing louder, closer.

Charles crouches, fingers darting into the deputy's pocket. Metal kisses his skin—the watch. He can feel it's warmth. He can hear its song. He snatches it back, its surface flawless and unharmed. No time for reverence. He palms it, shoves it deep into his own pocket, and spins on his heel.

The store sprawls before him, a battlefield of ruin bathed in strobe-light chaos. Red and blue pulses toggle through shattered glass, painting the smoke in feverish hues. Shadows writhe along the walls, demonic shadow monsters dancing to the siren's dirge. The front of the store is too dangerous now. The sirens are getting louder, closer. Charles bolts, lungs clawing for air that isn't laden with ash and chemical grit.

The back door slams open under his shove, hinges shrieking. Charles spills out into the night. Cool air slams into him. He clears the obstacles and sprints alongside the back of the buildings toward the alley.

The stolen sedan hides in shadow, its skin slick with dew. Charles dives in, fingers clawing for the keys. Metal bites his grip. A twist and the engine snarls alive. He slams the door, drops the shifter into reverse, and stomps the accelerator. Tires shriek, rubber whizzing against wet asphalt, carving dark scars into the alley's throat.

The car rockets backward, a torpedo of steel and fury. Smoke geysers from the exhaust as Charles wrenches the wheel hard at the end of the alley. He slams on the brakes, jams the transmission into drive and floors the gas. The front tires break traction, spinning wild, spitting asphalt like birdshot. The engine howls, a wraith's wail clawing at the night.

Headlights pierce a hole through darkness as the sedan rockets forward, devouring distance in savage gulps. Behind him, sirens crescendo, a chorus of doom clawing at his heels. Fire trucks loom at the intersection, their lights pulsating color into the void. Charles doesn't look back again. He can't. He won't.

—

The stolen sedan skids into the Dusty Spoke's lot, tires sliding atop gravel. A storm of dust erupts, swirling in sepia clouds that swallow the car completely. Charles bursts from the driver's seat. The dust coils around him like a living thing.

He doesn't pause. His boots pound the boards of the porch. The door groans under his grip, hinges shrieking sharply as he rips it wide. Light from the lot spills in, slicing the dim interior into pieces. Mandy's head snaps up, her eyes twin crescents of shock. She freezes mid-motion, a rag dangling from her fingers, as she drinks in the apparition framed in the doorway.

Charles stands there, a ruin draped in soot and blood, his clothes stiffening with gore, his face a mask of crimson. Behind him, the dust cloud writhes past the threshold, a phantom tide that ebbs and dies, leaving silence raw and ringing. He releases the handle. It slams shut with a hollow thud that reverberates through the wooden bones of the room.

He moves straight forward like a storm bottled in flesh. His eyes burn, pupils drowning in black-emerald fire, their glare a spike honed on rage and revelation. Mandy's breath stops, her pulse a trapped bird fluttering in her throat.

"Hey… honey. Everything okay?" Her voice fractures, brittle as sugar glass, words trembling on the edge of panic. This isn't the Charles she knows—the cool, tightly wrapped serpent of control. This is something else. Something unusual and unfamiliar.

Charles closes the distance until the bar top looms between them like a barricade. He plants his hands and leans in. Their eyes lock—hers wide and liquid, his twin emerald abysses swallowing light. She searches them, desperate for answers to questions she can't yet name.

"What is it?" Softer now, her tone a balm smeared over dynamite. She scans him—torso streaked in soot, fabric stiffening with blood, hair matted in clots. Her gaze ricochets back to his eyes, and what she sees there curdles her breath: a storm, black and bottomless.

Impact.

A slap of sound as Charles hurls the package onto the bar. It lands with a sodden thump, its paper skin blotched with blood and grime. Mandy flinches, pupils dilating as her gaze hooks on the relic sprawled between them. Her fingers twitch, inching forward, trembling like leaves in a phantom wind.

Charles's jaw muscles knot, teeth grinding into dust. His face burns crimson, veins writhing under hot flesh. A tremor ripples through him, subtle at first, then seismic. His eyes glaze, red-rimmed and fever-bright. Mandy's breath stutters. She reaches: slow, tentative, until her fingertip grazes the package.

Lightning.

Charles snatches up the envelope. His other hand simultaneously clamps her wrist, iron crushing silk. He yanks, ripping her from the bar's embrace, dragging her down its length in a blur of motion. Bottles rattle, glasses shriek against wood, as Mandy stumbles, her pulse pounding in her ears. Pain rises in her wrist. She cradles it as soon as he releases her, fingers kneading flesh in frantic circles.

Charles turns and seizes the mounted CRT television. Plastic groans under his grip as he wrenches it on its axis, angling it toward the back corner—a dead-end cul-de-sac draped in gloom. He slams the power button. The screen convulses, birthing a storm of static, white noise hissing like a pit of snakes from the speaker. He then punches the power button of the VCR tape player that sits on the butcher block table beneath the set.

The package is opened, spilling its secret: a VHS tape, its black skin void of grime. Charles grips it like a cleaver and rams it into the player's maw. The machine swallows, gears whirring, and the tape vanishes into its mechanical gullet.

———

Static flickers. White snow writhes, then collapses into image. Mandy stares, breath intermittent, as the screen exhales its first ghost of truth.

Charles turns his back to the screen.

The first frame stutters to life—a shaky, chaotic blur that digs at Mandy's nerves and brings on nausea. The camera jerks like a wounded animal, its lens sweeping fragments of a room in disjointed spasms. A lamp streaks past in a smear of light. A headboard ricochets into view, then vanishes. Ceiling tiles whirl like a pinwheel devoid of color. A picture frame flashes before the shot collapses into carpet fibers, coarse and colorless, filling the screen like static made flesh.

Clicks and thumps rattle from the speakers, hollow percussion echoing in Mandy's chest. The image convulses, then dies. White noise roars like a blizzard, swallowing sound and sight again. Seconds drag before the picture exhales again. This time, stillness. The camera has found its spine. The frame locks, rigid and sure, as though bolted to bone.

A wall dominates the shot: blank, mute, unnerving in its emptiness. Its surface glows under a pale corona of light, a circle burned into the center by a lamp crouching somewhere beyond view. Shadows gather in the corners, thick and oily, bleeding orange from a lone bulb gasping in the gloom. On the left, the arm of a chair, barely visible in the frame, like a severed limb. On the right, the edge of a television stand squats in silence. Below, carpet sprawls—a desert of lifeless beige.

Mandy leans in, inhaling in small gulps, eyes combing the void for meaning. Her pulse continues to increase, pumping pressure into her eyes. Every detail becomes a cipher: the grain of the carpet, the geometry of shadows, the sickly glare of that lamp. Her mind claws for clues, for context, for anything to anchor this dread.

Then—a voice. Male. Thick with smoke and authority. It slithers from the speakers, slick and serpentine: "Go ahead now, son. Step up. Don't be shy."

Mandy's head snaps toward the sound, pupils enlarging as if darkness itself has spoken. The screen remains unchanged: just the wall, the chair arm, the stand. But the air around the screen feels different now: charged, malignant. A shuffle scratches through the speakers, fabric dragging against wood. Then the voice again, sweeter now, sugar lacquered over rot:

"It's okay, son. It's fun. We'll make our movie and you'll be a famous movie star."

Silence crawls, slow and suffocating. Then—movement, not seen but heard. A scuffle, soft and furtive, like prey dragged across linoleum. The voice hardens, its edge honed to command:

"Go ahead and help him out."

A creak punctuates the hush—the groan of bedsprings surrendering weight. Mandy flinches, nails biting her palms. Another shuffle. Then—a sound that cleaves her marrow. A child's voice, thin and trembling, words quivering like moth wings:

"No... I don't want to. I want to go home."

Her throat knots. Breath curdles. The room around her dissolves, collapsing into that voice—a ghost dredged from innocence.

A second man speaks now, tone dripping with mockery: "Oh no. You don't want to go home now. The fun is just starting. Don't you want to make a cowboys and Indians movie with your friends? It'll be fun! Tell him, boys."

Then audio chaos erupts—two voices, high and bright, ricocheting like marbles across the dark. Children. Young. Giddy with something organic. "Ya! Come on, Stevie! It's fun! We get to jump on the bed all we want!"

The soundtrack devolves into giggles, breathless and punchy, punctuated by the rhythmic shriek of springs. Mandy's stomach knots, bile clawing her throat. Her eyes flick to Charles: his back a monolith, rigid, head bowed, hands clasped like a penitent before an altar of sin.

"You get to ride a horsey!" one voice yelps, syllables bouncing in disturbing sync with unseen leaps. The words splinter, broken with breathlessness: get—ride—horsey.

The bed groans again, a dirge of metal tortured by weight. Giggles swell, manic and merciless.

Then—the director's voice, slicing through the din: "Go ahead and put him in the shot."

A scuffle breaks out, sharp and sudden. Then—a cry. High, piercing, pitch ever rising, shredded with terror:

"Nooooooo..."

Mandy's breath expels at once. Her knuckles whiten against the table's edge. Onscreen, the wall remains blank, mute as a witness who will never speak. But the sound—the sound paints horrors no image should hold.

A boy no older than five jolts into view as if shoved there, and Mandy's breath catches mid-exhale like a stopper in her throat. Her eyes dart across the screen, desperate, refusing to believe what they see. White briefs, loose. A frame so thin it seems breakable, ribs etched like fragile bars across his chest. Stick-like arms crossed tight, as if he could fold himself out of existence. His eyes—wet, enormous, pleading, are oceans of fear.

A hairy arm shoots in from the side, its grip clamping down on the boy's shoulder with a violence that makes Mandy flinch. The hand is monstrous, crowned with a black onyx ring heavy in gold, glinting like a cruel eye. Tattoos crawl up the forearm: a black panther frozen mid-climb, claws raking imaginary wounds into flesh; above it, a stark Yin-Yang, and around the elbow, a spider web like a snare. Another hand juts in from the other side of the screen—just as brutal. The fist is in the boy's shaggy auburn hair, gaudy rings flashing as it jerks his head back. The boy whimpers, and Mandy feels the sound like glass shattering inside her chest.

"Straighten up! Look into the camera!" The command explodes in the room. Mandy's stomach knots. Her pulse rages in her ears as the boy obeys, wide-eyed, staring straight into the lens—and into her soul. She doesn't know him, yet something in those eyes feels achingly familiar, like a dream clawing at memory. Time stops. She lifts a trembling hand toward the screen, aching to cup his cheek, to shield him from everything. Her fingertips hover against cold glass.

A voice slices through the silence, sharp as a whip. Mandy jerks her hand back, shame flooding her like ice water for being so close to that voice.

"Tell me your first name and how old you are, son. ...Just your first name."

The boy doesn't move. Doesn't blink. His silence screams louder than words.

"Go ahead, son. Just tell me your name. It's not hard. It's easy. None of this is hard. You'll see." The voice is coaxing now, greasy and poisonous. "You can't be famous if nobody knows your name, right? Just tell us your name."

Those eyes—those drowning eyes lock on Mandy again, and she feels herself unravel. He stares so long it feels eternal, then flicks his gaze past the camera, toward the man behind it. A heartbeat later, his voice comes: small, broken, barely a breath.

"Steven."

"I can't hear you. Say it louder."

The boy startles, blurts out, "Steven! My name is Steven!" His voice cracks like thin balsa wood.

"Well see now, Steven? That wasn't so hard. Was it?" The voice presses, relentless. "And how old are you, Steven?"

"I'm five years old." He tries to sound brave, but the tremor betrays him. Mandy's nails dig deeper into her palms.

"OK, Steven. Very good. Are you ready to be in a cowboys and Indians movie?"

Steven nods, a tiny motion weighted with defeat. Mandy feels her heart cave in, a cavern collapsing under its own grief.

"OK, well the Indians are over there jumping on the bed. That's your camp," the director announces, voice slimy with false cheer.

Steven tilts his head left, eyes flicking toward the chaos. Off screen, two boys bounce on the mattress, shrieking war cries that twist Mandy's stomach into knots. The director's voice cuts again, sharp and commanding.

"Now you're the cowboy. The hero. You need to wrestle those Indians and keep them from wrecking your camp."

Steven glances back at him, then at the lens—at Mandy. That stare cleaves her in two. Inside her skull, she's screaming: Don't move! Stay safe! Please!

"Go ahead now, boy. Action!" Hands clap like gunfire. Mandy flinches.

Steven hesitates, gaze locked on Mandy through the glass, then shifts left and slips out of the right side of the frame. The camera jerks, chasing him. He stands at the bed's edge, staring up at two boys his size, in the same state of undress, pounding the mattress like dances of war.

"Woo, woo, woo, woo, woo…" They slap their mouths, rain-dancing in depraved parody. Mandy's throat burns.

"Go on, Steven! Have fun! Climb up there and pretend. Show those mean Indians they can't stomp your camp!" The voice drools poison disguised as play.

Steven climbs slowly, each movement weighted with dread. He turns, frozen in the lens's glare. All three boys fill the frame now, but Steven is a statue: arms limp, face hollow, eyes shadowed like bruises. Mandy feels her pulse suddenly stop.

"And… ACTION!" Another clap detonates. Steven startles, glances past the camera, then begins to bounce—mechanical, lifeless, like a fishing float on tiny ripples.

"OK, now Steven, take the Indians down. Shoot them with your gun."

Steven halts, turns toward the voice. His small hand rises, pointer finger stiff, thumb jerking like a broken lever.

"Pew, pew! Pew, pew!" The sounds scrape Mandy's nerves raw.

"Caleb, Blake... pretend to die now. The cowboy shot you."

"OK!" Blake chirps, bright and eager.

Mandy's breath gasps and catches. Her head whips toward Charles.

"Caleb and Blake?" Her voice cracks like new ice.

Charles doesn't move. Doesn't turn. He's stone.

Steven fires again, relentless. "Pew, pew, pew! Pew, pew!"

The other boys convulse, slapping themselves in appalling pantomime, collapsing into heaps. A snicker leaks from one pile. Steven stands over them, staring down at the mock carnage, his face drawn from sorrow.

"You did it! You're the hero, Steven!" The director's tone brightens, repulsive in its cheer. "Now call your trusty horse to haul these dirty dead Injuns back to town for your reward."

Mandy feels her soul faint, its nails dragging down the inner walls of her chest as it slumps. Hero. Reward. Words curdle in her ears like rot.

"Yay! Horsey!" Blake's muffled voice chirps from his heap, a soiled echo of innocence.

"Shh! Quiet, Blake! You're supposed to be dead!" snaps the director.

Steven freezes, confusion clouding his small face. His eyes drift past the lens toward the voice, searching for sense that will never come.

"Just call for your horse, Steven. He'll come to you," the director croons now, attention sliding from Blake's misstep. "If you had a horse of your own, what would you name it?"

Steven tilts his head back, gaze tracing the ceiling as if answers might hide in the tiles. Then, a fragile smile blooms. "Fred."

"OK then. Fred it is. Go ahead and call Fred, your horse."

Steven nods, hesitant, surrendering to the pretend he knows is hollow. His voice trembles like a reed in wind, "Freeeeeeeed…" he calls. "Come here, boy! Come on!"

He clicks his tongue, soft squeaks breaking suction against the roof of his mouth—sounds meant for kittens, not this nightmare.

"Come on, Fred. Here Freddy, Freddy. I need your help."

A shuffle stirs off-camera. Steven's head jerks toward it. Mandy's stomach convulses, dread clawing up her spine.

Then it happens—a man lumbers into view, sweat slicking his hairy back, white briefs clinging like shame. A rubber horse mask grins grotesquely where his face should be. He gallops in mockery, whinnying as if joy could live here. The fat on his sweaty body fights gravity with every gallop's landing.

The horse man turns his slickened mass, his hairy, pasty arm enters frame—thick, tattooed with the panther, the Yin-Yang, the spider web. Mandy's inhales quick and short. Her hand shoots forward, slamming the stop button.

"I don't want to see anymore!" Her voice trails as she spins from the screen, eyes drilling into the floor. Tears sting, hot and merciless.

Charles finally breaks free from his stone encasement, whirls, rage and resolve braided tight. He punches play, grips her shoulders, forces her toward the glow.

"No! I don't want to see anymore! It's sick! I've seen all I need to see!"

Her hand darts for the button. He swats it away. Charles presses and holds the FWD lever, scenes scream past in a blur of motion.

Mandy catches shards: flashes of flesh, shadows of harm. Tears flow down her cheeks and fall from her quivering chin.

Then snow devours the frame. Silence. Until the wall returns: blank, sterile, anxiety-inducing in its stillness.

"Go ahead, son. Go up there and tell us your name and how old you are." The voice slithers back.

A boy drifts in from the left, no older than five. White briefs sag on his brittle frame. His hair is matted, his cheek swollen pink like a wound blooming. He stands slumped, a spent rag doll.

"What's your name, boy?" The voice sharpens.

"Mark Wheeler," he blurts, terror cracking his tone.

"Just your first name," scolds the voice.

"Just Mark." The reply quick and sharp.

Mandy's gaze slices to Charles. His nod answers before her lips can shape the question.

"Wheeler?"

Another nod, slow as grief.

"And what do you want to be when you grow up, Just Mark?" The question drips false sweetness.

"I want to be a space man."

Forward again. Chipmunk voices squeal as time flies on tape and stops in the bar. Mandy looks away, fist clamped to her mouth, bile clawing her throat. Tears spill unchecked. Charles hooks her arm and turns her back. Flashes stab her vision: boys, helmets, offensive fragments of flesh. Too much. Always too much.

Blank wall. Another boy. Blonde, silent, cheek bruised like a fading sunset. His eyes lift, Emerald green embers embedded in dark hollows beneath a lowered brow. A cross-shaped scar brands his throat.

"This is Charles," the voice purrs. "And he wants to be a big bad biker when he grows up. Isn't that right, Chuckie?"

The child nods, slow, mechanical. Mandy's heart caves in. She folds into the man beside her, arms cinching his waist, tears soaking his shirt.

"Oh Charles, I am so sorry!" Her sobs shudder through the room.

Forward again. Flashes slice her eyes—helmets, hair, horror. She buries her face in his chest, wishing blindness. He makes her watch. Blank wall. Another boy. A circus clown dream. Forward. Blank wall. Another boy. A wrestler's wish. Forward. Each name a dagger. Each face a ghost grown into men she knows now—men bound by scars and secrets, baptized in cruelty.

Mandy clings tighter, grief roaring silent in her veins. The tape spins on, a carousel of broken childhoods, and she cannot stop it.

Charles presses forward, holding the button until the tape gasps its last breath in a storm of static. White noise devours the screen, a blizzard of nothingness. His finger shifts—rewind now, dragging time backward until the blank wall reappears like a ghost. He lets the tape roll.

The frame is empty, but the voice slithers in from somewhere unseen, tangled in shuffling sounds.

"OK, say the final lines and let's get the hell out of here. I'll take the tape home and start editing tonight. We should have it to our clients first thing Monday morning."

Mandy stiffens—clients: the word curdles like old milk in her ears.

Silence implodes, then ruptures. A figure lunges into view, obscene in its cheer: the horse-headed man, sweat-slick and no doubt a demonic grin unseen behind rubber. His arms fling wide, jazz hands tickling the air.

"Hey now!" The muffled cry punches through the mask, jolting Mandy like a live wire. He prances, a rotten parody of joy, voice rolling like a carnival barker.

"We hope you've enjoyed viewing our current selection! If any of our products tickle your fancy, you know how to reach us! We value you as clients, and as always, your transaction is one hundred percent private and secure. Thank you again—and expect a fresh catalog soon!"

Each word slams into Mandy like a stone. Her stomach heaves. Her breath splinters. Products. Clients. Catalog. Language dressed in civility, rotting at its core.

"Perfect! That's a wrap," the director crows. "You boys did great too!"

"Thank you, Mr. Kerrington," the horse-headed man replies, his masked face lunging close to the lens until it devours the frame.

"Thank you, daddy!" Two voices chirp from the shadows—bright, innocent, tainted.

The camera jolts, rattling like bones in a box. Then—static. Endless, merciful static swallowing the screen. Mandy stares, hollowed out, the sound hissing in her ears like the pressure releasing in her head. Its storm of pinpoints swirling like a galaxy collapsing in silence.

Slowly, she turns to Charles. Her eyes brim with sorrow so heavy it seems to bend the air. Her hand rises, trembling, and settles on his shoulder as a fragile anchor in a sea of despair. She presses gently, urging him to face her. Charles resists for a breath, then allows his head to turn, his movements sluggish, weighted with shame. His gaze flickers, collides with hers, then skitters away like a wounded animal. When it returns, it is sunken, gutted, drowning in guilt.

Charles feels filth clinging to his skin, burrowing into his soul. He cannot scrub it away. He cannot outrun it. Mandy sees it—the grime of memory branded into his eyes, and her heart crumbles. For a fleeting moment, pity softens her face. Then disgust surges like a backed-up sewer pipe, raw and unstoppable.

"We have to tell Banks." The words rip from her throat, resigned and urgent.

Charles jerks his head in a violent shake. No. His lips clamp shut, a barricade against the idea.

Mandy grips his arms, fingers digging in as if she could anchor him to decency. Her voice trembles with conviction. "We can trust him!"

Their eyes lock, a battlefield of fear and pleading. Mandy searches his gaze, desperate to plant her truth there, to make him believe. "You know we can trust him," she presses, her tone fierce, almost breaking. "He's a good man, Charles. He was a service man. He has integrity. He would never be part of this— and he wasn't in the video."

The silence stretches like a tightwire. Charles's chest heaves. Shadows of thought flicker across his face: war, loyalty, shame, the weight of secrets. Finally, his head dips in a slow, reluctant nod. Yes.

Mandy exhales like a dam bursting. She spins toward the telephone, urgency propelling her. Her fingers clutch the receiver, knuckles blanching as she dials. Words spill in a rush: sharp, clipped, desperate. Then, a slam. The handset crashes into its cradle, echoing like a gunshot.

She returns to Charles, her breath ragged, her pulse at its peak. He stands rigid with guilt. Together they wait, silence pressing down like a tomb, both of them drowning in the gravity of what comes next.

—

Twenty-five minutes crawl by like hours before the low rumble of Banks' motorcycle shivers through the night. The sound rolls closer, heavy and foreboding, until it dies in a sudden hush. Mandy's breath catches. Charles stiffens, his shame a weight pressing him deeper into shadow.

The front door bursts open, slamming against the wall like a wrecking ball. Banks strides in, a storm bottled in leather and steel. His pistol gleams at his thigh, gripped tight, half-hidden but ready; a silent vow of violence if needed. His eyes sweep the room, sharp and unyielding.

"Mandy... Charles... Everything alright?" His voice cuts straight to the bone. "What's the emergency?"

Mandy lifts a trembling hand, palm down, urging calm. "Put the piece away, Dan." Her tone strains for steadiness, but the tremor betrays her. "It's not like that. We have to show you something. Come here."

Banks slides the weapon into its holster with a fluid motion, then closes the distance in brisk, pounding strides. He rounds the TV, stepping into the cramped corner where Mandy stands like a messenger of sorrow. Charles lingers behind, his silence louder than usual.

"You don't need to watch the whole thing," Mandy warns, voice low, thin as thread. "And you aren't going to want to. But you need to see this, Banks."

Her fingers hover, then press the play button. The machine whirs, a mechanical sigh that seems to suck the air from the room.

Charles recoils, peeling away from them, retreating to a booth like a man fleeing his own reflection. He drops into the seat, shoulders hunched, head bowed. He tries to shut it out: the voices, the images, but they seep through, insidious. The director's tone slithers into his ears. Mandy and Banks whisper like concerned parents. The tape chirps in fast-forward, a shrill, relentless sound that drills into his skull.

Minutes bleed away. Then footsteps approach, slow and heavy with mourning. Mandy and Banks slide into the booth across from him. Silence settles like ash around them. Three figures, heads bowed, eyes locked on the scarred wood of the table, as if it could swallow their knowledge.

Finally, Banks lifts his gaze, steel meeting shadow. "Do you know where our movie stars are now?" His words land like a carpet bombing.

Charles doesn't look up. His head tilts in a slow, broken shake. No.

"I do." Mandy's voice slices the quiet, plain and cold as truth. "I know exactly where they are."

Banks throws a side-eyed glance to Mandy. How would she know where those guys are? She's just a bartender.

She elaborates.

Upon hearing Mandy's final word, Banks moves like a trigger snapping. He slides out, boots striking the floor with purpose. He rises, a tower of resolve.

"Stay here, Mandy." His command cracks the air. Then, to Charles: "Let's go."

The words hang. Charles pushes to his feet.

———

The sky bleeds faint streaks of blue and pink along the horizon, a fragile promise of dawn clawing through the dark. Charles and Banks stand before the motel door, shadows stretched long across cracked pavement. The number looms large on the chipped wood: confirmation, cold and absolute. Mandy's intel was right.

Banks leans in, voice a low rumble laced with grim humor. "Thirteen Sixty-nine. Perfect. One unlucky cocksucker in there for sure." A sharp snort escapes Charles—a brittle sound, humor strangled by tension.

Then the chaos explodes. The door bursts inward under Banks' boot, splintering wood with a crack that ricochets down the silent row. Darkness shatters as twin beams of light slice through smoke and stale air. The room convulses in chaos—dust swirling in beams of light, shadows writhing. A bed looms in the center, sheets tangled like entrails. Flashlight beams whip across the walls, carving frantic grooves in the black.

A flash of skin. A partially covered face contorted in horror. A hairy torso jerks upright. A sheet erupts skyward, a pale ghost flailing in the artificial dawn. At the foot of the bed, a man crouches on hands and knees, naked, exposed, his eyes wide saucers of shock and terror are all that can be seen in the shadows beneath the sheet. His hands shoot out in surrender, trembling, pleading.

Banks' pistol rises. The man snatches the sheet, drags it over his head, cocooning himself in a shroud of false safety—as if cotton could deflect bullets, as if blindness could erase fate.

The first shot silently delivers death. Then another. And another. Each muffled crack punches the sheet inward, ghost fists striking from nowhere. Charles watches, detached, almost mesmerized. Blood blooms like dark flowers across the fabric. Then gravity claims its due—the sheet collapses, dragging its cargo down. A limp arm spills free, dangling over the mattress edge, twitching like a dying rodent. Crimson threads slither down fingertips, drip-drip-dripping onto the warped floorboards.

Half the sheet still protrudes upward, trembling. Charles smiles, a grim slash of satisfaction. He grips the fabric, yanks it away.

Blake Kerrington crouches there, naked and cornered, his body curled tight against the headboard, eyes wild with primal fear. The sheets pooled at his feet are sodden with blood, a scarlet sea lapping at his skin.

Charles slides his pistol into his waistband, fingers curling around the hilt of his hunting knife. Metal silently slips free of leather. Blake jerks backward, spine pressing harder into the headboard—a dead end, immovable, merciless. He shoves against it as if sheer will could make it vanish, could provide him an escape.

The blade plunges—not into flesh, but into the mattress at Blake's feet. Foam sighs under steel. Blake recoils, legs snapping tight against his torso, breath toggling in uncontrolled gasps. Charles cuts a strip from the blood-soaked mattress, movements precise, surgical. Then, in a blur, his hand fists Blake's hair. He yanks hard. Blake's scream rips the air, high-pitched and childish.

The gag comes next—a crimson rag rammed between teeth, choking off sound. Banks moves without pause, duct tape hissing as it winds around Blake's head, sealing the horror in silence. Blake's nostrils flare, sucking frantic breaths. His eyes dart, white-rimmed and wild, ricocheting between predator and accomplice. Sweat slicks his skin, beads racing down like panicked tears.

The room reeks of fear, blood, sweat and smoke. It drowns in silence, other than the nasal suck and blow of Blake's labored breath and the faint tick of a warped air exchange fan somewhere in the ventilation system. Charles stands rigid on one side of the bed, Banks on the other. Between them, Blake writhes, gag muffling his frantic pleas into meaningless noise. His eyes bulge, wild and desperate, darting like trapped birds.

Charles

The flashlights rest now on the nightstands, twin halos casting harsh pools of light that slice through the gloom. Dust motes swirl in the beams, tiny ghosts dancing above the blood-soaked sheets. Charles and Banks loom over Blake, their stares heavy, lit from hellfire.

Banks suddenly moves, explosive. His fist rises high and crashes down, a sledge swung by rage. The blow, powered by the weight of his body, collides with Blake's face. The sound is sickening: a dull, wet crack. Blood erupts in a compressed release, spattering across Blake's cheeks like crushed fruit. His head snaps sideways, gag jerking against his teeth.

Charles lunges, animal-quick, vaulting onto the mattress. Springs shriek under his weight. He rises to his knees, hunting knife clenched in his fist, steel gleaming like a promise. His arm pistons down—not the blade, but the knuckle-wrapped hilt, slamming into Blake's shattered nose. Teeth shear free, snapping at the gums, white shards vanishing into the crimson ruin of his mouth—trapped there by the gag. His lip bursts wide, spilling blood in thick ropes.

Pain has no time to radiate before the storm breaks. Charles's fists rain down, left-right-left, a brutal rhythm pounding flesh into pulp. Eyes, nose, lips. Each strike is a beating of vengeance. He boxes Blake's ears, savage blows that echo in the hollow chamber of the room, then drives his fists back into the face, relentlessly.

Blake thrashes, hands clawing for cover, but Banks clamps him down, iron fingers locking his wrists. The gag muffles screams into strangled sobs. Blood slicks the sheets, spatters the walls, paints the air with metallic tang.

Finally, silence. Blake slumps, limp. Charles stops dead, chest heaving, sweat forming rivers down his temples. Banks straightens, breath grating like sandpaper. Both men peel

367

themselves from the bed, slow, deliberate, movements heavy with exhaustion and grim purpose.

Charles turns toward the bed, flashlight in hand. Its beam cuts a circle in the dark, landing on the first corpse sprawled beneath the bloody shroud. He grips the sheet, yanks it free. Light floods the dead man's face—

Steve Mack.

Recognition flares, cold and vivid. Charles and Banks lock eyes, a silent exchange overflowing with meaning.

Then their gazes drop to Blake. He lies naked, battered, a ruin of flesh and fear, barely clinging to life and choking on his own blood and snot. The Wicked Ones tattoo sprawls across his chest, stark and bold against the bruised canvas of his skin. Charles feels the weight of inevitability settle like lead. Banks meets his stare, nods once. No words. None needed.

Both men turn their eyes back to Blake. The room holds its breath. Dawn presses at the windows, but inside, night still reigns.

They roll Blake onto his belly in one smooth motion. Charles at the wrists, Banks at the ankles. Charles drags both wrists together and pins them high between the shoulder blades. Banks folds the legs, heels to hands, until joints lock and tendons stand out under skin. The duct tape hisses open in the dim and then wraps tight around flesh, layer after unyielding layer. The final rip snaps, and the bundle won't bend. Together they lever Blake onto his right side.

The Wicked Ones emblem sprawls across the upper left chest—collarbone to nipple, eight inches wide; ink sunk deep along the curve of the pec. Charles climbs onto the bed and settles on his knees. He cages Blake's head between his thighs, a vise of bone, muscle and anger, and bears down on the left shoulder until the ribcage rotates, turning the tattoo up like a target. He looks to Banks. Banks reads it, the whole history in a glance.

"We shouldn't, bro. Not yet," Banks warns, low. "Not without a vote."

A long moment of seriousness passes between their eyes before a wide smile spreads across both faces.

"Unanimous," declares Banks.

The flashlight drops to the mattress, and hard white glare spills across skin. Charles pins both shoulders, fury burning behind his eyes. Banks answers by drawing steel.

The knife slides free with a soft whisper. He sets the tip over the left chest, where heartbeats knock against cartilage and muscle. A bead of blood wells, dark and glossy, at the point of contact. Gentle pressure. The outer skin gives with a tight little snap—epidermis punctured, and then the blade finds the dermis, that red bed of capillaries that starts to weep at the slightest insult. The line that follows looks drawn with a thin red pen: clean, continuous, widening as vessels open and ooze. He traces the perimeter of the ink, deep enough to meet yellow fat, the subcutaneous layer that glints slick under light. Behind the blade the cut joins itself, forming a closed border.

Banks glances to Charles. Charles wants to watch. The flashlight rolls, pooling more glare. Banks sets his jaw and continues.

He eases the edge under the red seam. Blake snaps fully awake—eyes bulging white, gag wrenching his jaw. The scream that follows hits the tape and dies there, breaking into animal sounds. He bucks hard, shoulders and hips jerking, but Charles bears down, turning weight and forearms into pins.

Banks sprawls his weight across the lower half, pinning thighs and knees. The knife moves in brutal cadence—short strokes, back and forth, separating skin from the layer beneath.

Fat gleams yellow; small vessels shear and spill bright threads that trickle along ribs toward the waist. Blake arches, muscles locking into a full-body clench, then drops slack—shock wiping him clean. Breath bubbles from one nostril. Limbs sag.

Banks doesn't stop. He works the edge downward until the tip peeks from under the lower border of the tattoo. His left hand slaps over the ink, palm sealing blood. He grips and balls the freed skin in his fist—a rubbery bundle warm and wet, dermis slick against his knuckles.

An upward yank peels the flap back, exposing striated pectoralis fibers beneath, intercostal spaces glistening with red. Curtains of blood sheet along the ribcage, pool at the waist, and patter to the mattress. The blade kisses the last bridge of tissue; one decisive slice. The fillet comes free.

Banks holds it high. Blood threads drip through his fingers, spattering Blake's side in thin, bright lines. He presents the prize to Charles, and for a heartbeat they stare through the dripping fist—two men glaring across a red ruin. Their mouths curl into grim, tooth-bared grins; a nod passes between them like a contract.

Then Banks whips his arm down and spikes the flap onto Blake's belly. The impact lands with a wet slap that twists the gut—raw meat against tile. The fillet slides, painting a red comet tail across the abdomen before settling in a glistening heap.

Blood loss paints Blake in grotesque artistry: chest, belly, arms, thighs smeared in crimson swirls like a child's finger painting gone mad. Sheets cling wet to his frame. He looks dead, slack and pale beneath the gore. Charles and Banks stand leering on either side of the bed, their shadows long in the harsh pools of flashlight glare, eyes locked on the ruin they've made.

For a moment, silence reigns supreme. They drink in the sight—their work, savage and irreversible. Then Charles moves.

He bends low, left hand steadying the knife, its tip kissing the fresh wound at the center of Blake's chest. His right hand snakes upward, clamps Blake's nostrils shut in a cruel pinch. Banks reads the cue without words; he folds down, weight crashing onto Blake's shoulders, pinning him deep into the mattress.

Seven seconds stretch like wire unspooled. Then Blake convulses back into life. His body tries to arch, a violent surge of instinct: spine compressing, muscles firing in blind panic. He tries to sit up, to breathe, but the human vise crushes him flat. His lungs drag against emptiness; against vacuum, clawing for air through a pinched nose already clogged with blood and ruin. Tendons stand out along his neck: ballooning, straining under skin, roots of an oak clawing for purchase. His chest heaves, ribs sawing against flesh as his diaphragm jerks in futile rhythm.

The gag seals his mouth; the tape bites deep. Air becomes a myth. His eyes bulge, sclera gone raw, pupils blown wide in terror. Charles snickers—a low, guttural sound, and toys with the knife, tracing lazy circles over the wound as if doodling death. Blake thrashes, head whipping side to side, desperate to shake free of the grip crushing his nose. His movements grow frantic, jerks snapping like a fish on a hook.

A final violent twist, and his nostrils tear free from Charles's clamp. Blake drags air in the tiniest of forced sips, sucking life through broken, blood-choked channels. Each breath sucks wet, thin, but it's something. Cool oxygen threads into starved alveoli. Not enough. Never enough. His chest convulses, lungs straining like bellows against iron bands. Darkness still prowls at the edges, licking closer.

His eyes roll, whites flashing as consciousness frays. Banks chuckles. Charles joins him, grin emerging in shadow, knife still grazing the wound. Blake teeters on the brink, body trembling, breaths shredding into shallow gasps.

Then—impact. Charles's open palm cracks across Blake's face, snapping his head sideways. Another blow follows, backhanded, splitting the rhythm. A third lands hard, open-handed, jerking his jaw. Blake moans and claws his way back from the abyss. His breathing lengthens, deepens, panic bleeding into raw survival. His eyes, still rimmed in terror, lock on Charles.

Charles leans closer, closing the distance until his shadow swallows Blake's face. Their gazes collide—predator and prey, bound in a silence thick with menace. Charles sees coherence flicker back in those bloodshot eyes. And his smile grows.

The knife spins slow in Charles's grip, its tip teasing the wound carved into Blake's chest. Each tiny twist—clockwise, counter-clockwise, sends white-hot nerve fire screaming through his body. Pain blooms like lava, searing deep, radiating outward in pulsating waves.

Blake stirs, a broken manikin clawing for life. His head lifts in trembling increments, neck cords straining like high-tension wires under pale, blood-slick skin. His shattered nose drips crimson as his gaze crawls downward. He sees it—the wound peeled open, the steel dancing inside, cruel and deliberate. Every rotation feels like a fresh dagger, a new betrayal.

His eyes drag upward, locking on Charles. Emerald irises blaze cold, merciless fire. And then—recognition ignites. A spark flares in Blake's mind, igniting memory. Childhood specters surge forward, faces and voices colliding in a flood of clarity. Horror grips him. He knows who Charles is. He knows why this is happening.

Their gazes fuse, a silent corridor opening between them. Words vanish; thought becomes signal. Blake pleads without sound—stop, or finish it. Charles answers in kind—intent chiseled into the hard planes of his face. For a breath, they share something primal: guilt and judgment, punishment and acceptance. Two men, two verdicts, bound in a moment that feels eternal.

Then steel speaks. Charles drives the blade down, hard and true, plunging at an angle between ribs, ripping through intercostal muscle, piercing the pericardium in a single savage thrust. The heart yields with a wet pop, chambers rupturing under cold steel.

Blake involuntarily lunges upward as if to meet the blade, to welcome its kiss. His eyes balloon, pupils drowning in crimson glare. His face floods dark red, veins bulging like wet wool yarn under skin. Breath halts. Silence devours his scream. He stares, bug-eyed, into Charles's emerald fire—and then the light gutters out. His body slackens, limbs spilling like cut stage ropes. Blackness claims him.

Peace falls heavy, sudden, absolute. The room exhales. Rage evaporates like morning mist, leaving stillness crisp as day. It feels like an exorcism—an angry demon ripped from the walls. Charles and Banks ease their grips, hands sliding from cooling flesh. They rise slow, deliberate, movements weighted with aftermath.

Flashlights click alive. White cones dance across the ruin sprawled on the mattress. Blood pools in dreadful halos. Skin pale beneath rivers of red. They stand silent, breath pulling hard, hearts pounding in grim synchrony. For a long minute, they simply look at the corpse, at their work, at the darkness that binds them.

A sound slices the silence—a thin, broken whimper, fragile as a flower petal. Charles and Banks snap from their trance like a light switch has been thrown, heads jerking toward the noise. Flashlight beams whip across the room, twin spears of white dissecting the dark. They land on a corner—and freeze.

There, crumpled in shadow, a boy stares back. His face is a pale mask, pasty and hollow, eyes drowned in black circles and brimming with tears. His small frame curls tight on the faded cushion of a Queen Anne chair, knees welded to chest, arms cinched around shins like iron bands. He squints against the glare, flinching as light drills into his sockets. His body is bare save for sagging white briefs, fabric swallowing his thin hips.

The sight cleaves Charles open. For a heartbeat, the room tilts, reality warping around that fragile silhouette. He turns, searching Banks' face for anchor—but Banks is gone. Vanished like smoke. Panic flickers. Charles spins, scanning corners, shadows, blood-slick sheets. Alone now: with the boy, the dead, and the truth.

He moves for the door, boots silently padding over carpet. Fingers stretch for the handle. A glint hooks his eye. In the far corner, black metal rises like a tower: a tripod. Perched atop, a camera stares with its single glass eye, red light burning above the lens like a demon's ember. Alive. Watching. Recording.

Charles follows the invisible line from lens to bed, to Blake's ruin, to the crimson-smeared mattress. That eye has seen everything. Every scream. Every cut. Every sin. And more— things older, fouler, etched into the walls like rot.

He steps closer, breath controlled now, but pulse still pounding in his ears. The camera seems to breathe—the tape rolling, mocking him in the silence. In his mind, it speaks: I've seen everything. And I'm telling on you.

The words slither through his skull, slimy, undeniable.

Rage rears up. Charles lunges, hand snatching the camera free. Plastic creaks under his grip. He rips the cassette from its gut and jams it into his pocket. Then he hurls the camera with all the force pent up in his spine. It sails and smashes against Blake's bent kneecap with a crack. The corpse absorbs the blow, deflects, lamp shade crumples under ricochet, bulb pops.

The camera snaps free of its tripod, tumbles, skids, spins to a halt—a lifeless carcass on the carpet. Charles doesn't see. He's gone, out the door, heading for escape. The automatic closer hisses, door sealing slow, bleeding the last sliver of the room's light into oblivion.

In the black, the boy whimpers again; a small, broken sound that curdles the air. Alone now, except for the dead men and the ghosts that will never leave him.

Night air slaps Charles in the face as he trudges through the lot, lungs pulling in the cold air like a gift accepted. Outside, the lot sits in silence except for the metallic tick of cooling engines and the distant whoosh of passing tires on asphalt. Banks stands by his bike, phone pressed to his ear, posture loose, calm; untouched by the storm Charles carries inside.

Charles closes the gap in bounding strides. Banks lowers the phone, thumb killing the call, and slips it into his vest. His face is unreadable, shadowed under the brim of his helmet. Charles's eyes burn questions. His chin jerks—a silent demand: Who was that? What did you do?

"I called Dusty, man," Banks says, voice flat, matter-of-fact, like he's reporting the weather. "He'll know what to do about this mess."

The words hit Charles like a slap. Dusty. Another name in the blood-soaked ledger. Fury detonates in his chest. He lunges, hands clamping Banks' shoulders, fingers digging through leather to bone. His face twists, eyebrows knotted, eyes screaming: Why? Why drag him into this?

Banks doesn't flinch. His hands rise, gripping Charles's forearms with steady force. "Whoa! Easy there, bro. It's cool." His tone is calm, almost soothing, but steel lurks beneath. "Dusty got nothin' to do with any of this shit. He wasn't on the tape. He's a good guy. We can trust him."

Charles stares, emerald lasers boring into Banks' dark eyes. For a heartbeat, silence stretches like a balloon. Then it pops. Charles rips free, arms snapping upward, breaking Banks' grip like brittle twigs. He spins, storming toward his bike, rage crackling off him like static. His palm slaps Banks' seat twice—hard, sharp, an unspoken command: Mount up. We're gone.

He straddles his own machine, muscles still tense, breath barely under control. Hands move in a blur: key twist, switch flick, throttle pump. The bike rolls backward, tires crunching and pinging gravel like Tiddlywinks, until it cuts perpendicular to Banks' ride. Charles halts, head swiveling. Banks hasn't moved. He stands rooted, a Redwood grown from defiance, cigarette dangling from his fingers like a fuse waiting to burn.

"Come on, bro. He said to wait here," Banks calls, voice rising to span the widening gulf. "He's gonna see the tape and see this shit and he ain't gonna blame you, or us, for doin' none of this."

Charles points—first at Banks' bike, then down the black ribbon of road stretching into oblivion. His gesture is a cobra, striking in the night.

Banks shakes his head slow, deliberate. "Naw, man. We should wait."

The words hang in the air, saturated with risk. Charles feels the weight of choice pressing his spine. Then motion erupts. He kicks the starter, throttle twisting thrice, engine coughing before it roars alive. The sound shreds the quiet, a war cry ripping through the dark. Charles settles on the seat, drops his left foot hard, slams the gear. One last glance—Banks frozen, eyes locked, silent pleas ricocheting between them like bullets: Stick together. Don't break.

Charles answers with fire. Clutch snaps, throttle screams, and the bike lunges forward, carving a savage arc through the lot. Gravel spits under tires as he blasts out of the motel's shadow, engine howling rage into the night. Behind him, Banks stands still, a lone figure in the wash of exhaust and fading light, waiting for Dusty—and for the storm that's coming.

—

The phone slams into its cradle with a crack that shatters the stillness. Dusty glares at the glowing red digits on the clock—mocking him, screaming in neon blood. Not even dawn. The hour feels wrong, heavy with unfinished dreams and the stink of sweat-soaked sheets.

He props himself on one elbow, muscles groaning under the weight of sleep. The room crouches in darkness, corners thick with shadow. Outside, the world is ink, sky bleeding nothing but hints. His mind drags through fog, gears moving slow. A grunt escapes his throat, followed by a fart that stinks of stale beer and bad choices. He mutters nonsense, words slurred and senseless, particles of thought clawing for meaning.

His hand gropes for the handset, fingers clumsy, numb with fatigue. Plastic meets skin—cold, slick. He drags it close, breath sucking through clenched teeth. The keypad glows faint under the clock's red glare. His fingers stumble, punching keys in crooked rhythm.

Seconds stretch. Then—a click. A voice crackles in his ear, gravel-thick and dripping toxins.

"Someone better be dead!" The words land blunt and brutal.

Dusty straightens, spine snapping stiff. Sleep burns off like fog under fire. His tone hardens, iron poured into syllables. "Hey. It's me. Get everyone together and meet me at church. Right now."

No room for questions. No mercy for hesitation.

He slams the phone down, plastic cracking against wood. The sound ricochets through the room, a firecracker in the dark. Dusty swings his legs over the edge of the bed, feet thudding to the floor. The boards groan under his weight. He sits there, chest heaving, eyes locked on the red digits that still glow like a wound. Dawn is coming, but not fast enough.

—

Banks stands beneath the lone security light, its orange glow bleeding down in a cone that barely pushes back the dark. Shadows cling to the edges of the lot, mysterious and silent. He flicks his lighter, flame igniting like a tiny sun cupped in his palm. The tip of the joint catches, paper crackling as fire kisses green. He draws quick, sharp breaths, feeding the ember until it glows steady. Smoke coils into the night, thin ribbons twisting away on a lazy breeze.

He stares at the joint, turning it between thumb and forefinger, evening the burn. The first real pull hits his lungs like velvet fire. He holds it deep, chest swelling, then exhales slow, watching the smoke ascend into the orange haze. Warmth spreads through his veins, a narcotic tide smoothing rough edges. His pulse steadies. Muscles unclench. For a moment, the world feels soft. He spins the joint again, touches saliva to paper to tame a runaway burn, then drags deep, savoring the bitter-sweet taste. Comfort settles over him like a worn blanket.

Banks saunters to his bike and leans against the seat in a lazy side-straddle, legs stretched out like he owns the night. The chrome gleams dull under the gas light. He exhales, smoke

378

feathering across his face, and lets his gaze drift to the motel door. Numbers stare back—1, 3, 6, 9; stark against peeling paint. His mind slides loose, thoughts dissolving into static. The joint burns down, ember crawling, as Banks drifts inward, sinking deep into the quiet cave of his own head. Here, he feels safe. Here, the blood and screams don't reach.

The motel door creaks. A sliver of black splits open, and a small face peers out—a pale moon carved with fear. Banks snaps upright, senses slamming back like a breaker switch. The boy's eyes glisten, wide and wet, rimmed in shadow. Then he vanishes, swallowed by the dark.

Banks moves fast, hands rising, palms out—a gesture of peace, of promise. "Hey there, little fella. Everything's cool," he says, voice low, gentle as dusk. He steps inside. Light from the lot spills across ruin. The boy curls tight in the Queen Anne chair, knees welded to chest, arms locked around shins, face buried deep.

"It's OK, little man," Banks murmurs, inching closer. "I'm not here to hurt you. I'm here to help. OK?"

Silence answers. The boy doesn't move.

Banks glances at the slaughterhouse scene on the bed and quickly rises. Three strides. He grabs blankets, draping them over the dead, hiding the horror under folds of faded fabric.

"See, kid? There you go. No more bad guys." His voice softens, coaxing calm. "Everything's cool, little bro."

Still, the boy stays curled, a trembling knot of bone and fear. Banks scans the room, spots the comforter crumpled on the floor. It is clean, untouched by gore. He lifts it, shakes it open, and approaches slow. He drapes it over the boy's tiny frame, tucking warmth around shivering shoulders.

"You just stay right here, little dude," he says, words struggling with something he's never had, never had to give—a father's gentleness.

The joint smolders between his fingers. He takes one last drag, smoke twisting from his lips as he sinks onto the bed's edge. A bloody foot juts from the sheet beside him, pale toes stark against red. It doesn't faze him. He exhales, watching the boy. The joint burns to a nub. Banks pops it into his mouth, tongue sizzling for a heartbeat as the ember dies in spit. He swallows, bitter heat sliding down his throat.

He feels it before he hears it. A low rumble swells into a roar. Headlights ignite the window curtains in brilliant, dancing light and slice through the partially opened door, cutting the dark to ribbons. Motorcycles flood the lot, engines snarling like lions. Banks lifts his head toward the door, eyes narrowing.

Nobody notices the last bike in the formation; the one far enough behind to be out of earshot; the one with no lights running. Nobody notices when the bike silently coasts off the road.

Charles tucks back, shadow enveloping him as he falls deeper into the tree line, slightly down and across the road from the motel. His bike gently crunches backward into the dark, the sound nonexistent under the thunderous rumble emanating from across the street. He pauses: deep enough to suit his purpose, hidden among gnarled branches, eyes locked on the motel and the scene unfolding.

Banks steps into the door frame, orange glow from the lot spilling across his boots. He moves toward the gang, shoulders squared, core tight—a man bracing against a storm he can't stop. Dusty's bike screeches to a halt, front tire biting curb. He swings off with authority, eyes sharp as razors.

"Where's the tape?" Dusty barks; his hand already outstretched to receive.

"Charles has it with him," Banks answers, tone steady but nerves flicker in his eyes.

Dusty closes the gap, fury pressing to be unleashed. "Well, where's Charles?"

"He took off, bro," Banks says, words tumbling out. "He was a little worried."

"As he should be." Dusty's reply drips ice—and then the night blows wide open.

Jardini steps from shadow, shotgun rising. The blast erupts, a muffled roar that punches the night into daylight. Fire belches from the barrel, and Banks' chest burst into a rose of red ruin. His vest shreds, shirt tears, flesh bursts open as lead pellets rip through muscle and bone. The crater opens wide, a grotesque flower spilling petals of blood.

The force hurls Banks backward, breath blown from his lungs, body airborne for a breathless instant before slamming into the door. Wood shrieks, hinges scream, and the door bursts inward under the impact. Banks crashes through, limbs flailing. He lands hard, leather and denim skidding across carpet.

Charles watches wide-eyed from the tree line across the road, horror clawing up his throat. He knew this was coming, but knowing doesn't take the edge off. Banks was solid. Banks was good. And now Banks is dying.

—

Inside, the room spins. Banks sprawls on the floor, chest a crater of gore, blood pumping in thick, arterial surges. His fingers twitch, clawing at air, reaching for something—anything. His lips part, a broken moan leaking out, thin and wet. Eyes glaze, golden flecks drowning in shadow. He fights for breath, lungs shredded, pulling empty gulps that gurgle through blood. Each inhale is a blockade, each exhale a surrender.

The light fades from his face as life drains rapidly, pooling on the carpet in widening puddles. His body jerks once, twice, then slackens, limbs spilling like anchor chains. Silence swallows the room.

Banks is gone.

—

Across the street, Charles grips his bars until knuckles could tear through his skin. His jaw locks, teeth grinding grief and rage into dust. Banks deserved better.

—

Dusty and Wheeler enter the room. Banks' eyes are rolled aimlessly toward the ceiling, glazed and vacant. Jardini's shotgun stays trained on Banks, its black maw promising oblivion. Dusty grips a fistful of sheet and yanks hard, fabric snapping free to unveil Blake's mutilated corpse. Blood pools like swamp water, flesh carved into ruin. Dusty stares, teeth clenched, silence boiling into a rolling rage.

Banks right hand suddenly claws weakly at his chest wound, fingers twitching in a dying mimicry of life. His mouth gapes, eyes unfocused.

Jardini skirts past, shotgun never wavering, and crouches low. He rips another sheet from the floor, exposing Steve's corpse beneath. Dead eyes stare glassy into nothing. Jardini looks up, meeting Dusty's glare over the mattress. Fury arcs between them.

Dusty turns, boots grinding gore into carpet, and storms for the door. His voice trails as he crosses the threshold:

"Find Chuck and kill him." The words slice the night, cold as a cleaver.

Chaos sparks. Men scatter, boots sliding, leather creaking. Steeds mounted. Kickstands snap up, metal clanging like swords drawn to shields. Ignition switches click, headlights flare—white lances piercing the dark. Engines cough, then roar, a savage chorus shaking the lot. The air reeks of gasoline and vengeance.

Before the last bike snarls to life, Wheeler's shout rips through the din: "There he is!"

Every eye follows the beam of Wheeler's light. It spears the tree line, cutting through shadows to reveal chrome glinting like a found treasure. Charles. His bike crouches in the gloom, boney branches seemingly hold it fast to the earth. Other beams swing, converging, flooding him in harsh glare. The prey is marked.

Charles stomps the kick starter, boot slamming down, engine coughing before it catches with a guttural snarl. He squeezes the clutch lever, smashes the shifter down and twists the throttle. The rear tire spins, forest floor exploding in a storm of leaves and twigs. The bike fishtails, then blasts through the brush. Both wheels leave the ground as the bike launches onto pavement. Headlamp and taillight stay dark and Charles vanishes into the black.

Behind him, fury erupts. Engines bellow like beasts unchained, waiting for clutches to grab. Dusty rockets off first and the pack falls in line, single file, chrome fangs gleaming under the lamplight glow. The Wicked Ones tear from the curb, chasing blood at breakneck speed. The roar fades and the night reclaims its own sound.

The motel door creaks open slow, bent hinges sighing in protest. A small head pokes out—a boy's face, pale and hollow, eyes wide with terror. He sees emptiness, hears only the fading thunder. Bare feet press against asphalt as he steps out, clad in nothing but sagging briefs. Alone, he drifts toward the road, a survivor in the wake of monsters.

—

Headlights flare in Charles's mirrors like long arms reaching for his back. His pulse quickens. He gooses the throttle, twisting hard until the engine screams like a wild animal. The bike rockets forward, tires clawing asphalt, exhaust ripping the night apart. Wind slams his face, tearing at his jacket, howling in his ears like a scream.

The road ahead is a black runway, straight and unyielding. His eyes strain against the dark, pupils huge, nerves wired. He can't see more than a hundred feet—just a ribbon of shadow and the faint gleam of center lines. He rides blind now, trusting memory, praying the pavement stays true. If there's debris, a pothole, a stray animal—he's dead. No margin. No mercy. Behind him, the Wicked Ones thunder, engines snarling, rage riding pillion. Two out of three endings mean mutilation. He twists harder. The bike answers with a savage roar and torque.

The straightaway gives way into curves as he veers left, diving into the industrial zone. Brick giants loom on either side, windows black, steel doors glinting under industrial lamps. The air thickens with the stink of oil and rust, shadows gathering together in every alley. Charles leans hard, pegs scraping against pavement, sparks spitting like fireflies. His breath saws in his chest, heart pounding a brutal rhythm. He risks a glance. No headlights now, but they're close. He feels them, a pack of wolves scenting blood.

He rips left between two mill buildings, tires skidding over grit. Ahead, a chain-link gate bars the alley, padlock dangling loose. He releases the throttle, leaps off and moves to the gate. Fingers claw the chain, metal biting skin. He unwinds it fast, gate groaning as it spans open. Charles scrambles back, mounts up, and guns through the gap. He leaves the gate ajar.

The alley spits him into a vast graveyard of industry. Fences bristle with barbed wire, teeth glinting under gray moonlight. Stacks of lumber rise like ancient towers, their edges sharp against the gloom. A mountain of sand crouches in the far corner, pale and silent beside heaps of crushed stone, white as sun-bleached bones. Straight ahead, a mound of peat moss steams in the cold, vapor curling like breath from a sleeping beast. The air reeks of sawdust and damp earth, thick enough to taste.

Charles veers right and hugs the flank of a brick warehouse. Its walls loom high, scarred with soot, windows blind. He skids to a stop beside a steel overhead door, kills the engine, and kicks the stand. Silence falls down, disturbed only by the distant snarl of pursuit.

He runs, boots heavy on the concrete, past the sealed garage door to a smaller steel entrance. Fingers seize the knob and twist. It gives. The door swings inward with a groan, exhaling stale air thick with the musk of lumber and oil. Charles ducks inside, heart stammering, shadows welcoming him. He reaches for the latch, hesitates—bikes growl closer, their fury bleeding through the night. He snaps the door shut and plunges deeper into the warehouse's dark belly.

Inside, darkness sprawls like a blanket. The scent of resin and rust clings to the air. Rows of timber loom in serried ranks, hulking shapes stacked to the rafters. Overhead, steel beams crisscross like bones in a giant's ribcage.

Somewhere beyond, a choir of death howls.

—

Engines growl low as the Wicked Ones creep down the main artery of the industrial park, their headlights bouncing and flickering in the gloom. Shadows cling to brick facades, windows blind and black. Each rider scans hard, eyes flicking left and right, probing alleys for movement. There's only one way in and out. They know Charles is trapped. The hunt drones in their veins.

Dusty rides point, his silhouette outlined in chrome and menace. Suddenly his arm shoots left, finger stabbing toward an alley spanning between two mill buildings. The gate there stands wide open, chain dangling like a severed noose. Dusty kills his engine and dismounts. Wheeler rolls up beside him, silent, waiting. Dusty's gaze locks on the mill's front doors—heavy steel, chained tight from the outside.

"Chained from the outside," he mutters, voice flat as iron.

Wheeler follows his stare, catching the glint of padlock and chain cinched around the double handles.

Dusty mounts his steed, fires the beast to life, turns the bars and throttles into the alley. Wheeler falls in behind. "Lock this up when we get through," Dusty orders, tone sharp enough to cut through the rumble. "Nobody gets in or out."

Wheeler nods, face muscles tight, and Dusty pushes through the gate. Engines rumble behind him, echoing off brick walls in a thunderous reverberation. The alley amplifies their fury, sound bouncing like a volley of gunfire. They break into the yard—a sprawl of shadows and monolithic stacks. Dusty's eyes rake the scene, and there it is: Charles's bike staged near the wall, chrome twinkling under halogen light. Dusty backs his machine beside it. One by one, the pack falls in line, kickstands snapping down like triggers cocked. Boots hit asphalt. They cluster tight, a knot of violence pooling in the dark.

Wheeler seals the gate, chain clinking through links, padlock clamping shut with a metallic bite. He idles forward, parks, and joins the circle.

Dusty scans the yard. Lumber towers loom like silent warriors, their edges blocky against the night. Piles of sand hunch in corners, pale mounds beside heaps of crushed stone sharp as broken teeth. Steam coils from a mountain of peat moss, curling spirit-like into the cold. Barbed wire crowns the fence, glinting like a crocodile's long grin.

Dusty's gaze hooks on the building's flank: one overhead door sealed tight, one standard steel door shut and waiting. He approaches, apprehension trying to hold him back, and fishes out a cigar. Flame appears, licking tobacco as he draws deep, smoke wreathing his head like a warlord's crown. His free hand tests the handle. It turns easy. The door opens an inch. Dusty slams it shut.

Men fan out as they scour the yard. Shadows swallow them behind lumber stacks and stone piles. Minutes bleed away. One by one, they drift back, faces drawn and empty.

"Nobody out here," Jardini growls.

"He's inside." Wheeler spits, eyes hard. "No way out. Windows boarded. Front door chained."

Dusty drops his cigar, heel pressing it into pavement, twisting slow, rage simmering in the grind. His face knots, disgust etched deep. He wrenches the handle, steel shrieking as the door slams wide, ricocheting off brick. Dusty ducks low, pistol flashing into his fist, and plunges into the dark interior.

One by one, without being ordered, the pack streams in behind Dusty, splitting ranks alternately: right, left, right, left; fanning out in lethal symmetry. The space echoes with boots scuffling across sawdust-covered concrete and the clicking of hammers being cocked. The hunt has breached the walls.

Dusty moves like a shadow across the vast floor as he slips to the far side of the room. The double steel doors loom behind him, chained tight, a barrier sealing the world outside. His fingers hover over a panel studded with eight heavy-duty switches. One by one, he uses the second knuckle of his forefinger and throws them down.

Each flip replies with a metallic bang, echoing through the cavernous dark. High-voltage surges vibrate like distant thunder, feeding life into the veins of the building. Overhead, massive gas-filled bulbs stir sluggishly inside their steel hoods, glowing sickly orange and blue— faint light bleeding into shadows. Six switches in, and the gloom barely flinches. Darkness clings stubbornly to the rafters, a shadow demon refusing to retreat.

Dusty's hairy knuckle kisses the seventh switch and the first bank of lights erupts, blazing white fire across the steel bones of the ceiling. A heartbeat later, the second set ignites, then the third, each flare cracking the dark like lightning. The bulbs roar awake in sequence, preheating to full fury until the warehouse floods with brilliance. The men squint, eyes watering, pupils shrinking against the onslaught. Shadows scatter like vermin. Dust motes swirl in the sudden glare, glittering like ash in a furnace.

The space is enormous. Thirty feet overhead, girders crisscross, suspending rows of industrial lamps in neat formation. Their steel hoods gleam over the blaze, casting hard-edged pools of light across the floor. Along three walls, balconies jut out fifteen feet high, wrapping the room in a steel embrace. Each balcony thrusts twenty feet toward the center, its underside bristling with smaller lamps that spill harsh light downward.

The men fan out beneath these overhangs, weapons drawn. From their vantage, they can't see the tops of the balconies above their own heads, but across the gulf, they glimpse the labyrinth rising opposite. Steel shelving towers from floor to ceiling, climbing the walls like iron vines. Every section crammed with lumber—planks stacked end-first into pigeonholes, regimented rows like soldiers at attention.

The sight arrests them. From floor to rafters, the walls burst with a mosaic of grain and color. Pale pine and creamy birch gleam beside blood-red cherry, mahogany deep as wine, oak rich and golden. Some boards lie rough-cut, edges raw and splintered; others gleam satin-smooth, polished to perfection. The smell rolls over them in waves: wet resin, sweet sap, earthy musk—a perfume of forests slain and reborn. It clings to the air, pungent yet soothing, an ancient balm that almost calms the pulse pounding in their throats.

At the front, the balcony breaks its rhythm. No shelves climb here—only a boarded picture window, high up on the wall, glaring blind at the night. Far below it, an equipment cage of chain link sits alone. Dusty peers through the fencing, catching glimpses of crates. Above, an antique chandelier dangles from a chain, absurd in its opulence. Three tiers of crystal droop in dusty cascades, prisms dulled by neglect. Once, it must have blazed like a beacon, glittering for passersby beyond the glass. Now it hangs entombed, a relic strangled in shadow, its sparkle smothered by years of silence and a boarded window.

Dusty turns slowly as his eyes sweep the cavernous space. From his vantage point near the chained double doors, the warehouse stretches open like a steel arena—immense, echoing, its silence thick enough to choke. He can see both flanks of the building, the far wall crowned by the massive overhead door. Yet for all its size, the room feels eerily hollow, a void masquerading as emptiness.

The floor expands wide, a slab of stained concrete scarred by years of labor. Splinters scattered like shrapnel across its surface, mingling with curls of sawdust that whisper underfoot. Dirty tire tracks carve a path dead-center, running from the overhead door almost to Dusty's boots. Black stains travel along the route, slick memories of machines that have bled here before. Forklifts crouch like sleeping beasts on either side of the path, mammoth silhouettes with tusks of steel, their paint scabbed and peeling.

Crates litter the expanse in chaotic order—some squatting alone, others stacked two, three high, their wooden skins bruised and splintered. Pallets sprawl beneath many of them like squat feet. One crate dominates the center, a monolith planted square in the oil-streaked track, its bulk looming like a fortress. Beyond, more crates perch on the balconies above, scattered like forgotten relics. Fifty, maybe more—but the sheer scale of the room dwarfs them all, reducing their presence to clutter swallowed by immensity.

Dusty's gaze drags back toward his own corner. Nothing but a lonely desk crouches there, its surface an unkempt graveyard of neglect. The desk looks more kitchen table than command post, its veneer dulled by years of filth. A dust-choked computer slumps beside a tan rotary phone, its cord curled like a dried sandworm. A calendar mat sprawls beneath, scarred with scribbles and doodles. A meager stack of invoices leans drunkenly against a blotter, flanked by wood shavings that cling like dandruff.

Two file cabinets hunker against the wall, their drawers sealed tight, secrets locked in steel. A single chair slouches nearby, its cushion cratered by years of weight. Beside the desk, a sealed crate hunkers on a pallet, mute and unassuming.

Dusty exhales, breath whistling through clenched teeth. His eyes comb every angle, every shadow. There's no cover here. There's no blind spot; no refuge. The Wicked Ones have diced the floor into a grid of vigilance, their positions stitching the space shut. Charles isn't behind the crates. He isn't crouched beneath the desk. Down here, the ground level lies naked under their gaze.

If Charles is here, he's above them—in the steel labyrinth of balconies, in the hidden shadows where the light falters. The thought burns in Dusty's gut like boiling oil. Somewhere in this castle of timber and iron, an apparition is waiting.

Dusty's voice bellows, ricocheting through the steel cavern: "Check inside the plank shelves!" The command booms, shattering the hush, echoing off girders and timber stacks.

Men scatter, weapons flashing under harsh light. They dart between shelving towers, eyes probing pigeonholes like frantic scavengers, climbing steel ladders, peering into shadowed recesses where a man might fold himself small.

Dusty moves slower, deliberate. He's done a quick scan. Now it's time for a more detailed look around. His boots swirl sawdust as he drifts toward the crate near the desk, its bulk squatting like a silent gravestone. He lowers himself onto its edge, the wood groaning under his weight. From his vest, he draws a fat cigar, fingers working with ritual precision. Zippo snaps with a metallic pop, flame blooms, licking tobacco until it glows ember-red. He exhales a plume of smoke that billows upward, mingling with the resin-scented air. The taste is bitter, grounding. He watches his men scurry, their shadows racing across the floor like snakes on an algae-covered swamp.

Where could Charles hide? Dusty's mind ticks through possibilities. Crates—dozens of them; most nailed shut, their lids clenched like jaws. The opened ones burst with contents: propane tanks gleaming cold, bubble wrap spilling like entrails, foam peanuts drifting in lazy eddies. Too small, too full, no refuge there.

His gaze moves to the balconies. Men snap-to at his barked order: "Check upstairs too!" The command cracks sharp, sending four figures climbing into the Erector Set.

A flicker.

Dusty's eyes snag on the crate in the center of the room, a monolith planted square in the oil-streaked path. Too tall for Charles to climb into in the short time he had, but yet its lid sits slightly ajar. No footprints have recently disturbed the dust immediately surrounding the crate. He narrows his gaze, reading the stenciled letters bleeding across its flank: STRONGARM HARDWOOD FLOOR COVERING. Innocuous. Ordinary. But the loosened top bristles with menace.

Dusty rises, joints creaking, cigar clamped between teeth. He draws deep, smoke flooding his lungs, then exhales slow—a dragon's sigh curling into the charged air. His boots puff sawdust from beneath as he stalks toward the crate, eyes locked, pulse ticking like a countdown. Halfway there, something catches his vision: a slit carved into the wood, thin and black, lurking just beneath the lettering. At first glance, it mimics a scuff, a careless gouge. Its edges are too clean, too deliberate.

He circles, pistol sliding into his fist, muzzle tracking the crate as he moves. Another slit reveals itself on the next side. Then another. All four faces bear the same surgical cut, neat and uniform, like vents on a coffin. Dusty's breath draws deep. The crate churns with possibility.

"Hey!" His shout cracks the air.

Heads snap. Boots scuffle as then men emerge from their respective locations. The Wicked Ones converge, weapons drawn, eyes wide with anticipation. They form a ring around the crate, steel teeth bared, muzzles kissing wood. The silence that follows is a living thing—fluid, electric, pulsing with the question clawing at every throat: Is Charles inside?

Charles

Dusty raps twice against the crate's wall, the butt of his pistol thudding like a judge's gavel. The sound obliterates the still.

"You have to the count of three to stand up and come out of there!" His voice booms, rolling across the cavernous space, echoing off girders like distant thunder.

The Wicked Ones tighten their circle, muzzles dragging on wood, breath held. Sweat beads on brows, trickling down temple lines. The buzz of the overhead ballasts drone like an insect swarm, mingling with the faint creak of steel under tension. Dusty's cigar smolders between his teeth, ember glowing like a coal from hell.

"One!" His shout cracks. The hammer cocks with a metallic click.

The crate remains mute, lid frozen, its loosened edge barricading answers.

"Two!" Dusty roars, voice serrated with rage. "…And we're gonna make Swiss cheese out of this crate and its contents!"

Silence bites down again, smug and mocking. The only sound is the electric hum above.

Dusty stiffens, arm locking, pistol leveled dead-center. His finger curls, tendons taut. "THREE!"

A shot erupts: deafening, brutal. The concussion boxes every ear, leaving them ringing.

For a heartbeat, the world drops into dead silence. Slowly, senses return to the men. Their eyes start scanning the crate's wall for the bullet hole. Certainly, Charles will drop to the floor of the box, dead weight.

But no—the truth slams in like a freight train as three horrified words annihilate the hush.

"What the fuck?" The question blurts from somewhere.

Heads turn. Dusty stands there; cigar in teeth, emotion drained from his face.

His head is half blown apart, right temple erupting in a geyser of blood and brain. Red mist is fanned across the faces of the two men flanking him, painting them in gore. Their mouths gape, eyes wide, frozen in disbelief as chunks of flesh and brain slap wet against the floor.

Dusty drops in a sloppy heap.

Before thought can form, the warehouse crashes into chaos. Crates perched on balconies—assumed nailed shut, explode upward with splintering force. They rocket skyward and crash down, wood shards raining like shrapnel. From each box erupts a Hellfire & Brimstone soldier, leather-clad demons springing from coffins. Rifles gleam in their fists.

Sweat sprays from brows as bodies surge upright, jack-in-the-box nightmares armed to the teeth. In a blink, the upper tier bristles with death—Hellfire men, some still standing in their crates, encircling the Wicked Ones from above like vultures on steel perches. Their weapons angle down, sights locking on targets below.

"Drop 'em!" The command booms, a voice forged from iron. The Wicked Ones jerk, eyes darting, panic ricocheting between them. Their leader lies crumpled in a crimson halo; skull shattered.

No plan. No escape. Just the weight of inevitability pressing like a boot on their throats. Eyes flick from brother to brother, then upward to the ring of rifles crowning them. Wheeler's gaze hooks Jardini's—two animals, low on the food chain, cornered, minds sparking the same savage thought. Their eyes speak in silence, a telepathic snarl: Surrender is rot. Fight is blood. And blood is all that's left.

In blood and desperation, they forge a silent pact. Together, they snap upright, rifles jerking toward the balconies. Fingers curl on triggers, tendons taut, hearts thumping in their chests.

They never fire.

The warehouse erupts before their hammers can fall. Gunfire crashes like thunder, a deafening barrage that splits the air into shards. Muzzle flashes strobe, white-hot tongues licking steel and timber. Hellfire & Brimstone unleashes hell from above. Rifles bark in savage rhythm, brass casings spitting like sparks from a forge.

Bullets rain down in torrents, ripping through flesh, shredding leather, pulverizing bone. Wheeler jerks as rounds punch through his torso, body convulsing like a marionette controlled by a toddler. Jardini folds under the storm, skull bursting in a crimson geyser that spatters the men beside him. Blood atomizes into mist, hanging in the air like a macabre halo. Shards of bone ping against steel columns, ricochets whining like banshee screams.

The Wicked Ones scatter, instincts clawing for cover. Boots skid across concrete slick with gore. They dive behind crates, roll under shelving, firing blind into the blaze above. Their shots crack wild, splintering wood, chewing holes into shadows, but hitting nothing. The balconies spit fire in reply, disciplined, merciless, focused. Each round finds meat.

The air thickens into chaos: gunpowder smoke billowing like storm clouds, choking lungs, stinging eyes. The sweet musk of lumber drowns under the acrid stench of spent shells and blood. Splinters explode from shelving, raining down like wooden confetti. Crates burst apart, vomiting Styrofoam and steel fragments across the floor. The roar is endless, a symphony of slaughter echoing off girders until the warehouse itself seems to tremble.

Silence falls sudden, absolute, like a guillotine blade. The last echoes die in the rafters. Smoke rises in lazy layers, veiling the carnage sprawled below. Blood pools widen, their sheen dulled as dust drifts down like ash. The hum of the overhead lights creeps back into awareness.

Hellfire & Brimstone stands frozen: rifles leveled, eyes scanning the ruin. Below, the Wicked Ones lie broken, bodies twisted in unnatural ways, weapons slack in lifeless hands.

Caleb's voice cuts through the charged air, booming with triumph: "Perfect!" His grin gleams under the harsh industrial lights as he thrusts both thumbs skyward, rotating slowly so every Hellfire brother can drink in his approval. Their rifles glint, their faces split with savage pride. Caleb's arm sweeps wide, commanding: "Come on down!"

Boots clang steel as men cross the catwalk and descend the steps, weapons holstered and slung, laughter crackling like static. The storm has passed. Caleb drops to the floor, swagger in every step, pistol riding easy at his hip.

Then—a sound.

A creak: thin, out of place. Every head pivots, eyes narrowing toward the crate crouched next to the desk. The crate that has no bullet holes in it; thanks to that desk.

The Hellfire crew gathers behind their leader in a V-formation. Caleb halts at the desk, gaze locked on the crate's shadowed crown. His men fan out, forming a semi-circle of muscle and menace. Rifles rise, barrels hovering like black adders.

"Why don't you come on out of there now," Caleb says, voice calm, brimming with authority. His knuckles rap the lid—three sharp knocks that echo like nails driven into the wood.

Seconds stretch. Then, the whole crate jerks, popping loose from its flooring with a splintered scrape. Men flinch, grips tightening, muzzles kissing air. The crate tilts, as if by magic, teeters, and then crashes to the floor with a sodden thud.

Crouched on the crate's remaining flooring is Charles.

He rises like a revenant, hands lifted high, fingers splayed in surrender. Blood streaks his shirt, sawdust clings to his jeans. His eyes burn green fire, but his face wears resignation—a man walking the razor's edge of death. Caleb steps back, folding into the semi-circle, his stare a straight razor honed on Charles's throat.

"Go ahead and step off," Caleb murmurs, voice silk over steel. "Nice and slow."

Charles inhales deeply, holds it and steps off the short platform before exhaling—a condemned man savoring his last breath. He stands alone, ringed by rifles, the hum of lights droning like a funeral dirge.

"Take that piece of shit off and throw it down," Caleb snaps, chin jerking at the Wicked Ones PROSPECT cut clinging to Charles's back.

Charles grips the leather, fingers curling around its edges. His gaze locks on Caleb's, emerald boring into obsidian. Time slows.

"Do it," Caleb hisses.

Slowly, Charles peels the vest from his body. It lands with a slap, sprawled in a crimson mirror.

"Now piss on it," Caleb sneers, venom dripping from every syllable.

Charles unzips, movements deliberate, eyes never breaking Caleb's stare. Silence is broken by the hollow patter of urine striking bunched leather. The stench rises, acrid and pungent, mingling with gunpowder and resin.

Caleb joins him, zipper rasping, stream splashing in defiance. One by one, Hellfire men unzip, encircling the cut in a momentous ritual. A fart pops from the back of someone's drawers. Their laughter curdles the air as rivers of piss flood the patch—a baptism of desecration.

Flies zip shut. Boots shuffle. Caleb steps close, shadow swallowing Charles. His voice drops, cold as an ice pick: "You know what this means, right?"

The smiles drain from the faces of the other men, their happy masks swapped for those of serious business.

Charles nods, slow, solemn. His gaze falters, sinking to the floor.

"It means it's over for you," Caleb says, plain and lethal. "You're finished—done."

Caleb's hand slides into his vest, fingers curling around a just reward. Charles feels the weight of inevitability crush his spine. This is it—the full stop at the end of his bloody sentence. He waits, breath shallow, pulse pounding like end times.

Caleb's arm whips free of the vest's inside pocket. Black flashes—a gun? No. Leather gleams, rich and red under the lights. Caleb's grin splits wide, wild and bright.

"Put this on," he roars, thrusting the Hellfire & Brimstone cut toward Charles. "It's all over now. Welcome home, brother!"

Relief drops like a bomb. The rifles dip. The joke is over. The vacuum seal in the room ruptures and the air rushes in again. Cheers erupt from the gaggle of men. Charles stares at the vest, fingers squeezing tight as they clutch its weight. He lifts it high, the patch blazing like a sigil of rebirth. His smile spreads: slow, savage, unstoppable. With a snap, he swings it onto his shoulders. The leather drops in place and hugs him perfectly, like destiny fulfilled. It should fit well. It is his after all.

His fingers brush the patch over his heart: SGT. AT ARMS.

Caleb lunges, arms wide, crushing Charles in a bear hug. The pack surges, laughter erupting, hands slapping backs. They swarm him, rustling his hair, pounding his shoulders, voices rising in a chorus of brotherhood. Blood and piss stain the floor, but joy floods the room like fire.

For a moment, the warehouse forgets its horrors. For a moment, Hellfire roars louder than death.

Caleb slings an arm over Charles's shoulder, voice warm with triumph: "Let's get you home, cleaned up and debriefed, bro. I'm sure you could use a good night's sleep." His words roll easy. "Men..." Caleb barks, tone snapping like a whip. "Search the bodies. Take anything of value and look for bike keys."

Hellfire scatters, hands rifling through pockets oiled with blood. Rings, wallets, keys—loot stripped in seconds. Their laughter ricochets off steel beams, giddy and childlike, a victory chorus echoing through the fortress of timber and iron.

Within a minute, the dead lie naked of worth. The brothers regroup, swagger thick in their stride, voices bubbling with jokes and praise. They swarm Charles like zealots at an altar, fingers grazing his shoulders, smacking his back, rustling his hair. He's a rock star, a war god, and they crave his aura like addicts chasing heat. Compliments ooze, grins split faces, the celebration bleeding out the door into the night.

—

Outside, the back lot sleeps under a bruised sky. Motorcycles crouch in a neat row, chrome winking under halogen lamps.

Caleb spins, barking orders sharp as a whipcrack: "Bobby, you, Drake, Slug—get the van. Meet us at the clubhouse. The rest of you, pick a bike and let's move!"

Men scramble, keys clinking like coins of fate. Those without keys mount machines already primed, fingers curling around throttles. Caleb swings onto Dusty's bike, leather creaking, grin flashing at Charles, who kneels by his own ride. Ritual unfolding: petcock twist, fuel slithering down clear tubing, choke knob yanked, throttle pumped thrice. His hand grips the kicker, muscles coiling for the strike.

Then, before the first revolution of a single motor churns—sudden daylight engulfs the lot.

A metallic CLACK snaps the night, loud as a rifle bolt. Overhead, a spotlight ignites—a white-hot sun erupting from the warehouse roof. Its beam slams down like judgment, bleaching the lot in blinding brilliance. Heat lashes their faces, searing eyes until lids clamp shut. Shadows vanish, burned to ash under the glare.

Another spotlight flares, then another—giant all-seeing eyes opening along the roofline, spewing fire across steel and flesh. The men stagger, hands shielding brows, curses ripping from throats. Chaos crackling like static.

A voice booms from behind the blaze, disembodied, amplified through a bullhorn: "Drop your weapons and lie face down on the ground!" The command parts the air, iron and final.

Before breath can form, the perimeter erupts. Spotlights pop in staccato bursts, circling the chain-link fence like a halo of wrath. White beams chase away the remnants of dark, turning the brothers into prey. Confusion ramps up—heads snapping, eyes darting, guns jerking in frantic search of an unseen target. Muzzles swing, blind and desperate, fighting light with impotent steel.

Between the beams, shadows writhe—figures crouched low, rifles braced, death embodied in every silhouette. Red dots bloom like malignant stars, dancing across chests, crawling up throats, caressing foreheads. Three per man. Sometimes four. Laser sights jitter in crimson constellations, painting Hellfire in an astrology map of mortality.

The air saturates with dread. Sweat beads, trickles, stings. Fingers twitch on triggers, hearts slam ribs like fists on iron doors. The celebration curdles into terror, laughter strangled into silence. For a breathless beat, the lot holds its scream.

Then—nothing moves. Just the hum of lights, the hiss of spotlights, and the taste of fear coppering every tongue.

The night splits open with a roar that swallows every other sound. A helicopter bursts into view above the lot, its blades chopping the quiet into chunky pieces. Whop-whop-whop-whop—the rhythm pounds, louder than any bike engine these men have ever trusted. The air trembles under the bass growl of the machine, a mechanical beast descending from the void. Its compression jellies the guts of the men below.

From its underbelly, a spotlight ignites—a white sun tearing through the black sky. It floods the gang in merciless brilliance, blanching their faces, erasing shadows and features, stripping them bare. The beam quivers with the vibration of the rotors, flickering like a strobe. Every heartbeat feels exposed beneath that glare.

"DROP YOUR WEAPONS AND LIE FACE DOWN NOW, OR WE WILL OPEN FIRE!" The voice crashes down from above, amplified, metallic, godlike.

The men freeze. Confusion ripples through them like a disease transmitted from one to another. Eyes dart, searching for escape, for meaning, for Caleb. Always Caleb. One by one, they turn toward their leader, their anchor in this storm. His gaze sweeps across their faces—brothers forged in chaos—and something ancient ignites behind his eyes. A spark. A promise. A death sentence.

Caleb tilts his head back, defiance carved into every line of his jaw. His weapon rises fast and sure, like a black fang against the artificial sun. His scream rips through the night: "FUCK YOU IN THE FACE!" The words are raw, primal, a curse hurled at heaven itself. Then, as he bolts, the gunfire begins.

Bullets spit upward in furious streaks, chasing the phantom bird. The others follow suit, their weapons barking, their rage blooming in muzzle flashes, their legs working to avoid becoming a stationary target. They aim for the lights, for the eyes of judgment, as if shattering glass could rewrite fate. The helicopter jerks sideways, spotlight sliding off them briefly, then slashing back to pin them again. A rooftop lamp explodes, raining shards and sparks that hiss against flesh.

Then all hell breaks loose.

Figures on the roof erupt in flame and thunder. Shadows outside the fence dump lead into the lot. The air becomes a storm of metal. Blood spatters the warehouse wall in gory Rorschach tests. Flesh bursts like overripe fruit. Brothers fall—some crumple silently, others twitch in tortured spasms. Holes bloom in chests, skulls cave like rotten pumpkins. The ground drinks greedily, pooling crimson rivers that glisten under the merciless light. Brain matter smears across blacktop like pale worms crawling from shattered shells.

"CEASE FIRE! CEASE FIRE!" The voice booms again, but it's too late. Silence descends like ash after a firestorm. Smoke floats upward in a final, contained layer, tasting of iron and burnt leather. The lot is an animal graveyard now.

One man moves—a ruin dragging itself through blood. His arm trembles, pistol clutched like a dying prayer. He lifts it toward the roof. A single shot cracks the silence. His skull erupts sideways, painting the pavement with gray pulp. His head slams down hard, a period at the end of his sentence.

Charles lies face down beside—almost under his bike, hands locked behind his head. Caleb mirrors him, their bodies aligned like fallen statues. Slowly, they raise their chins, eyes locking in a silent communion. No words. Just the truth: this is the end. Time itself seems to hold its breath.

The watch in Charles's pocket becomes warmer, reminding him that it is there. It calls to him and begs him to reach in and retrieve it. Charles doesn't dare flinch.

Ropes slither down from the roof like vines. Black-clad figures descend, faceless executioners. Boots hit pavement. Weapons produce in their fists, black dragons of death. More figures surge through the fence, slicing holes in the chain link like surgeons cutting flesh. Sixty-five shadows converge, sixty-five muzzles aimed at two skulls. The math of annihilation.

Charles sees it—the flicker in Caleb's eyes, that old flame roaring back for one last dance. Before thought can form, Caleb rolls, weapon flashing upward. His first shot punches a man in the chest, folding him backward. The vest saves him, but gravity drags him down. Then the swarm answers.

Bullets hammer Caleb, jerking his body like a rag doll in a madman's grip. Holes blow out across his flesh, red petals opening in violent succession. Still, he fires, blind, rabid, spitting lead into the void. A final round kisses his skull. The back of his head erupts in a fan of gore, painting the pavement with gray and red. His face smashes down, eyes wide, staring through Charles into nothing. Time resumes its march.

Charles's eyes lock wide, frozen in a stare that feels trapped in ice. Inches away, Caleb's head lies shattered, his blood-soaked hair clinging to the pavement like a squid in a crimson tide. Charles cannot look away. The wet strands glisten under the harsh spotlight, each one a thread unraveling the last vestige of brotherhood. The world narrows to that image—Caleb's ruin, and the silence between heartbeats.

Then violence crashes back in. A knee slams down on Charles's neck, grinding collar bone against asphalt. Air flees his lungs in a strangled gasp. Another knee drives into the small of his back, crushing him into submission. Hands seize his arms, wrenching them backward until pain radiates like fire along his shoulders. Cold steel bites his wrists. Around him, a forest of muzzles remains trained, black eyes of executioners watching for the slightest twitch.

The two men pinning him move with mechanical precision, hauling him upright as if lifting a corpse from the ground. The toes of his boots scrape against the pavement, leaving faint parts in the blood-slick surface. Caleb's body lies behind him now, but Charles feels its gravity pulling at his soul.

A figure approaches—a man whose presence bends the air. His uniform is immaculate, his movements deliberate, his silence heavier than the weapons surrounding them. He stops inches from Charles, studying him as though reading a language etched in ancient stone. His eyes narrow, perplexed, searching for something human in the mask of blankness Charles wears. Charles returns the stare, hollow and unblinking. His face is a dead sea, no ripple of fear, no storm of rage. Only stillness.

"Take him back to headquarters." The words fall like a gavel, sealing fate. No explanation. No emotion. The leader pivots and walks away, boots striking the pavement with the rhythm of inevitability.

The grip on Charles tightens. His escorts snap to life, dragging him toward the alley where a black van crouches like a leopard in wait. Its paint drinks the light, its windows opaque as coal. Ten feet before Charles and his captors reach the van, the side double doors explode open, revealing a void framed by steel. Two dark-clad silhouettes surge forward, arms reaching from the darkness like claws. The handoff is seamless—a choreography of control. Charles is swallowed whole by the van's interior.

Hands vanish. Doors slam shut with a metallic clack. The engine awakens, puking smoke before roaring into fury. Exhaust vapor flows from the tailpipe, knotting into ghostly tendrils. Tires shriek against the pavement, spinning so violently that smoke spins around them, wrapping the wheels in a cyclone of burnt rubber. The alley becomes a tunnel of chaos—gray clouds boiling, swallowing light, erasing form.

The van lunges forward, a beast unchained. Its tires carve black scars into the asphalt. Charles feels the surge, the centrifugal pull as the world outside dissolves into smoke and shadow. In seconds, the vehicle, and the man inside, vanish behind a curtain of darkness, leaving only the stench of scorched rubber and the echo of a life severed from everything it knew.

—

The glass doors of FBI headquarters automatically slide open like the jaws of some beast, swallowing Charles. His boots scuff against polished tile as two uniformed escorts drag him forward, wrists cuffed tight behind his back. The lobby buzzes with fluorescent light and the low murmur of voices, a hive of motion where agents and clerks dart like worker bees behind bulletproof glass. Phones trill. Papers slap against desks. The air smells of toner and cold authority.

They march him straight toward the main desk—a fortress of steel and glass, its surface gleaming under harsh fluorescent lights. The escorts stop before a circular constellation of drilled holes in glass, the only breach in the barrier. One leans in, voice sharp and official: "SEC requested to see this suspect. Charles Watkins is the name."

Behind the glass, a woman barely glances up. Her left index finger rises like a commandment while her right hand snatches the phone. She cradles it between cheek and shoulder, nails clacking against keys—three quick strikes, then silence. Her finger hovers midair, frozen in ritual. Charles watches her lips move, but the words dissolve into muffled static. Two sentences, maybe three, before she stabs four more keys and spits a final phrase into the receiver. The phone drops. Her verdict: "They'll be right out." No warmth. No curiosity. Just procedure.

She vanishes into a forest of black filing cabinets, papers clutched like shields. Charles barely has time to breathe before the buzzer shrieks like a metallic insect whining from the steel-framed door. Two men in black glide through, faces emotionless. They don't speak. They don't blink. Hands sweep over Charles in a perfunctory pat-down, fingers probing for secrets. Then, without ceremony, the handoff happens. Charles and his bag of belongings are passed off like a customer during shift change. His original escorts melt away as new shadows seize him, spinning him toward the next threshold.

The buzzer drones again. A door swings open, unaided. They shove him through, past the desk, into a corridor that stretches like a subway deep into the building's heart. Another glass barrier looms ahead, guarded by twin sentinels in black. Five feet from the door, the lock buzzes and one figure swings it wide. Charles is thrust forward, slammed against a wall so hard his teeth clack. Cold plaster kisses his cheek. Pressure grinds into his spine, another hand crushing the back of his skull until his vision doubles. The world dulls, blurs. Whispering floats through the air—low, conspiratorial, but the words slip away like flying insects in the night. A latch clicks.

Then the storm hits. Hands rip him from the wall, spinning him like a dance partner. They shove, yank, propel him down the artery of chaos. The hallway seethes with bodies: agents striding with folders, clerks juggling stacks of paper, voices colliding in a cacophony that scrapes against Charles's skull. Offices flank the corridor like glass aquariums, each one a silent drama. Some glow with light, others brood in darkness. Inside some, mouths move in urgent choreography, but the glass swallows every syllable. Charles catches fragments, gestures, glances, but no sound, as if the world beyond those panes exists in another dimension.

Eyes flicker toward him. Some linger, curious, before snapping back to screens and files. Most don't bother. To them, he's just debris swept along by the current like so much before it. A dirty biker. A criminal. Nothing more.

"Come on. Keep it moving." The escort's voice blasts through the din. A hand slams into Charles's shoulder, jolting him forward. He stumbles, and would hit the floor if not for the iron grips anchoring his arms. Pain sparks along his joints. He steadies, turns his head, and locks eyes with the man who shoved him. For a moment, the world narrows to that stare. Charles's gaze is cold, emerald, icy, promising storms.

The guard flinches, then masks it with bravado. Another shove, harder this time, a punctuation mark of dominance. "Keeeeeeep walking!" he sneers, voice dripping contempt, syllables stretched like a whip crack. The hallway consumes them, a river of glass and steel carrying Charles deeper into the labyrinth.

Charles keeps his head rigid, eyes locked forward. The cuffs bite his wrists with every step, metal gnawing at wrist bone. His escorts flank him like wolves, their grips iron, their pace relentless. The hallway churns with motion: agents slicing through the current, voices ricocheting off glass walls, the hum of fluorescent lights drilling into his skull. Chaos presses in from all sides, yet Charles moves like a ghost, silent, unyielding.

Then it happens. One particular window slides into his peripheral vision, and time stops. The man behind the desk glances up, distracted, gaze skimming over the silvered crown of the woman seated across from him. His eyes snag on Charles; just for a heartbeat, then flick away, unimpressed, as if Charles were nothing more than a smudge on the glass. But the woman feels the shift. Her head rotates, slow, curious, following the invisible thread of his attention.

She peers through the glass. Charles's vision zooms then pulls right back.

Abigail Kerrington.

The name resounds in Charles's mind, silent but seismic. The hallway noise collapses into a muffled roar, like ocean surf in his ears. Everything slows—the swing of arms, the shuffle of boots, the window passing by. He floats past the glass as if suspended in amber, his gaze locking on hers, searching for a flicker, a spark, a hint of recognition.

Nothing.

Her eyes are clear, calm, untouched by memory. No storm. No shadow. Just the cool, professional glaze of someone anchored in a world that never burned. Her face holds no tremor, no fracture of the past. She studies him for half a breath: clinical, detached, then turns back to her business, her voice resuming its silent dance behind the glass. The man across from her leans in, reclaiming her attention as if Charles were never there.

The ache in Charles's chest is a knife twisting slow. Though it is nearby, he feels the short distance between himself and the watch, the echo of its ticking bleeding through time. But he says nothing. Shows nothing. He walks on, swallowed by the tide. He knows the watch will be in his possession again soon.

The chaos surges back: voices barking, doors closing and opening, phones ringing, voices mingling. His escorts shove harder now, impatience crackling in their grips. "Move it," one snarls, punctuating the command with a brutal jab to Charles's shoulder. He stumbles, rights himself, jaw clenched in a forced grin, eyes dead ahead. The hallway stretches, pulsing toward the heart of something cold.

Finally, they reach it. A door unlike the rest: oak, solid, no glass to bleed secrets. Its surface gleams under harsh light, branded with three stark letters: SAC. Authority carved in black.

The agent on Charles's right hammers twice, knuckles cracking against wood.

"It's open!" The voice booms from within—sharp, commanding.

The knob twists. The door swings open. Charles is propelled inside, the air shifting from chaos to something heavier, denser, like judgment settling on his shoulders.

A man waits—a figure cut from steel and protocol. Grey hair, razor part, suit pressed to perfection. He stands behind a fold-out table, eyes drilling into an open file clutched in his left hand. A pen taps against his teeth, a metronome of thought.

Then the agent's voice slices the air: "Sir… The suspect you requested."

The man looks up over his glasses. His eyes narrow. The pen freezes mid-tap. In one motion, the file slaps down on the table, a sound like a backfire. He moves straight for Charles.

The air in the room becomes solid before the SAC's voice shatters it like a block of ice. "Are you fucking kidding me?" His tone is boiling, fury spilling into every syllable. His eyes blaze behind the lowered rim of his glasses, drilling through the agents like bullets. "What the fuck did you do here?"

He moves; closing the distance in three strides. His hands lash out, sweeping the agents' grips from Charles's shoulders with a force that leaves a sting of pins and needles. The sound of flesh striking flesh cracks through the office. Charles sways under the sudden release. Before he can steady himself, the SAC's hands clamp down on his shoulders—firm, possessive, almost trembling with heat. His face hovers inches away, carved in crimson rage, eyes burning like coals stoked by a storm.

Then something shifts.

The SAC spins Charles around, a whirl of tailored fabric and raw command. His voice erupts again, but now it's aimed like a blade at the escorts. "Uncuff this man immediately, you idiots!" The words bounce back off the walls, sharp enough to flay pride. Beads of sweat form across his forehead, catching the fluorescent glare like flakes of glitter. His jaw grinds, teeth bared in a grimace that barely cages the beast inside.

The agents freeze, faces blushing under the onslaught. One fumbles for keys, fingers jittering like broken machinery. The other stammers, breath sticking in his throat, as if language itself has abandoned him.

The SAC's fury deepens, veins bloating along his neck, voice vibrating with a wrath that feels biblical. "Do you fools have any idea who this man is? Get this shit off him. You—" His finger spears the air, pinning one agent like an insect. "Go get him some water."

The command lands. The agent bolts, a scolded child fleeing punishment, shoes squealing against tile. The remaining escort wrestles with the cuffs, metal clinking in frantic rhythm. Charles stands silent, an oak in the storm, eyes locked on the SAC's face—a face that trembles now, not with rage, but with something else clawing its way to the surface.

The cuffs fall. Steel kisses the floor with a hollow clatter. And in that instant, the SAC transforms.

His hands soften, curling around Charles's palms with reverence. His thumbs trace slow circles over the raw grooves etched by restraint, massaging gently as if erasing violence with touch. His voice melts, warm, coaxing: "Come here, Charles, please. Sit down. Sit. Sit. Take a load off." He guides him toward the folding chair, every gesture tender, almost ceremonial, as though seating a king on a throne disguised in steel.

"Can I get you anything?" His words tumble out, urgent, almost pleading. Then his head snaps up, fury flaring anew—not at Charles, never at Charles, but at the void where obedience should be. "Where's that water?" The shout cracks the air, then collapses back into honeyed tones as his gaze returns to Charles, drinking him in like a long-lost relic.

"Are you hurt? Did these idiots rough you up?" His voice trembles with indignation, but beneath it peeks something deeper: a current of joy barely leashed. His smile twitches at the edges of his mouth, fragile yet real, as if the sight of Charles has torn open a vault of light inside him.

"I'll tell you; the communication around here could use some work. That's for sure!" He laughs a short, bold sound, then falls silent, eyes locked, glowing with a hunger the room cannot name.

Charles nods, then shakes his head, then nods again; caught in the erratic rhythm of excited words. The SAC's voice rolls like distant thunder, a torrent of sentences spilling across the sterile office. Charles struggles to keep pace, his head bobbing in awkward sync, but the smile on his face never falters. It's genuine, drawn from something deep—a relief that grows beneath his ribs. After years of shadows, this light feels almost blinding.

James S. LaMarca. Friend. Boss. Anchor in a storm that lasted half a decade. The name beats in Charles's mind like a paddle wheel as he watches the man pace, gesturing with a pen that slices the air like a blade. LaMarca's energy crackles, electric, his words tangling into themselves as if racing to outrun time.

The door bursts open. Escort One barrels in, clutching a flimsy plastic cup sloshing water like a miniature tide. Droplets leap free, spattering across the floor in erratic globules. He slams the cup onto the table, and a ring of liquid spreads instantly around its base.

LaMarca stiffens to a more official posture, voice sharpening into command. "Gentlemen—" The word slices the air, pulling every gaze toward him. His tone shifts—no longer the rambling storm, but something honed, deliberate, heavy with meaning.

"Allow me to introduce you to—" He pauses, savoring the silence, letting it stretch like tasting a fine wine. "—Special Agent, Charles Watkins."

The syllables land like flash bangs. For a breath, the room holds still. The agents stare, confusion etched into their faces, eyes flicking from LaMarca to Charles as if the universe no longer makes sense. Charles meets their gaze, calm, unflinching, offering a nod that feels like a god acknowledging unbelievers.

Their expressions widen then wane—shock bleeding into shame, then flushing crimson across cheekbones. Embarrassment ebbs like waves as recent memory claws at them: the shoves, the cuffs, the barked commands.

LaMarca twists the knife with a smile that gleams like polished steel. "Agent Watkins here has been undercover for almost five years now." His voice bubbles with pride, each word a stone laid in the foundation of revelation. "And thanks to his unwavering dedication, we've dismantled the Kerrington child exploitation network—every rotten limb, every shield they hid behind."

The agents inhale sharply, the sound awed, reverent. They know the name now. Watkins—the ghost in the machine, the phantom stitched into Bureau legend. A case older than their careers, older than some of their lives; brought to its knees by the man standing before them, wrists still raw from their ignorance.

"Pleasure to meet you, sir." Escort One steps forward, hand extended like an olive branch trembling in a storm.

Charles lifts his gaze, eyes locking on the man's flushed face. He doesn't move. Doesn't take the hand. His silence is a scalpel, peeling back layers of guilt. His expression speaks louder than words: Don't you have something else to say?

The agent stutters, tongue tripping over shards of apology. "I—I am so, so sorry, sir. I had no idea. We thought you were just—" He falters, choking on the word. "A scumbag perv. I mean—no! Not you! I just—nobody told us—"

Charles watches the man unravel, sincerity bleeding through every fractured syllable. Then, slowly, he stands, reaches out and grips the offered hand with a firmness that halts the spiral. The agent exhales, relief flooding his face as Charles's smile widens: warm, disarming, a lifeline tossed into deep water.

The handshake breaks. Escort Two steps in, eyes steady, voice stripped to its bones. "I'm sorry, sir. We thought you were one of them."

Charles nods, understanding etched into the curve of his mouth and the acceptance in his eyes. He clasps the second hand, sealing forgiveness in silence. The weight lifts, dissipating like mist.

"Your belongings, sir," says escort two as he offers a clear bag.

Charles can see his prized possession inside, safe and sound. It calls to him. It wants to be in his pocket. He leaves it in the bag to avoid drawing any more attention to it.

Behind him, LaMarca beams. A grin splits his face, wiping years from his features. It's a smile few have seen, an artifact resurrected by triumph. His eyes gleam with pride, with something fiercer, older: a bond soldered in fire and time. He nods, slow, deliberate, his voice a low rumble of approval as the room exhales around them.

"I don't know how you do it, son." LaMarca's voice softens, the storm spent, leaving only the steady vibe of admiration. His words roll slow, deliberate, like stones dropped into still water. "You are such a young agent with such keen skills. I can't imagine how far you'll go in this agency—or in this life, for that matter. But if you keep doing what you're doing—" He pauses, eyes narrowing with thought, then brightening with conviction. "—I imagine you'll lay claim to a life most men only dream of."

He exhales, long and heavy, as if releasing years of tension in a single breath and takes his seat. The chair groans under his weight as he leans back, hands clasping behind his head in a gesture of surrender to peace. For a moment, he looks less like a titan of law and more like a man who's crawled from the coal mines of chaos, soot still clinging to his soul, finally tasting clean air. Satisfaction ripples through him: completion, closure, the sweet ache of victory earned in blood and time.

"I don't know exactly what your distant future holds," he continues, voice mellow now, rich with promise. "But I can assure you this—you will be rewarded for your bravery, your loyalty, your service. Not someday. Soon. Very soon." His eyes gleam, twin shards of steel softened by pride. "I can tell you that right now."

Across the table, Charles absorbs the words like sunlight breaking through storm clouds. Pride swells in his chest, warm and heavy, a tide rising against the rocky shore of exhaustion. There's a twinkle in his eye: a flicker of triumph, but beneath it hides something darker, quieter. A whisper threading through the marrow of his bones:

Now that this is over; what's next?

The question slithers in, cold and relentless:

This has been your whole life. So, what's left when the mission ends?

He shifts in his chair, muscles loosening for the first time in years, yet the weight doesn't lift. It only changes shape. Five years of shadows, of masks and lies, of blood spilled in silence. Five years of becoming someone else until the mirror forgot his name. And now? The task is done. The empire burned. The ledger balanced. But the hollow space is cavernous, a void where purpose used to live.

Charles smiles: genuine, steady, but inside, the question echoes like a distant gunshot fading into night.

What's next?

—

The concrete steps of FBI headquarters ripple with life. A sea of bodies is gathered under a sky polished to steel. Nearly a hundred people press close, their murmurs weaving into a thrum that vibrates against the stone facade. Camera crews line the front rows in the crowd: reporters checking sound, cameramen checking white balance. Agents and officers stand rigid on the first landing, a tableau of discipline framed by flags snapping in the wind. At the center, a podium rises like an altar, its microphone jutting forward, an ear waiting to hear the message and pass it on to the crowd.

The voice comes: amplified, resonant, slicing through the crowd's restless tide: "Your attention, please."

A hush falls over the crowd and they direct their attention to the staircase stage.

"For extraordinary and exceptional meritorious service in a duty of extreme challenge and great responsibility; for extraordinary and exceptional achievements in breaking a major criminal case and for exhibiting decisive, exemplary acts that resulted in the protection and direct saving of the lives of children who were in jeopardy—" The cadence is ceremonial, heavy with reverence. "—The FBI is proud to award Special Agent, Charles Belial Watkins the FBI Medal For Meritorious Achievement."

A ripple of applause surges, cresting against the marble steps. The speaker pivots sharply, militant precision in every line of his body. Another sharply-dressed man steps forward, bearing a felt-covered tray where the medal gleams like captured sunlight. The speaker lifts it high, a glint of gold flashing against the gray day.

Charles, wearing a fine three-piece suit, moves: one step, then another, heel striking heel as he halts. He turns left, squares himself before the podium. The medal descends, cool material kissing the back of his neck before the weight of 5 relentless years settles against his chest. The handshake follows: firm, brief, three deliberate pumps, and then they break, pivoting in perfect symmetry to face the microphone once more.

The voice rolls on, echoing off glass and concrete. "For bravery and courageous acts occurring in the line of duty on the task force; for leaving family and friends to go undercover for an almost five-year operation, putting himself in grave situations and crisis confrontations—" Another pause, another swell of pride. "—The FBI is proud to award Charles Belial Watkins the FBI Shield of Bravery."

Charles

The ritual repeats: presentation, placement, handshake; a choreography of honor etched against the backdrop of history. Charles returns to his place in line, medals glinting like twin novas on his chest. His breath feels heavier now, not from strain but from the gravity of what these moments mean.

Then the air shifts.

"For extraordinary and exceptional meritorious service in a duty of extreme challenge and great responsibility; for extraordinary and exceptional achievements in breaking a major criminal case and for exhibiting decisive, exemplary acts that resulted in the protection and direct saving of the lives of children who were in jeopardy—" The words are familiar, but the name that follows hits like a silent bomb. "—for her sacrifice of almost five years of undercover work, with little to no contact with her family or friends, the FBI is proud to award Agent Mandoline Anne Russell the FBI Medal For Meritorious Achievement."

Mandy.

She steps forward: calm, composed, her uniform crisp as winter frost. The medal hovers through the air, settling against her collarbone with a brush of metal on fabric. Her handshake mirrors Charles's: three pumps, firm, disciplined, but her eyes betray the storm beneath. A sparkle ignites, fierce and fleeting, before she reins it in with the steel of professionalism. She returns to her spot beside Charles, shoulders squared, chin high. For a heartbeat, their gazes lock in a silent exchange, heavy with history and secrets soldered in fire.

The crowd buzzes, oblivious to the undercurrent pulsing between them. Today is a good day. Life is good. Or so it seems.

Charles lets his eyes drift downward, past the landing, past the podium, to the throng below. And there, front and center, framed by sunlight—stands Annie James; his foster mother. Alive. Whole. Her smile blooms like spring after a nuclear winter, radiant and unbroken. She lifts a camera, hands steady, eyes shimmering with pride. Charles answers with the smallest smile—a secret folded into the curve of his lips, meant for her alone.

The flash erupts, a burst of white fire freezing the moment. In that instant, time feels elastic, stretching back to a night drenched in blood and headlights, to a watch swinging from a rearview mirror like a pendulum of fate. He doesn't think about it—not consciously, but the echo reverberates in his bones: some debts were paid in seconds, some lives bought with borrowed time.

The applause swells again, drowning the whispers of memory. Medals gleam. Cameras flash. And beneath the roar of celebration, the quiet truth winds tighter: the cosmos is not done with its surprises.

Chapter 21: November 10th, 1996 – Age 29

One year later, the town breathes under a hazy winter sun, its streets washed in muted gold. Charles rides slow, the rumble of his motorcycle a low hymn against the hush of morning. The wind brushes his face like a blessing, cool and forgiving.

He has chosen to stay here—this town of ghosts and secrets, this soil where his roots tangled with shadows. He has conquered this land, vanquished its demons, and now he moves through it like a pilgrim tracing the stations of his own redemption.

A paper sack rests in the saddlebag, corners damp from fresh produce. Tonight, he will cook. A simple meal. A ritual of normalcy after years of masquerade and blood.

His tires whisper over asphalt as he slowly drifts past storefronts, each one a relic of memory. Rangle's Pharmacy crouches on the corner, boarded and silent, its windows blind. The truth burned it hollow—the rot behind the counter exposed, the man who peddled poison unmasked. The charred boards still stand like ribs of a carcass, a monument to justice paid in flame.

Further on, color moves against concrete gray. A sleek car idles at the curb, chrome flashing like a signal mirror. The driver steps out and rolls around to the other side. The door swings open, and Abigail Kerrington steps out, her heels striking pavement with the rhythm of a life reclaimed. She moves toward a flower shop, coat cinched tight, hair catching light like spun copper. For a breath, Charles watches her—this woman who once danced on the edge of oblivion, now radiant, whole. She does not see him. Does not know him. Her laughter spills into the air as the shop entrance swallows her, and Charles feels something loosen in his chest, a knot untied by the simple grace of survival.

The driver, Abigail's butler, strolls around to the driver's door and ducks inside to wait. His posture is perfect and professional.

The bike motors on, slow as thought. Ahead, a car glides toward him, its paint slick as an eel. Time dilates, stretching thin. Through the windshield, a face emerges from shadow—a girl's face, ivory skin aglow, cheeks kissed with healthy pink. The innocent. The one lost to the ledger of his sins. Her eyes catch his, bright as spring water, and her lips curve into a smile—a stranger's smile, soft and guileless. Fingers lift in a wave, casual, kind. She does not know him. Not the man who once stole her breath for the sake of a mission. To her, he is no ghost, no monster—just another traveler passing through a single frame of her long life ahead.

Warmth floods Charles's chest, fierce and sudden, like sunlight breaking through storm clouds. He watches her vanish into the stream of traffic, and for the first time in years, the weight shifts—not gone, but lighter, as if the world has granted absolution.

There—a white flash by the fish market snags his eye. It is Abigail's chef. He is in uniform; clean and bright. His arms are weighted down with brown paper bags. The content smile on his face shows that he loves what he does. He's heading for the car. He must have hitched a ride into town.

The town unfurls around him, a tapestry stitched with echoes. There—McCreedy's Bar, its neon sign dark, the laughter that once spilled from its doors now silenced by daylight. Beyond it, the old mill, windows shattered, gears rusting like bones.

In the park, children scatter across frost-tipped grass, their shrieks stabbing the quiet—a hymn to life unbroken. He sees faces among the crowd; fragments of old nightmares now softened by daylight. Men who crawled from ruin. Women who stitched their lives back together with trembling hands. Survivors, all.

Charles rides through it like a man moving inside a dream, every turn a revelation, every shadow pierced by light. The watch hangs in his memory like a pendulum swinging in the dark, buying seconds, bending fate. He does not speak of it. Does not name it. But as the horizon opens and the sky stretches wide, he feels its echo in his pulse, steady and sure.

Just at the edge of town, Charles sees a pickup truck heading his way from the opposite direction. It pulls over next to a roadside farm stand. The driver hits the horn: musical 're-mi-do-re'. Two dogs erupt in barks and howls from the bed of the truck. Buzzy steps out of the driver's side and rounds the front of the truck toward the stand.

Charles rubber-necks as he slowly cruises by.

He continues motoring out of town, building and dwellings becoming more and more stark. Another mile or so down the road and Charles sees a van parked next to a mailbox on the side of the road. A cone in the road warns other drivers to give space. In front of the van, a ladder leans against a pole. Charles coasts by. He reads the branding on the side of the van: CableCast.

Floyd is at the top of the ladder, stripping Internet cables and making connections. He peers down from his perch as the stranger on the bike below rumbles by.

All of these people have one thing in common: they each experienced a strange, unexplainable blip in their life. For some it was just a blink that made them momentarily pause whatever they were doing or thinking: the butler, dusting, feeling a sneeze that never comes; the chef, a full-body shiver, mid slice; Buzzy, losing his sense of direction for just one dizzying second. Each of these subtle experiences was either quickly brushed off or not really registered at all.

Some of them experienced a little more than a blip—the girl, for example. Poor thing went outside, started her car to warm it up and went back in. Less than ten minutes later, she stepped out of the house to find her car missing. She never even hit the road in that car that morning. Insurance purchased a new one for her. No harm. No foul.

Probably the worst experience was had by Floyd, the poor bastard. He blinked and found himself completely naked atop a twenty-eight-foot ladder—in one of the most affluent neighborhoods in town. Thankfully he was able to climb down, unseen, and with a flushed face, scoot to his van. That's where he found his clothing, strewn about the floor in the back. He was confused, his brain sprung like an overwound clock. He was also completely oblivious to the fact that Charles had pulled the ladder out from under him that day.

The good news is that Floyd took a few days off and cut way back on his drinking.

Charles gives the throttle a little twist and accelerates into the long straightaway. He is home now. Not in the way of geography, but in the marrow-deep sense that the war is over. The demons are dust. The friendly ghosts have faces again, warm and living. And as the bike carries him forward, slow and solemn, He lets the wind take the last fragments of the past, scattering them like ash across the streets he has claimed for peace.

There—in the distance, off to his right, stands the prison—now closed and still under investigation.

The prison, where it all started. The prison, where Charles was born. The prison, where the guards wore uniforms when on duty and patched cuts of leather when off. The prison where young girls would find themselves with child, even if they've been behind bars for longer than nine months. The prison where babies were stripped from young mothers, by a prison doctor who knew just where to rehome them: Kerrington's agency. It was quite the racket; an assembly line of abuse from start to finish. It was a factory, churning out one damaged product after another. With help from men like Rangle, protection from men like Dobson and Elderkin, and muscle like the men in the clubs, the Kerringtons pretty much had the narcotics and human trafficking game locked up. Now, those were involved are locked up—or dead.

The beast, that was lurking beneath the quiet, unsuspecting, dot-on-a-map town, has been slain. Its evil heart smashed to pulp and its long, black, slimy tentacles severed and burned.

After some miles on the black, winding dragon of road, with nothing but forest lining both sides, Charles winds the bike down, gear by gear until he comes to a stop in front of a lone mailbox at the end of a long, narrow dirt driveway that seemingly ends in the sky. The mailbox is all but hidden from those who don't know where to look.

This is not just any mailbox. This is his mailbox. This is his driveway. This is his home, in geography as well as marrow. The Lincoln house and all of its property are his now, bought and paid for.

Sure, the town got its fifteen minutes of fame. It bustled with law enforcement, news crews and tourists for a while after everything went down, but the public is fickle; its memory short. The buzz only lasted for a couple of weeks and died down completely in six.

This town is on the map now, not as unassuming as it was, but quiet again; peaceful. It's not a peace like that after a storm.

It is a peace brand new; a fresh canvas. A springtime blossoming after winter has had its bitter season.

This is his town, his house, his driveway—and his mailbox; which he's been staring at way too long.

He reaches for the metal loop protruding from the arched door and pulls. The door lowers and the mailbox's interior reveals: hollow, aluminum, desolate—except for that thin, four-by-six card, leaning against the side.

Charles reaches in and snatches the card out. With the same hand, he flips the box's cover upward. His knuckles set the lid tight. He balances upright on the bike and inspects.

It's a postcard.

The photo on the front depicts a sunlit paradise: white sands, the bluest of oceans, sparkling under a perfect sky. Palm trees shade beach chairs in the foreground. Droplet-covered bottle necks protrude from a sweating ice bucket that sits on a wicker stand.

Standing in the cold, November air, Charles can almost feel the sun's heat radiating from the image. He can almost taste that beer.

He flips the card.

His own address stands out the largest. It still makes him smile to see that. Above and to the left, the sender's address changes his smile to a snort as he reads:

Mike Hunt

~~1369~~ 1368 Lucky Lane

Paradise, Island. OU812

Classic—Charles understands the address of anonymity. He catches the Van Halen reference. He gets the joke behind the 1369—a faux military MOS number for an unlucky cocksucker. He doesn't quite understand the line scribbled through it though, or the 1368 written next to it—until he reads the message scribbled in the big box on the right:

(68—You blow me and I'll owe you one.)

Charles almost blows snot out of his nose. Through the tears that are trying to form he reads the next and final line:

Congrats on the house.

That's it. No updates on how he's doing. No signature. Just classic Burns: short and to the point, saying all that needs to be said in as few words as possible. Funny as fuck if you know him.

Burns is not on the run. The law is not after him. Nobody is chasing him. Charles knows exactly where he is—but he's not talking.

Burns disappeared after that night at the motel. He had nothing to run away from; nothing to fear. He just needed to get away. Something in him cracked that night, or so he felt. Maybe it was the brutal violence that had occurred inside the room. Maybe it was the gut-wrenching discovery of an innocent soul, forever stained, huddling in a chair. All he knew is that something happened that night—an epiphany? He wasn't sure. He was only sure that it was real.

He was standing there, speaking with Dusty. He saw Jardini step from behind Dusty, saw the shotgun barrel rise. His heart had enough time to panic; to alert his brain that this was the end. His brain had enough time to send the signal to the muscles that control his arms, ordering them to rise and protect. They didn't have time to so much as twitch before he saw the inside of the barrel glow with a hellish orange—

—And then he was alone. Standing in the same spot, his arms finishing their defensive block, covering his eyes. No blast came. No black took him. There was only silence. He thought he must be in the afterlife, surprised that there was no pain involved when death came, but when he finally lowered his arms, he saw the truth: He was alive and alone, in the motel lot, under a clear sky. Far in the distance, thunder rolled.

Thunder continues rolling; up the long, dirt driveway as Charles crests the hill—and goes home.

Chapter 22: November 10th, 2059 – Age 92

The porch creaks beneath the slow rhythm of Charles's rocking chair, each sway a tick of time folding in on itself. The November air drapes around him like a cool shawl, crisp yet tender, carrying the scent of fallen leaves and distant woodsmoke. Noon hovers near, its pale light spilling across the pond—a sheet of glass unbroken, mirroring the fire of autumn trees that stand like shaman in robes of crimson and gold.

In the palm of his hand rest the watch, pristine as new. He flips it over, shakily to view the underside. The dexterity in his arthritic fingers certainly isn't what it used to be. There is not a single scuff, not even the tiniest of hairline scratches anywhere to be seen. He pops the lid. The sound still envelopes him as it always has and he still welcomes it.

Charles utilized the powers of the watch for the entirety of his FBI career and in those years, he learned many of the unspoken rules, powers and needs of the watch. There's a piece of him that wishes all of the instructions were whispered to him that day at the river, but the whisper from the old lady was only the key. The rest was to be learned; not by the bearer of the watch—by the watch itself. The watch only asked: What do you want to do? It never gave suggestions or directions.

What it did give—was multiple chances to do things right, through patience, trial and error, to properly navigate to an acceptable destiny.

The watch never tells anyone what to do. It simply gives the rightful owner free will. Use it or don't. Do it this way or that.

The basic power of the watch is simple: when the bearer of the watch opens the lid, a marker in time is set for all living things. When the watch is closed, by anyone, time resets to the marker. It's as simple as that. Anything that happens to a living thing while the watch is open, even death, is erased when the lid is closed and time resets. Those offended, injured or killed will simply be in the same place and time they were when the watch was opened, completely unaware that anything has happened.

It all sounds simple until the bearer realizes that the time reset does not affect things not living. An inanimate item moved while the watch is open is still moved when the lid is closed and time resets. An item stolen or destroyed while the watch is open is still stolen or destroyed when the watch is closed.

Deep inside all this seemingly innocent magic, provided by the watch that relies solely on the free will of the bearer, is a darker motive and Charles figured this one out a little later than he wishes. You see—the watch is hungry for souls, or even just the taste of souls. It needs to be in the hands of the right bearer. When the watch is closed, any souls provided by the bearer are consumed in full. They are the power that winds the watch. The watch hungers for them. But souls collected while the lid is open are on loan, to be merely tasted and savored until the lease expires and the lid is closed.

Charles always kept this in mind, once he learned about it. He kept the souls of the innocent in mind when he utilized the power. When it came to his family, he was content knowing he never used the watch to manipulate them or their situations. Never once did he let the watch taste the soul of a loved one. If it ever came down to it, to save a life of a loved one, he is certain he would have and thankful he never had to.

It took him a lifetime to learn the nuances of the watch, the way it works with its bearer. He hasn't used its power in many years. The last time he almost used it was when Mandy died. It took everything he had to not open that watch before she died and close it after, just to bring her back for another moment. But he knew that was selfish. To bring her back to her suffering just to ease his own. He had to let her go that day. The watch never left his pocket.

The last noticeable side effect of the watch should have been obvious to him. It turns out, the bearer's body still ages at a normal rate when the watch is opened. When the watch is closed and everyone is reset to the same age and health they were before, the bearer isn't so lucky. Every minute the watch lid is open is a minute the bearer ages beyond their calendar years.

Charles bobbles the weight of the watch in his palm, giving it a last few moments of appreciation. He stares at the pruned skin of his hands, wrinkled beyond their years. It reminds him of the restraint the watch taught him. Every use has a consequence. Sure, he could have been financially rich. He could have manipulated life for his family, but he never did. He never used the watch to enrich himself financially or to help his family cheat at life. He was the richest man in the world. The man who got everything he ever wanted in the end.

Charles lowers the watch to his side.

On his lap rests an album, its leather cover cracked, its pages worn thin by decades of touch. His fingers linger on the cover, trembling not from weakness but from the weight of memory pressing through the years. He tucks the watch into his pocket and with full attention focused, opens the album slowly, reverently, as though unlocking a vault of souls.

The first photo greets him—a boy frozen in time; eyes bright with the emerald spark of youth. His foster mother took that picture on a day steeped in sunlight and laughter. Charles stares into those eyes, searching for the glimmer that once burned like a beacon. His own eyes now are veiled in milky cataracts, emerald reduced to a haze beneath the wash of age. Yet the joy remains, pulsing faintly like an ember refusing to die.

He lifts his gaze to the pond, to the cabin he claimed as sanctuary—the Lincoln house, stone bones rooted deep in earth.

The pages turn, and with them, the tide of years. Mandy's smile blooms from the paper, radiant in white silk, her hand clasped in his beneath a trestle of flowers. Another page—two figures beside a gleaming car, chrome glinting in the sun. Then a hospital room, sterile walls softened by the miracle cradled in Mandy's arms—a child swaddled, new as dawn. More pages, more echoes: birthday candles flickering like tiny stars; laughter spilling across backyards; faces ripening from innocence to grace. Proms. Graduations. Triumphs stitched into the fabric of family.

Charles drinks it all in, savoring each image as though tasting wine perfectly aged in the cask of time. His heart swells, tender and fierce, until he reaches the last page. A photograph of fullness—a porch bathed in golden light, two rocking chairs cradling him and Mandy like thrones of quiet majesty. Around them, an abundance of children and grandchildren, faces alight with joy, eyes shimmering with the promise of tomorrows. He touches each face with the tips of his fingers, tracing the contours of love etched in silver halide. His breath catches, a prayer without words.

The album closes with a crackling sigh, but Charles does not let go. He flips it over, opens it anew, drawn to the genesis of his story. A tucked photo peeks a corner from the slot created where leather cover meets hard cover. Charles plucks it from its hiding place. The image—a woman in a long, white spring dress, leaning against an oak whose roots claw deep into earth. Her hair lifts in a breeze, a frozen gesture of grace. Black and white, yet vivid as blood in his mind. He never knew her—not in flesh, but her presence thrums through his veins like life. His mother. The woman who gave him life and vanished into shadow.

He remembers the day his foster mother, Annie placed this photo in his hands, her voice hushed, her eyes heavy with truths too sharp for childhood. Seventeen years old, and the world cracked open: real names, real histories, the ache of origins. That night, he dreamed of flight, of soaring through darkness with the emerald-eyed lady in white, her arms a sanctuary he never touched.

Now, at ninety-two, the longing has not diminished. He traces her face, the curve of her cheek, the eyes that hold no motion yet brim with imagined warmth. He wills her to speak, to breathe, to step from the sepia hush into his world. He yearns for her embrace, for the life of her heartbeat against his ear. In his mind, he feels it—the weightless drift of love unbroken by time.

The chair rocks. The pond glimmers. The trees stand guard in their autumn fire. And Charles stares into the eyes of his mother as she stares back through the veil of years, two souls tethered by a thread no blade can sever. Love radiates, fierce and eternal, spilling through the cracks of time like sunlight through shattered glass.

Chapter 23: November 10th, 1967

The steel door looms like a monolith, its black surface exhaling cold into the narrow corridor. Eliza Marie Watkins stands inches from it, her breath fogging against the chill, her nose grazing metal that feels like the skin of death. Her head is shorn bare, scalp gleaming under the institutional light, a crown stripped away for the ritual to come. Thirty years carved into her face like fault lines—years of hunger, hurt, and hollow promises. She looks older than her span, as if sorrow has been aging her in secret.

The buzzer sounds, harsh and metallic, nerve-grating. A hand slaps the door, a grunt follows, and the slab groans open on hinges that scream like the tortured. Two men flank her, their grips iron, their faces masks of procedure. They usher her forward into the chamber—a room that oscillates with sterile menace, its walls sweating shadows.

The chair waits at the center, a throne of annihilation forged in black oak and steel. Leather straps dangle like flesh. Eliza moves toward it with the gait of a sleepwalker, her emerald eyes; those eyes that once shimmered like spring leaves, are now dulled to moss.

They still glint with defiance in the dying light.

Officials swarm around her, buzzing like flies over carrion. Voices murmur, pens scratch, papers shuffle—a symphony of bureaucracy played against the drumbeat of doom. Eliza does not hear them. Her gaze pierces the plate-glass window, into the witness room beyond. Empty chairs gape like toothless mouths. A handful of men linger in the shadows— lawyers, officers, strangers drafted by law to watch her vanish. They sip coffee, trade jokes, flick ashes into paper cups. One man exhales smoke in lazy spirals, his indifference curling through the air like a taunt.

Her thoughts crack, splintering into shards of memory. A life measured in losses parades before her mind's eye: hands that struck instead of held, lips that lied instead of kissed, promises that rotted before they bloomed. Love was a rumor she never touched. Safety, a myth she never believed. Even now, stripped of hair, of clothes, of dignity, she wonders why she was summoned into this world at all. If there is a god, she plans to spit her question into his face: What sin did I commit to earn this sentence called life? Rage writhes in her gut, hot and bitter, a serpent striking at heaven.

But then—something shifts. Reality blurs at the edges, colors bleeding into black. The voices recede, muffled, as if sinking beneath water. She drifts inward, deeper, spiraling into the caverns of her mind. Perhaps it is mercy. Perhaps madness. She cannot stop it—this reverse pull, this undertow dragging her through the corridors of time. Faces flicker. Moments ignite and vanish. She is thirteen again, barefoot in summer grass. She is five, clutching a doll with one glass eye. She is newborn, lungs screaming for air. The reel spins backward, faster, faster, until even thoughts dissolve into shadow.

A crack snaps her back—the slam of a black telephone handset against its cradle. The world rushes back in, brutal and bright. She is strapped now, leather biting wrists and ankles, steel kissing her temples. The microphone arcs into view, its head hovering before her lips like an executioner's blade.

"Do you have a last statement?" The voice is flat, scraped clean of mercy.

Eliza lifts her gaze, emerald eyes flaring one last time, molten with secrets no one will ever mine. The room stills. The men freeze mid-motion, their chatter strangled into silence. She surveys them slowly, savoring the discomfort prickling their skin. Then her lids fall. A breath swells her chest, deep and deliberate. She exhales, long and slow, and a smile ghosts her mouth—a curve of smug serenity. She shifts in the chair, a subtle wriggle, as if settling in for a journey only she can chart.

The clock looms on the wall, its red second hand slicing toward twelve. Three hands poised for judgment. Three-click—

Two-click—

One.

The switch slams. Voltage screams through copper veins. The chamber erupts in a chorus of hums and crackles, a savage hymn of current and consequence. Eliza's body arcs, rigid as stone. Muscles knot, tendons bulge, veins swell like starving vipers. Her face ignites crimson, foam frothing at the seam of clenched lips. Bubbles foam, multiplying and fragile, bursting against the heat. Smoke coils upward, thin and ghostly, a soul unraveling into vapor.

And then—blackness. Not silence, not peace—just the infinite dark swallowing her entirely, as the emerald fire gutters out forever.

Chapter 24: November 10th, 2059 – Age 92

Old man Watkins feels it before it strikes—a whisper of pain blooming in his chest, then a fist of fire crushing his heart. His breath snags, sharp and ragged, as his hand claws instinctively toward the ache. The world tilts. The porch blurs. Above him, the sky yawns wide, pale and endless, as if inviting him home.

The rocking chair groans in protest as he slips from its cradle, knees colliding with the wooden planks. The photo album tumbles from his lap, a muted thud splitting the hush. It lands hard on its spine; pages splay open like wings. The first image exposed—the woman in white, frozen in eternal grace. His mother. Her eyes—fierce even in monochrome, flare up at him like a beacon through the fog of pain. The eyes call to him. They calm him. They tell him what he needs to do.

Fighting against his own muscles, Charles jams his uncooperative hand into his pocket, grips the warm treasure inside and removes it from within. He gazes at it and then he gazes past it.

Loose photographs are scattered across the porch like cards on a poker table. Faces from decades past stare up in silent witness: Mandy's smile, children's laughter, fragments of a life stitched together by love and sacrifice. Charles reaches, fingers trembling, nails scraping wood. The pressure in his chest is a vise now, crushing, merciless. He grits his teeth, vision tunneling into a smear of light and shadow.

He collapses forward, cheek grazing the cold grain of the porch. One arm curls under him, clutching the watch tight to his chest as if to cage the agony. The other stretches, desperate, toward the album lying just beyond salvation. His fingertips quake, two inches from the edge—a gulf as vast as eternity. He strains, muscles screaming, and pinches the corner of one loose photo between trembling fingers. He drags it close, squinting through the blur.

It is the picture of his birth mother.

The album remains scattered—a relic of everything he was, everything he loved. With a guttural groan, Charles summons the last ember of strength flickering in his bones. He rolls his body over, inch by brutal inch, until the back of his head rests on the porch, photos haloed around. He raises the photo from his chest, just high enough to view it one more time. His breath rasps, shallow and broken, as his eyes lock onto hers—the woman in the spring dress, leaning against the oak, hair caught in a phantom breeze. His mother. His origin. His unanswered prayer.

From the sepia, Emerald eyes sparkle and stare back through the veil of decades, luminous and vivid even in this grayscale image. He drinks them in, parched for a love he never touched, clinging to the illusion as darkness pools at the edges of his sight. His lips part, shaping words no one will hear. A tear escapes, carving a silver path down the map of his weathered cheek.

Charles releases the latch on the watch. A *click—pop* resounds in the hush; this one louder than any before. His hands drop to his chest again, the watch and photo with them. He uses the last ember of strength left in his failing body to roll onto his side and curl into a ball. The watch stays tightly gripped and pressed into his chest. His head lays on the forearm of the hand that holds the photo inches from his view.

The blackness swells, vast and unstoppable. He does not fight it. He lets it take him, cradling the image like a talisman, his gaze fused to hers until the world dissolves into shadow. Her face—the last light he knows, burns in his mind as the abyss closes, soft and silent, like a curtain falling on the final act of a long, relentless play.

Chapter 25: November 10th, 1950

The basement breathes darkness, its air thick with the musk of earth, rot and secrets. A single shaft of moonlight pierces the gloom through a narrow window, a shard of silver slicing across the floor. It mists everything in the space with a pale gray wash. In its beam sprawls a circular symbol, painted on the floor in blood that glistens like fresh wounds. Its design looks ancient, not accidental. Around the outside of the symbol, tokens of intent crouch like pieces on a game board: a pocket calendar marked with today's date in a crimson X, a green candle guttering in brass, a lock of hair curled like a question, a chicken egg pale as bone, and at the center of the design—the severed head of her pet cat, its glassy eyes staring into nothing. Its gray fur is matted. One ear is missing its tip, but that injury is long healed, a battle wound no doubt earned years earlier in a street fight.

A young girl, thirteen years of age today, kneels at the edge of the symbol, her breath shallow, her lips murmuring something that barely scrapes the edges of silence. Her hands tremble, smudged with red. The mutilated body of her pet lies pinned belly-down, thin spikes biting through flesh into splintered wood beside her. Its tail is rigid in death.

Shadows cling to the walls, watching.

Then—movement. A shadow eclipses the moonbeam, swallowing its silver thread. It falls long and dark across the macabre display; and the girl. She stiffens, head snapping toward the window. Her face is shadowed. Something stands between her and the moonlight now—a silhouette swelling, bending low. Her breath knots in her throat as the figure leans closer, hood sagging like a shroud, face emerging from darkness.

An old man. His skin is parchment stretched over bone, fissured with time. Cataracts cloud his eyes, milky and spectral, yet in one orb a faint green ember smolders—a memory of color. Wrinkles carve his cheeks into maps of sorrow. His presence crackles like static, a frequency older than language.

She cannot move. Fear roots her to the blood-slick floor as his face looms closer, vast and all-encompassing, until it fills her world.

She doesn't know this old man, yet feels a connection in his gaze, which she cannot break.

Charles knows her though. He had met her in the past, or maybe it was the future. He had met her in the photo Annie gave him, in the dream he had that night and by the river, when he was small and she was old—and he had met her in that cold, gray prison cell, the morning he was born.

She is Eliza Marie Watkins—his birth mother.

With lightning speed, his hands strike, gripping her shoulders with a force that jolts breath from her lungs. He hauls her upright, spins her to face him. Her head stays locked, eyes welded to his, a tether of terror, awe and—something else.

The robe sways around him, heavy as earth, its folds blowing in a wind that does not exist in this dank space. His hands, gnarled and trembling, slide down her arms like rivers seeking their delta. They find her palms, cradle them, and press something cold into their hollow. Metal kisses her skin—a weight, a promise. He leans close, cheek grazing hers, his breath a riddle against her ear. Words spill, hushed and urgent, syllables that taste of eternity.

He draws back, loosening his grip so moonlight can reveal the gift. A watch gleams in her hands, its case gold, its lid wide open like an eye. Inside, gears glint like captured stars, frozen mid-spin. His fingers fold hers over it, tender, deliberate, until the lid snaps shut with a click that sounds like fate smacking its lips.

Her gaze clings to his, wide and drowning in wonder. His smile blooms: soft, sorrowful, radiant with something deeper than joy. He lifts a hand, pointing toward the symbol sprawled on the floor behind her. She turns to look, heart fluttering, and the world skews.

The blood is gone. The symbol is clean, its lines mere chalk. The gray cat—whole, except for a missing ear tip, breathing. It purrs as it coils around the leg of a dust-choked chair, tail flicking in lazy twitches. Its eyes gleam, alive, unbroken. The girl staggers, blinking, her mind clawing for sense. She spins back, seeking the old man, the anchor of this impossible tide.

He is gone.

The shadow has vanished. Moonlight floods the room again in his place, pure and merciless, washing the floor in silver. She stands frozen, the warming watch clutched in her fist, as the cat winds around her ankles, purring contently.

The watch was never just a keeper of hours; it was a hinge between lives, a covenant that one must fall for the other to rise. Time only borrows faces.

Its hands bargain in blood and grace—exchanges, second chances, the story returning to start.

Eliza can feel all of this and more in the warmth of the watch. She stares at it as the words last whispered by the old man echo to silence in her head.

The moonlight sharpens, spearing through the dark. She peers at the cat once again and then lifts her gaze to the window. The moonlight strikes and her eyes catch fire.

They explode a brilliant emerald green.

www.ingramcontent.com/pod-product-compliance
Lightning Source LLC
Chambersburg PA
CBHW030539260626
47157CB00006B/2097